PROMISE OF PERIL

Leonie could not forget how the Duke of Thornbury climbed up to her balcony and invaded her room.

"You're very lovely, too lovely for my peace of mind," he told her, before taking her in his arms and pressing his lips down on hers.

Only the arrival of Leonie's maid had stopped him from proceeding with his villainous seduction.

"Get out of here," Leonie said to him then. "And don't ever come near me again."

He had met her angry gaze with a smile as confident as it was chilling. "I still want you, Leonie. I don't think you realize how much. I'll be out of London over Christmas, but when I return, I promise that you'll hear from me again."

Leonie had dismissed his words, for at the time she was very well protected by her family name and all the privileges of a lady of high station. How could she have foreseen that when the duke returned, he would find her in a position where he need only stoop to conquer. . . .

A Change
of Fortune

SIGNET Regency Romances You'll Want to Read

A Change
of Fortune

by Sandra Heath

A SIGNET BOOK

NEW AMERICAN LIBRARY

SIGNET, SIGNET CLASSIC, MENTOR, PLUME, MERIDIAN AND NAL BOOKS
are published by New American Library,
1633 Broadway, New York, New York 10019

First Printing, October, 1985

1 2 3 4 5 6 7 8 9

PRINTED IN THE UNITED STATES OF AMERICA

1

The young lady and her maid had no idea they were being closely observed as they walked among the crowds beside the frozen Serpentine that clear, cold December morning. It was 1813 and so far the winter had been the most bitter in living memory, and Hyde Park was pale and brittle with weeks of unbroken frost. There were skaters on the frozen lake, their laughter echoing sharply through the still air, and the two young women stopped to watch.

A tall, fashionable young gentleman lingered secretly among the winter trees. He had been following them for some time. The maid was of no interest to him, for she was plain and of little consequence, but her mistress was a different matter; she had a loveliness which had claimed his full attention from the first moment he had noticed her. He took a long breath, leaning back against one of the trees, his tasseled cane swinging idly in his gloved hand. He wore a stylish Polish greatcoat which could only have come from one of Bond Street's foremost tailors, and his gleaming hessian boots looked Hoby's at the very least. His top hat was tipped rakishly back on his light brown hair, and his long-lashed hazel eyes bore a look of pensiveness. His fine aristocratic face was handsome, but its expression now was calculating; it was not an expression which would have been appreciated in the slightest by the young lady toward whom it was directed.

Their airing evidently at an end, the two turned from the lake and began to retrace their steps in his direction. He could see her more clearly now, and his practiced glance swept her slowly from head to toe. She was a little above medium height, and slender, although her figure was concealed by the fur-trimmed cream mantle she wore. She had silver-fair hair, he could see the soft curls framing her face beneath her pink-ribboned bonnet, and with her pale, clear complexion she should have had blue eyes, but her eyes were a magnificent, arresting dark brown. Who was she? He had never seen her before, and yet surely she must be out in society for she seemed at least nineteen years old and she was certainly from a wealthy family, that much was clear from her clothes and her manner. Oh, how cool and demure she looked, and yet there was a warmth which promised so very much to the man fortunate enough to engage her heart. For the first time in many weeks he was aroused from the boredom which had descended over him after a long and tedious Season; but how to succeed with her, that was the problem. She wasn't a lady of easy virtue, and so could hardly be openly approached and propositioned. No, in this case a certain subtlety would be required, else his lovely prey would too swiftly perceive the true nature of the chase.

They had almost reached him now, and suddenly he hesitated. Perhaps subtlety would take too long and his purpose be better served after all by a direct but disarming approach. Would she believe him if he confessed to being carried away on the spur of the moment by an overwhelming admiration? Would she melt before such abject "honesty"? But even as he pondered what to do, she looked coldly through him as if he simply did not exist, walking past with such a deliberate air of indifference that for a moment he was caught off guard. It was a very obvious snub, and belatedly he realized that she had become aware of his close scrutiny. The maid knew too, for her cheeks were a little flushed and she glanced coyly at him from beneath lowered lashes before hurrying on after her mistress.

Annoyance flushed hotly through him. He had thought himself undetected, and therefore at an advantage; overconfidence had cost him that advantage, and maybe a great deal more. He watched as they approached the gates into noisy, congested Park lane, one of London's busiest thoroughfares. As they passed from sight, he suddenly determined to see where they went, for he wasn't defeated yet and meant to proceed with the conquest of his lovely unknown.

On the pavement outside the park gates, however, he came to a halt, for there was no sign of them. A constant stream of carriages, wagons, gigs, and curricles passed him by, moving slowly over the icy road, and there were other pedestrians strolling to and from the park, but it was as if the two young women had vanished into the cold, thin air.

Something made him look suddenly across the way, and he saw them again, standing at the door of a large white house almost on the corner of Curzon Street. It was an elegant building, one which he had passed countless times in the past. As he watched, a liveried Negro footman admitted them and the door closed again, the crimson ribbons of the Christmas wreath upon it trembling a little afterward.

Threading his way through the traffic, the man stood on the pavement outside the house. It was indeed a fine building, with wide bow windows and beautiful wrought-iron balconies which were protected by handsome roofs. He glanced at the polished brass plate beside the discreet dark green door: MISS HART'S SEMINARY FOR YOUNG LADIES. He smiled a little, for this was a very exclusive establishment, more exclusive than ever since a certain Russian countess from the highest echelons of society had decided to graciously bestow her patronage upon it. To this seminary came the daughters of the very wealthy, to be educated from childhood to the age of eighteen, by which time they were ready to enter society and the Marriage Mart. So, his fair incongnita must be one of Miss Hart's "young ladies," there could be no other explanation since she was far too elegantly and fashionably attired to be one of the teachers, and she was too young to be a parent. It was possible that she was merely visiting, of course, but somehow he didn't think so, he felt certain that she was one of the privileged pupils, which would explain why he hadn't seen her before, for she couldn't yet be out in society.

He smiled again, for one snub wasn't sufficient to discourage him, especially as he knew that it was possible to gain invitations to this feminine stronghold. With such an invitation he would be able to see that he was formally introduced to the beauty who had so bewitched him.

His cane still swinging, his steps noticeably lighter now, he returned to quiet Curzon Street, where his carriage awaited him. Dame Fortune was smiling upon him after all this fine December morning, for it just so happened that recently he had become acquainted with a certain ambitious and scheming young woman fresh from St. Petersburg. This young woman, Miss Nadia Benckendorff, was the cousin of the seminary's distinguished benefactress, Countess Lieven, and was about to have her hitherto rejected advances unexpectedly welcomed.

Climbing into the carriage, he instructed the coachman to drive to the Russian embassy in Harley Street, where Dorothea Lieven's husband was the ambassador, and where Nadia had resided since arriving in London barely a month before. He leaned his head back against the carriage's excellent velvet upholstery, and after a moment he smiled again. Countess Lieven took her duties as benefactress very seriously indeed, and she frequently took tea at the seminary. He glanced out again as the carriage passed the tall white house. Soon he would be admitted through that exclusive door. . . .

2

A week later the seminary closed for the Christmas holiday, and all but one of the thirty pupils returned to their families. The one who remained was Leonie Conyngham, the young lady in the park.

At nineteen she was, strictly speaking, a little old to be at the school, but she was waiting for her widowed father to return from Madras, where he had been many years in the service of the East India Company. Richard Conyngham was now a nabob of the first order, and when he arrived in England early in the new year he was going to purchase a great country estate and a London residence, and his only daughter was going to be mistress of both. Leonie would then be launched in society with every possible advantage, and because of all that she would one day inherit, she would be very much sought after. It was an exciting prospect, and one which she now awaited with increasing impatience. Never had a winter seemed to drag by so slowly, and never before had she so wished Christmas to be over and done with.

It was very early in the morning, and she lay drowsily in her huge four-poster bed. Her room was the principal bed-chamber at the seminary, as befitted the most senior pupil. It was a handsome room, with a balcony overlooking Hyde Park. Its walls were hung with pink-and-white Chinese silk, and there was a pink stucco frieze around the ceiling. On the polished floor rested a fine floral carpet, and the draperies of the bed were of a particularly elegant deep rose brocade, which same material had been used for the window curtains

9

and the upholstery of the chairs. In one corner of the room stood an elegant little mahogany table on which there was a large porcelain jug and bowl, while in another there was an immense wardrobe, containing her extensive array of fashionable clothes. Apart from that, the only other item of furniture was her dressing table, which had white muslin hangings and was covered with a clutter of cosmetics jars and boxes, scent vials, jewel cases, pins, brushes, and combs.

A newly kindled fire crackled in the marble fireplace, having just been attended by a chambermaid. At Leonie's request she had drawn back the curtains and folded aside the heavy shutters, allowing the chill morning light into the room. The day looked bitterly cold and uninviting. The freezing fog which had descended over the capital three days earlier showed no sign as yet of lifting, and the boundary wall of the park was indistinct in the gloom. Beyond it the trees were white and ghostly, and the Serpentine was hidden from view. There were icicles on the wrought-iron balcony and suspended from its roof, and there was a thick rime of ice on the naked branches of the fig tree growing against the wall. Park Lane, usually busy even at this early hour, was almost deserted. It was very quiet, almost too quiet for one of the world's greatest cities.

Leonie shivered, wriggling further into the depths of the warm bed. Soon her morning tray of coffee and Shrewsbury cakes would be brought, but in the meantime it was good just to lie where she was, luxuriating in the comfort of the finest bed in the house, finer even than Miss Hart's. She smiled a little as she thought of the headmistress, who, for the benefit of the ladies and gentlemen of rank and fashion who entered her domain, gave an outward display of deference and humility, which qualities were quickly abandoned in private. Emmeline Hart was ambitious, more so than ever since the advent of Countess Lieven, and she was filled with a longing for the more magnificent things of life, as the purchase of her green velvet bed had revealed. What other grand items she had purchased for her private rooms could only be guessed at, since they had been carried in covered with discreet dust sheets, but the bed had been too large and cumbersone, and a great many people had witnessed its arrival. Leonie's smile faded a little then, for while it was possible to smile at Miss

Hart, it wasn't possible to like her at all; she was simply not a likable person, being too hard and cold for that, although she strove all the while to conceal her true self behind a veneer of sweet smiles and charming words.

Thoughts of Miss Hart vanished then, for Leonie suddenly remembered the forbidden book she had concealed so carefully the night before beneath her pillow. Sitting up, her silver-fair hair tumbling down over the shoulders of her lacy nightgown, she quickly put on her warm shawl and removed the book from its hiding place. It was Lord Byron's latest work, *The Bride of Abydos*, and was said to be very shocking indeed because of its theme of illicit love. This would have been shocking enough on its own, but was rendered more so than ever by the scandalous rumors in circulation concerning the poet and his half-sister, Mrs. Leigh. In the opinion of Countess Lieven, whose word was now law at the seminary, such a book was not at all suitable reading for proper young ladies, and she had promptly instructed Miss Hart to ban it from the premises. Unfortunately, as is frequently the consequence of such prohibition, acquisition of the forbidden volume immediately became a matter of the utmost importance, and to Leonie's certain knowledge there were at least three other copies reposing in various secret places throughout the building! This disobedience had as much to do with a general desire to flout the countess's wishes as it had to do with a genuine interest in Lord Byron's scandalous writings and affairs, since it was known that the countess was being very hypocritical indeed. She presumed to pronounce upon the protection of virtue, and yet was known to be actively engaged upon the pursuit of Lord Byron, whom she dearly wished to secure as her latest lover. Such double standards cried out to be challenged, although only in secret, since the countess was not a lady anyone wished to offend, her importance in society being far too great for that.

Leonie did not much care for Dorothea, Countess Lieven, whose interest in the seminary had meant the introduction of far too many petty rules and regulations, most of them brought in simply because they had applied at the countess's old school, the great Smolny Institute in St. Petersburg, which establishment had received the patronage of her imperial guardian, the Empress Maria Feodorovna. It was a wish to emulate this great royal lady that had prompted Dorothea to bestow her own patronage upon a similar school in London. Leonie sighed, for on her own, Dorothea Lieven was bad enough, but now she had been joined by her cousin, Miss Benckendorff, another ex-pupil of the Smolny, and heaven alone knew how many more new rules would be introduced as a result. The more Leonie dwelt upon it, the more glad she became that soon she would be leaving the seminary forever.

Opening the book and removing the embroidered marker, she settled back to read.

As Leonie defied the rules upstairs, downstairs in the headmistress's private parlor the small staff of resident lady teachers, including Miss Hart herself, was taking a breakfast of hot buttered toast and fine pekoe tea. The parlor was a pleasant room, warmed by a large fire which cast a flickering light over the crimson-and-white-striped wallpaper, the festoons of Christmas greenery, and the exceedingly handsome and expensive furniture. The furniture was far too opulent for a mere headmistress, but it expressed to the full Emmeline Hart's high opinion of herself. There were two items which in particular gave her much conceited pleasure; one was the splendid golden sofa upon which she sat in regal splendor, and the other was the portrait of Dorothea, Countess Lieven, which gazed severely down from the chimney breast.

Emmeline Hart was forty now and very plump, but twenty years earlier her looks had procured her all that she now possessed. Coming to London as a penniless but very shrewd adventuress, she had trapped a very married lord into an unwise liaison, and had then threatened to tell his jealous terror of a wife all about it unless he paid a certain price—the then vacant property in Park Lane. He had paid with some alacrity, and Emmeline Hart had donned the cloak of respectability, turning the house into an exclusive seminary for young ladies and conducting herself at all times in a most exemplary and decorous manner. Success had been assured from the outset because of the establishment's desirable and exclusive address. Each day the *beau monde* drove past its door, and as they took a turn in Hyde Park they could always see the elegant balconied windows gazing discreetly at them through the trees.

For almost twenty years now society had been sending its daughters to the seminary, to be taught English, French, German, arithmetic, history, geography, botany, embroidery, needlework, painting, etiquette, deportment, and manners, and those daughters had emerged as poised young ladies, ready to take their place among their peers. Recently, however, the arrival on the scene of Countess Lieven, and her immense influence, had made the seminary more exclusive than ever, setting it far ahead of its rivals, for Dorothea, in London for little more than a year, was not only a very important lady, she was also a patroness of Almack's, the most fashionable assembly rooms in London. Every Wednesday night the *haut ton* flocked to the subscription balls at this temple of high fashion, regarding it as a social advantage second to none to receive a voucher to attend, and Dorothea had let it be discreetly known that she would consider with great favor any application made by a young lady who had been educated at the premises in Park Lane. The moment this whisper had got about, the seminary had been inundated with applications from parents eager to secure this singular advantage for their daughters, and Miss Hart's rivals had been able to do nothing but watch in furious envy.

The headmistress sat proudly on her golden sofa, her lips pursed primly as she sipped her tea and contemplated the very satisfactory way things were going on. She had a face of startling sweetness, round and rosy, but the real Emmeline Hart was very different, being hard, ambitious, and unfeeling. This morning she wore a blue wool dress, a white shawl crisscrossed over her ample bosom, and a large frilled biggin on her graying hair. She felt very contented indeed, glancing up with a smile at Dorothea's portrait. Things, she thought to herself, just could not have been better.

As far as her companions, Miss Ross and Mlle. Clary, were concerned, however, things could not have been worse, for they were now without the services of the much-put-upon assistant teacher, Miss Mathers, who had left the day before due to ill health, and who was not going to be replaced. Over the years they had managed to delegate many of their duties to her, and now they were faced with the prospect of having once again to carry out those duties themselves. It was not a prospect they viewed with pleasure, and as a consequence breakfast today was a very quiet affair, with only Miss Hart herself finding anything to smile about.

As she reached for another slice of toast, however, she could not have known that events were about to take a very difficult turn which would make life somewhat awkward for her, and all because Leonie Conyngham had taken a fateful walk in Hyde Park and had caught the eye of a very determined, very unscrupulous gentleman. Indeed, he had already set about achieving his goal, and before that very day was out, he would have gained entry to the seminary.

3

The teachers' silent breakfast had almost finished when there was a tap at the parlor door and a maid came in with Leonie's early-morning tray for the headmistress to inspect before it was taken up. The maid was the same one who had accompanied Leonie on her walk in the park. Her name was Katy Briggs, and she was a timid girl with a fuzz of dark hair and a liberal sprinkling of freckles on her round face. She went in awe of Miss Hart, and was therefore exceedingly nervous as she conveyed the tray to a table and tried to set it down without making a sound, but the cup and saucer rattled, earning her a very disapproving frown from the headmistress.

Katy swallowed and bobbed a hasty curtsy. "I'm sorry, ma'am."

Without a word, Miss Hart rose majestically from her golden sofa and came to examine the tray. On it stood a gleaming silver coffeepot, a blue-and-white porcelain cup and saucer, and a small dish of freshly baked Shrewsbury cakes. The headmistress gave a grudging nod of approval. "It will do."

"Yes, ma'am."

Then, with a darting movement Miss Hart snatched the girl's wrist and held her hand accusingly aloft to reveal the fingerless mittens which had been absolutely forbidden. "What is the meaning of this?" she demanded in a quivering voice.

"Ma'am?" Katy's eyes were huge.

"You are wearing mittens."

"But, ma'am, it's so very cold and——"

15

"Countess Lieven has expressly forbidden the wearing of mittens in the house, as you are perfectly well aware, Briggs."

"Yes, ma'am. I'm sorry, ma'am, I didn't think."

"Think? *Think?* You aren't here to think, girl, you're here to do as you're told!"

"Yes, ma'am." The maid's voice was scarcely audible.

Miss Hart slowly released her wrist. "Remove them immediately."

Katy hastened to obey, pushing the offending articles into her apron pocket.

"Disobey any rule in the future, or question anything, anything at all, and you will be dismissed immediately, is that quite clear?" This last was said with a sly sideways glance at Miss Ross and Mlle. Clary, upon whom the barb was not lost.

Katy was striving to hide her tears. "Yes, ma'am," she whispered.

"Very well, you may now take Miss Conyngham's tray to her. And, Briggs?"

"Ma'am?"

"Tell her that I would be most grateful if she would kindly assist at tea this afternoon. Countess Lieven will be here, with her cousin Miss Benckendorff and a gentleman guest."

"Yes, ma'am."

"And, Briggs?"

The maid's heart sank again. "Ma'am?"

"Be less clumsy with the tray as you leave. I dislike hearing teacups clattering."

"Yes, ma'am."

Thankfully Katy picked the tray up again, balancing it on one hand and biting her lip with concentration as she opened the heavy door and stepped out into the chilly passage beyond. The tray did not make even the slightest sound.

As she went up the staircase, Katy paused on the half-landing at the back of the house, looking out of the frosty window at the long, narrow garden which extended to the gardens of the houses in parallel South Audley Street. It was a pleasant garden, with plane trees, poplars, and a weeping willow which draped its graceful fronds over a frozen ornamental pond. Directly below, beneath the ground-floor windows of the visitors' room, stood two stone sphinxes, white with ice now as they gazed solidly at the wintry scene. Down one side of the garden extended the wing of the seminary which contained the schoolrooms, while the opposite side was marked only by the high brick wall which separated the property from the one next to it.

Katy stared out at the eastern sky, beyond the houses of South Audley Street. There was a certain luminosity about that sky as the sun rose behind the pall of fog. She knew by that luminosity that today the fog would at last lift. She smiled with anticipation. Perhaps she and Miss Leonie would be able to go for another walk in the park, and perhaps too they would see the mysterious gentleman who had so nearly spoken the last time. Humming a little, the maid hurried on up the stairs.

Leonie gave a guilty start and hid the book as the door opened. "Oh, it's only you, Katy. I thought I'd been caught doing the forbidden!"

Katy grinned, but all the same glanced a little nervously back into the passage, as if she expected to see Miss Hart standing there. "You mustn't call me that, Miss Leonie, Miss Hart'd have the vapors if she found out!"

"If I know Miss Hart, she's safely ensconced in her warm parlor and has no intention of leaving it for the time being, not when it's as cold as this."

Katy set the tray carefully on Leonie's lap and then hesitated, reluctant to leave straightaway. "May I stay for a while, Miss Leonie?"

"You know that you can—unless you have some other duties. You haven't, have you?"

"No, Mrs. Durham said I could talk with you if you did not mind."

Leonie smiled, sniffing the still-warm Shrewsbury cakes. "I see that Mrs. Durham has been busy in the kitchens already this morning."

"Yes, Miss Leonie."

"Would you like one?" Leonie held out the dish.

Shyly Katy took one. She loved these moments with Leonie, whom she adored because she was so kind and natural, and without the unkindness which seemed so often to be the mark of young ladies at the seminary. Suddenly she remembered the head mistress's instructions. "Oh, Miss Leonie, I almost forgot! Miss Hart said would you help at tea this afternoon."

Leonie groaned. "Not our beloved benefactress again!"

"Yes. And her cousin Miss Benckendorff and a gentleman."

Leonie pulled a face. "It sounds awful. Still, I suppose I will have to do as I'm asked. I'm glad I'm leaving this place. That wretched Russian woman has made it quite horrible here."

"Yes," agreed Katy with immense feeling.

Leonie looked quickly at her. "Has something else happened?"

"I forgot to take off my mittens and Miss Hart caught me. I'm to be dismissed if anything like that happens again."

Leonie smiled and leaned over to squeeze the maid's cold little hand. 'Well, you'll be leaving soon anyway, and then you can thumb your nose at all of them."

Katy smiled hesitantly. "I still can't really believe you want me to be your maid, Miss Leonie."

"I wouldn't go away and leave you here."

"Yes, but to be your personal maid! I mean, I don't know all the things I'll need to know, and—"

"And you'll soon pick them up." Leonie smiled at her again. "You'll make an excellent lady's maid, Katy, I know that you will." She glanced toward the window then. "It looks as horrid as ever out there, which I suppose means being cooped up inside again."

"I think the sun will break through soon. It looked as if it would when I looked out of the landing window." Katy went to the window and peeped out.

To the west, over Hyde Park, there was little sign of the hoped-for sun. It was still very cold and white, almost as if snow had fallen. The herd of cows from the dairy in Queen Street was being driven in through the park gates, their breath even whiter than the fog and frost. There was a little traffic in the street now; a private carriage was making its slow way north toward Tyburn, its team picking their way carefully over the icy surface, and a donkey cart laden with holly and mistletoe was proceeding in the opposite direction toward Piccadilly, where normally the congestion was so great at the narrow junction that tempers were always frayed.

"Well?" said Leonie. "Do you think it will be fine?"

"It's hard to tell from this side of the house, but I do think it's getting brighter." Katy glanced back at the bed. "Miss Leonie?"

"Yes?"

"Do you . . . do you think he'll be there again?" she asked hesitantly, for she knew Leonie's low opinion of the mysterious gentleman.

"I sincerely hope not, for there was something about him for which I didn't care in the slightest."

Katy was puzzled. "I know, because you said so at the time, but I don't understand why. I mean, he was so very handsome—"

"And was conceitedly aware of the fact. He wasn't at all nice, Katy, I could tell it by the look in his eyes. His interest in me was anything but gallant and honorable, and nothing on earth would have allowed me to acknowledge him had he indeed had the audacity to speak. I took considerable delight in cutting him, and I shall do so again if we see him."

"Even if he speaks to you?"

"Especially then."

4

Later in the morning the pale winter sun at last broke through, and Miss Hart grudgingly gave her permission for Katy to accompany Leonie on her walk. They set off shortly before midday, Leonie once again in her cream mantle and pink-ribboned bonnet, Katy in her neat gray cloak. The improvement in the weather lured many to the park. There was more skating on the frozen Serpentine, and as on their last walk, they stopped to watch.

Katy glanced hopefully around for Leonie's unwanted admirer, but to her disappointment there was no sign of him. Leonie felt no such disappointment at his absence, for she had meant every word she said about him and had no desire at all to be confronted by a man she instinctively distrusted and disliked.

Walking back toward the park gates afterward, Leonie found herself gazing at the seminary, which had been her home for so long now. Soon she would be leaving it forever, going through the little ritual farewell ceremony which she had seen so many others go through in the past. She would be invited to the visitors' room, where the entire school would be gathered and where she would take a glass of wine with Miss Hart. Then she would be presented with a bouquet of flowers and two handsome leather-bound volumes of prayers, each one embossed in gold with her initials. Inside, on blank pages provided specifically for the purpose, Miss Hart would have written: "Miss Conyngham, with every kind and affectionate wish." The headmistress would then give a carefully prepared speech, and after that Leonie Conyngham would step out of the house and into her father's waiting carriage, to be driven away to her dazzling new life.

She walked more slowly, remembering some previous departures, some decorous, others the very opposite. When impetuous, warmhearted Athena Raleigh had left, requested to do so on account of her rather-too-frequent meetings with young army officers in the park, Miss Hart had hypocritically delivered her usual speech, expressing her sorrow at losing so excellent a young lady; Athena had repaid this preposterous insincerity by delivering a retaliatory speech which left Miss Hart with a very red face and the rest of the school struggling to hide its delight and mirth. That day had certainly been the highlight of an otherwise dull term. Another term had been highlighted by the departure of Lady Imogen Longhurst, the tall, beautiful. spiteful daughter of the Earl of Wadford. Imogen's capacity for unkindness and insincerity more than matched Miss Hart's, and she was cordially disliked by most of the other pupils, especially Leonie, whom she had selected time and time again over the years as the object of her clever malice. The fact that the Earl and Countess of Wadford had been present at their daughter's leaving ceremony had produced in Imogen an amazing skill as an actress. Obviously concerned that her parents might wonder at the lack of sorrow the other young ladies showed at their daughter's departure, she had drawn all attention to herself by weeping copious tears and promising to visit them all again as soon as she possibly could. To everyone's immense relief, no such visit was forthcoming.

Reaching the park gates, Leonie paused on the pavement, pondering the unfairness of life, for Athena, who had had so many friends, had eloped to Gretna Green with a scoundrel who'd made her very unhappy and had then deserted her. She now lived in severely reduced circumstances in Bath, disowned by her outraged family. Cold, scheming Imogen, on the other hand, had become the undisputed belle of the 1813 Season, and in the new year would be announcing her betrothal to Sir Guy de Lacey, a very handsome and wealthy gentleman who had fallen hopelessly in love with her at first sight. Leonie could only unkindly conclude that there must be something seriously wrong with Sir Guy's eyes, as well as his judgment. Had there been any justice, she thought with a sad sigh, then things would have turned out in the opposite way, and odious Imogen would be languishing in Bath, while softhearted, lovable Athena basked in the adoration of a man like Sir Guy!

"Miss Leonie!" cried Katy suddenly, tugging at her arm and pointing behind. "He's there again, look!"

Leonie turned quickly and saw two gentlemen riding across the park toward the gates. The man who had watched them the week before was riding a fine gray thoroughbred. He was dressed in a dark green coat and beige breeches, and he had not as yet noticed them. Beside him, the other gentleman was mounted on a large black horse. He was taller than his companion and about the same age, and his thin face had a quick, clever look. His eyes were so blue that the clearness of the color could be seen even at that distance, and his hair was a rich auburn which somehow made him seem oddly familiar to Leonie. In fact, everything about him suggested that she should know him, and yet she knew that she didn't. She did know, however, that she instinctively disliked him as much as she did her unknown admirer. They were two of a kind.

At that moment her admirer saw her and reined in immediately, leaning over to point her out to his companion. The second man looked quickly toward her then, his blue eyes very sharp and shrewd.

Leonie didn't hesitate; she caught a startled Katy by the arm and propelled her across Park Lane, which was much more busy now. A brewer's wagon had to come to a sudden standstill or risk knocking them down, and the wagoner shouted furiously after them, waving his dirty fist, but Leonie didn't even glance around. Reaching the seminary door, she knocked anxiously, and to her relief, Joseph, the Negro footman, admitted them almost immediately.

"Miz Leonie?" he cried in astonishment as she and Katy almost rushed into the vestibule.

She didn't reply, but quickly peeped around the lace curtain of the tall, narrow window beside the door. The two riders had proceeded as far as the park gates, but no farther. They looked across at the seminary for a moment and then turned away, their horses moving at a mere walk toward the Serpentine.

Katy pushed close to her. "Who are they, Miss Leonie?"

"I don't know, but somehow I feel as if I should know the second man, the one with the bright auburn hair."

Katy nodded. "I know what you mean, he looked familiar to me too."

"He did?" Leonie turned quickly to Joseph. "Joseph, come here quickly. Do you see the two gentlemen on horses?"

"Yes, Miz Leonie."

"Do you recognize either of them?"

"No, ma'am. Except—"

"Yes?"

"Well, the one with the red hair reminds me, well, of Lady Imogen Longhurst."

Leonie stared at him and then looked quickly out again, but the two riders had passed out of sight among the trees. Joseph was right, the second man *had* looked like Imogen, and that was why he'd seemed familiar. Imogen had a brother, her twin, Lord Edward Longhurst, and he was a notorious rake. He'd also set a record because his name had appeared more often in White's betting book than anyone else's, which was quite an achievement in a society devoted to gambling and wagering of one sort or another.

Slowly she turned back into the firelit vestibule, with its cream silk walls and elegant crimson chairs and sofa. It had been no coincidence that those two gentlemen had been riding in the park like that; every instinct told her that they had been hoping to encounter her once more.

Katy glanced concernedly at her. "Are you all right, Miss Leonie?"

"Hm?"

"Are you all right? You've gone so very quiet."

Leonie turned with a brisk smile. "I'm quite all right, I was just thinking that in future I'll walk somewhere else, but definitely *not* anywhere near the park."

Katy nodded. "Yes, Miss Leonie."

Leonie took a deep breath and smiled at Joseph. "Do you think Mrs. Durham could be prevailed upon to make some tea? I'm absolutely freezing."

The footman smiled. "I'm sure she can, Miz Leonie. Oh, and, Miz Leonie?"

"Yes?"

"Miz Hart said to remind you when you returned that the countess will be here promptly at four."

Leonie sighed. "Very well. Thank you, Joseph."

He gave her a sympathetic smile and went away toward the kitchens.

Leonie glanced at the long-case clock in the corner and then grimaced. "Two and a half hours to go, and then it will be all manners and p's and q's, all Russia and Smolny, then more Russia and more Smolny, a few new rules, some criticisms, and then even more Russia and Smolny. Oh, how I wish the wretched woman would go back to her precious St. Petersburg and leave us all in peace. And I wish she'd take Miss Benckendorff with her, and probably the gentleman who's going to be with them today, for he's bound to be Russian too, and equally as odious!"

But the countess's gentleman guest certainly wasn't Russian, he was very English, and he had just taken his leave of Lord Edward Longhurst and was riding back through Mayfair to his magnificent town house in Grosvenor Square. There he would change before driving to Harley Street to join the countess and her cousin Nadia. In two and a half hours' time he would come face to face at last with Leonie, just as he had planned to do from the very outset.

5

Dorothea Lieven usually made a point of arriving late for appointments, but today she was early. The carriage which was to convey her and her two companions to tea at the seminary left the embassy in Harley Street at half-past three precisely. It was Count Lieven's carriage, and as befitted the czar's representative at the Court of St. James's, it was very grand indeed, with the imperial coat-of-arms emblazoned on its gleaming blue panels. Drawn by a matched team of four fine bays, it proceeded at a brisk pace along Oxford Street toward Tyburn and the northern end of Park Lane. The December sun was sinking in a blaze of crimson and gold beyond Hyde Park, and long, cold shadows were reaching over the frozen ground. Soon it would be dark again, and already the haze of mist and fog was beginning to gather beneath the trees.

Dorothea was twenty-eight years old and very tall and thin. She wore a small honey-colored fur hat and a similarly colored three-quarter-length pelisse, from beneath the hem of which spilled the delicate folds of her white muslin gown. Her little feet, of which she was very vain, were encased in neat ankle boots which were laced very fashionably at the back. In her arms she carried her pet pug dog, Baryshna, which had around its neck a Persian gold collar studded with turquoises. This collar had been a gift from the Empress Maria Feodorovna, and was therefore always on display, since it was necessary to remind the British of such a grand royal connection. Dorothea sat stiffly on the seat, glancing neither to the right nor to the left, but her clever black eyes missed nothing for all that, and she was aware of everyone she passed.

Next to her on the velvet seat was her cousin Miss Nadia Benckendorff, who at the age of twenty-one was possessed of a breathtaking golden beauty which was set off to the very best advantage by the wearing of white from head to toe. She had on a fur-trimmed pelisse, a bombazine gown, a fur hat and muff, and ankle boots, and all were the purest of whites. Her large green eyes were set in a heart-shaped face, and her lips were that rosebud shape which was all the rage. Her golden hair was cut short so that it curled prettily around her face, making her one of the loveliest creatures and turning many an admiring male head as the carriage swept past. Nadia's looks and lofty connections might have been expected to have won her many suitable offers of marriage, but they had not. The truth was that she was virtually penniless and was completely dependent upon the charity of other branches of her family. It was not a situation which she liked or appreciated, and she had left St. Petersburg determined to find herself a wealthy British husband; and like Emmeline Hart twenty years earlier, she was not very particular about the means she used to achieve her aim. Today she was feeling confident that soon she would succeed, for she had set her scheming, ambitious cap at the young man sitting opposite her in the carriage. He had initially been cool and indifferent toward her, but during the last week he had undergone a gratifyingly promising change of heart, as his presence at this rather dull visit to the seminary bore excellent witness. She looked across at him and smiled; it was a slow sensuous smile which assured him of so very much if things continued in the present vein. He returned the smile.

The carriage at last drew up at the curb outside the seminary. The gentleman alighted, pausing for the briefest of moments to look up at the balconied window of the principal bedchamber on the second floor. His glance took in the sturdy fig tree growing so conveniently next to it. He smiled a little to himself and then turned gallantly to assist Dorothea and Nadia to step down from the carriage.

The visitors' unexpected promptness caught Leonie unawares, and Katy was still putting the final touches to her hair as the carriage drew up outside. With a gasp she looked a last time at her reflection in the mirror, wondering if the light blue dimity gown and pearl necklace and earrings were right for the occasion. Katy handed her her shawl and she hurried out of the room, forgetting her reticule, which the maid hastily picked up and brought quickly after her. Leonie had descended the stairs as far as the half-landing, but there she came to a startled halt, drawing swiftly back out of view of those in the vestibule below. Katy hurried down to her and Leonie immediately put a warning finger to her lips before pointing down. The maid looked over the edge of the banisters and her breath caught as she immediately recognized the tall, handsome gentleman standing with Dorothea and Nadia.

At that moment Miss Hart bustled from the visitors' room at the rear of the house. She was all smiles and civility, her dull green taffeta skirts rustling, her best biggin trembling with ribboned bows. "Ah, Countess, Miss Benckendorff, how delighted I am to welcome you once more." She sank into a curtsy and then rose, looking inquiringly at the gentleman, whom she did not know.

Dorothea immediately effected the necessary introduction. Her voice was hard and dry, and had a heavy French accent, for French was the language of the court at St. Petersburg. "Miss Hart, may I present you to his grace the Duke of Thornbury."

"Your grace." Miss Hart dutifully curtsied again.

Leonie was astonished to learn the identity of her admirer, for Rupert Allingham, fourth Duke of Thornbury, was one of the most eligible and sought-after gentlemen in the realm!

Down in the vestibule, Miss Hart was attending assiduously to her duties as hostess. Still all smiles and affability, she murmured that they would all be much more comfortable in the visitors' room, and she led the way in that direction, followed by Dorothea, the plump pug still clasped in her arms.

Rupert was about to go with them, when suddenly Nadia put a hand softly on his arm. "A moment, milord." Her voice was husky and like Dorothea's had a strong French accent.

He was reluctant to linger. "I hardly think this is the time—"

"Please, milord," she persisted, "for there may not be another opportunity to speak alone with you today." She moved perceptibly closer to him. Her hand was still on his arm, and her green eyes were dark and lustrous. "I only want to beg you not to go to Althorp for Christmas, but to stay in London."

"I've already accepted the invitation."

"Make an excuse. Do it for me."

He smiled a little. "For you? My dear Nadia, I hardly see the point, since you will be in Streatham Park and therefore out of town as well."

"I could stay on at the embassy."

"And disappoint your cousin? No, we will leave our plans as they stand. Now, then, let us rejoin the others before they wonder what mischief we're up to."

She pouted a little, but then her hand dropped from his arm and she smiled. "I won't give up, milord. I shall keep on until you change your mind."

"You, madam, are astonishingly forward."

"In St. Petersburg we do not waste time in pretense."

"So it seems." He offered her his arm and they walked toward the visitors' room.

The two secret onlookers still stood on the half-landing. Katy turned anxiously to Leonie. "What will you do now? Will you still go down?"

"I don't know what to do, for if I go down, then I am certain to be formally introduced to him, and that is something I wish to avoid at all costs." She thought for a moment. "Perhaps I could cry off with a headache. Yes, that's it, you must go to Miss Hart and tell her I've been taken unwell and won't be able to join them."

But even as she said this, Miss Hart suddenly appeared at the foot of the stairs. "Ah, there you are, Miss Conyngham, I was wondering where you'd got to. Do come down, the countess and her guests have already arrived."

"Yes, Miss Hart, but . . ." Leonie broke off, for the headmistress had hurried away again without hearing.

Katy was dismayed. "Oh, now you'll *have* to go down."

Leonie nodded reluctantly.

"It'll be all right, I'm sure it will. You're probably completely wrong about the duke.'' The maid's voice lacked conviction.

''I'm not wrong about him. I only wish I was.'' Leonie took a deep breath and then went down the remaining stairs.

6

The visitors' room, as might be expected, was a particularly handsome chamber, for it was here that Miss Hart received all important visitors, and here that the young ladies entertained their families and friends. It was a blue-and-gold room, decorated with Christmas greenery and dominated by another portrait of Dorothea. A bright fire flickered in the gray-and-white marble fireplace, and a very fine cut-glass chandelier illuminated the elegant furnishings. The sofas and chairs were upholstered in sapphire-blue velvet, there was cream brocade on the walls, and the curtains waiting to be drawn at the tall windows were of a particularly rich and heavy dark gold.

Tea was to be served at a low table before two of the sofas. The best gold-and-white porcelain had been put out, and there were plates of little triangular sandwiches, cakes, and biscuits. It all looked very formal and precise, even to the carefully arranged bowl of Christmas roses in the center, and it didn't look at all inviting.

Outside the sun had almost set now, its dying rays resting blood-red on the roofs of the houses in South Audley Street. In the seminary's garden, the ornamental pool seemed as if petrified, as did the weeping willow hanging over it. The pale light from the windows illuminated the two stone sphinxes, but beyond them all was lost in the brief winter twilight.

No one had commenced tea as Leonie entered. Dorothea and Miss Hart were seated on one of the sofas by the table, while Rupert and Nadia were inspecting a painting in the alcove by the fireplace. They were so intent upon it that they did not hear the door open and close.

Dorothea was criticizing the windows. "I tell you they are naked," she was saying, "quite naked and *abominable*."

Miss Hart was a little bemused. "I . . . I'm afraid I don't quite understand."

"Naked, Miss Hart. I think you British have no idea at all how to make your houses agreeable in the winter. You keep them so cold, and you leave the windows bare so that one is forced to look outside and remember how dismal the weather is. In Russia it is the custom to place exotic plants in embrasures, so that the illusion of spring or even summer is created. Then one may forget that it is winter." She waved a disparaging hand toward the windows. "This is *most* discomforting."

"Oh. Oh, I'm so very sorry," cried Miss Hart in dismay. "I'll have the curtains drawn immediately!"

"Drawn? That will not do, unless you intend to keep them drawn all day as well as all night."

The headmistress did not know what she was expected to reply to this. "Well, yes," she said tentatively, "of couse, if that is what you wish."

"Mon Dieu," cried Dorothea in some irritation, "of *course* that is not what I wish. Why would I wish to sit in the dark all the time? You have obviously not understood what I've been saying."

"I haven't?" Miss Hart was mortified, her cheeks flushing very pink indeed.

"The plants, madam, the plants!"

In something of a daze, the headmistress gazed dumbly at the garlands of holly, ivy, myrtle, and mistletoe, which were the only plants in the room.

"Not those wretched things, Miss Hart, the plants for the windows!" Dorothea gave an impatient sigh. "I will see that some are sent from the greenhouses at Streatham Park."

"Streatham Park?"

"The country estate we have taken for the time being."

"Oh."

"I presume you know how to look after delicate plants?"

"Oh, yes, my lady," replied Miss Hart most untruthfully. "You are very kind."

"Kindness has nothing to do with it, madam. I merely think of my own comfort. I cannot abide naked windows."

Miss Hart noticed Leonie then and thankfully beckoned her forward. "Ah, Miss Conyngham, do come closer."

Rupert turned immediately, his glance raking Leonie. Nadia, who had still been discussing the merits of the painting, broke off in mid-sentence as she became aware of his sudden interest in the new arrival. Her green eyes hardened as she saw the look in his eyes, and she instantly formed a dislike for Leonie.

Miss Hart was relieved to be able to divert attention from the windows. She beamed at Dorothea. "My lady, you are of course already acquainted with Miss Conyngham, but I do not believe she has met either Miss Benckendorff or his grace."

Leonie curtsied to Dorothea. "Good afternoon, my lady."

Dorothea gave a gracious nod. "*Enchantée,* Miss Conyngham. How very charming you look, I do so like pearls with pale blue, there is something so very tasteful about such a combination. Now then, allow me to present you to my cousin, Miss Benckendorff. Nadia, this is Miss Conyngham, who is the most senior young lady here."

Nadia's acknowledgment was exceedingly cool; she inclined her head but said nothing at all. Leonie could not help but be aware of the other's dislike, and so she too said nothing, but she guessed why she was being received so very coolly, for one had only to glance at Rupert to see. He had not taken his eyes from her since the moment he realized she was there.

Dorothea's black eyes flickered curiously toward her silent cousin, but then Rupert stepped forward to be introduced. "Ah yes, Miss Conyngham," she said, "this is his grace the Duke of Thornbury. Your grace, allow me to present Miss Conyngham."

He took Leonie's hand and drew it warmly to his lips. "Your servant, Miss Conyngham."

"Your grace." Leonie's voice was not encouraging and she deliberately withdrew her hand at the earliest moment.

He seemed undeterred. "You are the seminary's most senior young lady? Am I to hope that that means you will soon be out in society?"

Before she could reply, Miss Hart spoke for her. "She will indeed, your grace, and it is my opinion that she will be to the 1814 Season what dear Lady Imogen Longhurst was to that of 1813."

He smiled, gazing into Leonie's eyes. "I'm sure you are right," he murmured.

Nadia gave a slight laugh. "How can there be anyone to compare with Lady Imogen?" she said, going to sit down on one of the sofas.

Miss Hart smiled at her. "You are acquainted with Lady Imogen, Miss Benckendorff?"

"She and I are very close friends indeed, Miss Hart."

"I do so hope that one day soon she will call upon us here—it would be so good to see her again. I would welcome the opportunity to congratulate her upon her forthcoming betrothal to Sir Guy de Lacey."

Nadia didn't reply. Her angry green eyes were still upon Rupert and Leonie.

Belatedly Miss Hart detected the undercurrents which had been stirred the moment Leonie had come into the room. Clearing her throat a little nervously, she turned once more to Dorothea, keeping a wary eye as she did so upon the pug, which had already snapped irritably at her hand. "I understand that you wish to discuss changes in next year's curriculum."

"I do, since at the moment there appears to be a very serious omission."

"Omission? Oh, surely that cannot be so."

"It can, madam. I refer to the subject of history."

Miss Hart stared. "History? But Miss Ross is an excellent teacher, my lady. I'm sure there cannot be anything wrong with her lessons."

"There is a great deal wrong when the history of the greatest nation on earth is omitted. I speak of Russia, Miss Hart."

Miss Hart's mouth opened and closed. "Russia?" she said at last.

"It is my opinion that Russian history must be taught here, and since from your reaction it appears necessary to explain my reasons, I will now proceed to do so."

As she began, Rupert suddenly offered Leonie his arm.

"Miss Conyngham, I'm intrigued by the sphinxes I noticed outside the window. Perhaps you would be good enough to explain them to me."

It was a ploy to get her away from the others. She ignored the proffered arm. "They are only reproductions, sir, and not in the least interesting."

"Nevertheless, I would like you to tell me about them," he replied, taking her hand and drawing it firmly through his arm.

Short of making a scene, she had no alternative but to go with him to the window, which was well out of the hearing of the others. She could feel Nadia's angry gaze following them.

He looked out at the two statues, pretending to discuss them, but in reality he spoke of something entirely different. "You don't seem pleased to see me, Miss Conyngham."

"You're very perceptive, sir."

"You're devastatingly honest."

"It seems necessary where you are concerned, sir."

"Come now, don't be cross with me. I haven't sinned so very greatly, have I?"

"I can hardly be cross with you, sir, since I'm completely indifferent to you," she replied dryly. She met his gaze. "You've wasted your time coming here."

He raised an eyebrow. "Do they teach all their young ladies to be so forthright?"

She didn't reply.

He looked at her for a moment and then glanced briefly back at Nadia, who was still watching jealously from the other side of the room. "Perhaps it is because you think I have an understanding with Miss Benckendorff," he said, "and if so, let me assure you that I don't. She means nothing to me and I've given her no reason to think that she does."

She stared at him, remembering the scene she and Katy had witnessed in the vestibule. "You're despicable," she whispered. "You're giving her *every* reason!"

His eyes became more guarded. "Whatever you may think, I promise you that Miss Benckendorff does not warrant your sympathy. She is interested only in my wealth and title."

"Perhaps such selectivity is understandable where you are concerned, for to be sure you don't appear to be particularly likable."

Anger flashed across his handsome face. "You are very rude, Miss Conyngham, unnecessarily so, if I may say so."

"You may say what you wish, sirrah, for if I'm rude to you it's because you deserve it. Your reason for coming here today is very insulting indeed, and so under the circumstances, I feel that my mild sarcasm is more than justified."

He gave a cool laugh, but he was angry. "Insulting? Since when has taking a cup of tea been an insult?"

"I'm not a fool, sir, and so pray don't treat me like one. When you saw me in the park you decided to try to seduce me. Your presence here now is merely further proof of that."

"My dear Miss Conyngham, you presume too much."

"No, sirrah, it is you who presume too much. In the park you thought yourself the end in subtlety and cleverness, and you were wrong. You're still wrong, for I will never be even mildly well-disposed toward you. And now, if you will excuse me, I am needed to assist with the tea." She left him just as the maids came in with the silver teapot and hot water jug. She sat down at the other end of the sofa where Nadia sat. There was malice in the glance Nadia gave her.

Rupert remained by the window, his back toward them, and as Leonie began to pour the tea, he showed no inclination to come and sit down.

Miss Hart was still enduring Russian history, and was glad of the diversion as Leonie handed her her cup. Conversation died away for a moment as Dorothea too took her cup and sipped it. Leonie turned to pour Nadia's tea, but Nadia immediately leaned forward and put her hand over the cup. There was a challenging look in her green eyes. "I don't drink tea," she said coolly. "I drink only strong black coffee topped with thick cream." She spoke as if Leonie were little more than a servant.

Dorothea looked at her in disapproving surprise and Miss Hart sat forward hurriedly. "Oh, dear," she said in dismay.

Nadia smiled, still looking at Leonie. "Do not be concerned, Miss Hart, for I'm sure that Miss Conyngham will be only too pleased to be of assistance."

Rupert had turned from the window now, his hazel eyes sharpening as he looked at Nadia. Leonie was extremely angry, but she hid this very successfully behind a sweet smile. She had no intention of letting Nadia get away with such unwarranted rudeness. "But of course, Miss Bencken-dorff," she said. "I'd be delighted to help you. Tell me, how thick do you like it?"

' Like it?" Nadia was caught unawares. "Like what?"

"The cream."

The green eyes flickered. "As thick as possible," she said, knowing that much of the cream she had sampled in England was far from thick.

Still smiling, Leonie got up to ring for Joseph, who came immediately. She went quickly to him, her voice low so that only he could hear. "Joseph, does Mrs. Durham still have some of that clotted cream her sister sent her from Devon?"

He looked at her in surprise. "Why, I believe so, Miz Leonie."

"Do you think she could be prevailed upon to part with a little of it? For me?"

He smiled. "I'm sure she could, Miz Leonie."

"Well, perhaps not exactly for me. Miss Benckendorff would like some strong black coffee topped with thick cream." She paused, a wicked gleam in her eyes. "I rather think Mrs. Durham's clotted cream would be the very thing, don't you agree?"

He grinned. "I do indeed, Miz Leonie. I'll attend to it straightaway."

Leonie returned to her place. Conversation was now turning upon school matters again. Dorothea was once more finding fault. "Miss Hart, I could not help but notice at church last Sunday how very untidy your young ladies looked."

Miss Hart gave a start. "Untidy, my lady? Oh, surely not!"

"Oh, individually they may be quite acceptable, but as a whole they present a rather disagreeable *mélange*. Uniformity is the key to excellence, as the magnificent example of the Smolny Institute proves beyond a doubt. Your young ladies must follow this example, they too must have a uniform. I've been giving the matter much consideration, for one must be careful about such things, and I thought that green stuff dresses with tippets and white sashes would be suitable for the winter. For the summer the colors could be reversed, with white muslin dresses and green sashes. What do you think?"

"Well, I—"

"*Bon*, it is settled then. I trust you will attend to it as quickly as possible."

Miss Hart nodded resignedly.

Joseph returned with a small tray on which stood a small silver coffeepot and a dish containing a portion of Mrs. Durham's clotted cream. He set the tray carefully before Leonie and then withdrew again. Miss Hart forgot all about uniforms as she stared in astonishment at the thick yellow cream, which was so firm and unyielding that the spoon stood up in it. Rupert also noticed the cream, and glanced quickly at Leonie's demurely lowered eyes as she poured the coffee and handed the cup to Nadia. Then she picked up the dish of cream and held it out as well. "No doubt you would prefer to help yourself to the cream, Miss Benckendorff," she said lightly, her expression all innocence. "I trust it is thick enough for you."

Nadia gave her a venomous look and took the coffee but ignored the proffered cream. Leonie said nothing, but replaced it on the tray. Tit for tat, she thought with some satisfaction.

At that moment Joseph returned to the room and hurried across to Miss Hart, who looked up with some irritation. "Yes? What is it? You know I do not like being disturbed when I have guests."

"Excuse me, ma'am, but Sir Guy de Lacey has called. He says he wishes to see over the premises with a view to sending his niece here."

Miss Hart was a little flustered, for Sir Guy was a man of some importance, but at the same time she had no wish to neglect Dorothea. "Joseph, perhaps you could find Miss Ross and ask her to attend to Sir Guy."

Nadia put her cup down quickly. "Oh, surely there is no need for that, Miss Hart," she said with a sugary smile, "for you have an ambassadress *par excellence* in Miss Conyngham. Could she not assist Sir Guy?"

It was an attempt to remove Leonie from Rupert's vicinity, something which Nadia obviously thought would annoy and dismay her, but the very opposite was the case and Leonie leapt at the chance. She rose immediately to her feet, smiling at Miss Hart. "I'd be delighted to be of assistance, Miss Hart."

The headmistress beamed with relief. "Oh, my dear, would you really? Perhaps you could invite Sir Guy to join us for tea, and then I would be able to conduct him personally over the seminary afterward. If that is not agreeable to him, then I would be most grateful if you could show him around for me."

"Very well, Miss Hart." As Leonie withdrew, she noticed how quickly Nadia got up and went to Rupert by the window. They richly deserved each other, she thought, for they were surely well-matched. As she closed the door and proceeded toward the vestibule where Sir Guy de Lacey waited, she wondered if he and Imogen Longhurst were equally well-matched. Somehow she simply could not believe that a man who was of true quality and sensitivity could fall in love with a woman as cold and hollow as Imogen.

7

Sir Guy de Lacey was about thirty years old, tall, handsome, and very manly, with a clean strong profile and dark arresting eyes. At first he did not hear her approach. He stood by the fireplace in the vestibule, one hand resting on the mantelshelf as he gazed thoughtfully into the glowing flames. His tousled black hair was a little longer than present fashion dictated, giving him an individuality which was set off perfectly by his impeccable taste in clothes. He had on an oyster brocade waistcoat, a frilled white shirt, and a close-fitting gray coat. There was a small diamond pin in his starched cravat, and it glittered now and then in the firelight. He had evidently ridden to the seminary, for he wore breeches and top boots, and there was a riding crop on the table with his hat and gloves. There was something disconcerting about him, for he was at once rugged and authoritative, and yet elegant and refined. He was the sort of man toward whom women were inexorably drawn, and in spite of her desire to dislike him because of Imogen, Leonie found that she was no exception; indeed when she looked at him she thought him devastatingly attractive.

He became aware of her then and turned. She was very conscious of how dark and compelling his eys were. It was as if he was able to read her every thought. A strange, totally unexpected nervousness beset her for a moment. She lowered her eyes as she curtsied to him. "Sir Guy?"

"Your youthfulness amazes me, Miss Hart," he said dryly.

"Oh, I'm not Miss Hart," she replied quickly.

"I'm relieved to hear it, for I cannot envisage entrusting my niece to the care of a woman who somehow manages to look younger now than she apparently did twenty years ago." He studied her for a moment. "If you are not the redoubtable Miss Hart, may I inquire who you are?"

"My name is Miss Conyngham, Miss Leonie Conyngham. Miss Hart sent me to see if I could be of any assistance to you."

"Conyngham? I rather think your name is known to me."

No doubt it was, she thought, for Imogen was bound to have mentioned her, and not in a flattering light! She cleared her throat a little uncomfortably. "Miss Hart wishes to know if you would care to join her guests for tea."

He gave a short laugh. "Take tea with the Borgias? Perish the thought."

"I . . . beg your pardon?"

"Her guests are Countess Lieven, Miss Benckendorff, and the Duke of Thornbury, are they not?" He paused. "On second thought, maybe I insult the Borgias. No, Miss Conyngham, I do *not* wish to take tea, I've merely come to see over the premises with a view to sending my niece here."

"Perhaps I could conduct you?" she suggested tentatively, feeling inexplicably awkward in his presence.

He seemed to find her hesitancy amusing. "I don't know, Miss Conyngham—can you? Perhaps you do not feel sufficiently well-acquainted with the building."

She flushed. "I'm perfectly well-acquainted with it, sir."

"Then by all means show me around." He glanced at the long-case clock in the corner. "And I suggest that you do so promptly, for I have an early dinner appointment and wish to have this mummery over with as soon as possible."

Mummery? What manner of word was that to use of something concerning his niece's future?

"Do I detect a gleam of disapproval in your eyes, Miss Conyngham?"

"It isn't for me to approve or disapprove, Sir Guy."

"I'm glad you realize that fact."

She was beginning to dislike him. The initial sense of attraction was still there, but although Guy de Lacey might be the most handsome of men, his manner left a great deal to be desired, and his ill-concealed impatience grated very much indeed. "Perhaps," she suggested coolly, "you might find it more convenient to call another day, when you have more time."

The dark eyes swung quickly toward her. "No, madam, I would not find it more convenient, and since Miss Hart has evidently dispatched you to assist me, might I suggest that that is precisely what you do?"

She felt hot, angry color flooding into her cheeks, and quickly she turned to pick up a lighted candelabrum from the nearby table. "If you will come this way, Sir Guy." She walked toward the schoolroom wing at the rear of the house.

They entered the music room first. Dancing was also taught there, and on a sunny day it was a bright, cheerful room, its windows overlooking the adjoining house on the corner of Curzon Street, but now it was dark and cold, the shutters closed and the velvet curtains tightly drawn. Their steps echoed on the gleaming parquet floor, and the shivering light from the candelabrum illuminated the dust sheets over the pianoforte and harp. The chandeliers moved slightly in the draft from the open door.

Leonie's voice sounded hollow as she explained the various lessons which took place in the room, but she was aware that he was paying very little attention to what she said. His thoughts appeared to be elsewhere. On his dinner engagement? On Imogen? Wherever they were, they did not seem to center upon his unfortunate niece, on whose behalf he was here. He was, Leonie decided, merely going through the motions of being the concerned uncle and guardian, and he was doing it very gracelessly. The more she was with him, the more disagreeable she found him, and the more she thought him extremely well-suited to a woman as odious as Imogen Longhurst! Her growing dislike almost became too obvious when he suddenly took out his fob watch and again looked at the time. Her voice died away and her lips pressed closed. What point was there in explaining anything to this man? He quite palpably was not interested.

"Have you finished, Miss Conyngham?"

"There doesn't appear to be anything else to say, Sir Guy." It was as close as she dared come to letting him know what she thought.

His dark glance rested thoughtfully on her. "No doubt

there isn't," he murmured, "since you've been extremely informative and efficient."

She doubted if he'd heard a single word she'd said, let alone been able to judge if she'd been either informative or efficient. "Shall we proceed, sir?" she inquired, turning back toward the door, the sudden movement making the candles smoke and stream.

He said nothing more as she conducted him over the rest of the seminary. She showed him the classrooms, the dining room, the small dormitories where the youngest pupils slept with either Miss Ross or Mlle. Clary to watch over them, and the single bedrooms where the older pupils were allowed much more privacy. The circuit almost completed, she led him through the kitchens, and then the bathhouse, finally taking him to the small punishment room, where Mlle. Clary presided over the dreaded reclining board. The board was where miscreants were sent and ordered to lie motionless for a prescribed time. Leonie had herself been dispatched there only once, and she had found the experience so unpleasant that she had vowed never to be so punished again. Imogen, it went without saying, had never been sent there at all; it also went without saying that Athena Raleigh had spent a great deal of time there, reflecting upon her many sins, and repenting none of them.

At last the tour was over and they returned to the vestibule. Miss Hart and her guests were still in the visitors' room: Leonie could hear the low murmur of their voices. She put the candelabrum back upon the table. "I trust you find the seminary to your approval, Sir Guy."

"I do, Miss Conyhgham, but then, it is hardly likely that I would *not* approve of the establishment attended by the lady I am to marry."

"I think your niece will be very happy here."

He gave an ironic laugh. "My dear Miss Conyngham, Stella de Lacey would refuse to be happy in paradise itself at the moment. To be perfectly honest, she may be only twelve years old, but she has recently become a veritable monster, a tyrant, intent only upon having her own way, come what may. She is rebellious, rude, vindictive, and unreasonable, and she has decided to resent the fact that I am shortly to be married. All this manifests itself in a campaign against Imogen, who is completely innocent and does not deserve to be subjected to such a despicable display."

Leonie stared at him.

He gave a faint smile. "You seem at a loss for words, Miss Conyngham."

"You surely are not surprised."

"No, perhaps I'm not. But believe me, I don't exaggerate anything. Stella is indeed as horrid and unmanageable as I've said."

"Has she always been like that?"

"No, it has been a very recent thing."

She looked away, afraid that he might read her thoughts. Recent? Yes, she'd warrant it was, as recent as the arrival of Imogen Longhurst in Stella de Lacey's life!

"Miss Conyngham, no matter what you might think of me, I have my niece's best interests at heart. I've tried sweet reason, I've tried everything I can think of, but she will *not* promise good behavior—unless, of course, I agree to end my association with Imogen. That, quite obviously, cannot be, since I am not prepared to be dictated to by a chit of just twelve. I will be the master in my own house, and Stella is going to have to accept that what I wish is the law. I want her to come here, where I trust she will learn to mend her ways, for if she does not, then she will remain here until she does. I sincerely hope that her stay will not be a long one, for it is my desire to have her return home to Poyntons, my estate near Windsor, in time for the betrothal celebrations at the beginning of February. There is to be a very large house party, a number of balls, and so on. It is my fervent hope that this will prove an irresistible lure, for Stella adores house parties and dearly wishes to attend her first ball. If she is sent here as a salutary lesson, I believe that she will promise to be on her best behavior and that the whole of this disagreeable affair can be forgotten. Imogen is in complete agreement with me, indeed it was her suggestion that Stella should come here."

Leonie said nothing. Imogen suggested it? Yes, that was just the sort of thing she would do, and she'd do it with the full intention of never allowing Stella back into the de Lacey household! Imogen wasn't one to even attempt to understand a twelve-year-old girl's unhappiness—she'd think only of herself—and Guy de Lacey was obviously little better.

"You're very quiet, Miss Conyngham." He was looking at her. "I doubt if I would be far from the truth if I guessed that your sympathies are quite obviously with my niece."

She flushed a little. "She's only a child, Sir Guy."

"Aye, and what a child," he replied with some feeling. "You know nothing about my niece, Miss Conyngham, and I wonder if perhaps you instinctively sympathize with her because she has set herself against Imogen. Come now, don't look so astonished, for I know full well that you and Imogen cordially loathe each other." He gave a faint smile. "I also perceive that you feel more or less the same way toward me."

Her cheeks were still hot. "I wouldn't presume to like or dislike you, Sir Guy."

"Looking at you at this moment, Miss Conyngham, I'd say that you are the sort of young lady who would indeed presume, if she felt strongly enough about it. One way or another, you've left me in little doubt as to your opinion of me, and since you've allowed me to become aware of that opinion, I can only wonder if the grooming provided by this establishment is as completely efficient as it might be." His eyes were cool as he held her gaze. "I know that you are soon to be launched upon society. I can only trust the *monde* deals summarily with you. You need taking down a peg or two, Miss Leonie Conyngham, and if you cross my path again at some future date, you may be sure that I will be quite ready to do just that. Good day to you." Picking up his hat, gloves, and riding crop, he left. A breath of freezing air swept over her as he slammed the door behind him.

8

Stunned, she remained where she was. Her face felt as if it was on fire and her heart was thundering in her breast. She had never been been spoken to like that before, which was bad enough, but to think that she had suffered such humiliation at the hands of so uncivil and unpleasant a man! After all of which he was so patently guilty, he had had the gall to rudely criticize her! Oh, how she wished she'd told him *exactly* what she thought of him, and his loathsome bride-to-be, to say nothing of their joint unkindness to a mere child! But she had held her tongue, and so allowed him the privilege of the last word. She quivered from head to toe with anger and frustration, and at that moment she heard the door of the visitors' room opening. The thought of encountering Miss Hart's guests at this particular moment was too much, and she quickly gathered her skirts and hurried into the deserted school wing.

She took refuge in the music room, intending to remain safely out of sight until the visitors had departed, but as she opened the door something brushed past her legs and she gave an involuntary cry, but it was only Mrs. Durham's cat, which had evidently been shut in when she had been conducting Guy de Lacey over the premises. Quietly she closed the door behind her, and the icy darkness of the music room seemed to fold over her. Everything was so very quiet that she could almost hear her own heartbeats, but then gradually she became aware of footsteps approaching. She held her breath as she saw the swaying light of candles shining beneath the

45

door. The footsteps halted, and her heart almost stopped as the door was suddenly flung open and she saw the silhouette of a man, his identity at first impossible to see because of the brightness of the candelabrum he held.

"Miss Conyngham? Are you all right?"

It was Rupert. Her heart sank in dismay then, and sne stepped involuntarily back. "Sir?"

He came in and set the candelabrum down upon a small table. "I heard you cry out. Are you all right?"

"Perfectly. The cook's cat startled me."

He glanced around. "I'm hardly surprised if you are given to wandering around in the dark."

She flushed, but he could not see that in the candlelight. "I'm not wandering around, as you put it, sir, I merely came to see if I had left everything in order after conducting Sir Guy around."

He gave a short laugh. "Did you indeed? And how, pray, did you expect to see anything without a light? It's dark, Miss Conyngham, or hadn't you noticed? Come now, admit that you crept in here to avoid me."

"If that was my intention, sir, I appear to have been singularly unsuccessful."

He slowly pushed the door to, but did not close it completely. "Just as I," he said softly, "appear to have been singularly unsuccessful in my efforts to know you better."

"I dislike obviousness, sir."

"Then I ask you to forgive me; obviousness is the last thing of which I wish to be accused. Please, Miss Conyngham, can we not begin again? I wish to be your friend, but I seem to have got off on the proverbial wrong foot."

"You haven't got off on any foot at all, sir," she said coldly. "I don't like you and I will never trust you. Maybe you aren't used to having your advances spurned, maybe your looks, wealth, and title have hitherto always assured you of success, but you will never succeed with me."

"I don't give up easily, Leonie. I shall have you, I promise you that."

She stared at him, her eyes huge with disbelief. "How dare you," she whispered. "How dare you say such a thing to me!"

"I dare because it is the truth." He came closer suddenly,

taking her by the arms. "I want you, Leonie Conyngham, I wanted you from the very first moment I saw you. You're right, I'm not used to having my advaces spurned, and I don't intend to become used to it. You aren't going to be an exception, Leonie, because you're going to surrender to me just as all the others have in the past."

She wrenched herself away from him, at once frightened and furious. "Never!" she breathed. "Never!"

He smiled, watching as she hurried to the door. "We shall see," he murmured, "we shall see."

She heard him, but she didn't look back. As she emerged thankfully into the passage, she saw something white moving quickly out of sight into the vestibule. It was Nadia. In that split second Leonie realized that the countess's jealous cousin had been listening at the door and had probably overheard everything that was said. Nadia already loathed her; now that loathing had probably spilled over into a bitter hatred.

Leonie was relieved when it was time at last to retire to her bed, for this had been a day she wished to forget. She tried to relax before putting out the candle by reading more of *The Bride of Abydos*, but she simply couldn't concentrate on it. Every time she tried to read, she kept hearing Guy de Lacey's scornful voice promising to take her down a peg or two when next she was unfortunate enough to cross his path. She didn't think at all about Rupert, Duke of Thornbury, it was as if he didn't exist anymore, but she couldn't put arrogant, odious Sir Guy de Lacey out of her thoughts.

She heard a noise at the window, a scratching sound as if something was trying to get in. Then she heard a mewing. Mrs. Durham's cat! With a sigh she slipped from the bed and went to the window, drawing back the curtains and folding aside the cumbersome shutters. The cold seemed to breathe over her as she opened the window, and the bitter night air swept relentlessly into the room, making her breath catch. She looked quickly for the cat.

"Puss? Puss, where are you?" Surely the wretched creature hadn't decided to go away again!

"Well," said a masculine voice from very close at her side, "that's the first time I've been called that." It was Rupert; she could just make him out as he leaned back against the wrought-iron balustrade of the balcony. He had climbed up the fig tree.

With a cry she stepped back into the room and began to close the window, but he moved too quickly and was in the room before she could stop him. The candlelight gleamed in his hazel eyes as he closed the window behind him and drew the curtains across. "That's better," he said softly. "Now we can be much more comfortable."

"Get out," she breathed. She was very frightened. but she tried desperately not to show it.

"Oh, come now, don't be disagreeable," he murmured, flinging his top hat onto the dressing table. "I've only just arrived, and already you try to send me away."

"You are here without invitation, sir."

"If I'd waited to be invited, I'd have had a very long wait, wouldn't I?" he said reasonably. His eyes swept warmly over her, taking in her loosely brushed hair and the way the soft folds of her nightgown outlined her figure. "You're very lovely, too lovely for my peace of mind."

"Please leave," she said. "If you leave now I will say nothing of this."

"I'll leave when I've persuaded you that I'm really a very pleasant fellow."

"Pleasant? Is that what you call this?"

He came closer then, reaching out suddenly to seize her hand and drag her into his arms. Her lips parted to scream, but he put a rough hand over her mouth. "Now, now," he said softly, "that won't do at all. Be sensible, admit that to struggle will avail you nothing, but that to surrender, to meet me halfway, would mean so much pleasure."

She struggled to get away from him, but he held her too tightly. Then, miraculously, she heard someone at the door. It was Katy. He heard too, and for a moment was sufficiently distracted to allow Leonie the chance of dragging herself from his grasp.

"Katy!" she cried. "Katy, come in!"

The door opened and the startled maid looked in, her eyes widening as she saw the scene within.

Rupert straightened, giving a short laugh. "If you know what's good for you, girl, you'll leave," he said to the maid.

Katy stared at him then at Leonie. "Miss Leonie?"

"Stay, Katy. But you, sir"—Leonie turned toward him—"you can leave immediately."

He saw that for the moment the cards were stacked against him. He smiled, picking up his hat. "Very well, if that's the way you wish it. But remember this: if you say anything about what has happened, it will simply be your word against mine. Think of your reputation, Leonie—it will be sullied forever, and you're not even out yet."

"Get out of here," she whispered contemptuously, "and don't ever come near me again."

He met her angry gaze. "I still want you, Leonie. I don't think you realize how much. I'm away at Althorp over Christmas, but when I return, I promise that you'll hear from me again." He turned then and slipped out onto the balcony again.

Leonie hurried to the window, watching as he climbed over onto the fig tree. As he disappeared from sight, she emerged nervously onto the balcony. She had to see that he left; she wouldn't feel entirely safe until then. The cold didn't seem to touch her this time as she leaned over the balcony to watch him climb down to the frozen ground below.

The fog swirled clammily in the darkness, veiling the park across the street. There was ice on the wrought-iron rail beneath her hands as she watched him walk quickly away from the seminary toward the corner of Curzon Street. It was then that she realized he hadn't come alone, for another man was waiting with two horses by a streetlamp. The fog seemed to thin for a moment and she saw that the second man was a gentleman, clad in a costly fur-trimmed cloak and a top hat. As she stared at him, he suddenly looked up directly at her. It was Edward Longhurst.

She drew back quickly then, stepping into her room once more and closing the window and shutters firmly behind her.

"Are you all right, Miss Leonie?"

She turned quickly as Katy spoke. "Yes," she said quietly, "yes, I'm all right, but I don't know what I'd have done if you hadn't come when you did." She drew the curtains and went to sit on the bed. "I heard a noise on the balcony and thought it was Mrs. Durham's cat. I made it so easy for him, he just had to walk in."

"You weren't to know," said the maid comfortingly.

Leonie was silent for a moment. "He was right, you know. I would be taking a dreadful risk if I said anything about this."

"That's the way of it, isn't it?" replied the maid with a sigh. "Men can do things like this and be thought of as fine lusty fellows. Women must always think of their reputations. It isn't fair."

Leonie nodded, toying with the lace on the cuff of her nightgown. She looked up suddenly. "Why did you come?"

Katy smiled a little. "Mrs. Durham sent me to see if you wanted a glass of hot milk before you went to sleep."

Leonie couldn't help giving a wry laugh. "I think I shall be eternally grateful to her."

"Would you like some?"

"Yes, I think I would."

"I'll go and tell her." Katy went to the door and paused. "Will you be all right?"

"Yes."

As the maid hurried out, Leonie climbed back into the bed. She glanced a little nervously at the window. Had she fastened everything properly? Now that Katy had gone, the room seemed so very quiet. . . . She took a deep breath to steady herself. She had to push it all from her mind and think of something cheering instead. Like her father's return and the wonderful new life that lay ahead.

9

On the evening of the twenty-third of December, there was a grand ball at the Russian embassy. The weather was as cold and inhospitable as ever, and the freezing fog was, if anything, even more dense than before. Every vehicle on the streets of London had to be preceded by a man carrying a lighted flambeau, and the smoke from these, and from thousands of chimneys, added to the murk. It was being said that if the cold continued for much longer, then the Thames would freeze over and there would be another frost fair on the ice, just as had happened occasionally in the past. The cold seemed to seep into everything, and even the royal family was not exempt from its attentions. Princess Charlotte, the Regent's daughter, had been heard complaining that her rooms at Windsor Castle were so cold that in spite of fires a bowl of water had completely frozen over.

The weather, harsh as it was, did not deter the many guests attending the ball, and as eight o'clock approached, Harley Street was a crush of carriages. The embassy was ablaze with lights, but the brilliance was so obscured by the fog that little could be seen more than a few yards away. The smell of smoke hung heavily in the brittle air, and the sound of music drifted through the night.

Inside, the light from hundreds of candles made everything dazzling and bright. There were flowers and Christmas leaves everywhere. The green houses at Streatham Park had provided a colorful profusion of chrysanthemums, primulas, and camellias, as well as the exotic plants which filled every embrasure. Garlands of holly and ivy were draped around paintings, columns, balustrades, and statues, and golden baskets of mistletoe were suspended from the ceilings between the immense crystal chandeliers.

The babble of laughter and the drone of refined conversation vied with the orchestra as the guests assembled in the magnificent mirror-lined ballroom. Their reflections were repeated again and again in the polished glass, so that it seemed as if the ballroom stretched away into glittering infinity on all sides.

Dorothea was not in a good mood as she stood at the top of the ballroom steps with her husband, greeting the guests as they arrived. She was dressed splendidly in a red velvet Turkish gown, with a matching turban, and there were opals at her throat and in her ears. She looked very elegant, and there was a smile on her lips, but her eyes were sharp with displeasure, and beneath her hem her foot was tapping irritably. The cause of her discontent was her lack of success in acquiring either of the men of her choice as a lover. First there was Lord Byron, who had had the audacity to turn down an invitation to the ball, and who was about to leave town for an unspecified period; and second there was handsome young Lord Palmerston, a government minister of very romantic and charming inclination, who had more than caught her eye at the Almack's subscription ball the night before, and who had danced far too many dances with her friend and fellow patroness, Lady Cowper. Emily Cowper was very beautiful and fascinating, and Lord Palmerston hadn't looked at another woman all evening. It was all most frustrating and disagreeable, and Dorothea felt decidedly out of sorts as a consequence.

At her side, her husband stood in wary silence. Count Lieven was thirty-nine years old and reasonably good-looking, but he was far from impressive, in spite of the light blue cordon of St. André across his breast. He wasn't of the necessary caliber to be the czar's ambassador, owing his advancement solely to his mother's influence at St. Petersburg, and he was very much in the shadow of his forceful and clever wife.

Nadia stood a little behind them, her ostrich-feather fan wafting slowly to and fro. Tonight she had forsaken her favorite white and wore a pale pink satin gown with a low, square neckline and an overgown of rich blond lace. Her golden hair was hidden beneath a close-fitting pink velvet hat from which sprang a feathery aigrette, and she wore a magnificent diamond necklace which she had borrowed from Dorothea. She gazed over the crowded floor, thinking about Rupert, now so inconveniently on his way to Althorp. She had been so sure she would succeed with him, but her confidence had been severely shaken by the events at the seminary. Now she was forced to accept that Leonie Conyngham posed a very real threat to her plans; indeed there was even the unpalatable possibility that Rupert had engineered the whole thing in order to gain an introduction to Leonie. Nadia's lips pressed angrily together and her fan wafted more busily to and fro. She, who was so used to using others, had in turn been shamefully used herself, and her pride had received a considerable blow. But she was still set on winning Rupert, who was too great a prize to let slip through her clever fingers now. From now on she would be much more on her guard, she would play her cards very carefully indeed—and she would make Leonie pay dearly for her interference.

Her wandering glance fell suddenly on Edward Longhurst as he lounged on a red velvet sofa at the side of the ballroom. He sat alone, and looked supremely bored. He wore a tight-fitting blue coat and a ruffled shirt, and there was a quizzing glass swinging idly in his white-gloved hand. His thoughtful, cynical glance surveyed the dazzling gathering, and there was a perpetual half-smile upon his lips. She felt a surge of dislike. Why hadn't *he* gone to Althorp instead? She loathed him, having from the outset realized that he was no friend to her where her pursuit of Rupert Allingham was concerned. Outwardly he was always polite and friendly, but she could never rid herself of the feeling that he was laughing at her behind her back, as if he found her faintly ridiculous. There was, she decided, something rather malevolent about him; it was there in his sharp, incredibly blue eyes and in that irritating, contemptuous curve on his fine lips. He was not a man to trust, for he would always set himself against her. She studied him for a long moment. He was very like his sister in appearance, but there the similarity ended, for where he was

sly and untrustworthy, Imogen was all that she could have
wished for in a useful friend.

Nadia's glance moved over the crowded floor again, seeking out Imogen, who a moment before she had noticed dancing with Guy. She saw them almost in the center of the floor.
Imogen wore a primrose silk gown and her red hair was
twisted up beneath a dainty gold satin hat from which curved
a most elegant ostrich plume. She wore the superb Longhurst
pearls, a matching necklace and bracelet of the largest and
most perfect pearls imaginable, and she looked eye-catching
enough, thought Nadia grudgingly, but she could have looked
even better had she had the wit to wear blue. The Longhursts
all had such magnificent blue eyes, even the loathsome Edward, and in Nadia's opinion Imogen revealed a lamentable
lack of true fashion sense when she neglected always to
emphasize this feature. However, in spite of this failing, she
was still undoubtedly one of the loveliest women present,
although Nadia's charity did not extend to allowing her the
title of *the* loveliest, since that was an accolade she accorded
to herself alone.

How handsome and distinguished Guy looked in black
velvet, the diamond pin in his intricate cravat sparkling in the
warm light. Nadia smiled to herself. He was a man for whom
any woman would throw caution to the winds. He had every
quality she found desirable in a man: he was titled, more than
a little attractive, wealthy, and was possessed of, when he
chose, a devastating charm. Her lips pursed in puzzlement as
she watched them, for it was a mystery to her how someone
as shallow and insincere as Imogen had won the heart of a
man like Guy de Lacey. He seemed the sort who would be
drawn by a woman's inner qualities rather than by her looks
alone, and yet his choice of bride indicated that looks were
after all his sole desire, for Imogen Longhurst had beauty and
an infinite capacity for selfish scheming, but precious little
else. As Nadia made this detached, disloyal criticism, it did
not occur to her that the faults she found in Imogen were just
as prevalent in herself.

Imogen didn't speak as she and Guy danced; indeed she
hadn't spoken to him for some minutes now. She kept her

beautiful eyes downcast, and there were telltale spots of angry color on her pale cheeks.

"How long is this to continue?" he asked suddenly.

"As long as you persist in your attitude toward Nadia."

"I simply don't like her."

"She's my friend."

"I'm fully aware of that, but I still don't like her. Nor am I best pleased that you've invited her and the Lievens to Poyntons in February for our betrothal. The Lievens may be all that society desires at the moment, but they aren't exactly to my taste."

"Are you to choose my friends for me when we're married? Is that the sort of husband you intend to be?" Her eyes filled with tears.

His fingers tightened around hers. "Don't wrong me, you know that there isn't any truth in that," he said gently.

"But you wrong Nadia. Please, Guy, like her for my sake." She looked imploringly at him, determined to make him do as she wished.

"Imogen, I love you dearly, but I think you are very misguided in your choice of confidante. Nadia Benckendorff is an adventuress, and her breeding and background shouldn't blind you to that fact. She has come to London solely to find a husband."

"Isn't that what every woman wishes to do?" she countered. "Isn't that why I was launched upon society?"

"It isn't quite the same thing, and you know it."

She stopped dancing then. "You cannot love me if you say such things about my dearest friend."

"Imogen, you aren't being fair," he said, drawing her hand through his arm and leading her from the floor before attention was drawn to the friction between them.

She halted by a column, drawing away from him once more. Her cheeks were still a little pink and she wasn't yet prepared to be mollified. She was too angry with him to be reasonable, and she was determined to make him give in, even though she knew full well that on this occasion, as on many others, she was the one who was in the wrong. Her voice was haughty. "You may speak of fairness, Guy de Lacey, but are you being fair yourself? If you despise Nadia and the Lievens so very much, you shouldn't have accepted the invitation to come here tonight.''

''I accepted because you begged me to,'' he reminded her.

She drew herself up furiously then. ''So, it's all *my* fault, is it?''

He sighed inwardly, for she was quite impossible when she was in this mood. He had no desire to quarrel, but she was making any other course very difficult indeed. He tried again, putting his hand gently to her cheek and smiling. ''No, my darling, nothing's your fault—in fact I really cannot imagine why we're arguing.''

She looked sharply away. She didn't want to accept the olive branch. The argument was outwardly about Nadia, but she was also angry with him on another count—his attitude toward his niece, Stella de Lacey. The girl was impossible, and Imogen was determined to be rid of her for all time, but all she'd so far achieved was the promise that the brat would be sent to the seminary for a few weeks, with a view to her returning home in time for the betrothal! That didn't suit Imogen at all, although she'd managed to hide the fact ade—quately enough behind a screen of concern about the child's welfare. Guy loved his niece and took his responsibilities as her guardian seriously. He'd been loath to agree to send her to the seminary; indeed he'd only been persuaded to a temporary measure after yet another bitter argument and floods of re—proachful tears from his future wife. As Imogen deliberately reminded herself about all this, she was making herself angry all over again, but then, quite unexpectedly, a sudden thought struck her. When Stella was sent to the seminary after Christ—mas, Miss Hart would be requested to send Guy frequent reports on her conduct, a favorable report being necessary if the girl was to return home. It would be a simple enough matter to persuade Miss Hart to send only *un*favorable re—ports, for the headmistress would be willing enough to please her favored ex-pupil. If Stella was apparently not mending her ways in the slightest, Guy would be placed in a difficult, if not impossible, position. Stella had been told that she was being sent to the school because her behavior was impossible and unacceptable; he could hardly capitulate in the face of out-and-out defiance! Imogen's fan tapped thoughtfully, and then she smiled at him. She would have her way yet. ''For—

give me," she said softly, slipping her hand into his and moving closer. "I've been disagreeable tonight, I'm always disagreeable when I have a headache." She lowered her eyes in a way calculated to look conscience-stricken.

"A headache? You should have told me earlier," he said in concern. "Would you like me to take you home?"

"Oh, no," she said quickly, for that was the last thing she wished. "Perhaps we could sit for a while in the orangery?"

"Of course." He drew her hand through his arm again and they walked through the press toward the steps. The Lievens had left their post there now and were nowhere to be seen, but Nadia stood at the top of the steps. She came down toward them, her glance flickering momentarily to Guy before she smiled at Imogen. "Oh dear, you surely aren't leaving already?"

"No, we're going to the orangery," replied Imogen, deliberately halting even though she knew Guy would have preferred to walk on and cut the time spent with Nadia to an absolute minimum.

Nadia smiled again. "What a fortunate coincidence, I was just about to retreat there myself. It's so very noisy in here, isn't it? One cannot hear oneself think."

Guy strove to hide his exasperation, for he could tell by Imogen's manner that she had decided to renew the battle. There were times, he reflected, when he simply couldn't understand why he loved her so much.

She was smiling at Nadia. "You were going to the orangery too? Oh, I'm so glad, for you can come with us. Can't she, Guy?" Her eyes flashed challengingly toward him.

His own anger stirred them. "If you and Miss Benckendorff wish to go to the orangery together, I'm sure you won't mind if I leave you to your chatter," he said smoothly.

Imogen's lips parted in astonishment, for she hadn't been expecting this response. Her fan snapped open then and her eyes flashed. "Very well, if that's the way you wish it," she said coldly, slipping her arm through Nadia's.

He watched them walk away, but they'd hardly gone out of sight before a voice suddenly spoke behind him. "Well, Guy, my laddo, it looks as if you've put yourself beyond the pale again."

He turned with a quick smile to see his old friend Sir

Henry Fitzjohn standing there. "Harry! I thought they'd dispatched you to Bengal!"

"To all that heat and curry? Perish the thought. No, the East India Company, bless its heart, decided that I was indispensable here after all." He took out a snuffbox and flicked it open with a slight movement of his wrist. "I never thought I could become so attached to Leadenhall Street, but I fear that of late it's become a positive paradise as far as I'm concerned." He was a tall, thin man with sparse brown hair which was receding permaturely. He looked older than his thirty-five years, the more so because he was shortsighted and had a habit of wrinkling up his eyes in order to see into the middle distance. He was dressed informally, and consequently looked very out of place.

Guy glanced curiously at his clothes. "Aren't you a little ordinary for a Lieven diversion?"

"I'm not a guest, I've come to beg a favor of the countess."

Guy gave a quick laugh. "Good God, what a picture that conjures!"

"Not that sort of favor!" Harry smiled. "Guy, would you mind if I made use of you?"

"That depends."

"It isn't anything very much. You are acquainted with the countess, I'm not, and I merely wish you to introduce me to her."

Guy looked at him. "I presume you have good reason?"

"I do." Harry sighed. "I only wish that I didn't."

"What's wrong, Harry? Something at the East India?"

"In a manner of speaking. Does the name Richard Conyngham mean anything to you?"

Guy hesitated. "As a matter of fact it does, although I don't know him personally. Why do you ask?"

"He's dead, Guy, and what's more, he died impoverished and at the center of a dreadful scandal."

10

Guy stared at him. "Dear God above," he murmured. "But he was a wealthy man, a nabob! Surely there's some mistake."

"No mistake. He lost everything, and from all accounts, he had no one to blame but himself." Harry paused. "I find it hard to believe of him, though, for I knew him and always thought him the most honest and upright of men."

Guy was silent. Leonie's face seemed to hover before him. He took a deep breath. "What has all this to do with the countess?"

"Conyngham has a daughter."

"Leonie."

Harry looked quickly at him. "You know her?"

"Yes."

"I'm told she's very beautiful."

Guy smiled a little. "Yes, I suppose she is."

"Someone has to break the dreadful news to her not only that she's penniless but also that her father's name is soon to be at the center of an unwelcome scandal. In the absence of any other relatives, it was deemed prudent to approach the countess, because of her . . . er, interest in the seminary Miss Conyngham attends."

Guy was incredulous. "Do you honestly believe that that Russian lodestar is the right person for such a delicate and sensitive task?"

"No, I don't, but it's been decided in high places and is

out of my hands. I'm merely the messenger boy.'' Harry glanced at him. "Will you effect the introduction, Guy?''

"Under the circumstances, I don't seem to have much choice.''

"If you don't mind my saying so, you're being a little strange about this.''

Guy nodded a little. "Yes, I suppose I am. It's just . . .''

"Yes?''

"It's just that I was remembering the last time I spoke to Miss Conyngham, and I was wishing unsaid some of the things I said. Well, come on, let's find La Lieven and have done with it.''

Dorothea was in the orangery with Nadia and Imogen. The glass-domed chamber was warmed by numerous stoves in order to protect the almost tropical foliage which grew so profusely all around, and the air was stiflingly hot. There was a heavy smell of damp earth and citrus leaves, and high above, the glass roof was running with condensation. The only sound, apart from the conversation of the three women seated upon the sofa by a trellis, came from a beautiful macaw in a high gilt cage.

Dorothea was in the middle of describing the delights of a Russian winter to an entranced Imogen. "What a pity you British do not often have much snow, Lady Imogen,' she said, "for it means that you are denied the diversion of *les montagnes russes.*''

"Russian mountains? I don't understand.''

"Oh, they are excellent amusement. The snow is piled up into a hill about seventy feet high, and steps are carved up one side while the other is made very smooth. Then each gentleman takes a lady down at great speed on a cushioned toboggan. It's most entertaining. Some mountains are made even higher, so that larger toboggans can be used and more people go down together.''

Imogen, who disliked anything which took place at a pace, looked a little faint at the thought of these particular diversions. "How . . . delightful,'' she murmured.

Nadia gave a sigh. "Oh, how I wish there was snow like that here. Especially now.''

"Why now in particular?'' inquired Dorothea.

"Because that wretched agent in St. Petersburg has seen fit to dispatch my sleigh to London along with everything else. I distinctly remember instructing him to sell—" She broke off hastily, a flush leaping to her cheeks. It wouldn't do at all to reveal to Imogen how truly parlous were her financial affairs.

Imogen affected not to notice the slip. "A sleigh? Oh, Nadia, how very exciting. Do tell me what it's like. I'm told that the imperial sleighs are particularly magnificent."

Nadia gave a quick laugh. "Oh, but mine isn't an *imperial* sleigh. They have gold and scarlet trappings and are lined with sable, and they have at least twelve horses to draw them. Mine is only a little troika lined with blue velvet, but it's very pretty, don't you think, Dorothea?"

Dorothea raised an eyebrow. "Pretty? It's merely a sleigh, like any other sleigh. So, we are to have the embarrassment of having it delivered here in Harley Street, are we?" Her foot tapped irritably.

"It isn't my fault, Dorothea, it's the fault of that incompetent agent."

"Hm." Dorothea looked up then and saw the two men approaching. "Ah, Sir Guy, there you are. I was beginning to think you had deserted poor Lady Imogen."

Imogen gave him another haughty glance and then looked stiffly away.

He smiled a little. "Desert her?" he said to Dorothea. "How could I possibly bring myself to do that when I have only just succeeded in persuading her to accept me?"

Dorothea smiled and then glanced questioningly at Harry.

Guy quickly introduced him. "May I present Sir Henry Fitzjohn? Harry, this is Countess Lieven, and her cousin, Miss Benckendorff. Imogen you know already, of course."

Dorothea extended a gracious hand. "Sir Henry."

"Madam."

She glanced shrewdly at him. "I detect a conspiracy of some sort, sir. Why have you been so particularly introduced to me?"

He seized gladly upon the opening. "You are too perceptive, Countess. I see that nothing of importance slips past you."

"Nothing at all, sir. Am I to believe then that you wish to speak to me on a matter of importance?"

"It is my earnest hope that you will be able to grant us a favor, my lady."

"Us?"

"The East India Company."

"Indeed? How very flattering. What is this favor?"

He glanced at Guy and then launched into his explanation. Dorothea's smile faltered a little, her black eyes widening with astonishment, and Imogen stared in open amazement. Nadia, however, reacted in an entirely different way. Her breath caught on a gasp of ill-concealed delight, and a gloating smile curved her lovely lips. At one divine stroke, her hated rival was destroyed! From being a dazzling heiress, Leonie Conyngham was become a pauper.

Guy watched her with distaste. He knew of her pursuit of Rupert Allingham, having overheard that gentleman at White's when he related to Edward Longhurst all that had happened that afternoon at the seminary. Guy found Rupert, Duke of Thornbury, thoroughly despicable, and Nadia he found to be the equal in every way to the man she was pursuing so determinedly.

Dorothea recovered a little from her initial surprise, and her eyes were a little guarded. "Sir Henry, you mentioned a scandal, but you did not elaborate. Before I agree to do anything for you, I must be in full possession of the facts, since it would hardly be in my interest to involve myself in anything . . . er, untoward."

"Oh, I quite understand, madam," he said quickly, "and of course I will explain in more detail. It seems that Mr. Conyngham decided to risk all on a gold-mining venture with a partner by the name of Bourne, Mr. Philip Bourne. Both gentlemen agreed to put their fortunes into the mine, which became very successful indeed, inordinately successful, in fact. Then Conyngham fell fatally ill with a fever, and at almost the same time it was discovered that far from putting his own money into the business, he had embezzled his share from the East India Company, having previously squandered all his own at the gaming tables. On his death, his partner, Mr. Bourne, promptly recompensed the company for the vast sum it had lost, but by the terms of the legal agreement he and Conyngham had had drawn up at the beginning of their partnership, the default of one partner meant that everything

wer.: to the other. Mr. Bourne, therefore, now has everything, and everything in this case means a great deal. A great
deal. However, as far as Richard Conyngham's daughter is
concerned, the whole venture might as well have failed, for
she receives nothing at all. She's completely destitute, there
is no other family to take her in, and on top of that, she will
have to endure the notoriety which the whole case is bound to
achieve when news gets out.''

Dorothea nodded. ''The young woman is indeed in a most
unenviable position, Sir Henry.''

''She is, which is why we are so anxious that a lady of
sensitivity and understanding should be the one to tell her of
the terrible tragedy which has befallen her.''

Guy had to look away. Sensitivity and understanding?
Dorothea Lieven? God help Leonie Conyngham.

Dorothea smiled at Harry. ''You were quite right to come
to me, Sir Henry, and I will of course do as you request. We
leave for Streatham Park tomorrow for Christmas, but I shall
make it my business to call at the seminary first.''

''You are very kind, madam.''

She nodded and extended her hand once more. He kissed
it, bowed to them all, and then withdrew.

Imogen exhaled very slowly. ''Well, who would have
believed it? So Miss High-and-Mighty Conyngham isn't so
high and mighty after all.''

Dorothea shrugged. ''They were hardly a family of breeding anyway.''

Nadia could barely contain her delight. ''Well, to be sure,
it is as well that Miss Conyngham has reasonable looks, for
she will need them if she's to find a protector.''

Guy watched them. Dear God, how society adored a scandal, and how little sympathy it showed for innocent victims.
Imogen's attitude angered him, but Nadia's stirred his complete and utter loathing. He was filled with a desire to wipe
that feline smile from her lips. He toyed with his cuff. ''Oh, I
don't think the lady will need to resort to that sort of protection, Miss Benckendorff,'' he said smoothly.

''No? What else do you suggest for someone without
anywhere to go, and without a penny to her name? And what
a name!'' She laughed, contemplating the forthcoming stir
the whole affair would cause.

"What do I suggest?" he replied lightly. "Oh, I was thinking more along the lines of a post as companion."

Nadia sat up a little. "Oh. Well, I suppose there are such positions."

As you know well enough, he thought, since that is exactly what you were in St. Petersburg. He smiled. "Yes, there are indeed such situations, and it so happens that I know of the perfect one for Miss Conyngham."

"You do?" Nadia was wary now, having caught the steely glint in his dark eyes.

"Yes. The Duchess of Thornbury is seeking a companion."

Nadia froze. "Oh, no, I think you are wrong, Sir Guy."

"So do I!" snapped Imogen angrily.

Guy was angry himself, and for once completely immune to Imogen. He pursued his course. "I'm not wrong," he said quietly, "for I spoke to her only this morning."

Nadia's green eyes flashed and she looked away from him. The thought of Leonie being the duchess's companion was simply not to be tolerated, for Rupert lived in his mother's town house.

Guy was taking great delight in ruffling her spiteful feathers. "The duchess was bemoaning her loneliness," he went on, "and as you well know, she is a very kindly lady, so she would most certainly show compassion to one as unfortunate as Miss Conyngham. Yes, the more I think of it, the more I'm convinced that it is the perfect solution. I must make a point of calling on the duchess."

Nadia loathed him suddenly, knowing that he would do just that. He was right about the duchess: she was indeed too soft and kindhearted, and she was quite likely to take Leonie under her motherly wing. That was something which must at all costs be avoided.

Imogen looked crossly at him, rightly suspecting him of deliberately trying to upset Nadia.

He felt the moment had come to withdraw. He glanced at Imogen. "Would you care to dance?" he asked.

"No," she replied, "I would not."

He said nothing, but turned on his heel and walked from the orangery

11

The ball was over and the guests had all departed. Dorothea was in her boudoir reclining on a chaise longue. She was sipping hot chocolate from a silver cup, and she was offering tasty tidbits to her pug. She glanced up as Nadia entered. "I wondered how long it would be before you came. I suppose you want to talk about this wretched Conyngham business."

"You know that I do."

"I can't do anything about it. If Sir Guy calls upon the duchess as he threatened, then that is the end of it."

"I don't want Leonie Conyngham anywhere near Rupert."

"I'm sure you don't, she's far too pretty."

Nadia looked angrily at her. "I don't need reminding of that. Oh, Dorothea, we have to do something."

"Would you like me to ask Sir Guy not to do anything?" inquired Dorothea a little sarcastically.

"Don't be disagreeable, Dorothea."

"It's you who are being disagreeable. I've had a very tiring day and merely wish to relax—you come here with all your troubles."

"Don't you want me to be the next Duchess of Thornbury?"

Dorothea looked at her and then nodded, putting down the dish of tidbits. The pug immediately jumped down to snuffle at them. Dorothea fondly stroked its head. "Ah, Baryshna," she murmured, "how you love your little treats." She sat up then, giving Nadia her full attention. "So, we must see to it that Leonie Conyngham does not go to the Duchess of Thornbury. Am I correct?''

"Yes."

"It's simple."

Nadia's lips parted in astonishment. "It is?"

"Of course. We must see to it that she remains at the seminary.''

"How?"

"The assistant schoolteacher left recently. It will be a simple matter to persuade Miss Hart that Leonie Conyngham is an ideal replacement. After all, she *does* know everything they teach there.''

Nadia stared, but then gave a dismissive laugh. "I can't imagine anyone in her right mind preferring such a post to being companion to a duchess!''

"Then she must be prevailed upon," replied Dorothea a little testily. "There must be outstanding fees which can be demanded of her, a sum which she would feel honor-bound to pay back. Miss Hart must draw up a rather inflated bill, and there must also be a binding agreement, something which once signed will keep your wretched Leonie in her place. I will speak to Miss Hart in the morning and by this time tomorrow night your rival will be chained.'' She glanced shrewdly at Nadia. "That is not to say, however, that it will be the end of your precious Rupert's interest in her.''

"I know."

"It's up to you whether his interest strays, isn't it?" said Dorothea softly. "Now, then, I don't wish to discuss your tiresome *amours* anymore, especially as my own are in such a disagreeable state.''

"But—''

"Nadia! Don't be difficult. I've promised to do what I can. There isn't anything more to be said.''

Nadia got up and left, but as she walked back toward her own room, she thought of something which made her stop. Dorothea's plan was all very well, but it depended somewhat on Leonie not being able to pay the outstanding fees at the seminary. Nadia remembered the clothes Leonie had been wearing at tea that afternoon; she had had a pearl necklace, which, if sold, would more than meet any figure Miss Hart might present her with. And if there was a pearl necklace, who could say what other items there might be in her jewel box? And then there were her clothes and other accessories. The possibility was only too strong that Leonie would be able to pay any debts and still be free to go to the Duchess of Thornbury, which post would definitely be offered to her if Guy de Lacey had his way.

Nadia paused by the window, breathing on the frozen glass to stare out at the bitter night. The fog swirled secretively and Harley Street was almost completely obscured. She could just see the pale glow of a streetlamp, and icy, gleaming cobbles beneath it.

There were footsteps in the passage behind her and she turned to see a footman approaching. He was a tall, muscular fellow, with sly eyes and a smile which was just a little too ready. He was also one of the few Englishmen employed at the embassy, and she had very swiftly learned that he was prepared to do anything, no matter how far removed from the letter of the law, provided the price was right.

She smiled a little then, and waited until he had come closer. "I wish to speak with you," she said.

He halted, his crafty eyes sharp and quick. "Madam?"

"I have something . . . delicate for you to do."

"There's no one more delicate than I, madam."

"It's to be hoped you're right, for you mustn't be caught. Is that clear?"

"Perfectly, madam."

"Very well. I wish you to break into the seminary in Park Lane tonight. You will be well rewarded if you successfully remove certain items. You may dispose of them as you will. I have no interest in them beyond wishing them to vanish. Do you understand?"

"Yes, madam." He smiled.

Leonie awoke on Christmas Eve morning to the sound of music from the street outside. A fiddler and a blind penny-whistler were playing carols by the park gates. The fog was still thick, and the park white with frost. The fire in the bedroom had been lit for some time, the flames licking quietly around the glowing coals.

Katy brought in the early-morning tray. "Good morning, Miss Leonie," she said cheerily, for she adored Christmas.

"Good morning." Leonie sat up and pulled her shawl quickly around her shoulders as the maid put the tray carefully on her lap.

"It's as cold as ever outside," said Katy, going to the fire to warm her hands for a moment.

"You don't have to sound so pleased about it," replied Leonie, grimacing at the frost patterns on the window.

"I *love* Christmas Eve, it's my favorite day in all the year." Something suddenly caught the maid's eye. The wardrobe doors were slightly ajar, and yet she knew she'd closed them properly the night before. "That's strange," she murmured, going to close them, but as she did so she gave a start of dismay. "Oh, Miss Leonie!"

"What is it?"

"Your clothes! They've gone!" The maid flung open the heavy doors to reveal a virtually empty rail upon which only a plain gray wool dress remained. A white silk gown had fallen among the ransacked hat boxes at the bottom of the cupboard, but apart from those two items, everything else had gone, even the shoes and ankle boots. Katy turned quickly toward the dressing table, but the thief had been very thorough. The silver brushes and comb had gone, and all the little porcelain dishes. The jewel boxes had vanished. Everything of value had been removed.

Leonie stared, a cold finger of alarm touching her. While she had lain asleep, someone had been in her room, stealthily going through her belongings.

Katy hurried quickly away to tell Miss Hart, and a moment later the disconcerted headmistress had dispatched Joseph to bring a constable. The constable came straightaway to carry out a thorough examination of the premises and make a list of all the stolen articles, but he could give Leonie little hope of ever retrieving anything. Miss Hart reassured Leonie that she would be provided with sufficient funds to furnish herself with a temporary wardrobe, pending her father's imminent return. The constable then carried out a final inspection, closely examining all the windows, and in particular the fig tree growing against the balcony. He pointed to several broken twigs and the scrape marks of boots upon the trunk and said that in his opinion that was how the thief had gained entry. Leonie and Katy exchanged glances, knowing that the marks had been left by Rupert, but they said nothing at all. Miss Hart promised to see that the tree was cut back, and then the constable departed.

Miss Hart immediately provided Leonie with a cloak, bonnet, and shoes of her own, and dispatched her with Katy to a dressmaker in Oxford Street who was known always to have a number of clothes available for emergencies. The visit proved reasonably successful, and Leonie came away with two dresses, a warm cloak, and a bonnet lined with white velvet. The gowns, one pale green and the other a rather muddy donkey brown, were acceptable only for the time being, for they weren't exactly to her taste and she didn't at all care for their particularly large puffed sleeves, but under the circumstances she felt that they would have to do. She and Katy then proceeded to a nearby shoemaker's shop and purchased some shoes and another pair of ankle boots, then walked home through the cold to Park Lane. Dorothea Lieven's carriage was drawn up at the curb outside the seminary.

12

Leonie had just put on her new green dress when she was summoned to the visitors' room by a rather uneasy Mlle. Clary. The Frenchwoman was at great pains to avoid catching Leonie's eye, and she hurried away the moment her message had been delivered. Leonie was puzzled as she went down the stairs.

The moment she entered the visitors' room, she sensed that something was very wrong. The headmistress wasn't alone, Dorothea and Nadia were with her, and the latter looked sleek with vindictive anticipation, as if she could hardly wait for something to happen. The atmosphere was palpably strained.

Apprehension suddenly coursed through Leonie, and for the second time that day a cold finger of unease seemed to reach out to touch her. "You wished to see me, Miss Hart?"

The headmistress nodded. "I do, Miss Conyngham. I'm afraid that the countess is the bearer of sad news."

Leonie noticed that she wasn't invited to take a seat, but was left standing before them, almost as if she were on trial. "Sad news?"

Dorothea sat forward a little. "I'm sorry to have to inform you that your father is dead. Of a fever."

Leonie stared at her. "No," she whispered, "no, it cannot be—"

"It is so, Miss Conyngham," went on Dorothea's hard, dry, unfeeling voice. "News of his demise was brought to me last night and I was requested to tell you. There is more."

"More?" Leonie hardly heard her. Her head was spinning

and she felt almost faint. Please, don't let it be true. Don't let it be true.

"Your father died penniless and ruined."

How harshly it was said, without any consideration whatsoever. Leonie felt numb, her dark eyes huge with disbelief and anguish as she listened to the story of embezzlement and gold mines. "I don't believe it," she whispered when Dorothea had finished, "I don't believe any of it. My father wouldn't—"

"But he did, Miss Conyngham," interrupted Dorothea, "and as a consequence you are left in very embarrassing circumstances. There is a matter of outstanding fees and so on, matters which would be settled by relatives if you had any. But you don't, do you, Miss Conyngham?"

"No." Leonie's reply was barely audible. The awfulness of what had happened was beginning to be borne in on her. The chill in their eyes as they looked at her now was a solemn portent of what lay ahead.

Dorothea was relentless. "I understand that you would have had items of value which you could have sold to meet these debts, but that you have unfortunately had them stolen." The black eyes moved briefly toward Nadia, whose satisfied smile was a little too easy to read.

"Yes," replied Leonie.

"Well, I'm afraid that that leaves you in an even more embarrassing position, especially as I'm given to understand that this very morning you were provided with funds with which to purchase some replacement clothes. Is that correct?"

"Yes." Leonie was struggling to regain her poise.

"Then it must be obvious to you that something has to be done in order to settle these matters. You are no longer a privileged lady of leisure, Miss Conyngham, in fact you are the very opposite, and from this moment on you will have to work for your living." She paused. "We aren't without sympathy for your tragic situation, and it is our desire to help you if we possibly can."

"Help me?"

"By offering you a position here at the seminary. There's a vacancy for an assistant teacher, and I trust that you will see the wisdom of accepting, for that way you will at least have a roof over your head. You will also, of course, be able gradually to pay back the debts, which I'm sure you now feel to be your personal responsibility.''

Leonie felt trapped, bound by invisible cords which were tightening inexorably around her with each word that Dorothea uttered. Accept the post? What option did she have but to do that? Where else could she go? And how could she otherwise meet all these specified debts?

Dorothea gave a cold little smile. ''If you accept, you will be required to sign an agreement, for everything must be done correctly. You will be bound by that agreement until all debts have been satisfactorily settled. All that having been said, I would now like to hear your decision, Miss Conyngham.''

''I . . .''

''Yes?''

''I accept.'' She had to, there was no other course.

Dorothea glanced at Nadia and then rose to her feet, turning to Miss Hart. ''I trust that I may now safely leave matters in your hands. Pray do not forget the agreement.'' She indicated the table, upon which lay a hastily drawn-up document. Beside it stood Miss Hart's best silver-gilt inkwell and a new quill.

''I will attend to everything, my lady,'' replied the headmistress reassuringly. She then gave Leonie a cool nod of her head. ''I will speak with you in a moment.'' Then she escorted Dorothea from the room.

Nadia followed them, pausing in the doorway to look malignantly back at Leonie, her green eyes glittering with spite. She gave a low laugh; then the door closed and she was gone.

The room was suddenly very quiet. The fire shifted in the hearth, sending a shower of bright sparks fleeing up the chimney. She could hear her own heartbeats. An immeasurable sense of loss began to steal through her, but her eyes remained dry. There were no tears; they weren't even close. She listened to Miss Hart saying farewell to her visitors, and then the headmistress's busy steps were approaching the door again. Leonie turned to face her as she came in.

Miss Hart halted before her, her glance as chill as Dorothea's had been. ''Very well, Miss Conyngham, let us discuss your situation.'' She sat down close to the fire, very deliberately leaving Leonie standing. ''I will expect you to commence in Miss Mathers' place when the new term begins. You will, naturally enough, be the most junior member of the staff, and you will be at the beck and call of your colleagues. No doubt your many years with us have provided you with a clear notion of what your duties will be.''

"Yes, Miss Hart.''

"Very well. I trust that you also realize that you must immediately vacate the room you occupy at present. In future you will use the room previously allotted to Miss Mathers. It's on the third floor, at the front of the house. Obviously it's hardly what you've been used to, but you must consider yourself fortunate not to be out on the streets.''

"Yes, Miss Hart.'' Leonie gazed at the headmistress. It was like talking to a stranger. But then perhaps that was exactly what she was doing, for she was now seeing the real Emmeline Hart.

The headmistress pointed to the document. "I suggest you sign it straightaway.''

Leonie picked up the document and began to read.

Miss Hart was irritated. "You don't need to study it,'' she said sharply. "After all, you aren't in a position to challenge its contents, are you?''

Leonie was about to put the piece of paper down again when she caught sight of the figures mentioned in it. Her eyes widened incredulously and she looked accusingly at the headmistress. "But I know I can't possibly owe you that much!''

"Oh, but you do, missy, you do.'' Miss Hart's hard eyes did not waver.

"It isn't true!''

"Argue about it and you'll be thrown out.''

Leonie stared at her.

Miss Hart rose to her feet. "Sign the document, Miss Conyngham. I wish to be done with this disagreeable interview. Be thankful for the charity which is being extended to you, and think of the dreadful alternative should that charity be withdrawn.''

Leonie lowered her glance to the document. She didn't owe as much as the headmistress was making out, but why would Miss Hart inflate the sums so much? Resignedly she sat down and took up the quill. What point was there in resisting when the alternative to acceptance was indeed so very dreadful? She dipped the quill in the ink and signed her name.

Miss Hart immediately took the agreement away, placing it carefully in a drawer and locking it. She turned back to face Leonie, who immediately rose to her feet once more. "I have already issued instructions that you are to be moved to Miss Mathers' room. All your previous privileges will cease henceforth, and that includes the matter of meals. When the new term begins you will take your meals on the top table in the dining room with the rest of the teaching staff, the exception to this rule being breakfast, which you will take in my private parlor. It is at breakfast that matters concerning the school are discussed. Until the new term, however, since you are not strictly speaking on the staff until then, you will take all your meals in the kitchens with the servants. Do you have any questions?"

"No, Miss Hart."

"You may go now. Oh, and, Miss Conyngham . . ."

"Yes, Miss Hart?"

"Pray remember that from now on you are an employee. Do not give yourself airs and graces to which you are no longer entitled, and do not, on any account, draw unwelcome attention to the seminary because of the scandal attaching to your father."

"I don't understand."

"Your father was a villainous thief, missy, and I will not be best pleased by any misguided attempts on your behalf to clear his name. You are here only because the countess at present wishes it. If it were left to me, you would leave these premises immediately. I trust you understand me now."

Leonie looked at her with dislike. "I understand perfectly, Miss Hart."

The headmistress turned away.

Leonie withdrew from the room, but outside in the passage she paused for a long moment. She felt unutterably cold and numb, and she wished that it was all a nightmare from which she would soon awaken. But it wasn't a dream, it was all horribly true. Her father was dead and his name was about to be dreadfully maligned. He wouldn't have stolen any money, he was too honest, nor would he have gambled away his own fortune. She'd never believe such ill of him; she loved and respected him too much for that.

She stared blindly ahead as she walked toward the vestibule. She wanted to weep for him, and for herself, but she couldn't. It was if she was a hollow shell.

That Christmas Eve was the saddest and most desolate she had ever endured. Her new room at the top of the house was cold and sparsely furnished compared with her previous one. There was a hard, narrow bed, a small chest of drawers, a cracked mirror, and a plain wardrobe which would not close properly. The fireplace was small and barely adequate, and the coal provided was damp and of poor quality, smoking and hissing a great deal and not giving off much heat.

Darkness had fallen when she looked from the little window for the first time, gazing down over Park Lane and the park. It was the same view as before, but it seemed very different now without the elegant wrought-iron balcony. She opened the window and leaned out a little. The cold snatched her breath and she could feel the damp touch of the fog against her skin. There were carol singers in the street below, their lanterns glowing. Little bunches of holly were tied to their staves and their breath hung in silver clouds as they sang. But the doors of the seminary remained firmly closed: Miss Hart's seasonal goodwill was nonexistent when there were no young ladies present to be impressed.

Closing the window again, Leonie went to sit on the bed. Katy had tried to persuade her to go down to the warmth of the kitchens, but somehow she couldn't bring herself to face them all just yet. She needed time to compose herself and to absorb the bleak facts of her new, severely reduced circumstances. There would be no happy reunion with her father now, no great houses, no Season, and no dazzling future. It had all been whisked cruelly away by a bitter stroke of fate. Tomorrow she would emerge from this room and embark upon her new life, but tonight she would hide away, alone with her sorrow. She stared at the curving grayness of the smoking fire, the emptiness within her as melancholy and painful as ever, and still she hadn't shed a single tear.

13

The next morning there was no tray of coffee, and no one came to kindle the fire. She was awakened by Katy's hurried tapping at the door and a whispered warning that if she didn't get up quickly she'd forfeit breakfast before everyone went to morning service at the Grosvenor Chapel. But she wasn't hungry, and so she dressed in her newly purchased cloak, bonnet, and ankle boots and waited until she heard everyone assembling in the vestibule. Then, taking a deep breath to raise her courage, she went down to join them.

Miss Hart, Miss Ross, and Mlle. Clary waited by the front door, the rest of the servants assembled close to the foot of the stairs. The two teachers had swiftly followed Miss Hart's lead, for they gave Leonie cool glances and did not greet her beyond giving abrupt nods. The servants, however, showed compassion for her. She saw tears glistening in Katy's soft eyes, and kindness and understanding in the glances of both Joseph and little Mrs. Durham, the cook. The other maids and the kitchen boy looked sadly at her.

When Leonie had arrived, Miss Hart nodded at Joseph, who hastened to open the door. The headmistress sailed regally out into the bitter cold, her best mantle fluttering around her plump ankles, her new bonnet trembling with soft little pink feathers. Miss Ross and Mlle. Clary followed her, leaving Leonie to walk alone behind them. After Leonie came the servants, walking two by two.

The sedate little party walked north up Park Lane toward nearby Aldford Street. Christmas-morning bells pealed joyfully through the brittle air, and it seemed as if the sun might come out soon. The fog had retreated, but still clung stubbornly beneath the trees in the park, keeping their branches white with frost. Leonie noticed nothing as she walked along; it was as if she wasn't really there at all.

The Grosvenor Chapel, built originally for the family of that name, was in South Audley Street, facing straight down Aldford Street toward the park. It was an elegant yellow brick building, with tall round-headed windows and a plain pillared portico. As fashionable in its way as St. George's, Hanover Square, it was the place of worship for a great many of the *haut ton*, and many carriages were arriving as Miss Hart and her party approached.

Something made Leonie look at one carriage in particular as it drove past. It was a fine vehicle, with dark green panels and gleaming lamps, and it was drawn by four magnificent grays. As she watched, it drew up outside the church and a footman jumped down to lower the steps and open the door. There were three passengers inside: Imogen; her brother Edward; and Guy de Lacey. Leonie stared at them with both surprise and dismay, for they did not usually worship here; they attended St. George's. She wondered why they had chosen to attend this church instead, and her instinct told her that it had been entirely Imogen's idea, for it would amuse that lady to see Leonie Conyngham in such severely reduced circumstances.

Edward alighted first. He looked elegant to the point of dandyism in a tight-waisted, full-skirted overcoat which reached to his ankles. It was burnt orange in color and was adorned with military epaulets and frogging. His top hat was worn at a very precise angle on his dark red hair, and his cane swung idly in his gloved hand in a way which strongly reminded her of the Duke of Thornbury.

Guy climbed down next, and after the flamboyance of his future brother-in-law, he looked almost reserved in a plain charcoal-colored greatcoat, his top hat resting casually on his rather unruly dark hair. He didn't notice Leonie as he turned to assist Imogen down from the carriage, but Imogen noticed her straightaway. A cold little smile touched the perfect lips, but beyond that there was no sign of acknowledgment as she shook out the skirts of her apricot pelisse in order to fluff up the heavy white fur trimming. She looked very beautiful indeed, thought Leonie, but it was a beauty which was marred forever by the coldness which came from within.

The church was crowded, almost all of its twelve hundred places occupied by the Christmas-morning congregation. Organ music drifted mellowly above the whispering and general shuffling as Miss Hart's party took their places, Leonie sitting at the very edge of the aisle. The tall windows allowed the pale winter sunlight in to illuminate the golden vessels on the altar, and the pristine white walls seemed almost dazzling. Above the altar there was a domed ceiling of brilliant blue and gold, and these colors seemed to draw Leonie's gaze as she sat back after kneeling to pray. She hadn't been able to pray; her mind had been a blank. She stared at the blue and gold ceiling, wondering why she couldn't pray, couldn't even cry. It was as if all feeling had frozen and she was as much made of ice as the icicles suspended from the eaves.

She was careful to keep her eyes lowered as the service commenced, for she swiftly became aware that she was the center of much whispering and general interest. Imogen had begun it, leaning her head close to a neighbor and pointing Leonie out. The whisper had spread, hands had been raised to conceal mouths, and quizzing glasses had been turned in her direction. The Conyngham scandal had already begun to circulate.

It was almost the end of the service when Leonie at last turned her head to look across the aisle toward the Longhurst pew. It was with something of a shock that she found herself looking directly into Guy de Lacey's dark eyes. He didn't look away but held her gaze for a long, long moment, and she couldn't turn from him. Even in the midst of all her sorrow and wretchedness, and in spite of the acrimony of their previous encounter, she knew that she was still very drawn to him. There was something about him which made her heart almost stop, something which reminded her that she still had a heart and wasn't hollow inside. A flush began to steal into her cheeks and at last she managed to look away again.

The service ended at last, and as the congregation began to file out, she heard her name being whispered. She avoided all eyes as she made her way to the doors, but her ordeal wasn't quite at an end yet, for as they emerged into the cold day-light, Miss Hart was extremely gratified to receive a nod of acknowledgment from Imogen, who was standing by her carriage with her brother and Guy. The headmistress, never one to miss an opportunity to be seen mixing with the aristoc-racy, immediately halted to wish them all a very happy Christmas.

Miss Ross and Mlle. Clary, knowing their places only too well, prudently walked on, and Leonie followed them. As she passed Guy, however, she couldn't help looking at him again. He had been watching her, and their eyes met once more. He removed his hat immediately and bowed. "Miss Conyngham."

She hesitated, unsure of what to do, but then she saw the flash of anger in Imogen's eyes and the displeasure on Miss Hart's face, and she quickly hurried on without speaking.

On her return to the seminary, she at last went down to the kitchens, but if she feared there would be an unfriendly atmosphere there, she was very wrong. Her kindness toward them all in the past stood her in very good stead now, and they wanted to put her at her ease. She tried to join in the merriment, but it was very difficult, for she felt she should not laugh or even smile when news of her father's death was so fresh.

Four o'clock in the afternoon, the time Christmas dinner was served, arrived at last. The delicious smell of roast goose and all the trimmings filled the warm room. She enjoyed the happiness of the others as they teased a rather flushed Mrs. Durham that she hadn't seasoned the chestnut stuffing enough, and she clapped with them as the cannonball plum pudding was borne aloft to the table, its sprig of holly perched precari-ously amid the flames. Afterward they sat around the fire with some mulled wine, singing carols. Joseph often sang for them, for he had a deep, rich voice, and they all sat very quietly, clapping loudly when he finished. Mrs. Durham dragged in a sack of chestnuts and scattered some around the edge of the fire, where they began to blacken at once. Enjoy-ing the roast chestnuts and singing more carols, they whiled away an hour or so before someone suggested some games.

Leonie didn't participate in the games, and no one pressed her. The long day began to draw to an end, and Leonie knew that soon she would have to go up to the chill room on the third floor. She didn't want to go, she wanted to stay with the others.

Joseph seemed to sense her thoughts, for suddenly he leaned across to put his great dark hand over hers. "I've something to ask of you, Miz Leonie."

"Ask me?"

"Maybe it's a little impertinent."

She smiled a little. "I'm sure it can't be."

"Would you teach me to read and write, Miz Leonie?"

Mrs. Durham was cross with him. "Joseph, you great curmudgeon," she scolded, "you mustn't go asking Miss Leonie such a thing!"

"It's all right, Mrs. Durham," said Leonie quickly, "I don't mind at all, in fact I'd like to help him." She smiled at Joseph. "Of course I'll help you, I'm glad you asked me."

He nodded, his dark brown eyes shrewd but kindly. "We can help each other, Miz Leonie. I'll have some learning, and you'll have something to help keep your mind off other things."

"Shall we begin now?"

"I'd like that, Miz Leonie."

Mrs. Durham provided a sheet of paper and a pencil, and Leonie and Joseph adjourned to a quiet table in the corner, where they were soon joined by Katy. Thus another hour or so passed by, and it was midnight before a halt was called and Leonie at last went up to her room. She was accompanied by Katy, who insisted upon attending her, saying that Miss Hart wouldn't know and what the old toad didn't know about wouldn't hurt her.

In the cold room, Leonie turned quickly to the maid. "Katy, I'm so sorry."

"Sorry?" The maid looked at her in puzzlement. "Whatever for?"

"I promised you so much, but now it's all gone."

Katy put a gentle hand on her arm. "You mustn't apologize, Miss Leonie, it isn't your fault. I know you meant every word you said to me, and that's all that matters. One day it'll all be all right again, you see if it isn't."

But as Leonie lay in the darkness a little later, she knew that nothing would ever be all right again. It had all gone. Forever.

14

The year 1813 gave way to 1814, and the Christmas greenery was taken down, leaving everything looking oddly bare. The seminary made ready for the new term, and Leonie prepared to commence her new employment. She was anxious and unsure of herself, although she knew already from the lessons she was giving Katy and Joseph that she had a natural aptitude for teaching. The coldness of her colleagues, and more especially of Miss Hart herself, did little to help her through those early days of unhappiness and uncertainty, and she was especially apprehensive that she would be placed in charge of some of the older pupils, a number of whom she knew would resent and probably defy her because of her father. To her immense relief, Miss Hart decided that it would be more prudent to place her in charge of the youngest pupils, children who were new to the school and therefore did not know her at all.

The new year brought no improvement in the weather. Snowflakes were now frequently seen drifting aimlessly through the frozen air, but as yet there hadn't been a heavy fall. There was no relief from the fog, which occasionally withdrew a little to hint at an easing of nature's harshness, but which each time closed bitterly in again, cloaking everything with its icy shroud. The cold meant that there was ever-increasing speculation that the Thames would freeze over, and the newspapers dwelt at length on the possibility of a frost fair on the ice. The newspapers also dwelt at length on the Conyngham scandal, and Leonie was distressed to see her father's name much vilified, his guilt taken for granted. Her distress gave way to anger and indignation, and in spite of Miss Hart's dire warning about drawing unwelcome attention to the seminary through attempting to clear Richard Conyngham's name, she decided to go to the East India Company's headquarters in Leadenhall Street to challenge their charges against him.

At the end of the first week in January, two days before the new term commenced, she had an opportunity to slip unnoticed from the seminary. Miss Hart was much harassed by the arrival of a Russian gentleman, who informed her that he was the new history teacher, and who insisted upon a lengthy discussion of the syllabus he intended to employ during his twice-weekly lessons. He was immensely tall, with fiery eyes, a beard, and a deep, heavily accented voice, and he was quite determined to do everything his own way. Miss Hart virtually found herself being instructed what to do, and she was so nonplussed that she meekly led him to the visitors' room and sat there while he spoke at considerable length about Russian history. It was the second time the headmistress had received a lecture on the subject, and she found it as uninteresting on this occasion as she had on the first, but because he was there on Dorothea Lieven's instructions, she pretended to find it all most absorbing. While all this was going on, Leonie left the seminary and took a hackney coach to India House in Leadenhall Street.

The clerk who received her was all smiles until he realized who she was, at which point his willingness to be of assistance vanished and she was politely but firmly requested to leave. Shocked and unable to believe she was being treated in such a way, she at first stood her ground and demanded to see someone in authority, but to no avail; he merely called two of his fellow clerks and she had no option but to leave the premises. It was a mortifying experience, but it taught her a sharp lesson: her father was deemed guilty, and she was henceforth to be treated as the daughter of a felon, not of an honest and good man. Dismayed and humiliated, she returned to the seminary, entering as quietly as she had left. She told no one of the visit to Leadenhall Street.

That night the seminary was the scene of all the usual noise and bustle associated with the eve of a new term. There were cases and trunks in the vestibule, and carriages arriving outside. High-pitched girlish chatter resounded throughout the building, and the seminary seemed to come to sudden life again. The older pupils, who had known Leonie before, were split into two camps in their attitude toward her; some were sympathetic and agreeable, but many were the very opposite. The little girls who were to be her particular responsibility had no prejudices one way or the other; they judged her upon how kind and sympathetic she was when they felt suddenly homesick and alone and were trying to hide their tears. But if they spent that night feeling apprehensive, she did too. After giving Katy and Joseph another reading and writing lesson, she at last retired to her room. She couldn't sleep, she was far too anxious about the following day, and it was almost dawn before she fell into a fitful sleep.

But she need not have worried, for she slipped into teaching with an ease which astonished her. The familiar textbooks, which she remembered so well from her own early days at the school, were like a comfortable and well-loved cloak, at once warming and protective. At the end of her first morning she was feeling encouraged, and by the end of the day she felt almost confident. She would be able to endure.

In the relative seclusion of Streatham Park, Nadia and Dorothea were bored. It was the morning of Thursday, the thirteenth of January, the Russian New Year's Day, and the two cousins were seated at breakfast, gazing cheerlessly out at the frosty, deserted park, where a small herd of deer were being fed hay by a keeper. The room was warm and filled with the heady scent of Dorothea's favorite hyacinths, and the only sound was the steady ticking of the ormolu clock on the marble mantelpiece.

Nadia sighed. Today in St. Petersburg the Winter Palace and the Hermitage would be thrown open and forty thousand tickets issued. There would be such merriment and festivity. Even in London there would be *soirées*, dinner parties, or the theater. But they were out here, in virtual isolation, with absolutely nothing to do. She sighed again, glancing at Dorothea's vexed expression. How she wished her cousin and her dull-brained husband had not quarreled so bitterly that he had absolutely refused to please his wife by agreeing to return early to town. Now he was determined to stay out here for as long as possible, simply to irritate her, and if her present mood was anything to go by, he was certainly succeeding.

There was a knock at the door and a footman came in with a letter for Nadia. It was from Imogen, and it contained news which immediately made her get up agitatedly and go to the window.

Dorothea glanced curiously at her. "Is something wrong?"

"Rupert has returned early from Althorp. He's in town now."

"So?"

"So, I wonder why. He was going to stay there another week."

Dorothea shrugged. "He's changed his mind; there's nothing unusual about that."

"But this time I want to know why."

"You think it's because of Leonie Conyngham, don't you?"

"I don't know. I fear that it could be."

"Well, I warned you. The fact that she's no longer a great heiress doesn't make her less beautiful."

"I don't need reminding of that!" snapped Nadia.

"And if he chooses to go and see her, there's very little you can do about it."

"That is another thing of which I need no reminding. Oh, I should be there, not here! I have to know what's happening."

"*You* wish you were there? How do you think *I* feel, cooped up here with Lieven at his must dull and obstinate. *Mon Dieu*, I'd give anything to leave this wretched backwater."

"Why don't you, then?" asked Nadia carefully, wondering if Dorothea could be goaded into returning to the capital. "I don't understand you at times. You're the queen of London society, your word is law as far as the Season is concerned, and yet you meekly bow to Lieven's ridiculous pettiness."

Dorothea flushed a little at the scorn. "I merely attempt to keep up appearances."

"Why bother? Everyone knows your marriage is a pretense and has been for some time now."

"I've been in London for little more than a year, and I do not wish to jeopardize the position I have attained during that time. Lieven could make things very disagreeable if he wished. When I feel the time is right to put him in his place, then I will do it, but I hardly think now is that time. I haven't a pressing reason to flout his wishes by returning to town.''

Nadia gazed out of the window once more, watching the deer browsing on the scattered hay, their breath silver in the cold. "Imogen's letter contained other news. I know that you are no longer concerned with the activities of Lord Byron, but I rather think Lord Palmerston is of great interest to you.''

Dorothea looked up quickly. "What of him?''

"It seems that he and Lady Cowper have fallen out, in fact he's most definitely in a miff with her. He's been seen every night in his box at the opera house, while Emily Cowper is seen anywhere and everywhere but there.''

"Is Imogen sure of her facts?''

"As sure as it's possible to be. Emily Cowper told her herself.'' Nadia chose her next words carefully. "There seems little doubt to me that Lord Palmerston is ripe for the plucking. Your box is next to his at the opera house, isn't it?''

Dorothea didn't reply for a moment. Her long pale fingers drummed a little thoughtfully on the table.

"Will you seize your opportunity?'' asked Nadia softly.

Slowly Dorothea got up, tossing her napkin onto the table. "Yes.''

"We're returning to London?'' Nadia could hardly keep the delight from her voice.

"Yes.''

Nadia smiled. Now she would be able to discover why Rupert had returned so suddenly from Althorp. And she would be able to keep a wary eye on the seminary.

Before noon, after yet another acrimonious confrontation between Dorothea and the furious, resentful Lieven, the two cousins left Streatham Park in the traveling carriage. They drove north through the freezing fog, along a road which had deep ruts as hard as iron. Progress was slow and they didn't reach Harley Street until well after dark. Within an hour of arriving, they emerged again, dressed in evening elegance, and the town carriage took them across London to the opera house, where Imogen had said Lord Palmerston was to be seen each night, and where it so happened that Rupert, Duke of Thornbury, also had a box.

The opera house was reasonably crowded, and Dorothea was immediately gratified to see Lord Palmerston seated alone in the adjacent box. At twenty-nine, the young Secretary for War was very good-looking and elegant, and possessed a sensuous smile which told of an equally sensuous nature. He was tall and looked a little delicate. He had sandy hair and a high forehead; his skin was pale and his eyes seemed always a little lazy and amused. He noticed Dorothea immediately, and she left him in no doubt at all of her feelings as she smiled and inclined her head to him. His glance moved slowly over her, lingering on her so-slender figure in its sapphire-blue velvet gown, and on the whiteness of her bare shoulders. Then he returned the smile, and in that silent, knowing exchange an agreement was made. She sat back, exhaling with slow satisfaction. Her return to the embassy without Lieven would cause a stir, but if Palmerston was her lover she would be able to rise above it all, for he was as pressing a reason as any for making public her rift with her husband.

Beside her, Nadia was less pleased with the way things were going, for the Thornbury box opposite was empty. Her fan snapped open and closed, and the draft from it shivered the spangles adorning her green silk turban. She looked exquisite in a plain white silk gown, its low décolletage revealing the flawless perfection of her shoulders and throat, but although she attracted many admiring glances, she didn't notice any of them as she gazed across the auditorium at that other box. Where was Rupert? She had been convinced that he would be here tonight; some sixth sense had told her he would be, but it was now nearly time for the curtain to rise and still there wasn't any sign of him. Was he even now paying court to Leonie at the seminary? The fan stopped abruptly, for another disagreeable thought suddenly struck her. What if Leonie's attitude toward him had undergone a dramatic change now that she was impoverished? Was she now prepared to encourage so wealthy an admirer? Once this thought had occurred to her, she couldn't think of anything else, and she hardly glanced at the stage as the curtain rose and the performance began.

It was almost time for the intermission when suddenly someone entered the Thornbury box. It was Rupert. But Nadia's smile of relief faded a little when she saw that he wasn't alone; his mother and an unknown but exceedingly ugly young woman were with him. The young woman was short and rather thick-set, and her complexion was disagreeably sunburned. She wore a bright vermilion satin gown which did absolutely nothing for her, and she positively dripped with diamonds. Nadia had never seen so many diamonds; they were in her wiry dark brown hair, hanging pendulously from her ears, lying in glittering strands around her neck, and shimmering on her pudgy wrists and fingers. She was more dazzling than the stage. Nadia stared in astonishment at Rupert, whose attentiveness to this ugly creature could only be described as marked.

As the intermission commenced, Nadia still stared across at the other box, watching Rupert, who was at his most charming for the benefit of the creature in vermilion. Suddenly, as if he sensed the close scrutiny to which he was being subjected, he glanced across the auditorium, straight into Nadia's eyes. For a moment he seemed stunned, and then he got up, making his excuses to his companions and withdrawing from the box. Nadia knew he was coming to speak to her, and she too withdrew into the passage to wait for him.

He smiled as he approached. "Nadia," he said softly, drawing her hand to his lips and lingering over it for a moment, "I had no idea you were back in town."

"So I noticed."

He ignored the sarcasm. "I had to return early from Althorp. My mother was taken ill and Marguerite thought it wise to send for me."

"Marguerite?"

"Miss St. Julienne. She's the daughter of my mother's old friend, and she's come to England from her father's plantation in Jamaica. She's in my mother's charge, and will be here for the Season."

"She is, presumably, the creature who is with you tonight."

"Yes." His knowing eyes mocked her a little. "Don't underestimate her because she has no looks, for she's set to be the catch of the year. She is what is vulgarly known as a fortune, a vast fortune."

Nadia looked away, her mind racing. "Is that why you are paying her such ridiculously marked attention?"

"No, I'm being agreeable for my mother's sake. She

dotes upon Marguerite and wants me to be my most charming toward her.''

"You've more than obliged tonight, sir.''

"Oh, come now, Nadia—''

"Does your mother wish you to marry this vast fortune?''

"I rather think she does, but I have no such intention. My mother has been ill and I'm humoring her, that's all.'' He put his hand to her cheek. "You surely don't imagine that I would wish to take such a dreadful person as my wife?''

"I might have believed you, milord, had it not been that the dreadful person was also an immensely wealthy person.''

"I would have bowed to your statement had the person in question been within reason. Marguerite St. Julienne, you must admit, is not within reason. I don't care how wealthy she is, Nadia, I simply find her looks appalling. Looks matter a great deal; money doesn't necessarily sway me.''

She looked quickly at him, unable to help her next question. "So it doesn't matter that Leonie Conyngham is now so poor?''

He seemed startled. Then he laughed. "It wouldn't have mattered, had I really been all that interested in her, but I wasn't. Anyway, even if I had been, I would have dropped her the moment the taint of scandal attached to her name. One thing I cannot and will not tolerate is scandal.''

She searched his face, wondering how much she dared believe, but he met her gaze, and there seemed no hint of guilt in his eyes.

He put his hand to her face once more, his thumb gently caressing her cheek. "I'm not interested in Marguerite St. Julienne or Leonie Conyngham, but I *am* interested in you. I confess that being recalled from Althorp did not displease me, as it meant I would see you again.''

"But you thought I was in Streatham Park.''

"I hoped you would find it as dull there as I found it at Althorp,'' he replied smoothly. "Can I see you tonight? Alone?''

Her green eyes became warm and dark then. "Yes,'' she murmured.

He smiled. "I find you very desirable, Nadia,'' he whispered, bending forward to kiss her softly on the lips.

Exultation coursed through her, although she was careful to hide it from him. He was going to be hers after all, he *was*!

He drew back then. "The intermission's almost at an end." As he spoke, the bell sounded. "I must return to my box now, but I'll come to the embassy tonight."

She put her hand quickly on his arm. "I trust that you know where we may go in order to be alone? Properly alone?" Her eyes had never been more seductive. "You were right when you hoped I would find Streatham Park dull. I've missed you, milord, and tonight I wish to prove it to you."

Her glance caressed him briefly for a last time and then she went back into the box. Rupert remained where he was for a moment, a smile playing about his lips. He hadn't intended to continue his liaison with her; he'd found her of scant interest after seeing Leonie. But now Leonie was touched by scandal, and he abhorred scandal. Nadia wasn't touched by the scandal, however. She was simply a beautiful but rather too mercenary and ambitious adventuress, and tonight, after a surfeit of Marguerite St. Julienne's appalling looks and conversation, Nadia Benckendorff seemed like an angel. A fallen angel, of course, but what did that matter when she was going to be of only temporary interest? Smiling a little at her gullibility, he made his way back to his own box, steeling himself a little before going in to endure more of his mother's protégée.

15

The following morning, while Nadia and Dorothea slept late after their very satisfactory assignations with their respective lovers, Leonie rose early at the seminary and went down for the daily ordeal of breakfast in Miss Hart's parlor. She said as little as possible and endeavored to avoid the others' attention, for she was already learning how poor Miss Mathers must have felt when each day either Miss Ross or Mlle. Clary managed to delegate one of their own duties. This morning it was Mademoiselle who imposed upon her by requesting her to take some of her pupils for an airing in the park. In the face of Miss Hart's silence on the matter, Leonie had no option but to acquiesce, and shortly after ten she escorted the small party across Park Lane and through the park gates.

The fog had lifted and the weak winter sun shone down from an ice-blue sky. For once she found herself free of the barbed remarks of some of the pupils in her temporary charge, for they were far too excited about the news that there was now a thin layer of ice on the Thames. Their talk was therefore almost solely about frost fairs, and their chances of maybe persuading relatives to take them.

Returning to the seminary afterward, Leonie noticed a handsome dark red carriage drawn up at the curb. As she ushered her charges across the busy street, she saw Guy de Lacey alight from the carriage and assist Imogen down. Imogen wore yellow, a startlingly summery color for mid-January, and she looked very eye-catching indeed. She paused on the pavement, shaking out her skirts, and then she hurried on into the seminary, without waiting for Guy, who had turned once more to assist a third person down from the carriage. Leonie's momentary surprise at Imogen's haste to go inside was almost immediately forgotten as she looked at the third person. It was a girl of about twelve, and she knew it had to be Guy's niece, Stella de Lacey.

She was slightly built, with long dark ringlets tumbling from beneath her straw bonnet. She had large, melting brown eyes which looked huge in her small face. They were expressive eyes, and at the moment their expression was little short of mutinous. Her whole figure exuded defiance, and there was something in the set of her stubborn little mouth which promised a great deal of trouble in the days ahead. Stella de Lacey was not about to give in easily to her punishment, that much was certain.

Leonie's pupils filed past the carriage, glancing curiously at the new arrival, but Stella only glowered at them, not in the least intimidated. Guy became aware of Leonie then, quickly removing his hat and inclining his head. "Good morning, Miss Conyngham."

Unwillingly she met his eyes, for she knew that she found him too attractive. A flush leapt quickly to her cheeks, and she murmured a hasty acknowledgment and made as if to hurry on.

He put out a gentle restraining hand. "Please, Miss Conyngham, for I don't wish to remain at odds with you."

She had no option then but to halt, and she was aware of the giggling of the girls as they walked on into the warmth of the seminary.

He released her. "Forgive me, I did not mean to cause you any embarrassment."

"You did not, sir."

"I merely wished to tell you how very sorry I am about your father."

She felt unnecessarily defensive. "My father is innocent, Sir Guy."

"I wasn't expressing my belief in his guilt, Miss Conyngham, please believe me. I didn't know him, but I do know you, and I'm sorry that you are now placed in such a sad predicament."

A little confused, the color still touching her cheeks, she looked up into his eyes. "Thank you, sir."

He smiled a little. "After our first encounter I can quite understand that you think me a disagreeable bear of the first order, but I promise you that I'm not." He studied her for a moment. "I was surprised to hear that you had chosen to become a teacher."

"Choice didn't enter into it, Sir Guy. I had debts to meet and no roof over my head, and it was pointed out to me that the only honorable thing I could do was accept a post in order to solve both problems, the one for myself and the other for Miss Hart."

"I see." He glanced away, remembering Nadia Benckendorff's face at the embassy ball.

"Do you, Sir Guy?" She couldn't help the note of irony creeping into her voice, for he had never known what it was to be destitute. She herself knew that feeling of desperation only too well now.

"Yes, Miss Conyngham, I do, and rather more than I fancy you imagine." He held her gaze. "And I'm not referring to your unenviable position, I'm referring to certain circumstances which combined to make that position a great deal worse for you."

"Miss Benckendorff?"

He looked at her in surprise. "I hadn't realized you were aware."

"She came with Countess Lieven on the day I was told about my father's death. I would have had to be dull-witted indeed not to detect her hand in things."

He suddenly put his hand hesitantly to her cheek. It was an oddly tender gesture. He wore no glove and the warmth of his fingers seemed to burn like fire. "Miss Conyngham," he said softly, "I wish to forget how unforgivably rude I was to you when first we met. May we begin again?"

His closeness and the lingering touch of his fingers affected her so much that she felt almost weak. A giddy emotion was tumbling through her, confusing and distracting, as if she was under some sort of spell, and it was only with a great effort that she managed a light smile, drawing away a little. "Of course we may, sir."

He looked into her eyes for a moment more and then turned suddenly to his niece. "May I present my niece, Miss Stella de Lacey? Stella, this is Miss Conyngham, one of your teachers."

Recovering quickly now, Léonie smiled at the girl. "I'm pleased to meet you, Stella."

Stella scowled, her lips pressing rebelliously together.

Guy's anger rose sharply. "Where are your manners, Stella? Speak when you're spoken to!"

"Why should I?" declared the girl then. "I don't want to come here, I want to stay at Berkeley Street with you! Don't send me here, Uncle Guy. Please."

"Will you promise to behave yourself and be at all times polite and respectful to Imogen?"

Stella looked resentfully away and didn't reply.

"Very well," he said, "you leave me no choice. I won't be dictated to, Stella."

Stella gestured after the vanished Imogen. "*She* dictates to you!" she cried.

"Imogen is to be my wife," he replied, with forced patience, "and she does *not* dictate to me. She and I discuss things of mutual importance, and then we come to a decision."

"I'm nothing to do with her. She hasn't any right to—"

"Be quiet!" he snapped. "Imogen has every right, especially when I consult her. We've decided that until you are prepared to conduct yourself graciously, you are to remain here."

"*She* wants me to stay here forever. She doesn't want me ever to go home again!"

"That's nonsense."

"No, it isn't. She hates me!"

"She doesn't hate you, although by all that's holy you've given her every reason to loathe you. I don't know what's been the matter with you recently, Stella, you've changed so much that sometimes I think I hardly know you."

"We were happy until *she* came along!"

"Don't persist in talking about Imogen in that way," he replied angrily. "I won't have you home, Stella, not until you cease being such an obnoxious little tyrant. This disagreeable and downright willful defiance has simply got to stop."

Tears filled Stella's eyes and her lips quivered, but she didn't say anything more. Leonie's sympathy went out to her, for she could see the truth behind the girl's outrageous conduct. She was desperately unhappy and frightened about what the future held in store now that a woman like Imogen Longhurst had entered Guy de Lacey's life. Stella had said it all when she said that she and her uncle had been happy until Imogen came onto the scene. That was how it always was with Imogen: she was devoid of kindness and understanding.

Guy turned a little apologetically. "Forgive me, Miss Conyngham, I'm afraid that I've yet again let my temper get the better of me. In mitigation I can only plead that in recent weeks I've endured enough conflict to last me for the rest of my hitherto peaceful life." He smiled. "I sincerely hope that a stay here will have the desired effect upon my niece, for it goes very much against the grain with me that it's necessary for her to come here at all. Now, shall we go inside? Imogen has unfortunately to leave almost immediately for Windsor, as she has to wait upon the queen, and she cannot delay much longer before setting out."

And Imogen's plans must come first, thought Leonie critically. If Imogen had royal duties, then she should attend to them herself and leave Guy to do his duty where his niece was concerned. But no, that wouldn't do; Imogen needs must delay until the last moment and thus keep the friction at flamepoint, and thus also ensure that Guy remained at the seminary for the shortest time possible. Leonie knew Imogen too well, having in the past had ample opportunity to witness her methods at close quarters.

Preceding Guy and Stella into the seminary, Leonie wondered again about Imogen. Why had she hurried on in as she had? Surely she couldn't be eager to see Miss Hart, not after having stayed away for nearly two years now. No, she was up to something. But what?

Entering the vestibule, she saw Imogen and Miss Hart emerging from the visitors' room. They didn't notice her at first and so she saw how conspiratorial they were. "You may rely on me, Lady Imogen," the headmistress was murmuring. "I promise to do exactly as you have requested."

Guy came in at that moment and overheard. "And what have you requested?" he inquired of Imogen.

She turned with a sharp gasp. "Guy! I didn't know you were there!" She gave a nervous laugh then, a false little laugh which struck another warning chord in Leonie. "I was merely asking Miss Hart to do all she could to make Stella's stay a happy one, for I realize how dreadful she must be feeling and I want to make things as pleasant as possible for her."

Leonie looked suspiciously at Miss Hart, whose eyes were prudently lowered to a close study of the floor tiles.

Imogen smiled and hurried across to Guy, linking her arm through his. "I know I'm being difficult, sweetheart, but truly I must set off now for Windsor."

"I know. I'll just say good-bye to Stella."

"I'll wait in the carriage," she said, her deep blue eyes flickering momentarily to Leonie, whom she knew she hadn't fooled in the least. A faint smile curved her lips and then she was gone.

Guy turned to Stella. "I don't want to leave you here," he said gently, "but you must understand that you cannot impose your will upon me. Be good, so that Miss Hart sends me favorable reports of your progress, and I promise you that you will come to Poyntons for the house party on the ninth of February. Be disobedient and I shall remain firm in my resolve."

Leonie looked again at Miss Hart. So, that was it. Imogen had told her not on any account to send Guy approving reports!

Guy bent to kiss Stella on the cheek, but she averted her face. He hesitated, but then suddenly turned on his heel and left. Joseph hurried to close the door behind him.

The moment Guy had gone, Stella suddenly whirled about to face Miss Hart, her eyes flashing with defiance. "I won't stay here, I won't!" she cried, stamping her foot. "I'll run away, do you hear me? I'll run away back home, while that Longhurst creature's away, and I'll *make* Uncle Guy take me back!"

Miss Hart's eyes narrowed coldly. "You'll do as you're told, missy," she said icily.

"I won't!" cried Stella again. She rushed to the table and swept the dish of calling cards to the floor. It fell with a loud clatter that brought two maids hurrying from the direction of the kitchens. Joseph gaped in amazement at this display, but Stella was unrepentant. "I won't do anything you tell me to, I shan't stay here! I hate you all!"

"Indeed?" Miss Hart's eyebrow was raised. "Perhaps an hour or so on the reclining board will cool your tantrums. Joseph, have Mlle. Clary come here immediately."

Stella stamped her foot again. "I won't go to any reclining board! I won't do anything you tell me to, I'm going to run away tonight and there's nothing you can do about it!"

"I can certainly see that you're punished in the meantime," warned Miss Hart, almost beside herself with fury. "And I can make your escape as difficult as possible by seeing to it that you are guarded. Miss Ross will sleep with you."

Leonie stared at her. Miss Ross? But everyone knew that she slept like the proverbial log! The Battle of Hastings could take place outside her door and she'd sleep through it, so why on earth set her to guard someone like Stella? The answer came almost immediately. Miss Hart wanted Stella to try to escape, for it would enable her to send a first poor report to Guy!

Mlle. Clary arrived at that moment and, assisted by a very reluctant Joseph, bore a kicking, screaming Stella off to the punishment room.

Leonie turned hesitantly to the headmistress, knowing that she must voice her opinion, even though it would hardly be well-received. "Miss Hart?"

The headmistress held her gaze. "Miss Conyngham?"

"About Miss Ross. She sleeps so soundly that—"

"I do not require your opinion, Miss Conyngham."

"But—"

"It isn't your business, missy. Go to your duties immediately, and never again presume to question my actions."

Leonie fell silent. Miss Hart had laid a trap and Stella was going to fall straight into it.

16

Stella wasn't chastened by the punishment, and emerged only to create another astonishing scene, this time in the dining room before the entire school. It was another amazing display of furious defiance, accompanied by a great deal of screaming and foot-stamping, and it prompted a rather faint Miss Ross to recall tales she'd heard of Lady Caroline Lamb, or Ponsonby as she then was, when she'd been sent to Miss Frances Rowden's seminary in Hans Place, Kensington. Miss Rowden, it was rumored, had never fully recovered from the experience. Miss Hart, however, was made of sterner stuff. Apparently totally unmoved by the rather public tantrum, she promptly dispatched Stella back to the punishment room, under Mlle. Clary's continuing supervision. She remained there until it was time to go to bed.

Miss Hart allocated Leonie's former bedroom to Stella. It had remained unexpectedly vacant since the beginning of the new term because there were no less than three young ladies of equal rank and seniority who all aspired to occupy it. Since they could not all be obliged, the headmistress had decided to deny it to all of them. It had then been set aside for Stella, because the headmistress was mindful of the child's connection with Imogen, and therefore, somewhat tenuously, with Nadia and Dorothea Lieven. Imogen's subsequent secret request concerning the child had come too late to prevent arrangements being made, and so the rather chagrined Miss Hart had had to leave the seminary's most disruptive and difficult pupil ever in possession of the school's finest bedroom. Those who had been denied the coveted room did not like such apparent favoritism, especially as Stella's subsequent conduct had been so appalling, and so in the whole school, only Leonie felt any sympathy for the new arrival.

Miss Ross, who had not been taken into the headmistress's confidence about Stella, was only too aware of her shortcomings as a jailer, and was very unhappy indeed as she escorted the girl to the bedroom. Taking her unwanted responsibilities seriously, she decided not to take any chances, and so locked the door once they were both safely inside. She then put the key on a ribbon around her neck, and thus felt certain that Stella could no longer carry out her threat to run away that night.

Undressing and climbing into the spacious bed, Stella maintained a surly and resentful silence. She curled up into a little ball, her back toward the teacher's side of the bed, and she ignored an instruction to put on her night bonnet. Miss Ross sighed and did not press the point, for at least the wretched child was quiet for the time being. The teacher felt very hard-done-by as she too prepared for bed. Shortly afterward, the candle was extinguished and silence descended first over the room, and then over the entire building. Outside in Park Lane the traffic became gradually more quiet, until at last there was only the occasional carriage driving past. Somewhere the watch was calling, their cries echoing through the freezing fog.

A solitary light glowed in the seminary as Leonie sat by the fire in her room. She couldn't relax enough to go to sleep, and she hadn't even changed into her nightclothes. Her copy of *The Bride of Abydos* lay unopened on her lap, and she gazed into the smoking fire, thinking about Stella. The child's unhappiness reached out to her, and she knew that if Stella could possibly escape from the seminary tonight, then she would do it. The thought was unsettling and worrying, and after a long while Leonie got up and went to the window, gazing out at the misty darkness.

On the floor below, Stella lay awake, listening to Miss Ross's deep, steady breathing. As the teacher sank into a sounder sleep and began to snore, the child sat up carefully beside her. Miss Ross didn't stir at the movement, nor was she aware of the girl slipping from the bed and going to the dressing table to take a small pair of scissors from the reticule lying there. By the faint glow of the dying fire, Stella succeeded in cutting the ribbon around the teacher's neck. The key slipped easily into her waiting fingers.

Stella dressed quickly and silently, putting on her warmest clothes and not making a single sound. Miss Ross slept on, her snores loud and rhythmic, and she knew nothing as the door was stealthily opened and then closed again.

Stella slipped silently toward the top of the stairs, but she didn't see Mrs. Durham's cat in the shadows, and she trod on its tail. It gave a loud, pained yowl and fled spitting into the darkness. Stella froze, her heart pounding, but miraculously the building remained silent. After a moment she hurried on down the stairs.

Leonie heard the cat and ran swiftly from her room, instinctively snatching up her cloak, knowing that the noise had had something to do with Stella. She looked over the stair balustrade just in time to see Stella's fleeing figure at the bottom. The child disappeared from view then, running not to the main doors, but toward the school wing at the back of the house.

Tying on her mantle, Leonie hurried down after her, and as she reached the school wing, she heard a sound from the direction of the dining room. "Stella?" There was silence then, and she went into the dining room. A sweep of bitterly cold air passed over her and she saw that the French windows were open. As she ran out into the dark night, she saw Stella running toward the narrow path which led between the adjoining gardens and out into South Audley Street. She must have noticed the path earlier and decided then to escape that way!

Stella ran like the wind down South Audley Street toward Curzon Street, and she paused briefly by the wall of Chesterfield House on the corner, looking back to see if anyone was following. Her breath caught on a dismayed gasp as she saw Leonie running toward her.

"Stella! Please stop!"

With a cry, Stella ran on, turning into Curzon Street and fleeing east in the direction of Berkeley Street. She ran past Longhurst House, in darkness now because both Imogen and her brother were away from home. It was a handsome white building with a pillared porch beneath which carriages could drive and their passengers alight under cover in bad weather, and it commanded a prime position in the much-sought-after street, but Stella didn't even glance at it. It wasn't of any interest to her when her hated enemy was out of town.

She was nearing the eastern end of the street now, and she peered ahead for the entrance of Lansdowne Passage, the dangerous subterranean way which led between the gardens of Lansdowne House and Devonshire House, and which connected Curzon Street directly with Berkeley Street.

Behind her a dismayed Leonie realized which way the girl intended to go. Lansdowne Passage was the haunt of footpads and pickpockets, and had been used by highwaymen as an escape route until railings had been placed at the top of the steps at each end.

"Stella!" she called desperately. "Stella, don't go that way! Please!"

Stella hesitated, her face pale in the dim light of a streetlamp, but then she disappeared into the entrance of the passage.

Leonie reached the entrance a moment later. Her heart was thundering with fear and from the exertion of running. She was afraid to go into the dark tunnel. Overhead the bare branches of the famous Devonshire House elms loomed starkly into the night, and she could hear the echoing sound of Stella's fleeing footsteps. Taking a deep breath, Leonie went down the steps, and soon the faint light from Curzon Street had faded behind her.

The Tyburn River passed beneath the tunnel, and the paving stones rang hollow at one point. She could hear the sound of flowing water. Ahead of her Stella's footsteps had suddenly stopped. Leonie halted too, listening for any sound. She could see the steps leading up into Berkeley Street, their damp surfaces shining in the light from a streetlamp. As she gazed toward it, she saw a tall figure standing in the middle of the passage. It was far too tall and burly to be Stella! Then she saw Stella, pressing back terrified against the tunnel wall as several other figures gathered menacingly around her. Leonie's heart almost stopped. Then, unbelievably, she heard the watch calling in Berkeley Street. She began to scream for help, and the figures around Stella all whirled about in the direction of the screams. The watch had heard as well, and they appeared at the top of the steps, the welcome light of their lanterns swaying wildly down into the passage. The men by Stella fled then, their steps pounding on the paving stones as they ran toward Leonie, thrusting her roughly aside as they made their escape to Curzon Street.

Winded, she stumbled against the damp wall, pressing back as the watch gave chase, their whistles shrilling deafeningly in the confined space. One of them had stopped to assist Stella, who had almost collapsed with terror now. Leonie hurried to her. "Stella? Stella, are you all right?"

The girl gave a glad cry and ran to her. Leonie held her close as the watchman raised his lantern suspiciously, his quick glance taking in Leonie's tousled silver-fair hair, so vivid in the lanternlight and so strangely uncovered by hat or bonnet.

"Right," he said gruffly. "Let's be having your names and addresses, then."

"I am Miss Conyngham of the seminary in Park Lane, and this is Miss Stella de Lacey, the niece of Sir Guy de Lacey."

His eyes narrowed. "Oh, yes? And I'm the Queen of Sheba. Ladies don't go out alone at night, especially not in Lansdowne Passage. Let's have the truth now. Who are you, and where do you live?"

"I've already told you," replied Leonie.

"You expect me to believe that? One of your customers get out of hand, did he? Want more than he'd paid for?"

Leonie gasped indignantly. "How dare you speak to me like that! Do I look like a streetwalker?"

Stella clung to her. "Please," she whispered, "please take me to Uncle Guy's house."

The watchman looked uncertain then, but he still wasn't entirely convinced. "Right," he said after a moment. "Right, I'll take you to Sir Guy's house, and then we'll see if you're telling the truth, won't we? Come on." Holding his lantern high to illuminate the way, he escorted them to the steps into Berkeley Street.

Guy's house lay almost opposite the entrance to the passage. It was a dignified brick house, austere and beautifully proportioned, with pedimented second-floor windows and stone balustrades. Its round-headed door was approached by three shallow steps, and Guy's name was on the brass plate which shone very brightly in the lanternlight as the watchman knocked loudly. The sound echoed up through the house.

At first there was no response, but as the watchman continued to knock, they at last saw flickering candlelight within. A footman, his wig not quite straight and his dressing gown tied hastily around his waist, looked out cautiously. "Yes? Who is it?"

Stella pushed inside. "It's me, James! Where's Uncle Guy?"

"Miss Stella?" The footman stared at her in astonishment.

Leonie and the watchman followed her into the square entrance hall, which led through to an inner hall from which rose a magnificent double staircase. The walls were pale blue and contained gilded niches in which stood beautiful statues, but the first entrance hall, in which they now gathered, was dominated by a solitary painting hanging above the marble fireplace. It was a portrait of Imogen. She looked ethereally beautiful, her red hair twisted up into a loose knot and twined with tiny strings of pearls. She wore a very décolleté white gown which displayed her charms to the best advantage, and it seemed to Leonie that the portrait was watching her, its magnificent blue eyes haughty and scornful.

Guy's voice came from the staircase then. "What is it, James? Is there a disturbance?" He appeared at the entrance to the inner hall, wearing a floor-length dressing down made of green shot silk. Beneath it his frilled shirt was unbuttoned, and he still had on the tight-fitting trousers he had worn during the evening. His hair was disheveled and his dark eyes angry.

Stella gave a glad cry and ran to him. "Uncle Guy!"

Instinctively he caught her close. "Stella?" He looked across at Leonie then. "What's the meaning of this?" he demanded.

Before Leonie could reply, the watchman stepped respectfully forward. "Begging your pardon, Sir Guy, but I found them both in Lansdowne Passage, and they said the young lady was your niece."

"She is."

"Yes, Sir Guy. I can see that she is. There was some

trouble in the passage, and the teacher here called for help. It was lucky we were close by.''

Guy's eyes swung angrily toward Leonie again. ''You were in Lansdowne Passage with Stella? Have you taken leave of your senses? If this is a sample of the care shown to its pupils by your establishment—''

Stella drew away. ''It wasn't Miss Conyngham's fault, Uncle Guy. I ran away. I hate it there, and I wanted to come home. She ran after me to try to stop me. Then there were those horrid men in the passage . . .'' Her voice died away and she bit her lip, realizing more and more with each passing moment how much danger she, and consequently Leonie, had actually been in.

Guy put his hand to the child's chin and raised her face toward him. ''Are you all right?''

''Yes.'' The reply was barely audible.

''You're sure?''

''Yes.''

He turned to the watchman, taking some coins from his dressing-gown pocket and pressing them into the man's hand. ''You did well. I'm grateful to you.''

The watchman's eyes widened as he saw the amount. ''Thank you, Sir Guy! Thank you kindly!'' Still muttering his thanks, he withdrew to the door, and the rather bemused James showed him out into the night again.

Guy turned severely to Stella again. ''I'm disappointed in you,'' he said sternly. ''I thought that you truly meant to mend your ways, but already you show that you have no such intention.''

Tears filled Stella's eyes. ''But I only wanted to come home!'' she cried. She pointed accusingly at Imogen's portrait. ''I wanted to speak to you when *she* wasn't here!''

''That's enough,'' he snapped angrily.

''Please, Uncle Guy,'' she pleaded. ''You must listen to me. She's been making all the trouble, I swear that she has. She tells fibs about me, and says I've said and done things I haven't.''

''I said that's enough! I will *not* have you speaking about Imogen in that way. I'm going to marry her because I love her, and you, madam, are going to accept that fact or remain at the seminary. Is that quite clear? Tonight's little episode has merely convinced me all the more that you are quite unfit to return home. You are going straight back to Park Lane. You will not spend the night beneath this roof.''

Stella stared at him, her huge eyes filling with tears. She turned to Leonie then, running into her arms, weeping bitterly. Leonie held her close once more. ''It's all right, Stella,'' she whispered, smoothing the dark ringlets. ''Please don't cry.''

Guy was still angry, but Leonie could see that he hated having made his niece cry. He turned away, beckoning James. ''Have Mrs. Raikes rouse herself and bring some hot milk to the library. Then have my town carriage made ready. I intend to escort my niece and Miss Conyngham back to the seminary.''

''Yes, Sir Guy.'' The footman hurried away.

Leonie and Stella sat alone in the library, sipping the welcome hot milk while Guy went to dress for the short journey to Park Lane. The library was warm, its bookshelves reaching from floor to celing. The chairs were upholstered in dark green leather, and there were green velvet curtains at the tall windows. Guy had evidently been seated by the fire when he had heard their noisy arrival, for a half-finished glass of cognac and an open book lay on the small table by the lighted candelabrum. Leonie glanced at the book. It was Milton's *Paradise Lost*.

Stella cupped her glass of hot milk in her hands and gazed tearfully at nothing in particular. Guy's reaction to her flight had not been what she had been hoping for. She felt devastated, and rejected. Tears coursed slowly down her little cheeks, and every so often she sniffed.

Leonie went to sit beside her, putting a comforting arm around the trembling shoulders. ''You've gone about it all the wrong way,'' she said gently. ''You've made him angry now, but part of his anger is due to the fact that you put yourself in such danger. He loves you very much, Stella, and I know that he wants you to come home again.''

''No, he doesn't. He just wants to be alone with her.''

''You're wrong. If you want to go home again, Stella, you're going to have to be good. Continue as you are at present and you'll make things worse and worse and you'll only punish yourself.''

''Even if I'm good, that horrid Miss Hart won't tell Uncle

Guy the truth. Will she?'' Stella looked shrewdly at Leonie. ''I saw her with Imogen, and I know what Imogen's asked her to do.''

Leonie looked away, startled at the child's perception.

''There isn't any point in my being good. They aren't going to let Uncle Guy know, they're going to see that I stay where I am.''

''I'll let him know the truth,'' said Leonie suddenly. ''I promise you that I will.''

But Stella shook her head, tears filling her eyes again. ''He doesn't want me,'' she whispered. ''He won't listen to you.''

Leonie had no chance to say anything more, for at that moment Guy returned. ''The carriage is at the door.'' He wore the greatcoat she had seen him wear at the Grosvenor Chapel, and he was teasing on his leather gloves.

Stella got up silently, looking accusingly at him. Then she slipped her little hand into Leonie's, and they walked past him and down to the waiting carriage. It was very cold after the warmth of the library, and Stella huddled close to Leonie, her face averted from her uncle.

The carriage drove slowly through the deserted Mayfair streets, and the fog swirled eerily all around, glowing with light now and then as they passed a streetlamp. Guy asked Stella to tell him exactly what had happened since he had left her at the seminary, and his face darkened when she reluctantly obliged. Stella hid her face then, huddling even closer, and in spite of the motion of the carriage, Leonie could feel how much she was trembling.

At the seminary all was still in darkness. No one yet knew what had been happening. Miss Hart came hastily on being informed that Sir Guy de Laccy was demanding to see her immediately, and that his niece had managed to run away after all. She hurried into the vestibule, tying her robe over her voluminous nightgown. Her hair was tied in tight plaits beneath her floppy night bonnet, and in spite of her show of agitation and dismay, Leonie could see how sharp and clever her eyes were. ''Sir Guy?'' she cried. ''Whatever has happened?''

''My niece ran away tonight, madam,'' he said coldly. ''It seems that the entirely unsuitable guard you placed upon her proved as ineffectual as your damned punishment room. I don't want to hear again that you've treated my niece so abominably, nor do I wish her to be placed with anyone other than Miss Conyngham. Is that clear?''

Leonie looked at him in astonishment. He wanted Stella placed in her charge? Stella's lips parted and her hand crept gladly into Leonie's again.

Miss Hart looked displeased. ''Sir Guy, Miss Conyngham is a very junior member of staff, and as to my having treated Miss de Lacey abominably . . . well, I find such a suggestion totally unwarranted.''

''Possibly you do, but I find what you've done so far to be little less than barbaric. Place my niece in Miss Conyngham's charge, for if you do not then I will remove her, amid some rather unwelcome publicity. I'm sure you wish to avoid that.''

Miss Hart's cheeks paled a little. Unwelcome publicity and a risk to the seminary's reputation were the very last thing she wanted. She'd given her word to Imogen that she'd make Stella's stay at the seminary as difficult as possible, thus provoking the girl into continued bad behavior, but how could she still do that when faced with this threat from Guy? She had no option but to acquiesce to his demands, for the time being at least. ''Very well, Sir Guy, Miss Conyngham will have sole charge of your niece.''

''From this moment on,'' he insisted.

''Naturally.''

He turned to Leonie then. ''Forgive me for forcing this responsibility upon you, Miss Conyngham, but it is obvious to me that you are the one to look after her.''

''I will be glad to, Sir Guy.''

He smiled then. ''Yes. I know,'' he said softly.

She looked quickly away, afraid that he might see how much that softness in his voice affected her.

But he noticed nothing. He crouched down before Stella and put his hands on her arms. ''Stella,'' he said gently, ''I want more than anything to have you home again, but you *must* give me proof that you want to live in harmony with both me and Imogen. There cannot be any other way, sweetheart, and I hope that you can understand that. I cannot turn from Imogen simply because you don't like her. Besides, I'm sure that you're wrong about her, and if you meet her halfway, she will be more than glad to welcome you."

Briefly Stella glanced up at Leonie, but then she nodded. "I understand, Uncle Guy."

"And you'll try?"

She didn't reply.

His hands dropped away and he straightened again, the disappointment clear in his eyes for a moment. Then he picked up his hat and gloves and left. Joseph closed the outer door behind him and almost immediately they heard the carriage driving away.

Leonie turned to Miss Hart then. "Perhaps you will instruct Miss Ross that I am to stay with Stella from now on."

The headmistress's cold eyes flashed. "Don't give yourself airs and graces, Miss Conygnham, and don't presume to order me around." But she was in a cleft stick, and she knew it. Angrily she turned to Joseph. "Go to Miss Ross and tell her that she is to return immediately to her dormitory."

"Yes, ma'am." Joseph bowed, but his glance momentarily met Leonie's. Behind Miss Hart's back, he grinned.

17

Several days later the long-promised snow began to fall, and just as the frost had been the longest in living memory, so was the snow the heaviest. It lay in a deep mantle over the land, and the streets and squares of London were choked with drifts. The thin ice on the Thames was covered with soft whiteness, and some of the smaller vessels moored upstream of London Bridge were frozen in.

The fog had lifted the moment the snow began to fall, and now the air was clear and sharp. During the day the sun shone coldly down from a flawless sky, while at night a million stars glittered in a heaven as black as velvet.

The *beau monde* found its life fleetingly checked by this latest vagary of the weather, but the moment the streets were cleared, society emerged once more to continue enjoying the winter round of soirées, assemblies, balls, and dinner parties.

Imogen was inevitably delayed in Windsor, but at last, after a difficult journey, she returned to Curzon Street, and that evening she and Guy attended a dinner party at Devonshire House. The evening had not gone well, for on her return from Windsor she had been hoping to see favorable results from her secret agreement with Miss Hart; she had been far from pleased to discover the turn events had actually taken during her absence. She disliked the understanding which seemed to have sprung up between Stella and Leonie, and she liked even less the fact that Leonie was now only too likely to have contact with Guy. Dwelling upon all this throughout dinner, she was not at her most amenable, and the atmosphere between herself and Guy was a little strained when they at last left Devonshire House to return to Curzon Street.

They had Longhurst House to themselves, because Edward was temporarily out of town. Realizing that sulking was not achieving anything, she begged Guy to stay with her for a while and then instructed the butler to bring a bottle of iced champagne. She and Guy then sat in the firelit drawing room, he in a large armchair, she on the floor beside him, her head resting on his knee. The drawing room at Longhurst House was particularly beautiful, with vast mirrors and magnificent paintings on its gold brocade walls, and two intricate crystal chandeliers suspended from its decorative ceilings. The firelight flickered over red velvet chairs and sofas, and there was perfume in the air from the open potpourri jar in the hearth. Imogen's pale pink gown was blushed to deep rose, and the diamond comb in her hair glittered and flashed in the moving light. The flames were reflected in her eyes as she gazed into the fire; it should have been a perfect moment, but it wasn't, because she couldn't set aside the instinctive unease she felt because of Guy's dealings with Leonie. At last she could bear it no longer; she had to bring up the subject.

"Why did you insist upon Leonie Conyngham having charge of Stella?"

"Because she appears to have Stella's regard."

"But she's hardly qualified for such a responsibility!"

"That isn't the point in this instance."

"Oh?" She looked up at him. "What *is* the point then?"

"I should have thought it was obvious."

"Oh, yes," she replied a little acidly, "it's perfectly obvious."

"What exactly do you mean by that?"

"Come now, Leonie Conyngham isn't an experienced teacher, but she *is* rather attractive."

He was silent for a moment. "Am I to presume then that you suspect me of an ulterior motive where Leonie is concerned?" His tone was noticeably cool.

"Well, you could have, couldn't you? I mean, Rupert Allingham certainly had designs upon her before her disgrace."

"It's hardly *her* disgrace," he said shortly. "If blame must be placed anywhere, then Richard Conyngham appears to be the prime candidate."

"All right, it may not be her personal disgrace—what does it matter anyway? I was talking about Rupert's considerable interest in her."

"May I remind you that I'm not Thornbury and that my interest in Leonie Conyngham is due solely to my concern for Stella's welfare." His tone was still cool, and a little irritated as well now.

She got up angrily, knowing that she wasn't handling the situation very well. "It seems to me that Leonie is able to cause a great deal of trouble without ever seeming to."

"To what are you referring now?"

"Well, you and I are quarreling over her, and it was because of Rupert's unfortunate interest in her that Nadia was caused a great deal of distress."

"I'm not quarreling, you are. And as for Nadia Benckendorff . . . well, she doesn't merit any sympathy whatsoever."

"Guy!"

"It's true, she is the most callous, unfeeling, and generally disagreeable creature it has ever been my misfortune to encounter."

"I won't listen to you," she replied, turning away.

"Correct me if I'm wrong, but did she not ask Dorothea Lieven to keep Leonie at the seminary when news of Richard Conyngham's fate reached London?"

"I have no idea." She didn't look back at him.

"Don't treat me as if I'm a fool, Imogen. I know perfectly well that you are aware of Nadia's activities. She was afraid that I could carry out my threat to see Leonie installed at Thornbury House, and this business of unpaid fees has been disgracefully inflated to keep Leonie where she is. So don't expect me to sympathize with, or even like, Nadia Benckendorff."

Imogen felt stung. "If she did anything such as you suggest, it was because she loves Rupert."

"She *wants* him. There's a subtle difference. She won't win him, though, I can promise you that."

At last she turned. "What do you mean? Do you know something? If it's because he's still supposed to be infatuated with Leonie, let me assure you—"

"On this occasion it has nothing to do with Leonie. I was thinking rather of Marguerite St. Julienne."

She stared at him, and then gave an incredulous laugh. "Don't be ridiculous. She's the ugliest and dullest creature in London!"

"And one of the richest. Rupert Allingham may like wagering on any damned silly thing, but I'll warrant he won't take a gamble where his wife is concerned. He'll want a fortune, Imogen, and the St. Julienne fortune is handsomer than most. Nadia must suspect something of the sort, for she has recently thrown all caution to the winds. But then you probably already know."

"Know? Know what?"

He looked at her in surprise. "Don't tell me you aren't party to her every thought? Miss Benckendorff, determined to make sure of the Duke of Thornbury, has embarked, as they say, on the voyage to Cythera. She's his mistress, Imogen."

She looked at him in astonishment. "I can't believe it."

"As you wish, but I promise you it's true."

"How do you know?"

"Thornbury, gallant gentleman that he is, told me himself. He isn't one to respect a lady's reputation, certainly not a lady he regards as nothing more than an adventuress. Scruples have no place in his character, Imogen, nor do they have any place in Nadia's, as her despicable interference in poor Leonie Conyngham's life reveals only too clearly."

She was stung, both by being excluded from Nadia's confidence and by this renewed defense of Leonie Conyngham. "Leonie! Leonie!" she cried. "Why do you always have to mention her? I'm beginning to think I was right after all, and that in spite of your noble denials, you *do* have a *tendre* for her!"

He rose angrily to his feet then. "Don't be so damned tedious, Imogen! I'm not in the mood for it. Perhaps it would be better if I left now, for this evening has hardly gone well, has it?"

She was alarmed at his reaction. Tears swiftly sprang to her eyes. "Oh, Guy, please don't go like this!"

At that moment they heard Edward's carriage entering the pillared porch outside, and Imogen knew that Guy would certainly leave now, for he and Edward disliked each other.

She ran quickly to him. "Please stay," she begged, slipping her arms around his neck.

He caught her close for a moment, but he didn't change his mind. "No," he said softly, "I think it best to forget tonight and begin anew tomorrow."

"But I have to leave for Oxford tomorrow—you know that Edward and I must attend my cousin's wedding! If I hadn't been delayed at Windsor, we would have had three days, but as it is—"

He kissed her on the lips. "Then we will begin anew when you return. No, Imogen, don't ask me to stay again, for if I did, then the evening would become a positive disaster. We are neither of us in the best of moods, and it would be wiser all round if we left well alone for the time being."

She nodded. He kissed her again and then left. She couldn't help but be aware of the reserve in him, and the unease that had been with her throughout the evening became more insistent. He could have stayed had he really wished to, and he could also accompany her to Oxford, for the invitation had been extended to him; but he had taken neither option. Why? Did he, as he had said, wish to stay in town because of Stella? Or was it maybe because of Leonie? Leonie. The name seemed to haunt her, and tonight it had almost been as if she had been with them at Devonshire House, and then here, in this very room. What exactly *were* his feelings toward the woman he had so carefully seen was in charge of his niece? Imogen's blue eyes were thoughtful and cold. She had never liked Leonie, not even when they had been children together at the seminary; now she hated her.

As Guy drove away from Curzon Street in his carriage, around the corner in Park Lane his niece was gazing out of her bedroom window at the snowy moonlit park. She was ready for bed and was wearing a warm wrap over her nightgown. Katy had just finished combing her dark ringlets and was tying on her little night bonnet. A moment later the maid had withdrawn, leaving Stella and Leonie to retire when they were ready. Stella's eyes were very pensive as she stared out into the night.

Leonie was seated at the dressing table, just as countless times in the past. It was good to be back in her old room after the cold discomfort of the floor above. It was good too to be again awoken each morning by Katy and the morning tray. Stella had quickly come to look forward to the maid's arrival each morning, for she enjoyed sharing in the unlikely friendship. There was no affectation about Stella de Lacey, Leonie thought approvingly; she was honest and genuine, and above all very likable indeed. Glancing at the girl, standing so motionless at the window, Leonie began to wonder why she was so quiet and thoughtful. "Stella? Is something wrong?"

"No. Why do you ask?"

"I'm not used to such silence from you. Has anything happened to you in class?"

"No, they're still refusing to speak to me. I don't care, though. Most of them are silly anyway, especially the ones who look down their superior noses at you."

"It's inevitable that some of them will feel like that about me, Stella."

"No, it isn't, they're just too stupid to think for themselves. They heard their families condemning your father unheard, and so they do the same to you. I couldn't care less if they never spoke to me my whole life through."

Leonie smiled. "What a tiger you are, to be sure."

"I like you," replied Stella simply.

"And I like you too, which is why I'm concerned about your odd silence tonight. Usually you chatter nineteen to the dozen."

"I've been thinking."

"I know." Leonie glanced at the copy of the *Times* which lay on the little table at Stella's side of the bed. Whatever had caused Stella's quiet mood had something to do with that paper, which she had so carefully begged from a very reluctant Miss Hart.

Stella turned to her then. "I've been thinking about Uncle Guy. You were right when you said that the only way for me to get home again is by changing my ways, and that is what I've been doing. I've attended all my classes, I've done my lessons, and I've obeyed all the teachers. I have been good, haven't I?"

"Yes, you have."

"I know that Miss Hart is on Imogen's side, but I also know that you aren't."

"No, I'm on your side."

"And you promised that you would tell him how good I was being, didn't you?"

"Yes."

Stella closed the shutters with a clatter and quickly drew the curtains across before going to the bed and sitting up in it, her knees drawn up and clasped with her arms. Her eyes were shining conspiratorially. "I'm going to be so good that Uncle Guy won't know me when next he calls. I'm going to be a positive angel."

Something about her caught Leonie's sudden attention. "What are you up to?" she asked suspiciously.

"Up to? Me?" Stella's eyes were all innocence.

"Yes, you. I may not have known you for long, but it's been long enough to know when you're plotting something. I only hope for your sake that it isn't anything foolish."

Stella looked positively sleek, the gleam in her eyes more anticipatory than ever. "All right, I admit that I'm up to something. I won't tell you what it is, but I promise you it isn't anything foolish." Her glance moved fleetingly toward the newspaper beside her.

"Is it something to do with that paper?"

"Well, in a way. It just gave me the idea, that's all."

Leonie was a little disturbed. "You do promise that you aren't going to be silly again, don't you?"

"Silly? Oh, I'm not going to run away or anything like that, honestly I'm not. I have it all planned, and all I want now is for Uncle Guy to come to see me again. He must come alone, though, that's all."

"Why?" asked Leonie suspiciously, still afraid that the girl was about to launch into something unwise.

"Because it won't work if *she's* with him, that's all." Stella smiled slyly. "And she's in Oxford at the moment, at her cousin's wedding. Oh, he must come soon, Leonie, he simply must!"

18

A week passed and Stella had begun to fear that Imogen would return before there was a chance to speak to Guy alone. It was another fine but bitterly cold morning when he went riding in Hyde Park, where the ways had been cleared and the snow piled at intervals beneath the trees. Seeing the white facade of the seminary, he decided that the time had come to visit his niece again. He had stayed away deliberately since the night she had run away, hoping that if she was left to her own devices she might come to realize that he did indeed mean every word he said concerning her unacceptable behavior. But even now he wasn't sure if the time was right to see her, for he had that very morning received a less-than-encouraging report from Miss Hart. However, since he had formed a dislike for the headmistress on meeting her, he decided that the best person to see about Stella's conduct would be Leonie. When Joseph admitted him to the seminary, therefore, he requested to see Leonie first, and then he went to await her in the visitor's room.

He deliberately avoided glancing at Dorothea Lieven's portrait, turning his back toward it and standing by the window to look at the garden. It seemed that few had ventured out into the deep snow that had drifted against the high walls, but someone had thrown crumbs out for the birds, and their tiny prints were everywhere. Something made him glance toward the school wing, and there, in one of the classrooms, he saw Leonie seated at a high desk. She was facing a group of small girls and appeared to be reading to them. His eyes moved

115

slowly over the slender figure in its plain donkey-brown dress. Her silvery hair was pushed up beneath a neat frilled day bonnet, but one curl seemed intent upon escape, tumbling down from its pins, only to be immediately pushed back into place. He couldn't help noticing how dark her eyes were, and how pale her skin; there was something about her which stayed in the memory long after she had gone from sight. There was no doubt, he thought, that had not events so cruelly intervened, she would have taken society by storm.

As he watched, Joseph entered the classroom to speak to her, and a moment later she had dismissed her class before going out herself. Then her light steps were at the door, and he turned as she came in. "Good morning, Miss Conyngham," he said, crossing to her and raising her hand to his lips.

"Good morning, Sir Guy. You wished to see me?"

"Yes. I hope I haven't inconvenienced you in any way."

"No, my class was just about to go to Herr Meyer for a music lesson." Oh, how good it was to see him again. Until this moment she hadn't realized how much he had been on her mind.

"Please take a seat," he said, escorting her to a chair close to the fire.

She sat down and then looked up at him. He didn't speak straightaway; it was as if he wasn't quite sure how to begin. He stood by the fire, one hand upon the mantelpiece and one foot upon the fender, and he gazed into the flames for a long moment. She was reminded of the day she had first seen him; he had been gazing into the vestibule fire in just that way.

He looked at her suddenly. "I wanted to see you about Stella. How is she?"

"She's very well."

"And her behavior?"

"Cannot be faulted."

He looked away. "There's been no disobedience?"

"No." She was puzzled by his manner. "Sir Guy, is something wrong?"

"I'm not sure. You see, what you've just said rather contradicts the report I received from Miss Hart this morning."

"Oh." She felt an embarrassed flush leap to her cheeks.

"And given that there is only one Stella, I find it perplexing to say the least that she is apparently an angel one minute and the devil incarnate the next. Which am I to believe, Miss Conyngham?''

The color heightened on her cheeks and she felt suddenly very hot. How could she possibly tell him the truth, that Imogen had ordered Miss Hart to tell lies about Stella?

He watched her. ''Is there something I should know?''

''No. At least . . .'' She got up. She had to say something—but what? ''Sir Guy, since the night that you insisted that I have charge of Stella, Miss Hart has actually had very little to do with her.''

''I can accept that. I presume, therefore, that Miss Hart consulted with you before writing to me.''

''No. She didn't.''

Anger and disbelief flashed into his eyes. ''She didn't bother to speak to you, and then still presumed to write to me expressing an adverse opinion?''

''I'm sure it was a misunderstanding,'' she said quickly. ''Believe me, Sir Guy, Stella is being very good indeed—in fact she is a model pupil.''

He searched her urgent face. ''Miss Conyngham, is my niece happy here now?'' he asked suddenly.

The change of direction startled her. ''Happy? She . . . she will only be happy when she's with you again.''

''Apart from that consideration, is she happy here?''

''She's happy when she's with me.''

''I note the qualification.'' He smiled unexpectedly. ''And I can well believe that she is happy with you, for it would be a very strange soul who would not be, but I am left with the fact that at all other times she is presumably not at all happy. Am I right?''

''Yes, but she endures it because she believes her reformed behavior will ensure an early return to you.'' She held his gaze. ''She is everything you could wish, Sir Guy, and when she does leave I shall miss her very much. I like her a great deal.''

He nodded. ''I wish that I could hear those words on Imogen's lips,'' he said softly, ''but I suppose I must acknowledge that Stella's past conduct didn't in the least encourage feelings of affection.''

She lowered her eyes. Affection? Imogen wasn't capable of any.

"Miss Conyngham, please forgive me if I've given the impression of disbelieving what you say about Stella. The truth is that I don't find Miss Hart at all to my liking, and indeed had it not been for your presence here, I would have removed my niece and placed her in another similar establishment." He smiled at the look of astonishment in her eyes. "The night Stella ran away and you tried to stop her, I saw then that there was a certain rapport between you. She responded to you in a way which made me very hopeful that an improvement in her conduct would not be long forthcoming. I love her very much indeed, but sweet reason was achieving nothing, and it seemed that the shock of being sent away was the only solution. I decided upon that course very reluctantly, for I have to admit that I disagreed with Imogen on the point, but due to your presence, Miss Conyngham, it seems that it was the right decision after all, and so I will be forever grateful to you."

She didn't quite know what to say, and she smiled in some embarrassment. "You . . . you have nothing to thank me for, Sir Guy."

"Oh, but I think I have. Now, it's time for me to see Stella herself."

"I will leave you, then—"

"No, please, I would like you to stay." He went to the bell and rang for Joseph, who immediately went to find Stella.

She came straightaway, and in such delight that she completely forgot Miss Hart's stern strictures about the inelegance of running. She virtually burst into the visitors' room, and without seeing Leonie, ran to her uncle, her arms outstretched and the white sash of her new green schooldress flapping wildly behind her. "Uncle Guy!" she cried. "I thought you'd forgotten all about me!"

He laughed and swung her into the air. "Forget a minx like you? There've been times of late when I've dearly wished I could!"

"Don't be beastly!" She laughed, slipping her arms around his neck and burying her face in his shoulder for a moment. "I'm sorry for having been so dreadful. I'm going to be good from now on, I promise."

He lowered her gently to the floor. "I trust you mean that,

for if you do, then you will soon be able to come home again."

"Take me with you today. Please, Uncle Guy."

"No, for I need to be convinced that this change for the better is a permanent thing, and not some temporary expedient you've decided upon in order to have your own way."

"Oh, Uncle Guy, as if I'd do such a thing," she replied, looking hurt.

"But you would, you minx, I know you only too well. So I shall require another good report from Miss Conyngham here before I definitely make up my mind." He smiled across at Leonie.

Stella turned quickly. "Oh, I didn't know you were here, Leonie," she said, smiling. There was something about the smile which warned Leonie that whatever it was that had been on the girl's mind for the past week was about to be brought out into the open.

Stella searched in the large pocket of her dress and took out a rather crumpled, sealed letter. "Uncle Guy, I would like you to give this to Imogen. It's a letter of apology for having been so odious toward her." Her voice was sweet and her eyes wide and innocent.

Slowly he took it. "Is it really a letter of apology?"

"Oh, yes, truly it is. I want to start all over again." She paused, her eyes sliding momentarily toward Leonie. "Actually, Uncle Guy," she went on, "I was hoping that you'd let me *prove* how genuinely sorry I am."

"Prove it? How?" His dark eyes rested quizzically on her, for such an overwhelming change was too much to believe entirely.

"Well, I know that she likes Shakespeare, doesn't she?"

"Yes," he replied guardedly. "I also know that you loathe him."

"But I want to try to like him, for her sake, so that in the future, when she is your wife, I will be able to go to the theater with her—as her companion."

He seemed dumbfounded for a moment, and then an irrepressible gleam of humor shone in his eyes. "Forgive me if I seem dubious, Stella, but the thought of you and Imogen toddling off to the theater together to watch Shakespeare is simply too much to take seriously."

"But I'm changed, Uncle Guy," she protested. "I really thought that if I could show her how much I mean to be good . . . I mean, she knows I loathe Shakespeare, but she'd have to believe I was trying to do the right thing if I went to such lengths just for her. Wouldn't she? I thought that we could get to like each other. After all, I won't be just twelve forever, will I?" She gave a wistful sigh. "Still, if you think it's a foolish idea, then of course I won't say anything more about it."

"I didn't say that," he said quickly. "I was merely taken a little by surprise. If you really would like to embark upon this, then of course I would be only too pleased to assist. What do you wish me to do? Provide you with volumes of his works?"

Stella studiously avoided Leonie's suspicious eyes. "No, actually I'd like you to take me to the theater tomorrow night."

He stared at her. "Take you to the theater?"

"Yes, *The Merchant of Venice* is going to be on at the Theater Royal, Drury Lane, and I *know* that it's one of Imogen's favorites. You told me that she played the part of Portia during the theatricals at Chatsworth—".

"Yes, she did," he said quickly, not wanting to recall the occasion, for Imogen had displayed a singular talent for overacting which had left everyone writhing in embarrassment.

Stella was intent upon pressing her point home. "I thought that it would be an ideal opportunity, Uncle Guy, because if I'm allowed to go to Poyntons for the house party, then I'd have something to talk to her about. Look, there was an notice in the *Times*, and I cut it out to show you." She searched in her pocket again and took out the piece of newspaper.

Leonie watched as she handed it to him. So that was what the business with the newspaper had been about!

Guy read it out. " 'On Wednesday, January the twenty-sixth, Mr. Kean of the Theater Royal, Exeter, will make his first appearance at the Theater Royal, Drury Lane, in the part of Shylock in *The Merchant of Venice*. To be followed by the farce, *The Apprentice*, with Mr. Bannister in the leading part.' " He glanced at Stella. "Who is this Mr. Kean? I thought at the very least that you'd be wanting to see Kemble in the role.''

"I just want to see the play, Uncle Guy," she replied meekly.

He smiled a little. "So you'd have me believe."

"But I do!" she protested. "Please take me, Uncle Guy, because I do so want to please Imogen." The insertion of Imogen's name was very deliberate.

He nodded. "Very well, Miss Slyboots, I'll take you."

"Oh, Uncle Guy!" she cried in delight, hugging him. She drew back then. "There's something else . . ."

"I hardly dare ask what it is," he replied dryly.

"Oh, it's nothing dreadful, truly it isn't. I was wondering . . . Well, I was wondering if Leonie could come too."

Leonie was thunderstruck, color rushing to her cheeks. "Oh, Stella, you mustn't ask such a thing!"

"Please, Uncle Guy," pressed the girl. "I would so like it if she could."

He smiled across at Leonie. "Of course you must join us, Miss Conyngham."

"You must not feel obliged to invite me, Sir Guy," she said, greatly embarrassed. "Of course I cannot accept."

"Please, Leonie!" begged Stella, going to her and taking her hand. "I do so want you to be there. Tell her, Uncle Guy."

"My niece is right to ask you, Miss Conyngham, and I would have invited you anyway, even had I not been prompted. Please say that you will join us."

The hot color still burned on Leonie's cheeks. "You're very kind, Sir Guy, but truly it's impossible for me to accept."

"Because of your position here? Do you think Miss Hart might object?"

"Yes." Of course Miss Hart would object, she'd be angry, and she'd be alarmed at the thought of what Dorothea Lieven and her cousin might have to say.

"I'll speak to Miss Hart before I leave," he said firmly. He paused then studying her face. "There's some other reason for turning down the invitation, isn't there?"

"There are two, Sir Guy. First, I don't think Lady Imogen would be best pleased. She and I have never got on, and I believe she would be much put out if I accompanied you and Stella.'' Much put out? That was putting it mildly!

''I'm hardly embarking upon a pursuit, Miss Conyngham, I'm merely asking you to join us for the evening. Stella is only twelve, and I believe it's considered proper for such young girls to be accompanied by a lady on such occasions.''

''Yes, but—''

''No buts, Miss Conyngham. I'm sure Imogen will understand the situation. So, we are left with your last reason.''

She took a deep breath. ''It may sound lame, Sir Guy, but it's simply that I don't have anything to wear, anything suitable for the theater, that is. My clothes and jewels were stolen just before Christmas.''

Stella's eyes shone. ''But you do have something to wear, Leonie, you have the white silk gown the thief dropped. Oh, you *can* come with us!''

There was nothing more Leonie could say. Still feeling very embarrassed, and cross with Stella for putting her into such a position, she accepted the invitation.

When Guy left shortly afterward, he kept his word and first spoke with Miss Hart. The headmistress was dismayed, and at first put up a number of implausible objections, each one of which Guy demolished with ease. Eventually she had no option but to give in and grudgingly consent to Leonie's being allowed to go to the theater. Angry at being put in a very difficult position, Miss Hart then retired to her private parlor and the solace of the golden sofa, where she sat disconsolately wondering what the outcome of this latest development would be. She glanced up at Dorothea Lieven's portrait. Oh dear, life was becoming difficult. Dorothea and Nadia would be absolutely furious to discover that Leonie, far from being completely shunned by society, was now to sally forth to the theater with one of London's most handsome and eligible men! Imogen would be equally furious, both because she loathed Leonie and because Stella was somehow still in her uncle's good books, in spite of all that had been done to the contrary. Miss Hart gave a weary sigh. One tried one's best to please everyone, and one ended up pleasing no one. What should she do now? Should she send word to the embassy and to Imogen about what was about to happen? Or should she prudently stay silent and hope that the event came and went without anyone's ever being the wiser? Even as she thought this last, she knew that it was far too hazardous a course. No, she would have to send word and thus rest in the knowledge that at least she had done all that could be humanly expected, for it was hardly her fault if a gentleman of Guy de Lacey's standing *insisted* upon having his own way! With another weary sigh the headmistress got up and went to her escritoire, sitting down to compose two suitable communications.

In the vestibule, meanwhile, a rather cross Leonie was waiting for Stella to come in from saying farewell to Guy. She heard him riding away down Park Lane toward Piccadilly, and then Stella was hurrying in, shivering with the cold. As Joseph closed the door and withdrew, the girl held her cold hands out to the fire, unaware as yet of how displeased Leonie was with her. "Oh, it's so *cold* out there," she cried, "but I really do think it's going to thaw! The icicles on the balconies are beginning to drip and—" She broke off as she caught Leonie's eye. "You're cross with me, aren't you?"

"Yes. By asking if I could join you, you placed both me and your uncle in a most difficult and embarrassing position."

"Uncle Guy wasn't embarrassed."

"I don't profess to know how he felt, but *I* most certainly felt embarrassed. How could you have asked such a thing, Stella?"

The girl's face fell. "Oh, please don't be angry. Uncle Guy doesn't mind, honestly he doesn't. In fact he . . ." Her voice died away on a guilty note.

"In fact he what?" demanded Leonie suspiciously, by now aware that Stella was capable of anything.

"Well . . ."

"I'm waiting."

Stella took a deep breath. "I told him I thought pink and white flowers for your hair and wrist would go absolutely perfectly with your white silk dress." She edged slowly away toward the staircase as Leonie's eyes widened with more angry disbelief. "And he said that he agreed and he'd send you some tomorrow," finished the girl in a rush. Then she gathered her skirts and made a dash for the staircase, not stopping or looking back as Leonie's voice echoed after her.

"Stella de Lacey! How *could* you!"

19

Neither of Miss Hart's communications reached its proper destination. Not knowing Imogen's address in Oxfordshire, the headmistress directed the note to Curzon Street, trusting that it would be forwarded, but as Imogen was expected back in two days anyway, the note remained in the silver dish in the grand entrance hall of Longhurst House. The note to Dorothea was delivered to the embassy, where it fell into Count Lieven's jealous hands. By now aware of his wife's infidelity with Lord Palmerston, the count was already suspicious about a stay with "friends" that she intended to make immediately after the following night's subscription ball at Almack's, and he was convinced that the note was connected with this. Trusting that not receiving the note would cause Dorothea some embarrassment, or at least inconvenience, he consigned it unopened into the fire, and said nothing at all about it.

Overnight the thaw which Stella had thought was in the offing became a reality, and London awoke the next morning to the sound of dripping water and the splash of wheels through puddles in the streets. Sleet was falling, adding to the wetness, and the thin covering of ice on the Thames began to break up, flowing slowly downstream once more, only to find its way almost barred by the narrow arches of London Bridge.

The thought that now there wouldn't be a frost fair after all hardly entered Stella's head; she was too excited about the visit to the theater, and as darkness at last fell and the time approached when Guy was to arrive at the seminary in his carriage, she almost drove poor Katy to distraction by changing her mind time and time again about which dress to wear. In the end she decided on the white velvet with the wide lace collar and crimson sash. With it she wore a gold locket bequeathed to her by her mother, and she carried a little satin reticule. Her ringlets were held back from her face by a white velvet band, and the outfit was completed by a very pretty cashmere shawl. She waited impatiently by the bedroom window, and Leonie watched her a little curiously. There was something about her excitement which wasn't entirely due to the outing; there was something else behind it. But what could it be? Leonie hoped with all her heart that the girl had heeded her warning and wasn't after all planning something which would make Guy angry and thus leave her in a worse position than she already was.

Finishing her own dressing, Leonie sat by the dressing table for Katy to put up her hair. Guy had, as promised, sent some little pink and white flowers, a spray for her hair and a posy to be tied to her wrist. They were rosebuds and lily-of-the-valley, and their scent was exquisite. Katy finished pinning her hair up into a knot at the back of her head, allowing three heavy curls to spill down, and then she picked up the spray of flowers and fixed it carefully to the side of the knot.

At the window Stella gave an excited gasp. "There's the carriage! He's arrived at last!" In a renewed flurry of anticipation, she snatched up her reticule and shawl and fled from the room before Katy had had time to tie the posy to Leonie's wrist. But soon the ribbon was tied, and the plain white shawl draped carefully over her arms. After giving Katy a quick hug, Leonie too left the room.

News of the outing had passed around the school, and it had caused a stir, not because such outings were very rare but because it was known that Miss Hart had not wanted Leonie to go. Consequently there was quite a large group of pupils gathered at the top of the staircase, peering over as Leonie went down.

Guy waited in the vestibule with Stella. He was dressed formally, as gentlemen were expected to be when attending the theater. His black velvet coat was cut very tightly, so that it could never be buttoned to conceal the ruching and frills of his shirt, and there was a diamond pin in his lace-edged cravat. He wore a white brocade waistcoat and white knee breeches with costly silver buckles. A *chapeau bras* was tucked beneath his arm, and he was carrying white kid gloves.

As Leonie approached, she thought how very handsome he was. It would be so very easy to fall in love with him. . . .

He sensed that she was there, and turned. His dark glance moved slowly over her and then he smiled and bowed. "Good evening, Miss Conyngham."

"Good evening, Sir Guy."

"I trust the flowers were to your liking."

"Yes, very much so." She knew that a telltale blush was once again stealing over her face, and she hoped that he could not see it in the light from the chandelier.

He glanced at Stella, who was virtually hopping with impatience by the front door. "I think, Miss Conyngham, that a certain young person will positively burst if we don't leave immediately."

She smiled. "I think you may be right."

He glanced up at the row of faces peering down from the top of the stairs, and as one they gasped and drew hastily back out of sight. "Good-bye, ladies," he said, and then he offered Leonie his arm and Joseph opened the door for them to go out into the darkness.

Stella preceded them to the waiting carriage. The night felt strangely mild after the recent bitter cold, and the sleet falling audibly, striking wetly on the road and pavement. It wasn't a pleasant sound, for it augured dirty streets, splashed hems, and soaked shoes. Leonie held her silk skirts clear of the pavement and was glad when Guy had assisted her into the carriage. The upholstery smelled faintly of costmary, and the windows were polished so much that she could see her reflection as clearly in them as if she were looking into a mirror. Beyond her other self, she could just make out the trees in the park. Beneath them the snow was darkened by the continuous dripping of melting snow and frost, and the paths gleamed a little in the light from the streetlamps.

Guy climbed in and sat next to Stella; then the door slammed and the carriage drew away.

Meanwhile, at the embassy in Harley Street, Nadia Benckendorff was preparing to go to the opera house, Covent

Garden, with Rupert. She was late and he had been waiting in the entrance hall for some time now, but she was determined to look her very best; and determined too, if a little belatedly, to make him feel less sure of her. Becoming his mistress had been a mistake, for it had not brought her any nearer her goal and had, if anything, left her feeling more uncertain of him than ever. She had seen little of him for the past few days, and so was determined that tonight would go well.

She wore a sheer white muslin gown which clung revealingly to her figure, and there were rose-colored plumes in her golden hair. Dorothea had already left for Almack's, and would then be going directly on to a secret address with Lord Palmerston, so Nadia had no compunction whatsoever about borrowing her ruby necklace, since it went perfectly with the neckline of her gown. Dorothea would have been furious if she'd known, but Nadia had no intention of allowing her to find out, and she concealed it from the prying eyes of servants by putting on her fur-lined evening mantle before leaving her room.

She went down to the entrance hall, but the warm smile died on her lips as she saw that Rupert wasn't alone, that Edward Longhurst was with him. Rupert came quickly toward her, the deep indigo of his evening coat looking almost black in the candlelight. He smiled, but as always she couldn't tell what he was thinking. As he raised her hand to his lips, she could feel Edward's mocking eyes upon her. Rupert was still smiling. "I trust you don't mind Edward tagging along."

Mind? He *knew* she minded, since he knew she loathed Edward Longhurst! Her anger was tinged with disappointment too, for he merely greeted her, without any particular show of affection. Her face was wooden as she turned toward Edward. "Good evening, milord. How surprised I am to see you. I thought you were in Oxford with your family."

He bowed, a lace handkerchief held lightly between two fingers. "Family get-togethers are too tedious for me, Miss Benckendorff."

"I was under the impression that the opera was equally as tedious as far as you were concerned, sir," she replied a little acidly.

His smooth, clever smile didn't falter. "Ah, but that is only when I'm not in your sweet company, Miss Benckendorff."

She said nothing more and a heavy silence descended suddenly over them. Then Rupert cleared his throat, exchanging a brief glance with Edward before offering her his arm. "Shall we go then?"

Nadia had barely taken her place in the carriage when she noticed something crumpled and white on the floor by her feet. When she picked it up, she saw that it was a lady's handkerchief, prettily edged with lace and embroidered with the initials M.St.J. Renewed anger flushed hotly through her. That creature had been in the carriage today. He had been with her again and he made no attempt whatsoever to hide the fact, even though he knew she was unhappy about the way he was seen so frequently escorting his mother's protégée.

She couldn't keep the bitterness from her voice as she thrust the handkerchief into his hand. "Miss St. Julienne's, I believe."

He accepted it without a word, which made her more furious than ever. For a moment she thought of getting out of the carriage again, but then the door was closed and the coachman touched the team into action. They drove in silence to Covent Garden.

Guy's carriage drew up outside the Theater Royal, Drury Lane, and it was immediately evident that the combination of the thaw and the fact that an unknown actor was playing the leading role had kept the crowds away. As Leonie alighted, she glanced up at the austere lines of the theater, rebuilt barely a year before after the previous building had been destroyed by fire.

There were few people in the vestibule, and the splendid double staircase ascending to the domed Corinthian rotunda was almost deserted. Usually the rotunda itself was an impossible crush before a performance, but tonight it too was almost deserted. They entered Guy's private box, and Stella immediately sat forward in her chair, gazing excitedly around the auditorium, which was barely a third full.

Guy drew out a chair for Leonie and she sat down. There were ladies in a box opposite, with diamonds in their hair and at their throats, and when she leaned forward a little she saw others, all of them sparkling with jewels. She was suddenly conscious of how unadorned she was with only flowers in her hair.

Beside her, Guy seemed to sense that she was thinking. "They look like St. Mark's Cathedral in Venice, as fussy and ornate as a reliquary."

She smiled a little self-consciously. "Maybe they do, Sir Guy, but nevertheless I wish that I was like them."

"You have no need of such aids, Miss Conyngham, you're very beautiful just as you are."

"And you, sir, are a master of the art of flattery."

"I never indulge in flattery, Miss Conyngham, for it is a singularly unrewarding pastime. If one flatters a woman and thus succeeds with her, she must be a shallow creature and not worth the winning. You, on the other hand, would never respond to empty flattery, which would make any such attempt on my part quite futile. So you see, when I pay you a compliment, you may rely upon its being said in all honesty."

At last the performance commenced, and at first it seemed as if it were merely an average production, as the unenthusiastic applause of the thin audience showed, but the moment Mr. Kean made his first appearance, an almost electrifying change swept tangibly through the house. He was a small, unimpressive figure, barely five feet, five inches tall, and his head looked far too large for his little body. He was a very strange Shylock, especially as he had dispensed with the traditional red wig and beard and wore black instead, and a surprised stir passed through the audience. But then he gazed from the stage with his burning eyes and spoke his first lines, and the entire audience knew instinctively that they were in the presence of a great actor. Leonie found she was holding her breath, and Stella was spellbound, her lips parted slightly, transfixed by the shuffling figure on the stage. Guy was motionless, at first with astonishment, then with admiration.

Absolute silence gripped the house, but then Kean's brilliance drew involuntary bursts of applause, and by the end of the first act he had so asserted his dominance over them all that the dropping of the curtain brought forth a wild enthusiasm which was all the more astonishing since the audience was so very thin. A seething excitement and babble of conversation broke out, and Stella turned at last to Leonie and

Guy. "I think," she said in a trembling voice, "that Mr. Kean is the most wonderful actor there's ever been."

Leonie nodded, a little shaken by the sheer intensity of the man's acting. "I think you may be right," she said. She glanced at Guy. "What do you think, Sir Guy?"

"He's certainly a genius," he replied simply, "and this won't by any means be the last we see of him." He leaned forward. "I see that word's getting out already."

Leonie looked down too, and saw several gentlemen leaving their places to hurry out of the theater.

Guy sat back again. "Before the performance is over, the house will be full, you mark my words."

Stella looked at him again, her smile sweet and her eyes as large and innocuous as could be. "What a shame Imogen isn't here to see it," she said.

At the opera house, the performance was very poor indeed, and the audience as thin as at the Theater Royal. The house was shuffling and dissatisfied, and already there had been a number of catcalls.

Nadia's fan moved slowly to and fro and she sighed. She doubted if she'd ever endured a more boring or irritating evening, boring because of the quality of the production, and irritating because Edward Longhurst was seated on one side of her. Dear *God*, how she despised him! Why had he had to come tonight, when she'd especially wanted to spend the evening alone with Rupert?

Gradually she became aware of a stir in the nearby boxes. People began to talk excitedly, even though the performance was still in progress, and then they began to leave their places. What was happening? She turned inquiringly to Rupert, and Edward got up to see what was going on. He returned to tell them that everyone was going over to Drury Lane to see the brilliant new actor playing Shylock.

Rupert glanced at the stage, where the cast had now been so disturbed by the noise from the audience that they'd missed several cues. "I vote we toddle over and see this new fellow, for to be sure, anything is preferable to this shambles." He got up and held his hand out to Nadia, thus not giving her any choice in the matter.

At the Theater Royal, the second act had been considerably

delayed by the turmoil in the audience. More and more people kept arriving and now most of the boxes were occupied and there were many standing at the back of the house. What had been a painfully thin house had now become a great crush.

Nadia, Rupert, and Edward took their places in Rupert's private box, and Nadia's mood was now more sour than ever. Her hem was wet and her satin slippers soaked through, and to make matters worse, they had come face to face in the rotunda with Lady Cowper, who had immediately noticed that she was wearing Dorothea's necklace. Emily was more than a little piqued at the way Dorothea had snapped up Lord Palmerston, and was therefore bound to mention the matter of the necklace to her, since she knew that Dorothea would never have consented to its being borrowed and would therefore be absolutely furious when told.

Nadia's fan wafted angrily to and fro as she gazed over the crowded theater, and then she stiffened in astonishment, staring across at the occupants of Guy de Lacey's box opposite. "Milord?" she said quickly, touching Rupert's arm. "Forgive me, but I have a dreadful headache and do not think I can endure this crush."

"A headache?" He looked at her, but then almost immediately forgot all about her as the curtain at last rose on the second act.

A prolonged burst of applause broke out, followed at last by a breathless silence as everyone waited for Mr. Kean to make his appearance. He was greeted with the thunderous acclaim reserved for conquerors, and he responded to his audience, going from strength to strength, and dominating the whole theater as no actor had done before.

The brilliance of the performance made little impression on Nadia, who was too busy dwelling on Leonie's apparent restoration to the finer things of life. Anger burned through her as she gazed across the auditorium, and she wondered if Leonie was not only a threat to her own plans, but to Imogen's as well, for Guy de Lacey did not look as if he were there under duress, and nor did he exude an air of ennui!

Rupert had at last noticed Leonie. His handsome face revealed nothing of his inner thoughts, but the fact that he glanced time and time again across at the other box conveyed to Nadia that he still found Leonie far too interesting. Nadia sat stiffly, toying with her fan, her loathing for Leonie written clearly in her vindictive green eyes. Maybe Dorothea was not there to lend assistance this time, but there was a new ally now, for Imogen would not be at all amused to learn whom her future husband had escorted to the theater tonight.

Behind his two companions, Edward lounged lazily in his chair, not a single undercurrent escaping his attention. So Rupert was still intrigued by the little schoolteacher, was he? And the Russian cat was as green with jealousy as it was possible to be. Oh, what malice there was in the glances she sent across to that other box. He smiled a little, watching as Guy spoke to Leonie again and she smiled and nodded. There was a rapport there which would no doubt be of considerable interest to Imogen, thought Edward, his glance moving slowly over Leonie's bare throat and shoulders. His blue eyes became even more thoughtful, and a faint smile touched his fine lips. He enjoyed making trouble, and what he had noted tonight offered infinite possibilities for following that favored pastime.

The Merchant of Venice came to a triumphant ending, and the audience erupted into wild and appreciative applause. Afterward the crush in the rotunda was so great that it was barely possible to move, especially as many were leaving, not feeling in the mood for the farce, *The Apprentice*, after the strength and magnificence of Kean.

Nadia, Rupert, and Edward found themselves at the top of one branch of the staircase, and looking across, they saw Guy, Leonie, and Stella descending the other side. Rupert watched Leonie until she passed from sight in the crowded vestibule, and his apparent absorption stung Nadia more than ever. She had to say something derisory about her hated rival. "Rosebuds in her hair and not a diamond in sight—how very rustic she is become."

For a moment he said nothing, but then he gave her one of his enigmatic smiles. "You must think me a dreadful boor, my love, for you told me earlier that you had a headache and I paid you scant attention. Allow me to make amends now. I shall, of course, be pleased to take you home. We will go immediately."

She stared at him, taken completely by surprise. "Now? But . . . but will you be staying with me?"

"My poor darling, how very brave you are, but I wouldn't dream of it, for I couldn't possibly impose upon you when you are feeling indisposed."

"But you wouldn't be—"

"Don't try to make me feel better," he interrupted, raising her hand smoothly to his lips. "I have been a poor escort tonight, and for that I must beg your forgiveness. Edward and I will take you back to Harley Street immediately."

Her green eyes fled to Edward's face. He smiled, his glance moving deliberately down to the vestibule, where last they had seen Leonie. Nadia's lips parted and then closed again, and she looked quickly at Rupert again. "Where will you be going after you leave me?" she asked.

"Why, to White's, of course."

It sounded so false, and she knew that that wasn't his intention at all. He was going to look for Leonie Conyngham, in order to begin pursuing her once more! In a daze, she accepted the arm he offered, and they began to descend the staircase. Damn Leonie Conyngham, damn her! She would be made to pay dearly for this latest humiliation!

20

Guy's carriage was moving west along Piccadilly, and Stella gazed wistfully out at the wet streets and the great piles of melting snow which stood on every corner. She sighed. "I suppose this thaw means no frost fair after all, and I was so looking forward to seeing one."

"Young lady," said Guy firmly, "if you fondly imagined I would permit you to visit such an unseemly gathering, then you were very much mistaken."

"Oh, but Uncle Guy—!"

"No. Frost fairs are the haunt of every disreputable part of society, and on no account would I have allowed you to go."

She pouted a little, but then forgot the fair. "I wish tonight wasn't ending," she said. "I want it to go on and on."

He smiled then. "It doesn't need to end yet. We could have dinner at Grillion's if you wish."

She stared excitedly at him. "Oh, *could* we? A real French dinner?"

"As French as it's possible to get outside France." He glanced at Leonie. "You are, of course, included in the invitation, Miss Conyngham."

"Oh, there's no need to feel—"

"Obliged again? I don't, I promise you. I would be pleased to have your company, and I'm sure that Stella feels the same."

"I do, oh, I do," said Stella quickly, looking urgently at Leonie. "Please say you'll come too."

Leonie smiled. "Of course I will. Thank you, Sir Guy."

He lowered the window and ordered the coachman to turn north into Albemarle Street.

Grillion's Hotel had in the space of eleven years become one of the most fashionable hotels in London. It had been opened in 1803 by Alexander Grillion, a French chef who had previously been in the employ of Lord Crewe, a nobleman renowned as a connoisseur of food and drink. Dinners at Grillion's were very expensive indeed, costing between three and four pounds, as Leonie knew only too well, so Stella's excitement now was understandable, for it wasn't every day that small girls of only twelve were taken to such grand and exclusive establishments. Nor, if it came to that, thought Leonie a little dryly, were assistant schoolteachers.

The hotel was at number seven Albermarle Street. The rooms above the street door had grand balconies on which stood a row of pots containing bay trees, and on the pavement by the door two liveried footmen paraded importantly up and down. As Guy's carriage drew up at the curb, they immediately hurried forward to open the doors.

Guy escorted Leonie and Stella into a very elegant and hushed entrance hall, from which rose a beautiful elliptical staircase. The maître d'hôtel hurried attentively to greet them. "Good evening, Sir Guy. Ladies. Do you wish to dine? . . . Ah, excellent, please come this way."

They followed him into the immense dining room, where ladies and gentlemen sat at candlelit tables and where a small orchestra played on a dais at the far end. The delicious smell of food hung in the air, and there was a drone of refined conversation. They were shown to a gleaming, polished table, in which the reflection of the candelabrum upon it could clearly be seen, and a small Negro boy dressed as a footman brought the menu card. Stella's eyes shone and she practically trembled with excitement as she gazed all around. Her glance met Leonie's for a moment, and without a word being spoken, Leonie knew that the girl was exulting in Imogen's absence.

Nadia had been returned rather ignominiously to Harley Street—at least she felt she had been treated ignominiously, although in fact Rupert had been almost too polite and attentive. She had tried to tell him her headache was better, but he refused to believe her, telling her again that she was being noble on his account and he wouldn't hear of it. He and Edward had then driven away again, evidently content that she was well and truly out of the way for them to go about whatever devious plan they now had in mind. Well, if they thought Nadia Benckendorff could be disposed of as easily as that, they were sadly mistaken. Taking a long, angry breath, she rang furiously for a footman, and was relieved to see when he came that it was the man who had so expertly stolen Leonie's belongings from the seminary.

"I want you to find me a hackney coach," she said.

He stared. "A hackney, madam? But there is a carriage—"

"I said a hackney, and I meant a hackney," she snapped. "Do you think I want everyone in London recognizing one of the embassy coaches?"

His eyes cleared. "Ah, I understand perfectly, madam. I will attend to it directly."

He hurried away, and in what seemed barely a minute he returned to tell her that a hackney was waiting at the door. She emerged again into the night, instructing the hackneyman to drive to St. James's Street and go very slowly past White's club. Then she sat back on the dingy seat, her hood pulled forward to hide her face from any passerby. One way or another she would find out where Rupert and Edward had really gone tonight.

But as the anonymous little coach drove past White's, she feared straightaway that her suspicions had been correct, for there was no sign of Rupert's carriage outside. In order to make sure, she instructed the hackneyman to drive past again, but still there was no sign of the other carriage.

She sat back angrily. So, he *had* lied to her. Maybe he was with Leonie even now! For a moment her fury threatened to get the better of her, but then she struggled to regain her lost composure. She must be logical about this. Rupert wasn't at White's, but that didn't necessarily mean he was yet with Leonie, for she had been with Guy. So the wisest thing to do now would be to see if Guy had taken his guests back to his house in Berkeley Street. After that, the seminary itself would have to be watched, to see who arrived back there with whom. Leaning out, she instructed the hackneyman to drive to Berkeley Street, and to draw up by Lansdowne Passage.

He looked curiously at her, but then nodded, cracking his whip at his tired horse.

Guy's house was in darkness, no lights in the drawing-room windows. Nor was there a carriage waiting at the door. Nadia gazed across, a little perplexed, and then quickly leaned out again and told the puzzled hackneyman to drive on to Park Lane and to stop opposite the seminary. Wearily he urged his horse forward again and set off in the direction of Piccadilly.

Turning the corner into Park Lane, the horse trotted steadily past the park wall, and came to a halt opposite the seminary, as directed. Nadia looked out once more, but there was no carriage. There were, however, some small boys playing marbles on the corner of Curzon Street, and somehow they looked as if they had been there for some time. She leaned out and told the bemused hackneyman to call the boys over. He carried out this latest instruction and watched as Nadia held up a coin to the boys.

"How long have you been on that corner?"

"An hour, maybe two," said the largest boy, his eyes on the coin.

"Has a carriage returned to the seminary?"

"A carriage? No miss."

"You are sure?"

"Positive, miss. We always wait around, hoping to be asked to look after horses and such-like, and so we'd know if a carriage came to the school."

She surrendered the coin and the boys hurried back to their post on the corner. The hackneyman looked down at her. "Where to now, ma'am?"

"Nowhere. We wait here."

"Here? Yes, ma'am." Wearily he put down his reins and drew his damp blanket more tightly around his cold knees. *Foreigners*, he thought darkly. Strange lot, all of 'em!

Nadia sat back in the darkness, but almost immediately she sat forward again, for a carriage was approaching down Park Lane from Tyburn. It didn't halt at the seminary, but drove on to Curzon Street and vanished from sight; it was Imogen. So she had returned at last from Oxfordshire. For a moment Nadia contemplated going straight to Longhurst House to tell her friend what had been going on in her absence, but then almost immediately she discarded the thought, for it would mean probably missing Leonie's return to the seminary. It was important to see who brought the schoolteacher and her wretched charge home, and so Imogen would have to wait for the time being. Shivering in the damp, cold darkness, Nadia settled back again to continue her vigil. She could hear the steady drip-drip of water in the darkness, and she thought longingly of the continuous hard snow of a Russian winter. This in turn brought thoughts of the imminent arrival of her troika. How foolish she would look now, taking delivery of a sleigh when there was no snow to be seen! Disgruntled, she shifted her position and started angrily out at the seminary's discreet dark green door.

Nadia had been mistaken when she thought Rupert and Edward were not at White's, although she could be forgiven for so thinking, since they had gone to some lengths to conceal their presence from her. Guessing that she would follow them, Rupert had left his carriage outside Almack's, in nearby King Street, and then he and Edward had walked to White's. Since arriving, they had been playing cards at a crowded table, but Rupert found no pleasure in the play. Throwing down his hand and tossing in his lost bets, he got up and went into an adjoining room, flinging himself down on a sofa and snapping his fingers to a footman to bring him some cognac. A moment later Edward left the table and joined him. "Your mind wasn't on your play tonight. Are you regretting dumping the fair Benckendorff after all?"

"If that was the case I could go to her swiftly enough. The lady has made herself tediously available."

"So it seems. But she evidently has . . . er, charm, for you go back to her."

"Gift horses, and all that."

Edward gave a short laugh. "Yes, I take your point." He beckoned to the footman, who immediately brought him a glass of cognac too.

"I knew she'd follow us tonight," said Rupert.

"You went out of your way to give her reason," pointed out Edward. "You hardly troubled to reassure her where the fair Leonie is concerned."

"Isn't there anything that slips unnoticed past you?"

"Very little. I'm very meticulous. You still have a fancy for the schoolteacher, don't you?"

"Is there any point in denying it?"

"Not really." Edward glanced slyly at him. "So, you're dancing attendance on Mama's appalling Jamaican, bedding the beautiful Russian, and all the while you lust after the delectable English rose. My dear fellow, your love life is a positive maze."

Rupert gave a slight laugh. "It may seem so to you, my laddo, but I know my way through the maze well enough."

"I'm sure you do. You're wasting your time with Leonie Conyngham, though, for the lady simply doesn't like or trust you."

Rupert was pricked by this. "Don't underestimate me."

"You seem very sure of yourself."

"I can succeed with her, if that's what you mean."

"Perhaps it would be intriguing to lay a small wager on the matter."

"You would lose."

"You think so? What if I were to bet you that *I* will succeed with her first?"

"You?" Rupert sat up in surprise. "I didn't know she was of interest to you as well."

"Because I haven't said anything until now doesn't mean that I'm immune to her considerable charm. I'm certainly interested enough to make an effort to beat you to her bed."

Rupert looked at him for a moment. "Very well," he said at last, "I accept your wager. We'll make it official by entering it in the betting book."

Edward smiled. "But of course," he said lightly.

They went to the table where the book was kept, and Rupert picked up the quill, pausing for a while in astonishment as he read some of the previous entries. "Good God above," he said, "I see that Percy Rosse and Lord Dunsdon have twenty guineas resting on a race between two woodlice."

"A fellow must amuse himself somehow," murmured Edward. "Besides, I understand woodlice have been known to go quite well."

"No doubt." Rupert was still perusing the book. "I had no idea there was such overwhelming curiosity about my matrimonial plans. There seems to be a staggering number of bets resting on them, a staggering number. . . .''

"You should have recourse to the sacred book more often, dear fellow, or you'd know about these things."

"You know everything, I suppose."

Edward nodded. "All that is necessary."

"Why do so many believe I will marry in September or thereabouts?"

"It may have been a chance remark of mine."

Rupert gave a short laugh. "If it was, my laddo, then you'd best get out your prayer mat that I do indeed come across on that date, for there are some names here which I would not wish to cross, and that's a fact."

"Cross?"

"Yes, for that is what you will have done if I fail to marry then."

"I can't imagine why I would be deemed to have crossed them, for the remark was made only lightly in passing, and I made it plain that it was merely a guess."

"Did you?" Rupert raised an eyebrow. "If this scripture is anything to go by, they think you've seen the word brought down from the mountain on tablets of stone. However, we digress." He dipped the quill in the ink. "How much are you prepared to risk on your skill as a lover? Five guineas? Or perhaps you're willing to back up your bragging by making it a hundred?"

Edward gave another smooth smile. "Why be so timid? I was thinking more on the lines of ten thousand—to make it more interesting."

Rupert stared at him. "Ten *thousand*?"

"You find that too steep? Dear me, you *have* been away from the good book for a long time, haven't you?"

"I don't find it too steep," replied Rupert a little coolly. "I was merely admiring your immense courage in the face of such overwhelming odds. Very well, ten thousand guineas it is." He began to write: "The Duke of Thornbury bets Lord Edward Longhurst ten thousand guineas that he will conquer the fair Leonie Conyngham first." He smiled at Edward then. "And since you wish to make it interesting, may I suggest a time limit? Say, three weeks? No, I have a better idea—we'll limit it to the day de Lacey's house party commences at

Poyntons, since that seems as good a day as any to choose. What do you say?''

"I agree."

Rupert added the necessary information and then tossed down the quill. "And may the best man win."

"Oh, he will, dear fellow. He will." Edward was still smiling. He watched as Rupert walked away. This was now set to be most diverting, for so much intrigue could be stirred by it. . . . He glanced again at the book, his eyes narrowing as he looked at the other bets to which Rupert had earlier drawn his attention. There were indeed a great many wagers on the wedding plans, and he felt just a little uneasy, for Rupert was right: there were names there which it would not do to cross. But for the moment, there were other, more pleasing things to think about.

21

At Grillion's they were almost at the end of their meal, and Stella was engaged upon her second large portion of apricot-and-chocolate *gâteau*. Guy had put himself out to be an attentive and amusing host, entertaining them with many anecdotes about famous figures in society. He was the personification of charm and consideration, and with each passing minute Leonie felt herself succumbing more and more to the spell he so effortlessly cast over her. She knew she was falling in love with him, and there was nothing she could do to save herself from the inevitable pain and heartbreak of such folly. It was Imogen Longhurst he loved; he merely pleased his niece tonight by being kind to her teacher.

The conversation, which had turned upon many interesting topics, now turned upon Richard Conyngham, and Stella stopped eating to look sympathetically at Leonie.

"It must be quite dreadful for you," she said. "I know how *I* would feel if such horrid and untrue things were said of my father. Isn't there anything you can do to clear his name?"

Leonie shook her head. "It doesn't seem so."

Guy looked at her. "Have you been to India House?"

She smiled wryly. "Oh, yes, I went there, and I was practically thrown out for my impudence."

His eyes darkened. "Surely not!"

"Oh, but it's true. I spoke with a clerk, who was all politeness until he heard my name, and then he asked me to leave."

"A damned clerk treated you like that?" cried Guy

143

incredulously. "I cannot believe it! Didn't you demand to see someone in authority? I happen to know that Sir Henry Fitzjohn would have received you sympathetically."

"Neither Sir Henry nor I had the opportunity to find out, Sir Guy. The clerk summoned some other fellows, and I was again requested to leave. Rather than be forcibly ejected, I decided to go of my own accord. Needless to say, I've never tried again. My father would never have done those things, Sir Guy, I know that he wouldn't."

He studied her for a moment. "You loved him very much, didn't you?"

She lowered her eyes. "Yes. I hadn't seen him for many years, but he wrote to me every month and his letters were kind and full of little things to make me laugh. That's how I remember him—when I was small and still living in Madras, before my mother died and I was sent back here." She stopped for a moment. "I grieve for him, Sir Guy, but I can't cry for him. I wish with all my heart that I could."

For the briefest of moments his hand rested gently on hers. "We grieve in different ways, Miss Conyngham, and for some of us tears come later rather than earlier." He took his hand away then, as if a little embarrassed at having made such an intimate gesture. "Would you like me to speak to Harry Fitzjohn about your father? Harry's an old friend of mine."

She searched his face, her eyes brightening. "Would you do that?"

"Yes."

"I'd be very grateful."

"Don't build up false hopes," he warned, "for a promise to speak with someone does not mean all will automatically come well."

She smiled. "I realize that, Sir Guy. I just want someone to consider the man my father really was—he was honorable."

At that moment Stella drew their attention by pointing across the room toward a man seated by himself. "Is that Lord Byron?" she asked.

"It's very rude to point," reproved Guy, "and no, it isn't Lord Byron, who looks nothing whatsoever like that gentleman. Why did you think it was he?"

"Because he limped when he came in." Stella studied the

man for a moment. "I suppose if I'd thought properly about it, I'd have known it couldn't possibly be Lord Byron, who must be far, far more handsome than that. Lord Byron *is* handsome, isn't he?"

Guy smiled. "There is a school of thought which would have it thus."

"School of thought? Oh, you mean every lady in London." Stella applied herself to the *gâteau* again. "I don't think *I'd* ever be so boring as to swoon over the same man everyone else was swooning over. *I* don't want to be another Countess Lieven."

"Countess Lieven?" Guy raised an eyebrow. "How does she come into it?"

"She was chasing Lord Byron."

"Was she indeed? And how do you know that?"

"I listen," she replied simply.

"At keyholes?"

"Certainly not!" she protested indignantly. "I merely sit there and they forget I'm present."

"They?"

"Yes. That's how I know that Countess Lieven wanted Lord Byron to be her lover, but he wasn't coming round to it, and so she turned her attentions to Lord Palmerston instead. *He's* her lover now."

"Miss de Lacey," reproved Guy, "I'm surprised and shocked."

"Why?"

"To think that my niece knows about such things."

"Well, if they will talk about it in front of me, what else do they expect? Anyway, they realized I was there then and dropped their voices and I didn't hear any more."

"I'm relieved to hear it. But who exactly are 'they'?"

"I couldn't hear what they were saying," she went on, not hearing him, "but I know they were being absolutely horrid about someone. They were like the three witches in *Hamlet*."

"*Macbeth*," he corrected automatically. "*Who* were?"

"Countess Lieven, Miss Benckendorff, and Imogen. They were being absolutely beastly—you could tell by the way they whispered together. Whoever it was they were talking about, I felt very sorry for."

Leonie's heart had almost stopped with dismay. Guy was

annoyed. "Stella," he said quietly, "since you couldn't hear what they were saying, I cannot see that you are in a position to make any judgment."

"I didn't have to hear them," she replied unguardedly, "I *know* what Imogen's like when she's plotting something."

"That's enough," he said abruptly.

She flinched a little, and then the old rebellious look crept back into her eyes. "I haven't said anything that isn't true," she said defiantly.

"Unless you intend to apologize for saying unkind things about Imogen, I suggest you hold your tongue."

"Apologize? Why should I? She's horrid, Uncle Guy, she'll make you dreadfully unhappy, and I hate her as much as she hates me!"

A dreadful silence fell upon the table. Leonie felt quite awful, and she could sense Guy's rising fury. Oh, Stella, Stella, she thought, why on earth did you have to spoil it all like this?

Stella had gone too far now to withdraw. "Please don't marry her, Uncle Guy."

"You've said more than enough," he replied coldly.

"Why can't you see her for what she is?" cried Stella, her voice rising emotionally. "She made you send me away because she hates me!"

"She didn't *make* me do anything. I sent you away because your conduct was unacceptable to me. Tonight I truly believed you had changed, but it now seems you are as rude and undisciplined as ever. You haven't improved in the slightest, and you can therefore forget any notion you may have of coming home, or of coming to Poyntons next month. You will remain at the seminary until you learn some manners!"

Stella's eyes were huge and tear-filled. With a sob she got up. "I hate her!" she cried. "And I hate you!"

Her voice carried clearly over the entire dining room, and all conversation died away as everyone looked at her in disapproving astonishment.

Hot, mortified color flooded into her cheeks, and she ran from the room, cannoning into a waiter as she did so. He stumbled sideways and knocked a vase of flowers from a sideboard. It fell with a resounding crash.

Leonie flung down her napkin and hurried out after the

sobbing girl, catching her in the vestibule and doing her best to calm her. But Stella was almost hysterical now, weeping inconsolably and causing a great deal of commotion.

Guy was pale with fury as he came out to them, and it was upon Leonie that he vented his wrath. "I trust, Miss Conyngham, that this isn't a sample of your influence, for if it is, then I made a very grave error entrusting my niece to your care!"

Her lips parted with hurt, and then she was suddenly angry. "The grave error you made, sir, was in entrusting your niece to anyone else in the first place! She should be with you, not with strangers."

"I'll thank you to keep your opinions to yourself," he replied coldly, "for I have no use for them."

"Have you any use for anyone or anything except yourself, sirrah?"

"Have a care, madam!"

"Why? So that you can be unspeakably rude to me again? Since you've chosen to find fault with me, I think it only fair that I should return the compliment. You handled things very poorly a moment ago, Sir Guy de Lacey. Indeed you handled it as well as a carthorse with a phaeton! You reduced your niece to tears, and you did it alone."

"It seems to me, Miss Conyngham, that the fault lay entirely with her. She only had to apologize."

"Evidently it has escaped your notice that she had been doing just that all evening. Why else was she doing her best to please you? But no, *you* had to leap instantly to Imogen's defense, when I can assure you that the lady is more than capable of defending herself. Mr. Kean's performance tonight has evidently gone quite to your head—you think you're Shylock and you want your pound of flesh and the blood to go with it!"

"That's more than enough, madam," he breathed furiously.

"Is it? I could go on."

"I'll spare you the effort by sparing you my presence! My carriage will convey you back to Park Lane. Good night to you." He turned on his heel and strode angrily away.

Stella was still weeping bitterly shortly afterward as she and Leonie drove away from the hotel, and Leonie herself was close to tears. An evening that had been almost enchanted had become an evening of disaster.

Nadia was so cold that she was on the point of ordering the hackneyman to drive on, but then suddenly Guy's carriage drove past and drew up at the curb outside the seminary. She watched as Leonie and Stella alighted alone and hurried inside. So, wherever they'd been and whatever they'd been doing, it didn't seem likely that they'd been with Rupert. Now it only remained for Imogen to be informed of the night's events, Leaning out, she instructed the dozing hackneyman to take her to Longhurst House.

As the coach turned around, she glanced out again at the seminary. Tonight she'd been forced to realize that Rupert's interest in Leonie Conyngham was far from over, in spite of her reduced circumstances and the scandal attaching to her father's name. Evidently it was not enough to keep her in a lowly position at the school; now something more would have to be done. Nadia's green eyes were vengeful. Leonie would have to go. She must be dismissed and thus sent away from all future contact with Rupert.

Imogen was seated in her boudoir, Miss Hart's note in her hand, when Nadia was shown in. Her face was pale and she crumpled the note. "I'm glad you've called, Nadia," she said quietly, "for it seems that during my absence—"

"When the cat's away, the mice will play?"

Imogen's blue eyes went swiftly to her face. "You know about the visit to the theater?"

"I was there, with Rupert. We both have cause now to wish something to be done about Leonie Conyngham. Don't we?" Nadia held the other's gaze. "We must talk."

Imogen nodded.

Leonie lay in the bed listening to Stella's muffled sobs beside her. The girl hadn't stopped crying since rushing from the dining room at the hotel, and nothing Leonie had said seemed to offer her any comfort at all. Oh, if only Stella had been a little more wise, if only she'd bitten back her comments about Imogen, or even if she'd had the wit to apologize when she had the chance, then things might have remained as they had been. As it was, Guy was furious with his niece again, and furious with Leonie herself.

Leonie stared up at the bed hangings. Never in her whole life had she so lost her temper with anyone as she had tonight. She'd said such things to him, and in a very public place. Maybe he'd merited every word, but that was still no excuse for having spoken as she had. She closed her eyes for a moment. She'd lost her temper because he'd hurt her. Tonight she'd fallen finally in love with him, and when he'd turned his anger upon her, it had been like a knife twisting in her heart. By reacting as she had, she had forfeited his good opinion of her, and no doubt the next day he would come to the seminary to remove Stella to another establishment. Her furious defense of Stella had probably cost her something else too, for it was hardly likely now that he would put himself out to speak to anyone about Richard Conyngham.

Stella was quiet now, her face turned away to the wall. Outside, the street was almost deserted, with the sound of only one carriage to break the silence. It came very slowly down from Tyburn, coming to a halt outside the seminary. There was no sound of opening doors, no voices, just a silence broken by the occasional jingle of harness and stamping of hooves. Leonie sat up, puzzled, and then slipped from the bed to look out. By the light of a streetlamp she saw the carriage drawn up opposite. It was a handsome vehicle, drawn by matched bays and driven by a liveried footman. There was a coat of arms on the door panel, but she couldn't make it out.

As she watched, the glass was lowered and a gentleman looked out, directly at her window. In the fraction of a second before she drew hastily back out of sight, she recognized Edward Longhurst. After a moment she heard the carriage drive on and turn the corner into Curzon Street. The night became quiet again.

22

Two days passed and there was no word at all from Guy; things were left just as they were. Stella was very quiet and withdrawn, never once mentioning what had happened at Grillion's. Leonie was very sad to see her brought so low after being so very happy, but there was nothing that could be done. Too many things had been said that night; now they simply had to wait and see what happened.

On the Friday, Imogen and Nadia came to the seminary, demanding to speak in private with a rather uneasy Miss Hart, who guessed what they had come about. She was right, for they immediately demanded Leonie's dismissal, and the headmistress was forced into the unenviable position of having to refuse them. She was all of a fluster, explaining that to grant their demand would be to risk Dorothea's displeasure, and that was something she simply could not contemplate, not even for ladies as exalted as themselves. She was willing enough to see Leonie go, but only if Dorothea gave her permission. They left in a fury, and Miss Hart took refuge on her golden sofa, calling for a glass of something strong to steady her ragged nerves.

Leonie watched the carriage drive away, and she wondered what had happened. She'd seen their determined faces on arrival, and then she'd seen their absolute fury on leaving, but what their purpose had been, she could not guess.

In the carriage, their frustration was immense, for Miss Hart's refusal to comply was a stumbling block neither of them had foreseen. Imogen's anger was doubled because as yet Guy had not mentioned the visit to the theater. He had had ample opportunity, but he had not said a word about it. His silence made her uneasy, and for some reason she found herself unable to bring up the subject herself. She had been banking on Leonie being dismissed from the seminary without further ado, but now that was not to be, not until Dorothea intervened, and Dorothea was still out of town with her lover and no one knew exactly when she would return. Nadia had hinted that it might not be for another two weeks yet, and that was a length of time which it alarmed Imogen to consider.

That night was very cold indeed, bringing the thaw to an abrupt halt. London awoke the next morning to find itself once again in the iron grip of frost. The melting, broken ice which had been flowing slowly down the Thames now became choked by the ancient piers of London Bridge, freezing together to form a solid, uneven expanse which stretched upstream as far as Blackfriars Bridge. Before the end of the morning people were seen on the ice, at first just testing it and then walking right across from shore to shore. By nightfall the first booths had appeared. The frost fair was beginning.

It was snowing on the Sunday morning when the entire seminary set off for church. Miss Hart had to admit grudgingly that Dorothea's uniforms looked very well indeed, the matching green hooded cloaks fluttering prettily in the cold wind blowing down Aldford Street.

Stella walked silently at Leonie's side, her eyes downcast all the time, and as they entered the church, she remained equally silent. Leonie was by the aisle, with Stella seated beside her, and they had been there for some five minutes, waiting for the service to commence, when suddenly Stella whispered to her, "You have an admirer."

"Admirer?"

"The Duke of Thornbury. He's behind us, on the other side of the aisle. He's been staring at you ever since he came in."

Leonie turned in surprise and found herself looking into Rupert's hazel eyes. He smiled and inclined his head, and she turned quickly to the front again. Why had he come to this church? He had never been there before. The service began and everyone rose to sing the first hymn. Leonie didn't look around again, but she could feel Rupert's eyes upon her all the time.

The sermon was a dull affair, delivered without sparkle, and soon the younger girls near Leonie were beginning to fidget. Not long after that the rest of the congregation began to shuffle, and it was with some relief that everyone rose at last for the next hymn. As the organ began to play, Leonie suddenly realized that they were all about to sing her father's favorite hymn. The Grosvenor Chapel seemed to melt away before her and she was no longer in wintry London, she was a small child in hot, sunny Madras, in St. Mary's Church, and Richard Conyngham's beautiful baritone voice was echoing poignantly in her ears. The memory caught deep inside her, and suddenly the loss of her father was as painful and fresh as the moment she had first been told. The tears which had been so long in coming sprang to her eyes, and she was afraid that she was about to break down completely. She had wanted to be able to grieve properly, but not now, in this public place. Gathering her skirts, she hurried out of the building. The hymn seemed to follow her, echoing all around.

Outside, the line of carriages waited at the curb, their coachmen and postilions standing together in groups. Snowflakes touched her hot cheeks, catching in her hair and on her cloak as she walked quickly past them to a quiet part of the street. The wind swirled the snow, making it eddy all around, and the coldness of the air was strangely soothing. She paused beneath the naked branches of a plane tree. The pain began to subside.

"Are you all right, Miss Conyngham?"

She whirled about to see Rupert standing behind her, a concerned look in his eyes.

"I'm quite all right," she said a little stiffly. She liked him as little now as ever she had, and she would never forgive him for having forced his way into her room.

"You seem distressed," he said, "and I wondered if there was anything I could do to help."

"Nothing at all, sir. Please don't trouble yourself further."

"It's no trouble, I promise you." His voice was soft, his glance unmistakably warm.

She moved perceptibly away from him. "I said that I am

quite all right," she repeated coldly, stepping aside to return to the chapel.

He put a quick hand on her arm. "Please, don't go yet."

"Sir, I don't think you and I have a great deal to say to each other."

"I wish to make amends for having behaved so poorly in the past."

"If that was an apology, sir, then consider it made. Now, please let me go."

"I cannot blame you for feeling as you do, but I'm truly sorry for trespassing as I did. Can we not be . . . friends?"

She was amazed. Friends? After all that he had said and done? "No, sir, we most certainly cannot."

"But—"

"How is Miss Benckendorff?" she asked deliberately.

He raised an eyebrow. "Very well, I should imagine. What has she to do with this?"

"I rather think *she* might think she has a great deal to do with it, sir."

"What she thinks is no concern of mine."

"I beg to differ on the point, sir."

He smiled a little. "May I call upon you?" he asked suddenly.

She stared at him. "Sir, I cannot prevent you from calling, as you well know, but I promise you that I will not receive you. I trust I have made myself perfectly clear?"

He still smiled, apparently completely unperturbed. "Oh, yes, Miss Conyngham, you've made it very clear, but I shall still call upon you."

At that moment the service ended and the congregation began to leave the chapel. Leonie walked determinedly away from him.

On the walk back to the seminary, something happened which was to put Rupert, Duke of Thornbury, completely out of her thoughts. The crocodile of green-cloaked figures was walking quickly down Park Lane, for the snow was falling more heavily than ever now, and there was a great deal of excited chatter about the frost fair, which everyone now knew had begun to appear on the river. The accident happened very quickly, just as they had almost reached the seminary. One moment Stella was walking quietly at Leonie's side, the next she had stepped into the road to avoid a very large lady with six excitable little dogs on leads. The hackney coach was approaching from behind, making no sound because of the snow, and the unfortunate hackneyman had no chance to rein in before Stella was knocked heavily to the ground and almost trampled by the terrified horse.

There was immediate chaos, the dogs yapping, the large lady having the vapors, and many of the pupils beginning to cry. The horse was alarmed, tossing its head and whinnying as the anxious hackneyman maneuvered the coach away from Stella, who lay motionless in the snow, her face drained of all color.

Leonie knelt beside her. "Stella? Stella, can you hear me?"

The girl's eyes flickered and opened. For a moment she looked up in puzzlement, but then she saw the coach looming above her and fear leapt into her eyes. She tried to sit up, but Leonie gently restrained her.

"No, don't move, you may have broken some bones."

Miss Hart pushed forward then, having taken a moment or two to recover from the shock of what had happened. She heard what Leonie said and she was angry, for the last thing she wished was for Stella to remain where she was and thus draw unwelcome attention to the fact that an accident had befallen one of the seminary's young ladies, especially since at the time of the accident the young lady had been in the care of no less than the entire staff! "*Miss* Conyngham," she said icily, "I hardly think it sensible or desirable to leave Miss de Lacey lying in the street." She turned to the hackneyman. "You, fellow, carry her into the seminary."

Leonie was alarmed. "She shouldn't be moved," she protested. "Not until a doctor has examined her."

"Any examination which may be necessary will be carried out in the privacy of the seminary," replied the headmistress, her eyes angry as they fleetingly met Leonie's.

The hackneyman hurried to do as he was told, picking Stella up very carefully and carrying her inside. The girl whimpered as she was carried up to the bedroom, but as she was laid gently on the bed, she passed out, lying there very still and ashen-faced.

Joseph was immediately dispatched to the doctor, with instructions that after that he was to go on to tell Guy what had happened.

While all this was going on, Imogen and Nadia were paying a morning call upon Imogen's ailing great-aunt, the dowager Lady Baswell, whose house was in Berkeley Square. Their duty done, they emerged into the snow to enter their waiting carriage. Nadia wore white, and looked coolly beautiful. Imogen was in brown, and beside Nadia's blond loveliness she felt at a disadvantage; indeed, it seemed that she often felt thus when with Nadia, and it wasn't a feeling she cherished. Imogen was forced to admit to herself that she did not often outshine her new friend, and it was galling, for why should a Russian adventuress be compared favorably with an earl's daughter?

Nadia sensed nothing of Imogen's jealous thoughts. "Imogen, has Edward mentioned anything to you about a wager he has with Rupert?"

"No. Why do you ask?"

"Oh, it's just that there's something going on and I can't find out from Rupert what it is."

Imogen gave a short laugh. "Indeed, and here was I thinking that I was the only one to be suffering from the disagreeable reticence of the man I love."

Her tone piqued Nadia; indeed a great deal about Imogen piqued her of late. "There is perhaps something else you should know, Imogen, since you've brought up the subject of reticence. This morning I was told that not only did Guy take Leonie Conyngham to the theater, he subsequently took her and his niece to Grillion's for an intimate dinner."

Imogen stared at her. "Who told you?"

"Emily Cowper, and she may be relied upon. It seems that Stella made a dreadful scene, and it also seems that Guy and Leonie had a very heated argument. She and Stella then returned alone to the seminary, which is when I saw them."

Imogen looked quickly away. The carriage was now driving from the square into Berkeley Street. So much had happened that night, and yet Guy still hadn't said a word to her. Why? She should have been exulting in the fact that Stella was again in disgrace, and Leonie apparently out of favor, but she gleaned little solace from the situation. Guy's silence disturbed her more and more, for she didn't understand it, and in this particular instance, what she didn't understand made her feel very vulnerable and uneasy. She wanted him to tell her all about it, to leave nothing out, but she knew in her heart that he wasn't going to do that. Eventually she was going to have to ask him herself, and she was beginning to wonder if she would like his reply.

At that moment they were passing his house, and Nadia sat forward suddenly. "Look, isn't that the footman from the seminary?" She pointed as Joseph hurried away from the house after delivering his message to Guy.

Imogen's every instinct warned her that this was a moment when she must be sure to be with Guy, for anything connected with the seminary meant not only Stella but also Leonie Conyngham. She quickly lowered the glass to order the coachman to halt, and as she did so she saw Guy's footman emerge from the house, glance quickly toward the halted carriage, and then step hastily back inside. A moment later Guy himself came out.

Imogen alighted and hurried to meet him. "Guy? I was passing and saw the footman from the seminary. Is something wrong?"

He took her hand and pressed it quickly to his lips. "Stella's had an accident," he said. "I must go immediately to see her."

"Oh, no!" she breathed, feigning anxious concern. "How very fortunate that I have my carriage ready and waiting. I can take you there straightaway. Come, we mustn't delay."

As he handed her back into the carriage, she exchanged a brief glance with Nadia, who had overheard everything. Nadia's smile was inscrutable. Imogen sat back, her hand resting reassuringly in his. Unease still swept through her, but at least she had the satisfaction of knowing her intuition had been right. Now she would be there when next he came face to face with Leonie.

23

Miss Hart was waiting in the vestibule when Guy arrived, accompanied by both Imogen and Nadia. "Good news, Sir Guy!" she cried, hurrying forward, the blue ribbons on her biggin trembling. "The doctor has examined Miss de Lacey and it seems that she was merely concussed. No bones were broken and he is sure there are no internal injuries. He says she must rest in bed for a few days, and then she will be able to resume her lessons."

He gave a quick sigh of relief. "How is she now?"

"A little shaken, but apart from that she is as well as can be expected."

"Your footman said that she had been knocked down by a hackney coach. Can you tell me exactly what happened?"

Her eyes slid momentarily toward Imogen and Nadia, whom she wished to placate after having felt obliged to refuse their demands concerning Leonie. "It . . . it was most unfortunate, Sir Guy," she said, "for I fear that much of the blame must be laid at Miss Conyngham's feet." She saw the smile touching Imogen's lips, and felt encouraged to proceed. "She had charge of Miss de Lacey, as you requested, but on the way back from church she neglected her duties by stopping to converse with an acquaintance and leaving your niece to walk on unattended."

At the top of the staircase, unseen by anyone in the vestibule, Katy listened indignantly to the headmistress's lies. The maid had seen the accident from a window, and she knew the truth of what had happened.

Guy held Miss Hart's gaze. "Yes. Go on."

"Well, that is more or less it, for Miss de Lacey wasn't paying attention to what she was doing and she stepped very unwisely from the pavement directly into the path of the hackney coach. I had her brought inside and the doctor was sent for immediately. I also instructed Joseph to convey the news to you. I trust that I have more than adequately attended to my responsibilities."

He didn't reply for a moment. "So," he said then, "you are telling me that you regard Miss Conyngham as being at fault, and that but for her failure to carry out her duties, the accident would probably not have happened. Is that what you are saying?"

She hesitated, but knew that she had already gone too far to withdraw now. Besides, it would be very difficult to disprove her word, for it was hardly likely that he would question anyone, and it was only to be expected that Leonie herself would deny culpability. She met his gaze as squarely as she could. "Yes, Sir Guy. I'm afraid that I can take no other view."

"I see."

His penetrating eyes seemed to see right into her soul, and in some consternation she quickly lowered her eyes.

Then he turned away, glancing up the staircase just in time to see Katy draw hastily back out of sight. "Miss Hart, may I see my niece now?"

The headmistress stared at him, taken completely by surprise, for she had fully expected him to demand Leonie's immediate dismissal. Miss Hart didn't quite know what to make of it, for she had done her level best for both Imogen and Nadia by trying to provoke Guy into taking matters into his own hands. The headmistress knew that had she taken the dismissal upon herself, even for Imogen and Nadia, then Dorothea would have been furious and might even have withdrawn her patronage. But Guy would apparently have had justice on his side, for his niece had been injured and he had been told that it was due to Leonie's neglect; Dorothea would graciously accede to his wishes and that would be the end of it; everyone would have been satisfied. Instead, he hadn't demanded anything of the sort; he had apparently decided to leave the matter and now wished only to see his niece!

Imogen and Nadia, their hopes raised by the headmistress's clever ploy, were also bitterly disappointed, Imogen in particular, for she saw his reaction as further evidence that she had every reason in the world to fear Leonie. Her immediate impulse was to pursue the matter of Leonie's responsibility herself, but there was something in his manner which kept her silent. She must be circumspect; there would be another opportunity, and when it came, she would seize it and put it to full use. She would destroy Leonie Conyngham.

Guy was still waiting for Miss Hart's reply. "Madam, I asked if I could now see my niece."

She almost jumped. "Oh, forgive me, Sir Guy. Yes, of course. Joseph, please conduct Sir Guy to Miss de Lacey." She turned almost gladly to the footman, who had at that moment returned.

Imogen went with Guy, but Nadia suddenly and unexpectedly declined to accompany them, a fact which drew a curious glance from Imogen, who guessed that she had an ulterior motive. Nadia watched them go up the stairs and then turned to Miss Hart, an eyebrow raised expectantly.

The headmistress immediately took the hint. "Miss Benckendorff, may I offer you some tea? Oh, I beg your pardon, I mean coffee. Black, is it not?" She turned to beckon Katy, who was now coming down the stairs.

"Yes, black," agreed Nadia. "Without cream," she added stonily.

Miss Hart gave her a weak smile. "Yes, of course. Without cream." She cleared her throat. "Shall we adjourn to the visitors' room? It's so much more comfortable and private there."

Imogen was still wondering what Nadia was up to when she and Guy were shown into Stella's room. Stella was lying asleep in the huge bed, her dark hair spilling over the pillow, her little face pale and wan, but it wasn't at the child that Imogen's glance was inexorably drawn, it was at Leonie, who was seated in a chair next to the bed. As Leonie rose immediately to her feet, Imogen's anxious glance moved swiftly toward Guy, to gauge his reaction, and to her immeasurable relief, he seemed hardly to notice Leonie; indeed he looked straight through her. For Imogen it was a moment of almost unbelievable comfort, allaying so many recent fears and dispelling the unease so swiftly that it might never have been. She was sure of him again, she felt secure, but as she watched Leonie hurrying out, the need for revenge was still there. Leonie had caused her a great deal of anxiety, and that could be neither forgiven nor forgotten.

Guy went swiftly to the bed, taking Stella's hands. She stirred immediately, her eyes fluttering open. "Uncle Guy?"

"How are you, sweetheart?"

The use of such an affectionate term brought tears of gladness to the child's eyes, and she struggled up to hug him. "Oh, Uncle Guy! I'm so happy you've come, and I'm sorry to have upset you so—"

"It's all right," he said gently, holding her close. "It's all forgotten now."

Imogen watched in silent anger, her face devoid of expression, and the only outward sign of her fury was the tightening of her hands on her reticule. Dear God, how she loathed the child. . . .

Suddenly Stella realized that she was there, and hesitantly drew away from Guy, her smile faltering. "G-good morning."

Imogen's lips curved into a tight smile. "Good morning, Stella. I trust you are not feeling too indisposed?"

"No. Just a little bruised." Stella's reply was halting. She could feel the other's hatred.

"Perhaps in future," went on Imogen, "you will pay more attention when you are out."

Guy looked quickly at her, a warning glint flashing in his eyes.

She didn't notice his reaction; she was too determined to put Stella in her rightful place. "I also trust that you will consider others and not continually give cause for anxiety and concern."

"Imogen—" began Guy.

"No, Guy, this has to be said," she replied, forgetting her previous wise decision to be circumspect at all times. "I saw how distressed you were when first you heard about the accident—you feared for Stella's very life! Now we discover that the accident was in part caused by Stella's own empty-headedness. It isn't good enough, and I can see that even if you can't. Which brings me to the matter of Leonie Conyngham's gross negligence. I think you are very ill-advised indeed not to demand her immediate dismissal."

"Imogen, I do not wish to discuss any of this, least of all now," he said angrily.

Stella was staring at her. "Leonie's negligence? What do you mean?"

"Come now, you know perfectly well," said Imogen coldly. "She left you to walk along on your own while she gossiped with an acquaintance."

"But that isn't true!" cried Stella. "It just isn't true!"

"I might have known you'd leap to her defense."

"I'm not telling lies, it really isn't true," protested Stella, turning to Guy. "Please believe me, it wasn't Leonie's fault, it was all mine, I wasn't paying attention!"

Imogen was relentless. "Are you telling us that Miss Hart is a liar?" she demanded.

Stella's glance fled back to her. "Yes," she whispered. "Yes, if she said those things about Leonie, then she's telling lies."

"I don't think so," replied Imogen icily.

There were tears in Stella's eyes now, and her lips were trembling. "She is!" she cried. "She's telling lies about Leonie!" She turned away then, flinging herself against her pillow and bursting into tears.

Guy was furious with Imogen, his face pale and his voice as icy as hers had been. "I think you've said enough, don't you? Perhaps it would be better if you withdrew for a while."

She stared at him, a disbelieving fury bubbling up inside her. Without another word, she turned on her heel and left.

There was no sign of Nadia when she reached the vestibule, which angered her all the more, since she was determined to teach Guy a lesson by driving off in a dudgeon and leaving him to walk back to Berkeley Street. How *dared* he treat her like that! How dared he side with that odious, odious brat! She trembled with a fury so great that she forgot how uncertain and anxious she had been about him only minutes before.

At last she heard the visitor's room open, and Nadia emerged. "Ah, there you are," she said briskly, but then something about the other's face made her pause. "Is something wrong?"

Nadia came slowly toward her. "I suppose you could say that."

"Well?"

"You know that Rupert told me that he was attending morning service at St. George's with his mother and Miss St. Julienne? Well, it was a lie. Miss Hart has just said in passing that he was at the Grosvenor Chapel this morning and that he went outside with Leonie Conyngham." Nadia's green eyes were thoughtful. "He's pursuing her, Imogen. I now know it for certain."

"Are you ready to leave?" asked Leonie abruptly.

Nadia looked at her in surprise. "Leave? But what of Guy?"

"I'm no mood to wait for him."

Nadia raised an eyebrow, but wisely left the subject of Guy. "I'll stay here a little longer. There's something I wish to do."

Imogen stared at her. "Do? What?"

"Gain Stella's confidence." Nadia smiled.

At that moment there was a knock at the front door, and Joseph appeared to attend to it. A delivery boy stood there, a very large basket of red roses in his arms. "Is this the residence of Miss Conyngham?" he inquired.

"It is."

"These are for her." The boy thrust the basket into Joseph's arms, waited for a small tip, and then hurried away.

Joseph carried the basket carefully to the table, watched all the while by Imogen and Nadia. The moment he had gone to find Leonie, they hurried to inspect the card that lay among the flowers.

Nadia picked it up. " 'To Leonie,' " she read out, " 'whose loveliness eclipses these poor blooms, and whose face haunts my every dream. R.' " Her face went very pale. "The writing is Rupert's," she said quietly, dropping the card back among the roses.

Imogen nodded. "So he isn't *always* reticent, is he?" she remarked dryly.

Nadia glanced coldly at her and then turned away.

Imogen smiled a little. "Well, I'm leaving now, and if you wish to change your mind and come with me . . . ?"

"No. I'll stay."

24

Meanwhile, Guy had at last managed to calm Stella down, and she was no longer crying, but from time to time she sniffed a little, and her lips trembled.

He sat on the bed beside her once more. "That's better," he said gently. "You mustn't tire yourself out anymore. You've had quite a morning of it so far."

"Miss Hart *is* fibbing, Uncle Guy, you must believe me."

"I do."

She stared. "You do?"

"Yes."

"Oh." She toyed with the coverlet. "If you knew she was fibbing, why didn't you say so? Why don't you take me away from here, and take Leonie away too?"

He gave a quick laugh. "Not so fast, young lady. It isn't as easy as that. I have my reasons for saying nothing, and they're good reasons, believe me."

She searched his face for a moment. "It's because of Leonie, isn't it? Because she needs to stay here?"

"Yes."

The reply satisfied her, but something else still did not. "But, Uncle Guy, if you and I can tell that Miss Hart isn't being honest about it, why can't Imogen see it too?"

"Perhaps she still feels a certain loyalty to Miss Hart. After all, she was a pupil here for some time. Now, then, can we talk about something else?"

"All right, but, Uncle Guy . . ." She hesitated. "I know I said a lot of things about Imogen at Grillion's—"

163

"From the tone of your voice I'd say you were about to express no regret whatsoever, and that being the case, I'd prefer it if you left it unsaid."

He'd anticipated her perfectly and she didn't like it very much. She looked away, her lips set a little rebelliously. "I do wish you didn't love her," she muttered.

"Stella—" he began warningly.

"All right," she said quickly, "I won't say anything else about her. Let's talk about the frost fair instead. Have you seen it yet?"

He relaxed a little, for the frost fair didn't seem a particularly difficult topic. "No, I haven't, but I understand it's set to be quite an attraction."

She glanced at the window. It was snowing heavily outside still. "Would you take me to see it? Oh, please say you will."

"No."

"Oh, but—"

"No! I told you the other night why I wouldn't, and nothing's changed since then."

Resentment bubbled up inside her then. Yes, something *had* changed since then; she'd spoken rudely about Imogen on two separate occasions. He'd have taken her to the fair if it hadn't been for that! She was being punished again because of Imogen! "*Why* won't you take me?" she demanded.

"I've already explained. Such a place isn't at all proper, and I will not countenance taking you."

"That isn't your real reason, is it!" she cried, tears leaping into her eyes again. "It's because of Imogen!"

"Don't be silly."

"I'm not being silly! You're angry with me because of her, and so you're punishing me!"

He stared at her. "I don't think you mean that," he said quietly.

"I do! I do!" she cried, her voice rising. "You'd do anything to keep her happy. You don't care about me at all!"

Slowly he got up. "Perhaps I'd better go," he said. "You're overwrought and it will do no good for me to remain here while you're in this state."

Stella turned away when he had gone, hiding her face in her pillow again, sobbing as if her heart was breaking.

Guy went slowly downstairs, halting as he saw Nadia waiting there alone. "Miss Benckendorff? Where's Imogen?"

She smiled a little awkwardly. "She . . . er, left a short while ago."

He sighed inwardly.

"Sir Guy, I was wondering if it would be permissible for me to sit with Stella for a while?"

He looked at her in surprise, for it was very strange that she of all people should make such an apparently kind, concerned offer. "Why, yes, I'm sure it would," he replied. "Although at the moment I think she's a little overwrought."

"But that is understandable, is it not? I will go to her—maybe I can help." Nadia smiled again, and walked past him to go up the staircase.

He watched her for a moment and then noticed the basket of roses, which still stood waiting on the table. He glanced at the card, and at that moment he heard Leonie's light steps approaching from the school wing. He turned as she entered the vestibule. "Good morning, Miss Conyngham," he said, and his voice echoed a little.

She started. "Oh! G-good morning, Sir Guy." She felt very much at a disadvantage. When he had ignored her earlier, she had been immeasurably hurt, believing it was because of the argument at Grillion's. That had been bad enough, but now Katy had told her what Miss Hart had said to him when he had arrived, which made the snub he had delivered appear in a very different light—it meant that he believed the headmistress.

He smiled a little, gesturing toward the roses. "You appear to have an ardent admirer."

The smile confused her. "Yes, I'm afraid that I do."

"Afraid?"

"I don't like the gentleman concerned and I don't intend to keep his flowers."

"I'm relieved to hear you say that, for he may be a duke, but he's neither trustworthy nor honorable." He smiled again. "Don't return the flowers, it would be a shame to waste them. No doubt there is the usual crop of winter ailments among the young ladies here, and I'm sure their sickrooms would be much brightened by such magnificent blooms."

She couldn't help smiling, although his apparent friendliness now still puzzled her. "That is an excellent idea, Sir Guy."

"Miss Conyngham, may I have a word with you in private?"

Her heart sank. "Of course. Please come through to the visitors' room, I believe it's unoccupied now." She was shaking a little as she conducted him to the empty room, where she turned to face him. "Sir Guy, if this is about the accident, I wish to say that I didn't neglect my duties."

"You think I don't realize that?"

She stared at him. "But—"

"I once told you that Miss Hart wasn't to my liking, and now I assure you that she's even less so. But she is your employer and I know how important this position is to you, and for that reason alone I allowed the matter to pass unchallenged. If it hadn't been for your situation, Miss Conyngham, I would most definitely have put the old toad firmly in her place." He looked at her. "You do know why she lied don't you?"

"No."

"In order to appease Nadia Benckendorff, who now wishes you away from here as ardently as she once wished you to stay."

"But why?"

"We need look no further than that basket of roses for the answer to that. She's jealous of Thornbury's continued interest in you, Miss Conynham, and I happen to know that she's already been here once to request Miss Hart to dismiss you— Miss Hart refused because she required Countess Lieven's permission before taking such a step."

"How do you know all this?"

"Imogen told me. Nadia wanted her to accompany her here, but Imogen would have nothing to do with it; indeed she advised Nadia not to come."

Leonie looked away. So that was what that visit had been about! And how typical of Imogen to slide neatly out of all mention of her own participation! Leonie's breath caught a little then, for why had Imogen come too? She had seemed as determined as Nadia, and she had left looking as furious— surely it couldn't be that she too was jealous! Slowly Leonie glanced up at Guy. Oh, if only such a jealousy could be well-founded. . . .

He hadn't noticed her thoughtfulness. "Miss Conyngham, I don't like to think of you enduring not only such severely reduced circumstances but also the considerable spite and vindictiveness of others. If anything like this should happen again, I want you to tell me."

"Oh, but—"

"No buts."

She searched his face for a moment. "I must thank you for your kindness, Sir Guy, but—"

"I said no buts. I shall expect you to turn to me in future, is that clear?"

She hesitated. "Yes," she said at last.

"Now then, all this having been said, I will come to the real point of wishing to speak in private with you. To begin with, I wish to apologize to you for my conduct at Grillion's, it was quite inexcusable and you were right to round upon me as you did."

Her eyes widened in renewed astonishment. "But I was dreadfully rude to you."

"Justifiably so, and as I recall it, *I* was the one who began the rudeness." He smiled a little ruefully. "It's quite some time since I've been torn off such a strip, and I'm glad that you saw fit to do it, for it revealed to me not only that you are a young woman of admirable spirit but also that you have a great affection for my niece. It is because of this last that I really wish to speak to you, for I wish to enlist your assistance."

"Assistance?"

"I've just left Stella in tears again. She persists in believing that I deliberately side with Imogen against her, which simply isn't true. I love Imogen very much, but I'm not blind to her faults. I also love Stella, but I cannot give in to her. You do understand that, don't you?"

She nodded. "Yes, I do."

"That's the crux of it, Miss Conyngham. You understand my position, and you're fond of Stella. I believe that she adores you and will listen to what you have to say."

"Oh, I think you overestimate my influence," she said quickly.

"I don't think so. Nor do I *under*estimate you in any way." His dark eyes held her gaze. "I'm convinced that if Stella gives *you* her word that she will behave, then she will abide by it. I want this whole situation to be resolved as quickly as possible, for I don't relish it in the slightest, and apart from that I'm anxious that she learns quickly that success doesn't come from such odious conduct. Unless she learns that, Miss Conyngham, I shudder to think how she will eventually turn out.''

She'll turn out like Imogen, thought Leonie uncharitably.

"Will you speak to her for me, Miss Conyngham? Will you try to extract a promise so that she can come home again? I'm due to be at Poyntons for the betrothal celebrations on the ninth of February, and that's not very far ahead now. I'd like her to be with me when I go.''

"I'll do my best for you, Sir Guy, but I cannot say that I will succeed.''

"I think that you will," he said softly. He gave a slightly embarrassed laugh then. "And for my part I'll attempt to reason with Imogen, if she'll deign to speak to me.''

"Deign? I don't understand.''

"She left a little . . . er, angrily, shall we say?''

"Oh.''

He smiled. "I'm beginning to fear I'm losing my touch with the fair sex. First there was the debacle at Grillion's, then my niece's unshakable belief that I am at all times a monster, and now my intended bride has stalked off in a veritable fury. I can do no right, and it's becoming quite depressing.''

She returned the smile. "Oh, I'm certain that your touch is as sure as ever it was, sir.''

There was a wry devilment in his glance then. "I wonder how I should take that remark, Miss Conyngham? I've already been on the receiving end of your tongue's unerring sting, and have thus learned a little caution. Are you saying that my touch is always flatteringly excellent? Or are you hinting rather that it's never been even adequate?''

"Which way would you like me to have meant it?'' she countered.

"Oh, most definitely the former.''

"Then so be it.''

He took her hand and raised it jestingly to his lips. "You're very kind, and my bruised pride is already fully restored.'' He became more serious then, still holding her hand as he looked down into her face. "You're wasted here in this wretched place, Leonie Conyngham. You should be out in society, where you belong.''

Her heart seemed to stop within her at the warmth in his eyes and in his voice. His fingers tightened momentarily around hers, and for a fleeting, breathless moment she thought he would kiss her. But then, abruptly, he released her. The spell shattered and it was as if the atmosphere which had suddenly sprung up between them had never been.

He moved away. ''I think it's time that I left, for no doubt you've many duties to attend to, even on a Sunday.'' He spoke lightly, but she knew that he was as conscious as she of the moment that had just passed.

''I . . . I will do what I can to persuade Stella.''

He looked at her again. ''Yes, I know that you will.'' He went to the door. ''By the way . . .''

''Yes?''

''I haven't forgotten my promise to you concerning your father. I've been in touch with Harry Fitzjohn at India House, and I'll be dining with him soon.''

''Thank you, Sir Guy.''

He nodded and then left.

She remained in the visitors' room, going slowly to the window to stare out over the snow-covered garden, where large, heavy flakes were still falling from the dark yellow-gray clouds above. She watched them curling and dancing through the frozen air, but she didn't really see them; she was thinking only of Guy de Lacey.

''I love you,'' she whispered. ''I love you with all my heart, but I will do my utmost to make things happy for you when you marry Imogen. . . .''

25

Nadia had gone when at last Leonie went up to see Stella again. The girl was still tired and shaken after the accident, and still upset about arguing with Guy again, but she seemed in slightly better spirits, due, so it appeared, to Nadia Benckendorff's kindness and understanding! Leonie was perturbed at how the girl sang Nadia's praises, for kindness and understanding were alien to the Russian's character, and so the concerned and friendly visit was very suspicious indeed. Leonie was careful not to say anything critical of Nadia, however, for Stella seemed very warmly disposed toward her new "friend" and wasn't inclined to listen to anything even remotely denigratory about her. It was as if she was determined to turn to Nadia no matter what, and Leonie was dismayed to suspect that it was because she knew how much Guy disliked her. The latest quarrel between uncle and niece was evidently a little more serious than Guy realized, for Stella seemed more hurt, and therefore more intractable, than before. It all made for a great deal of difficulty, and made Leonie's promise to him all the more impossible to carry out for the time being.

It was Thursday before the snow at last stopped completely and the sun shone down from the early-February sky. The snow had been cleared from the streets, but the ice remained, making everything smooth and glassy and very, very dangerous. Word spread that the frost fair was now a flourishing concern of at least thirty booths. There were swing boats, a skittle alley, coconut shies, Punch and Judy shows, several

170

wheels of fortune, and many other diversions, including even a printing press. The atrocious weather hadn't kept the people away, and already several thousand were said to have visited it.

At the seminary the pupils talked of little else, until Miss Hart let it be known that she disapproved and that on no account would anyone be permitted to go there. She told them that if she heard one more word on the matter, she'd write letters of complaint to the families of those concerned.

After breakfast, just before going to take her first class, Leonie went up to see Stella again, but she had barely sat down on the edge of the bed when Katy came hurrying to the door in great excitement. "Miss Leonie, I think you'd better come. Some more roses have been delivered for you."

Stella looked up curiously. "More? Have there been others, then?"

"Yes—" began the maid, but Leonie interrupted quickly.

"Oh, they weren't anything important," she said, looking warningly at Katy, because she didn't want Rupert's name mentioned, not now that Stella had begun to hold Nadia in such high regard.

Stella was puzzled. "But why didn't you tell me about them, Leonie?"

"I didn't think they were important. Besides, it's only someone playing tricks on me."

"Expensive tricks," said Katy, "for he's sent twelve baskets this time."

Leonie stared at her. *"Twelve?"*

"Yes, all exactly the same as Sunday's. They must have cost him a small fortune. Anyway, I just don't know where to put them all, and that's why I think you should come down and see them. They're causing ever such a stir in the vestibule, and Miss Hart's furious about it."

"I'll come straightaway," said Leonie, leaning over to kiss Stella on the forehead. "I'll come back and see you later."

The girl smiled and nodded. "All right. And, Leonie . . . ?"

"Yes?"

"*I'd* like some roses in here, if you don't want them."

"You shall have a whole basket to yourself."

As Leonie went down the stairs, she saw that there were indeed twelve baskets. She reflected that Rupert Allingham,

Duke of Thornbury, must have taken leave of his senses. Fortunately there was no one in the vestibule now—Miss Hart had driven them all away to their various classes—and so Leonie was able to inspect the card in the nearest basket without anyone watching. "Leonie, my adored one. I worship you with all my heart. R." Her lips parted on an angry gasp, and she picked up the next card, only to find its message equally as intimate and offensive. "My darling Leonie, please say you will soon be mine. R."

She went to all the other baskets, removing the cards and tossing them unread into the fire. "How *dare* he write such things to me and then send them in so public a way!"

"But suppose he means what he's written?" asked Katy, who had heard one of the pupils reading the cards out earlier.

"He doesn't, he's merely trying to seduce me, and he's so sure of himself that he thinks this will help him achieve what he wants. He's very much mistaken, for I despise him as much as ever."

Katy glanced at the roses. "Whatever will we do with them all?"

"Put them wherever you like, Katy, but be sure to take a basket to Stella, won't you?"

The maid nodded. "Miss Leonie . . ."

"Yes?"

"She's bound to find out about them coming from the duke, you know."

"Maybe she won't. I don't want to tell her just yet, not now that Nadia Benckendorff has charmed her so."

"There's a carriage outside," said Katy, hurrying to the window by the door. She turned quickly back. "It's him! It's the Duke of Thornbury, and he's coming to the door!"

Leonie was startled, but quickly composed herself to face him. "Open the door, Katy, but be sure to remain here with me. I don't want to be alone with him."

"Yes, Miss Leonie." The maid opened the door just as Rupert had raised his cane to strike upon it. He was momentarily surprised, but then he saw Leonie and smiled. He stepped inside, removing his top hat. He wore the gray Polish greatcoat he had had on the first time she had seen him in the park.

He came toward her. "Good morning, Miss Conyngham. I

confess I did not expect to be greeted in person." He made as if to take her hand.

She moved coldly away. "I merely happened to be here, sirrah, so pray do not read anything more into my presence than there is."

He glanced at Katy and then back at Leonie. "May we not speak alone?"

"No, sir, we may not. I have very unpleasant memories of the last time I was unfortunate enough to be alone with you."

"If I offended you then—"

"Offended me? Sir, I found you as repellent then as I find you now. I wish you would leave me alone, and I certainly wish you would stop sending me flowers, which, incidentally, I have given away. I don't like you, your roses, or the improper sentiments you've seen fit to write on the cards accompanying them."

"Improper sentiments? Leonie, I meant every word I wrote."

"I gave you no leave to address me so familiarly," she replied. "And I don't believe anything you say."

"But I'm serious about this," he said, pausing then to glance again at Katy, who could hear every word he said. "Leonie, I don't care if you don't like me addressing you in this way, but I think of you by your first name and to me that is how I should speak to you. I *do* mean what I'm saying to you now, but I know that in the past I've both offended and angered you."

He spoke quietly and looked so earnestly into her eyes that she could almost have believed him, had she not known better! She laughed a little incredulously. "Sir, you've missed your vocation, you should be vying with Mr. Kean on the stage."

"Damn you for that!" he cried suddenly, as if she'd touched him upon a nerve. "I *love* you, can't you understand? I love you and I want more than anything in the world that you should believe me."

She stared at him, astonished at the vehemence with which he spoke. Then, before she knew what was happening, he suddenly pulled her into his arms, kissing her passionately on the lips. He released her again almost immediately, but his eyes were dark and he seemed almost overcome with emotion. "I love you, Leonie," he said, his voice husky. "I love you, and you *must* believe me!'' Then he turned on his heel and left.

The suddenness of the kiss had startled her, but as the door closed behind him, she turned quickly to Katy, her eyes flashing with fury. "How dare he! There wasn't one word of truth in anything he said, and then he had the face to actually kiss me!''

The maid lowered her eyes. "But, Miss Leonie, I believed him. I really think he does love you.''

Leonie stared at her in astonishment.

Shortly afterward, when Leonie had at last commenced her first lesson of the day, Imogen came alone to the seminary. She wore a cream lawn gown under a fur-trimmed lilac pelisse, and her red hair was dressed up beneath a stylish beaver hat. She looked both beautiful and imperious as she instructed Joseph to conduct her to Stella's room. He did as he was told, for there was something in her manner which did not invite anything but immediate obedience.

She entered Stella's room unannounced, closing the door firmly on Joseph, who lingered nervously outside, wondering if he had done the right thing.

Stella sat up slowly in the bed, her face going pale. "Why have you come here?'' she whispered.

"I think it's time you and I had a little talk, don't you?'' replied Imogen smoothly, going to the window and gazing out over the snowy park. A basket of red roses stood on the table beside her, and her blue eyes flickered coldly toward them for a moment.

"Please go,'' said Stella.

"Not before I've told you your uncle's final decision concerning your future,'' said Imogen, turning to face her. "You aren't going to like this in the slightest, but there isn't a single thing you can do about it. . . .''

Leonie's English grammar lesson was almost at an end when Joseph suddenly burst agitatedly into the classroom. "Miz Leonie! Please come quickly, it's Miz de Lacey, she's screaming and crying, and Katy can't do anything with her!''

Leonie rose slowly to her feet, staring at him in dismay. "But whatever has happened?''

"Lady Imogen came to see her and when she left Miz de Lacey began to scream and scream! Miz Hart said I was to bring you straightaway!"

Leonie gathered her skirts and ran from the room, leaving a buzz of interest among her pupils. She heard Stella's hysterical sobs long before she reached the bedroom. The disturbance had attracted a great deal of attention and a group of pupils had gathered at the door, peering curiously inside. Leonie pushed her way through them and saw Stella lying facedown on the bed, sobbing as if her heart was breaking. Katy was attempting to calm her down, while Miss Hart stoo' nearby, looking tight-lipped and angry.

Seeing Leonie, the headmistress advanced to her. "So you are here at last, missy," she said icily. "I suppose one must be thankful that you do eventually attend to your duties, however belatedly. Well, since Sir Guy has seen fit to place you in charge of his niece, I believe it is now up to you to bring her under some semblance of control. I trust I do not need to remind you that the last thing I wish to do is send for Sir Guy, since that would reflect poorly upon the seminary. Am I quite clear?"

"Yes, Miss Hart." Oh yes, it's perfectly clear, for you still wish to please Imogen, and it wouldn't please her at all if Guy could no longer bear his niece's unhappiness and thought it best to take her home after all!

The headmistress turned coldly to Katy. "Briggs, you may leave Miss de Lacey now, you have other duties to attend to."

Miss Hart then dismissed the group of onlookers and swept out. Katy followed her, closing the door softly behind her.

Stella seemed completely unaware of anything that was going on around her. She wept distractedly, as if her little heart was bursting with utter despair. Leonie hurried to her, sitting on the edge of the bed and gently putting a hand on her heaving shoulder. "Stella? It's Leonie. Won't you tell me what's wrong?"

"Go away! Leave me alone!" The girl's voice was choked with sobs.

"I can't leave you like this."

"I don't want to speak to anyone! I wish I were dead!" Stella could barely speak, she was so overcome, and her words were muffled because she had hidden her face in the pillow.

"Stella, you must tell me, for if you do not, then I will have no option but to send for Sir Guy." And to the devil with Miss Hart and the seminary's precious reputation!

The effect of this on the girl was electrifying. The sobs caught on a gasp and she was suddenly very still. "No. Please, don't do that!" she implored, sitting up suddenly and turning her tearstained face toward Leonie. "Don't go to him, I beg you! You mustn't, Leonie, you mustn't!" She caught Leonie's hand tightly, her eyes pleading.

"Then tell me what's wrong."

"No!"

"You leave me no choice but to send for him, Stella. He has to be told that you're in such a dreadful state."

"He won't care! I don't want him to know! I hate him!"

Leonie stared at her. "Oh, Stella," she whispered, "you surely don't mean that."

"I do!" The girl was trembling again and fresh tears sprang into her eyes.

Leonie put her hand over the other's. "Imogen was here, wasn't she? What did she say to upset you so?" Stella didn't reply, but Leonie felt how she stiffened. "Stella, was it something Imogen said?" she asked again.

"I don't want to talk about it," whispered the girl. "I don't ever want to talk about it, not even to you. I hate her, and now I hate him too!" She took her hand away then, taking a deep, steadying breath to ward off the tears which were still threatening to engulf her at any moment. "There," she said almost defiantly, "I'm all right now, you don't need to send for him now, do you? Promise me that you won't, Leonie."

"I can't promise that, not when I can see that you're still very upset. Besides, he has every right to know. He loves you very much and he's ultimately responsible for—"

"He doesn't love me!" cried the girl, her voice rising a little again. "I don't want him to come here, I don't ever want to see him again! Promise me that you won't send for him or tell him anything about this. I won't cry anymore, I promise."

Leonie felt sad as she searched the girl's face. To agree to her pleas would be wrong, for Guy should indeed be told, but at the same time it was obvious that for the moment seeing him would be rather inadvisable, for Stella was very over-wrought and the subject of her uncle seemed only to make matters worse. Perhaps it would be better to temporarily agree to her request, in the hope that when she was more calm she would be ready to say what had happened. "All right," she said at last, "but only on one condition. If I truly feel that Sir Guy must be told about this, then I will do so."

"But, Leonie—"

"No, Stella, I cannot possibly promise what you ask. I'm your friend and I love you very much indeed, but Sir Guy loves you as well, no matter what you might think to the contrary at the moment."

"He doesn't love me at all," replied Stella in a quiet voice.

"You're very wrong."

"I don't want to talk about him."

Leonie nodded. "Very well." She smiled, leaning forward to push a stray curl of the girl's dark hair back from her hot forehead. "I think you should try to sleep now. You'll feel much better then. I'll go and see if Mrs. Durham will make you a hot posset to drink."

Stella nodded, lying back on the pillow again. She looked very tired, drained in fact, as if the dreadful weeping had sapped all her strength. "I do hate him now, you know," she said quietly. "I loved him so much, too much to want him ever to marry someone as hateful as Imogen. Now I think they deserve each other, and I hope they'll make each other very unhappy."

"Oh, Stella—"

"No, it's true, I *do* hope they do." The girl's eyes met Leonie's. "I wanted him to like you, that's why I made him ask you to the theater as well."

Leonie stared at her. "That was wrong, Stella."

"I know, but it was what I wanted. Now I wish I hadn't." She fell silent for a moment then, gazing toward the window. It was snowing outside again, small wispy flakes which spiraled aimlessly through the iron-hard air. "I wish Nadia would come to see me again," she whispered.

Leonie said nothing more.

26

At almost midday that same morning, Nadia Benckendorff was taking a very late breakfast in the orangery at the embassy. She had a sleepless night thinking about Rupert and Leonie, and now she had an abominable headache. More than anything in the world she wished to be rid of Leonie; she wanted her summarily dismissed so that the next time Rupert went to the seminary, she would have vanished from his life forever. Yes, that was what was required, but achieving it was still an apparently insurmountable difficulty, and would remain so until Dorothea at last returned from Lord Palmerston's ardent embrace. Half-formed plans and ideas there were in plenty, but nothing which offered a definite chance of success. The cozy little talk with Stella had been most illuminating, and now Nadia knew a great deal about Leonie's day-to-day duties and so on, but it was how to put all this information to the best use which was proving distressingly elusive.

Nadia sighed, settling thoughtfully back on her wrought-iron chair, gazing past the tropical foliage toward the snowy gardens beyond. For a moment she was reminded of St. Petersburg, and thoughts of Leonie Conyngham faded. Surely her troika would soon arrive, and then how grand and eye-catching she would look, skimming across Hyde Park behind three milk-white horses!

A footman bowed before her. "Miss Benckendorff, Lord Edward Longhurst has called."

She looked at him in astonishment. Edward Longhurst was

calling upon *her*? But he loathed the very sight of her, and the feeling was mutual! Curious to know what had brought him, she nodded. "Very well, I will receive him in here."

She poured some more thick cream on top of her black coffee, sitting back again then to watch as Edward approached. He was, she admitted grudgingly, rather handsome, and he certainly dressed very modishly, but his eyes were always so clever, and his lips curved in that perpetual half-smile which she had long since learned to mistrust.

He bowed to her, his glance moving quickly over her slender, graceful figure, revealed so subtly by the soft folds of her high-waisted white muslin gown. "Good morning, Miss Benckendorff."

"Milord." Her green eyes were cool and she did not return his smile.

"I trust I haven't called at an inconvenient time."

"Inconvenient? No. I confess I'm astounded that you've called on me at all, given the way you and I feel toward each other."

"I fear you must have misunderstood me, Miss Benckendorff, for I feel no animosity toward you. May I sit down?"

"Please do, for I'm most intrigued to hear what you have to say."

He lounged back on a sofa, reaching up for a moment to pull down an overhanging spray of orange leaves, sniffing the sweet-smelling flowers before releasing it again.

She was a little irritated. "I'm sure you did not come to admire flowers, milord."

"No, but nevertheless flowers do form part of my reason for coming here." The penetrating blue eyes were turned full upon her then. "Did you know that earlier this very morning twelve more baskets of roses were delivered to Leonie Conyngham, and that Rupert himself then called to see that she had received them? Ah, I see from your face that you did not know. It is a disagreeable state of affairs, in more ways than one, and if you and I have hitherto not exactly seen eye to eye, I rather think that now is the time for us to rectify the situation. Don't you agree?"

"I don't understand."

"I think we both have the same aim, Miss Benckendorff, we both wish to be rid of Leonie Conyngham."

"*I* wish to be rid of her, I make no secret of it," she replied, "but I had not realized that you were in any way concerned about her."

"Oh, yes," he said, suddenly serious, "and as I've already said, it's for more than one reason. Shall I go on?"

She still doubted his sincerity, regarding him with mistrust. "Please do."

"Very well. I will begin with my sister's unwise complacency where Guy de Lacey is concerned. I saw him with Leonie Conyngham that night at the theater, and the warning signs were there."

"They quarreled afterward, did you know?"

"Yes." He smiled. "I also know that they have since mended the rift."

She lowered her cup, a little surprised. "Surely not, for Imogen said he ignored Leonie at the seminary yesterday."

"He subsequently spent some time alone with her."

"How do you know?"

"Servants can be bribed, Miss Benckendorff, but then you know that already, don't you?"

She flushed a little, looking away angrily.

"Kitchen boys are very poorly rewarded for their labors, Miss Benckendorff, and at the seminary there is one who likes his palm to be crossed with a little silver now and then. *He* saw them in the visitors' room when he was sent out into the seminary garden to feed scraps and crumbs to the birds. He said they were most definitely *not* quarreling." The smile was playing about his lips again. "So, there you have my first reason: I wish to see Leonie Conyngham bundled away somewhere to keep her from harming my sister's happiness."

She sipped her coffee. "Very well, I accept that that is a good reason, indeed, an admirable one. I had not realized you were so fond a brother, milord."

"Nor had you realized that I hold you in high regard," he reminded her.

She stared disbelievingly at him. "Oh, come now, sir, don't treat me like a fool!"

"I'm not, I promise you. I happen to think that you are the very wife for Rupert Allingham, but I'm afraid that at the moment Leonie Conyngham is once again rather getting in the way of things. He is in danger of becoming infatuated with her, and that won't do at all, will it? That is my second reason: I don't want him making a fool of himself with a creature like that, Nadia. I may call you Nadia, may I not?'' He smiled.

"Please feel free . . . Edward," she replied dryly.

"That's better. I do so hate being formal. So, I think we are allies in this particular war, Nadia, for we both wish to destroy Leonie Conyngham."

"And the two reasons you've just given me are your only reasons?"

"Yes." He met her eyes without a flicker.

After a moment she nodded. "Very well, sir, we are indeed allies. How do you suggest we go about achieving victory?"

"I've been giving the matter a great deal of thought, but the answer did not come to me until I learned how cleverly you'd ingratiated yourself with that odious brat Stella de Lacey."

"Ah yes, Stella . . ." Nadia sipped her coffee, savoring the taste of the warm cream. "She must be the key, but I have not been able to think of the best way to use her."

"I've thought of a way, Nadia."

She looked quickly at him. "Tell me."

"I want you to go to see Stella again. After my sister's visit this morning I would imagine the child needs cheering up." He smiled. "Imogen has a way with children, don't you know? Anyway, you must toddle along to the seminary, with your friendly hat on, and you must offer her all the comfort and understanding in the world. Oh, and you must offer to give her her heart's desire, a visit to the frost fair."

Nadia stared at him. "Sir, forgive me if I'm being dull-witted, but how will all that achieve Leonie Conyngham's dismissal?"

"Have a little faith in me, Nadia," he reproved, a little offended. "Stella has been strictly forbidden to go to the fair, but at the moment she's so upset that she'd do anything to go against her uncle's wishes. She must be encouraged in this rebellion, and afterward it must all appear as if the fault lies solely with Leonie, who will have been . . . er, lured away for several hours at night while the visit to the fair takes place."

"Lured? How?"

"She will.be with her lover."

Nadia's eyes widened. "I did not know she had one. Who is he?"

"Why, I am he, Nadia." Edward smiled.

"You?"

"Well, yes, but she will not realize that until it is too late. She will think she's meeting Rupert. Let me explain. I will send a note to the seminary, accompanied by a red rose or two, and in it I will pretend to be Rupert, begging her to meet me in my carriage outside the seminary at nine in the evening. The note will be couched in such a way that she is bound to at least come down to speak to the sender, at which point she will be whisked away against her will and kept away. The moment Leonie has left, Stella must also leave, going the back way through the garden into South Audley Street, where you will be waiting in another carriage to take her to the fair. When both carriages have left, another note will be sent, this time to Guy de Lacey, and it will inform him that his niece has fled the fold for a while and that her teacher is languishing in the arms of her lover. I rather think that will bring him hotfoot to the seminary, where he will find it all apparently to be very true. There will be no mistake about his reaction this time; he will *definitely* demand Leonie's dismissal, and Miss Hart will have no option but to comply, Dorothea Lieven or no Dorothea Lieven. And I think that that will be the end of any interest de Lacey might have in Leonie, don't you agree? It will also be the end of Rupert's, for he will not be able to endure the thought of her having surrendered her all to his best friend."

Slowly Nadia got up, going to stand by one of the huge stoves that heated the vast conservatory. She was silent for a long moment, and then she looked shrewdly back at him. "It seems to me, sir, that you are being very clever, for while your plan will indeed achieve what we wish, it will also attach a great deal of odium to me, for having lured a child away and taken her to a place as disreputable as the frost fair."

"Come now, surely it is an easy matter to persuade Stella not to mention your part in it. Send someone else in the carriage to pick her up. You don't have to risk anything at all. All you are needed for in this is to persuade Stella to do as we wish, and since you've made yourself such a dear friend in a remarkably short space of time, I think it well within our capabilities, don't you?''

''Why use me at all? Indeed, why even use Stella? All you need to do is lure Leonie outside to your carriage.''

''Don't forget that I have my sister's interests at heart as well. I wish to rid her not only of Leonie Conyngham but also of that interfering, spoiled little brat. Guy de Lacey is in a cleft stick where his niece is concerned, for he's been forced to take a stand, and if she blatantly continues with her disobedience, then Imogen is assured of her absence from the forthcoming celebrations at Poyntons, possibly forever, if cards are played skillfully. Now then, are you convinced that my plan is good?''

Slowly she nodded. ''Yes. When do you wish to begin?''

''I wish it all to take place tonight.''

She stared. ''*Tonight*? But that is so soon.''

''Stella is particularly upset right now, and so now is the time to strike. Soon we will have Miss Conyngham packing her bags, her reputation in tatters, we'll have the Duke of Thornbury's faith in her destroyed, Guy de Lacey's faith not only in her but also in his niece equally destroyed, and Imogen will at last be happy. And you, my dearest Nadia, will be happy too, for you will be there to offer comfort to Rupert's bruised self-esteem. I don't think his attention will wander again after that, do you?'' Inwardly Edward was smiling, for he was thinking that at the end of it all, he would have won the wager, for he would have conquered Leonie, and that was really all he was interested in. The rest was incidental.

Nadia's green eyes were shining with anticipation now. ''I like your plan, Edward. Shall we discuss it in more detail?''

''But of course,'' he replied smoothly. Oh, what a gull the woman was; she actually believed she still had a chance of winning Rupert, who felt nothing for her and was merely amusing himself before soon casting her off forever. But in the meantime, her vanity and ambition made her a very useful tool. The winning of the wager with Rupert was all that mattered, and it didn't matter one jot what means were used for there was little time left now.

27

That afternoon a combination of the improvement in the weather and the unsettling effect Stella's outburst had had upon the younger pupils prompted Miss Hart to dispatch them for an airing in the park in the care of Leonie and Katy. The sound of scraping shovels echoed through the air as workmen continued the daunting task of clearing the streets, and even in the park itself there were now opened paths and tracks. The little party from the seminary set off between the trees, their ankle boots crunching in the snow, their cheeks and noses soon pink in the raw cold.

They had been gone only five minutes when Nadia called to see Stella. The girl was sleeping, and for a moment or two Nadia was content to let her remain that way. The scent of roses was quite heady in the warmth from the fire, and Nadia's heart hardened still more as she saw them, their rich color so vivid in the pale winter sunlight coming through the windows. She went across to them, running her fingertips softly over their velvet petals. Before another day was out, Leonie Conyngham's reputation would be worthless and she would at last be truly destitute; and Rupert Allingham, Duke of Thornbury, would never again wish to send her roses. . . .

Stella stirred in the bed, her eyes slowly opening. "Nadia? Oh, Nadia, I'm so glad you've come to see me again."

With a false smile, Nadia went to her. "Ah, Stella, my dear." She paused then, looking down with apparent concern. "My poor darling, how pale and tired you look. I was hoping to find you much improved today. Has something happened?''

Stella bit her lip and looked away. "Yes."

"Would you like to tell me about it?"

The girl hesitated, but then shook her head. "No, I don't want to talk about it to anyone. You don't mind, do you?'' she added anxiously, afraid she might offend her new friend.

Nadia gave a gentle, understanding smile, sitting on the side of the bed and taking Stella's hand. "No, of course I don't mind. Everyone has something they would rather forget, even I do, so we will talk of something else, something cheerful. Have you heard what is to happen at the frost fair tonight? They're going to roast a whole sheep over charcoal! Just imagine, one could sample fresh roast mutton, and then try brandy balls and gingerbread, and all the while out at night in the snow! What excitement there will be, with all the noise and music, and all the people enjoying themselves.''

"Yes." Stella's reply was barely audible.

"You aren't interested?"

"Yes, I am, but . . ." Stella sighed.

Nadia leaned forward a little. "Actually, it was because of the fair that I came to see you. I wondered if you would like to see it.''

"I'm not allowed to."

"That doesn't mean you can't."

Stella stared at her. "What do you mean?"

"You can come to the fair with me tonight, provided you are well enough, of course, and provided that you can slip in and out of here without anyone knowing.''

Stella's eyes shone. "Of *course* I'm well enough, I'm just feeling unhappy, that's all.'' But then her joy died away. "I couldn't do anything in secret, though. Leonie would know I'd gone and she'd make a fuss.''

"Leonie won't be here tonight."

"She won't? Why? Where will she be?"

"She's meeting her lover. You do know she has a lover, don't you?''

Stella was thunderstruck. "No," she whispered, "no, I didn't.''

"Oh." Nadia was all surprise. "I thought *everyone* knew."

"Who is he?"

"Ah, that is something of a mystery, for I don't think he wishes his identity to become known. Still, it doesn't matter, the thing is that she's going to meet him tonight and she'll be gone for several hours. So you see, you *will* be able to creep in and out without anyone here realizing. What do you say? Would you like to do it?"

Stella was still shocked at what she'd been told about Leonie, but now she quickly pushed it to the back of her mind. "Yes! Oh, yes, I'd love to come with you."

"Then you shall."

With a glad cry, Stella sat up to fling her arms around Nadia's neck, hugging her tightly. "You're my friend!" she cried. "My only true friend!"

Unseen by the girl, Nadia smiled. It was a hard, calculating smile, devoid of kindness.

Stella looked at her then. "How will we go? What do you want me to do?"

Oh, this was almost too easy. "I want you to wait until Leonie goes out to keep her assignation, then you must leave straightaway, going out the back way to South Audley Street. I will be waiting there in a carriage. Oh, there's just one thing . . ."

"Yes?"

"I might not be able to get there in time, so two of my friends, a lady and a gentleman, might be in the carriage instead, but they will be watching out for you, so you won't get into the wrong carriage by mistake." Nadia gave a light laugh. "That wouldn't do, would it?" She was a little concerned then. "You won't mind going with my friends if I can't be there, will you?"

"No, of course not, not if they're your friends."

"There is something you must promise me, Stella."

"Anything."

"You mustn't ever tell anyone what we've done, it must be our secret. Your uncle would be very angry indeed with me if he knew I'd helped you like this."

"I won't breathe a word to anyone."

"Especially not Leonie, for she would go straight to him, you know that, don't you?"

"Yes. I promise not to say anything. Cross my heart."

"Good. It's settled, then. Be ready at about nine, for that is when Leonie is meeting her lover."

It didn't occur to Stella to ask how Nadia knew so much about Leonie's private arrangements; the girl was too excited at the prospect of seeing the fair after all. She was also too triumphant at the thought of deliberately flouting Guy's wishes, even if he would never know she'd done it.

Leonie and Katy had taken their charges to watch the skating on the Serpentine. Skating was now a very fashionable pastime indeed, and a number of enterprising boys, who saw the chance to make a profit, had worked hard to clear the ice of snow. A large number of carriages had consequently arrived, and there were many skaters, their laughter and the slither of their wooden skates echoing all around.

The girls were enjoying the scene, and so was Katy, but Leonie's mind was on something else. She felt very unhappy about not telling Guy about Stella's upset that morning. Katy suddenly touched her arm. "Look, Miss Leonie, isn't that Sir Guy riding over there?"

Leonie looked in the direction the maid was pointing, and sure enough, it was Guy, riding a large, rather capricious gray horse. Her heart sank then, for he had noticed her and was turning the horse in her direction. She didn't want to face him now, not when she felt so very guilty, but there was nothing she could do about it, for he quite obviously intended to speak to her.

He reined in a few yards away from her, effortlessly controlling the horse, which was very willful and fresh. He wore a dark green riding coat with flat brass buttons, and close-fitting buckskin breeches. His dark hair had curled in the exhilaration of riding in the extreme cold, and he had pushed his hat rakishly back from his forehead. He dismounted and smiled at her. It was a smile which cut through her like a knife. "Good afternoon, Miss Conyngham."

"Good afternoon, Sir Guy."

"I'm so glad I noticed you, for it gives me an opportunity to ask how Stella is without presenting myself unannounced at the seminary. Before I say anything else, perhaps I should tell you that I know all about Imogen's visit and the fact that Stella had another tantrum."

Tantrum? Was that how Imogen had chosen to describe it? Leonie wondered how much he really knew, and how far he was prepared to let his future wife go. She remembered what Stella had said that morning. *I don't want him to come here, I don't ever want to see him again. He doesn't love me at all. I hate him.* Those weren't words of tantrum, they were words of heartbreak and desolation. What had Imogen told the girl, and had she said it with this man's full knowledge? Even as this thought entered her head, she felt ashamed, for when she looked into his concerned eyes, she knew that he would never have been party to anything so cruel.

He smiled at her silence. "I appear to have somehow struck you dumb, Miss Conyngham."

She colored, as she so easily seemed to whenever in his presence. "I . . . I was wondering what to say. You see, Stella was . . . well, very upset after the visit."

"That was why I deemed it wiser to stay away for the time being, since my niece will not believe good of me no matter what I do. If I see her now, I know perfectly well that she will accuse me of doing it with only Imogen's welfare in mind."

"She will always think that while she remains at the seminary," she replied before she could help herself. But it was true, and she could see so well why Stella felt as she did. He *did* do things because of Imogen; that was why his unfortunate niece had been sent away in the first place.

He glanced away, his riding crop tapping a little irritably against his boot. "Don't you think I'm fully aware of that fact, Miss Conyngham?"

She'd offended him! "Forgive me, Sir Guy," she said quickly. "I didn't mean to speak out of turn."

He looked at her again, smiling. "You didn't, I'm merely smarting because I know you're right, and I know that I've handled this whole business very badly from the outset." He took her hand and kissed it gently. "It is I who should be begging your forgiveness, Miss Conyngham, for I seem to be continually imposing my problems upon you."

She wore gloves, but it was still as if she could feel the warmth of his lips upon her skin. He was so very close to her, and she longed to feel those lips upon her own, longed to feel his arms tight about her, crushing her against his body. . . .

Without warning she felt perilously close to outright confession of her love. That way lay complete folly. With a slight gasp, she quickly withdrew her hand. Please don't let him be able to read her thoughts. Please.

Their eyes met, and she knew that again he was as aware as she of the atmosphere which had so instantly enveloped them both. He moved perceptibly away. "Having said all that," he murmured a little self-consciously, "I thought I would leave it up to you to suggest when it might be suitable for me next to call upon my niece. Whenever you think it wise . . ." His voice trailed away, and he looked at her again.

She avoided meeting his eyes. "I . . . I will inform you immediately, Sir Guy. I . . ."

"Yes?"

"I haven't been able to speak to her yet, as I promised. The moment simply hasn't been right."

"And Imogen's intervention hasn't helped, has it?"

She raised her eyes to his. "No."

He smiled then. "You are in complete agreement with Stella about my marriage, aren't you?"

She colored again. "I wouldn't presume to have an opinion, sir."

"What you really mean is that you're far too tactful to admit it."

"I want you to be happy, Sir Guy."

He searched her face for a long moment. "I know that you do," he said quietly. Then he looked quickly away. "I . . . er, I dine with Harry Fitzjohn tonight."

"I pray God that some good will come of it."

"I sincerely hope that it will," he said, meeting her eyes again, "for to be sure, Richard Conyngham must indeed have been the upright man of honor you say he was, for a lesser man could never have had a daughter as totally admirable as you."

"I'm not admirable," she whispered. "Indeed, I'm far from it." It isn't admirable to be filled with desire for a man who is engaged to another. . . .

"I disagree," he replied, his voice still very soft, "and before I'm further bewitched by those great dark eyes of yours, I think it best if I left. *Au revoir*, Leonie." He turned and quickly remounted, urging his horse away across the snow.

She was immune to everything but the remembered sound of his voice, and it was a moment or two before she realized that he had used only her first name when he had said good-bye.

28

The schoolday was over and darkness had fallen when Leonie was summoned to the vestibule by a rather anxious Joseph, who was still upset about mistakenly allowing Imogen to see Stella, and who was consequently not prepared to take any chances when he was even vaguely doubtful about something. The something in this particular instance was a rather disreputable-looking delivery boy who had very reluctantly obeyed when bade to wait inside. He stood in the vestibule, his sharp eyes darting all around, his tongue passing nervously over his lower lip. In his hand was the solitary rose he was delivering.

Joseph hurried to speak to Leonie before she went to the boy. "Miz Leonie, I would have just taken the rose, but there's things that don't seem quite right."

"What things?"

"To begin with, there's only one rose, not a basket, not twelve baskets, just a single flower. And since you've taught me to read, I know that the note with it is in different writing, and the man who wrote it has signed his full name this time, Rupert, not just R. Maybe I'm being too cautious, but I thought I'd speak up. Did I do right, Miz Leonie?"

She smiled. "Yes, of course you did, Joseph." She walked on toward the boy then, and her tone was guarded when she spoke to him. "I understand you have a rose for me."

He whirled about, not having heard her approach. "Miss Conyngham?"

"I am."

He thrust the rose into her hand and then pressed a rather dirty card upon her as well. "I'm to see you get these."

She glanced quickly at the note. Joseph was right, it was in an entirely different hand, and Rupert had indeed departed from his usual practice and had signed his full Christian name. Indeed, the whole tone of the note was different. "Leonie. If you have any kindness in your heart at all, you will take pity on me and at least see me once more. Grant me this one small wish, for I cannot go on this way. I will be outside the seminary in my carriage at nine o'clock tonight. Please speak to me. Rupert."

She looked suspiciously at the boy, who was anxious to get away. "Why is the writing different this time?"

His tongue again passed over his lower lips, and he only very reluctantly met her gaze. "Well, it's like this. The first one got spoiled and wet, and the gaffer had to write it out again. That's all."

There was nothing more she could say. She gave him a coin and watched as he almost ran from the building. Then she glanced again at the note. Certainly the spoiling of the original would explain the writing, but she still felt oddly uneasy about the change of signature. She breathed the fragrance of the rose. How beautiful it was, and how subdued the perfume of a single bloom after the lavishness of all those baskets. She couldn't help thinking of how Rupert had been when he had kissed her and begged her to believe in his love. A single rose was so much more expressive and believable than an extravagant, gaudy multitude. . . .

Shortly afterward, she went up to see Stella again, and she did so wondering what her reception would be this time, for after her walk earlier she had been greeted with decided coolness. Nadia Benckendorff had had something to do with the change in Stella, but what she had said or done was a mystery, for Stella refused to talk about it.

Entering the bedroom, Leonie took the rose to place it with all the others, then turned to look at the girl, only to find her cold, rather reproachful eyes already upon her. Leonie smiled. "How are you feeling now?"

"Much better. Thank you."

The tone was as distant as before. "Have I said or done anything to offend you, Stella?"

"No."

"There must be something—"

"There's nothing at all, Miss Conyngham."

Leonie stared at her. Miss Conyngham? She'd been "Leonie" practically from the beginning, and yet now, without warning or reason, she was being rejected and their relationship placed on a much more formal footing. Was she no longer to be regarded as a friend? Was there only room for Nadia Benckendorff? "Stella, why are you doing this? You're obviously angry with me about something, but how can I put it right if you won't tell me what I've done?"

"I'm not angry with you at all." Stella picked up a book and opened it, bringing the conversation to an end.

Leonie went out, pausing in the passageway. Something was going on, her every sense warned her of it, but what could it possibly be? What had Nadia Benckendorff put into the girl's trusting head?

A little later that evening, Imogen sat alone in the great drawing room of Longhurst House, and she was both bored and angry. She had wanted Guy to escort her to the theater, but he had had a prior dinner engagement with Harry Fitzjohn and had declined to break it, even though she had pleaded with him. That had rankled, and things had rankled still more when she realized that she would have to spend the evening entirely alone. Edward was out on some undisclosed deviousness connected with his secret wager with Rupert, there were no forgotten invitations which she could use at the last moment, and now her footman had returned from Harley Street to tell her that Nadia was not at home and would not, therefore, be able to dine with her. It really was too bad! She vented her frustration upon the unfortunate cream muslin gown she was embroidering, jabbing the needle in and out as if it had mortally offended her.

The double doors opened and a footman came in. "Miss Benckendorff has called, my lady."

She looked up in surprise. "Show her in immediately."

"My lady."

A moment later Nadia swept in, her white silk gown whispering and her long feather boa dragging over the polished floor behind her. Her golden hair was swept up beneath a gold brocade turban, and Dorothea's rubies glittered at her throat. "Imogen, *darling*," she cried. "I'm so glad to find you at home. I was afraid you would be out with Guy."

"I would have been had he not decided to place Harry Fitzjohn first." Imogen was disgruntled to see how beautiful Nadia was again.

"Harry Fitzjohn?"

"They're dining together."

"Oh." Nadia's smile faded a little. "At Guy's house?"

"No, at Harry's club, wherever that is. I was too annoyed with Guy to inquire. Oh, do sit down, Nadia, you make me feel quite uneasy standing there like that. Besides, you're in the light and I can't see what I'm doing."

Nadia obeyed, but as she settled back and automatically arranged her skirts, her mind was racing. Guy wasn't at home tonight? Would that make any difference to the plan? What if he hadn't returned by the time Edward's message arrived summoning him to the seminary?

Imogen went on embroidering for a moment, but then looked curiously at Nadia. "Is something wrong? You seem very preoccupied."

"Wrong? No, nothing at all. Oh, it *is* good to find you at home, for I was sitting all alone at the embassy wondering what on earth I could do with myself this evening."

Imogen was taken aback. "You were at the embassy?"

"Yes. Why?"

"Because I sent a footman around earlier to invite you to dine, but he returned to say that you were out."

Nadia gave a light laugh. "Yes, I was. I had something important to attend to. I must have returned after your fellow had left. Anyway, all's well that ends well, and I'm here now."

"True." Imogen's needle flashed in and out several times more. "I'm surprised that you are at the proverbial loose end as well tonight. Where's Rupert?"

"He is also dining, with his mother and that ridiculous St. Julienne creature."

"He's taking to extremes his willingness to be the dutiful and obliging son, isn't he? That must be the fourth time this week he's dined at home like that."

Nadia breathed in a little irritatedly. "I suppose it is," she replied shortly, "but it isn't the Jamaican who concerns me, it's Leonie Conyngham. You should be concerned about her too, Imogen."

"Guy isn't interested in her."

"You're a fool if you believe that."

Imogen bridled a little. "There's no need to speak to me like that—"

"There's every need, Imogen." Nadia hesitated. "There's a great deal you don't know about what's happening tonight."

"What don't I know?"

Nadia smiled. "If it all goes to plan, by this time tomorrow we will both be rid of Leonie Conyngham, once and for all. . . ."

It was nearly nine o'clock and Stella was lying in bed, the bedclothes pulled right up to her chin as she feigned sleep. Leonie was sitting by the fire, reading. She hadn't been able to reach past the barrier which Stella had placed between them, and she was no nearer finding out what it was all about. She felt very disturbed and uneasy, and that was why she was remaining in the bedroom rather than going down to the kitchens to give Katy and Joseph their usual lesson. She glanced at the clock, wondering if Rupert would indeed be outside at nine, and even as the thought crossed her mind, she heard the sound of a carriage approaching. It came to a halt before the seminary.

Leonie put her book down and went to the window, wiping away the mist to look down. Only the horses were in the light from the streetlamp; the carriage itself was in darkness. She hesitated. Was it so very much to ask that she allow him to speak to her? She glanced back at Stella, who was still sleeping soundly in the bed, then on impulse she took her mantle from the wardrobe and hurried out. The moment the door closed behind her, Stella flung back the bedclothes. She was fully dressed.

She hurried to the window, gazing down at the carriage. She saw Leonie emerge slowly from the front door and then pause, as if undecided. She also saw Edward Longhurst lean out of the carriage window away from Leonie, bending down to hand a piece of paper to a small boy waiting there. The boy ran away in the darkness, toward Curzon Street. Stella didn't wait to see any more; she ran from the room, tears in her eyes. She had trusted Leonie, believing her to be perfect in every way, but she wasn't, she wasn't!

Leonie still hesitated on the doorstep. Something was wrong, but she couldn't think what it was. Then suddenly she realized: the carriage was Edward Longhurst's; she'd seen it from the window the night of the theater! As she stared, she saw him look cautiously out, wondering why she wasn't coming any nearer. It was a trap! With a gasp, she turned back into the seminary, closing the door behind her and pushing the bolts across. She was just in time to see Stella's cloaked figure hurrying stealthily from the foot of the stairs toward the school wing.

In the carriage Edward cursed beneath his breath. Somehow she'd sensed it was a trap. Damn her to hell and back! For a moment he was undecided what to do. He'd been so confident of success, overconfident it seemed, for he'd already sent his message to Guy. It was too late to retrieve it now. He leaned his head back against the soft upholstery, his lips pressed together in a thin line, his blue eyes cold and angry. Then he leaned from the window and ordered the coachman to drive home to Longhurst House.

As he passed South Audley Street, he glanced out and saw another carriage waiting close to the alley leading from the seminary garden. It would wait in vain now, for Stella de Lacey would not be coming.

Stella had left the seminary the same way this time that she had done before, through the French windows in the dining room, and out into the snow-covered gardens. Her footprints were easy to follow, and Leonie hurried anxiously after them.

She emerged from the alley just in time to see Stella climbing into a waiting carriage. It drew quickly away in the direction of Curzon Street, and Leonie ran desperately after it, calling Stella's name. She was out of breath when she reached the corner. The carriage was passing Longhurst House, and she saw that Edward Longhurst was at that very moment alighting from his own carriage. In that fraction of a second she saw how sharply he turned to stare after the passing vehicle. He knew who was in it! Stella's flight was all part of the same trickery!

At that moment a hackney coach drove slowly along, and without hesitation Leonie stepped in its path to wave it to a halt. With a curse, the hackneyman reined his horse in. She ran to speak to him. "Are you for hire?"

"I was just going home—"

"I'll pay you well. I must follow that coach." She pointed after the vanishing vehicle, which was turning out of Curzon Street and was now driving south toward Piccadilly. Soon it would be impossible to find it.

The hackneyman gaped after it. "Follow that? With old Jupiter here? You must be jesting, miss."

"I'm not jesting, it's very important. Please help me."

He took a deep, resigned breath. "All right, I'll do my best."

She climbed quickly inside, and the old vehicle moved off as fast as its ancient horse could pull it. In her anxiety about Stella, Leonie had for the moment forgotten Edward Longhurst. She didn't know that he had seen her hail the hackney.

The other carriage drove east through the crush of Piccadilly, and from time to time the hackneyman lost sight of it, but he always managed somehow to find it again. Farther and farther toward the old city of London they went, and gradually the more nimble hackney closed the gap between the two vehicles, maneuvering in and out until it was almost directly behind.

They drove along the Haymarket and into the Strand. Soon Ludgate Hill and St. Paul's Cathedral lay ahead. Leonie gazed out with mounting concern. Where on earth was Stella being taken? And who was taking her?

At last the other carriage turned from the busier streets, driving south into a narrow lane near Queenhithe. The lane led toward the river, and there were now warehouses on either side, towering above the hackney as Leonie looked anxiously out. Then she saw a notice fixed to a wall, advising that the ice was safe to cross. At last she realized where Stella was going: the frost fair.

The carriage carrying the girl at last came to a standstill, for the lane led between two warehouses and was too narrow for such a large vehicle to pass. The hackney halted a discreet distance away, where the shadows were very dark and it couldn't easily be seen, and Leonie alighted. The noise of the fair was all around, although it was hidden from view by the crowding buildings. The flickering light of bonfires and torches reached far up into the night sky, and shone brightly through the narrow way where Stella was hurrying away with a man and woman Leonie didn't recognize. She called out to the girl, but the noise of the fair drowned her voice.

Leonie looked urgently up at the hackneyman. "Please wait for me."

"Miss, old Jupiter's in no state to go anywhere for a while yet. I'll wait, don't you fret."

She hurried after Stella then, and as she went between the warehouses, the confined space seemed to amplify the noise from the frozen river, making the mixture of voices and jangling music echo almost deafeningly. At last she emerged onto the wharf. The fair stretched over the uneven ice before her, a breathtaking sight lit by the dancing light of hundreds of torches. The ghostly shapes of icebound barges and ships loomed starkly into the night, and hundreds of people strolled among the many hastily erected booths and tents. Music seemed to come from everywhere, the notes of fiddles, drums, and penny whistles clashing into a single brash, cheerful noise which jarred the night. And all the while there was the laughter and shouting of people making merry.

She gazed in wonder at the incredible scene. There were swingboats, Punch and Judy shows, skittle alleys, a flat area where there was dancing and a little skating, there were wheels of fortune, printing presses, and numerous beer and gin tents, outside which ladies of doubtful virtue brazenly accosted any man who caught their eye. Leonie moved hesitantly to the very edge of the wharf. Where was Stella? She seemed to have vanished into thin air.

29

Leonie didn't know how long she'd been searching. She'd looked everywhere; she'd been jostled, pushed, sworn at, and propositioned; and now she was frightened, and becoming increasingly worried about Stella's safety in this rough, indecorous place. Tired and cold, she paused in the shadow of a barge, gazing helplessly over the milling, noisy crowds. The endless clamor seemed to echo in her aching head, and she felt close to tears.

Suddenly she was grabbed from behind and a dirty hand was clamped over her mouth as she was dragged back farther into the shadows. She was thrust back against the side of the barge, and found herself gazing in terror into the leering, drunken face of her assailant. He pressed against her. "Want some company, love?" His breath reeked of gin and she tried desperately to struggle free, but he merely tightened his hold, grinning and trying to kiss her.

As suddenly as he had seized her, he suddenly let go. He gave a grunt of pain and slumped onto the ice, lying there motionless at her feet, a little blood oozing from the blow he'd received on the back of the head. She stared down at him, still so terrified and shocked that she couldn't move.

"You all right, love?"

Slowly she raised her eyes, and found herself looking into the concerned face of the young soldier who'd saved her. His scarlet uniform was bright even in the shadows.

"You all right, love?" he asked again.

"Y-yes," she whispered. "Yes, I'm all right."

"I saw him grab you." He looked curiously at her. "You're not the usual run of it, are you? You don't look to me the sort that should be out on her own at night."

"I don't. I mean . . ." She was still shaken. "Th-thank you for saving me."

He grinned then. "Knight in shining armor, that's me." He looked puzzled again then. "Why *are* you all on your own here? It's just asking for trouble, you know."

"I'm looking for someone."

"Your feller?"

"No. A girl. I teach at a seminary and she's run away here tonight. I'm afraid for her."

"I can see that. Well, I've nothing else to do, so I'll help you, if you like. If I'm with you, you won't be bothered."

She gazed thankfully at him. "Would you do that for me?"

"Wouldn't have offered otherwise. Besides, I like helping damsels in distress, especially if they're pretty." He prodded the unconscious drunkard with his boot. "He'll be all right by and by. Bit of a headache, but that's all." He offered her his arm then. "Come on, we'll set about looking for your runaway. What does she look like?"

As they walked away from the barge, she noticed that he had a limp, as if he had been badly wounded recently.

Stella was in the canvas enclosure where the whole sheep was being roasted. She'd been there for a long time now and she was becoming frightened. She didn't care for the man and woman she was with—they didn't seem very respectable— and there was no sign at all of Nadia. The charcoal smoke was getting in her eyes, making them sting, but she knew that the stinging wasn't due only to the smoke; she was very close to tears as well. She wished more than anything that she was safely back at the seminary with Leonie and that everything was as it had been before it all went wrong. She wished that it was as it had been when she, Leonie, and Guy had set out to go to the theater. That had been good.

Stella's guardians for the evening were acquaintances of the embassy's obliging footman. The man was broad-shouldered and muscular, and his nose had once been broken in a prizefight. He was in his mid-thirties, with a fleshy face and thick lips, and like his friend at the embassy, he looked as if he could be persuaded to do anything, provided the price was right. His female companion was about the same age, although she endeavored to look a great deal younger. She wasn't slender anymore, her hair was henna-rinsed, and she wore far too much rouge. There was a patch at the corner of her mouth, and when she walked she swung her hips in a way just as suggestive as the women Stella had noticed waiting outside the beer tents. Stella didn't like her at all; she wasn't sympathetic, and she seemed totally preoccupied with the thought that at any moment the ice would crack and they'd all be drowned. She dwelt on this dread so much that Stella was beginning to feel it would happen, and it was so terrifying a thought that in spite of the cold, beads of perspiration appeared on her forehead.

Even now the woman brought up the subject again, poking at the ice with her toe. "It's goin' to go, I just know it is."

The man was irritated now. "It's as firm as 'Ampstead 'Eath! For Gawd's sake, Maisie, have some of this 'ere mutton and shut up. We're gettin' good money for this little caper, and it ain't as if we've got a lot to do!"

"I just don't like this ice! We're all goin' to be drownded."

She was overheard by the woman carving the mutton, a thin, wizened creature with a large, dirty mobcap and a clay pipe between her yellow teeth. "Drownded?" she said, her voice a little distorted because the pipe was clenched in her mouth all the time. "There was a feller drownded just back there by Blackfriars Bridge today."

Maisie's eyes widened. "What 'appened?" she demanded.

"A plumber he was, name of Davis. He was carrying a load of lead piping and decided to cross over the ice. Vanished between two blocks of ice and 'asn't been seen since. There's a few places like that—they looks safe enough, but before you know what's 'appening . . ." She snapped her fingers rather too expressively, grinning all the while at Maisie's terrified face.

It was the last straw. Maisie dropped her mutton and gathered her skirts. "That's it, I ain't stoppin' 'ere another minute!"

"Aw, Maisie—" began the man.

"I don't intend to be the second fool drownded 'ere today!'' she cried, pushing away through the crowds and out of the enclosure.

The man hesitated, glancing for a moment at Stella. Then he shrugged. He'd been paid already for getting the kid to the fair; what did she matter now? He hurried after Maisie, and the crowds seemed to fold over him as if he'd never been there.

Stella stared after them. ''No!'' she cried. ''Don't leave me!'' She tried to push through as well, but the people didn't part for her, she was too small. At last she managed to get out, but of her two guardians there was no sign. Terrified, she pressed back against the canvas side of the enclosure, tears pouring down her cheeks. She was afraid to leave that one place; she didn't know what to do or whom to turn to. She sank slowly onto the ice, kneeling there, her face hidden in her hands, her shoulders shaking as she wept.

Leonie and the soldier had almost given up hope, when suddenly he noticed the pathetic little figure by the enclosure. ''Is that her, miss?''

Leonie gave a gasp of relief. ''Yes! Yes, it is!'' She ran toward her. ''Stella? Stella, are you all right?''

Stella slowly took her hands away from her face, hardly daring to turn in the direction of the voice, but then she scrambled joyfully to her feet and hurled herself into Leonie's arms, bursting into fresh tears, but of thankfulness now.

''It's all right, sweetheart,'' murmured Leonie, holding her close. ''I'm here now and you're safe again.'' She smiled at the soldier. ''I don't know how to thank you.''

''That's all right, miss, I'm glad to have been of service.''

Stella heard the strange male voice and looked up at him in surprise. Then she looked at Leonie. ''But . . . where's Edward?''

Leonie took her gently by the shoulders. ''I neither know nor care, although tonight I've realized that for some reason *he* appears to be very interested in me. I've also realized that you, young lady, have a great deal of explaining to do.''

Stella's lips quivered. ''I know. Oh, Leonie, I wish I hadn't been so silly, but it's too late now, isn't it? I've done just what they wanted me to, and now Uncle Guy will never want me home again.''

Leonie looked sadly at her. "You're your own worst enemy, aren't you? But you're wrong about your uncle—he loves you very much and he does want you home with him again."

"He won't, not after he hears about tonight."

"We might be able to get away with it," said Leonie slowly. "I'm sure no one knew when we left the seminary, and if they still haven't discovered we're missing, we might be able to get back in as secretly as we left, Stella."

Hope leapt into the girl's eyes. "Do you really think we could?"

"It's possible—only possible, mind. But, Stella . . . ?"

"Yes?"

"If we succeed and I promise not to say anything to Sir Guy about tonight, you must promise something in return. It's barely a week now before he goes to Poyntons, and he wants you to go with him, but you must give me your word that you'll behave from now on and try to live in harmony with Imogen."

Stella's lips pressed rebelliously together. "She won't let me, she hates me!"

"It's the only way, sweetheart."

After a long moment the girl nodded slowly. "I know."

"And you'll give me your word?"

"Yes." Stella smiled ruefully at her. "I'll be as good as gold from now on . . . I really will."

Leonie smiled, ruffling her hair fondly. "I sincerely hope you mean to stand by your word this time."

"I do. I was afraid tonight, Leonie, more afraid than I've ever been in my life before, and if it hadn't been for you . . ." Her voice died away and she looked curiously up into Leonie's eyes. "If you don't like Lord Edward, who *is* your lover then?"

"My what?"

"Your lover. Nadia said that you'd—"

"Nadia Benckendorff has by far too much to say for herself, Stella de Lacey. I haven't got a lover, as you'd know well enough if you'd stopped to think. When on earth do I have the time to entertain a beau? . . . Well? . . . I teach all day and I'm with you all night, or had you forgotten that?"

Stella looked shamefaced then. "I didn't think."

"You most certainly did not."

"I'm sorry, Leonie, truly I am. Do you forgive me?"

"Of course I do, because I know how dreadfully upset you've been about things. Now then, I think it's time we went home." She turned apologetically to the soldier. "I know I've imposed most dreadfully on you tonight, and I'm ashamed to ask you to help again."

He smiled. "Ask away."

"Will you escort us back to my hackney coach?"

"It'll be an honor, miss. Come on."

Stella clung close to Leonie as they walked back to the shore, and to Leonie's immense relief, the hackney was still waiting, the driver huddled asleep inside. He woke with a start as the soldier opened the door.

As the hackneyman climbed wearily back onto his perch and Stella was seated safely in the old coach, Leonie turned to thank her rescuer again. "I'll be forever grateful to you, sir, you are a true gentleman."

"I'm just a soldier, miss."

"What's your name?"

"Whittacker, miss. Private John Whittacker of the Fifty-first Light Infantry Regiment, under the command of Lieutenant Colonel Mainwaring."

"Where are your barracks?"

"I'm not stationed back here in England, miss. I was wounded in Spain and got sent back here. I'm hoping to get over there again soon—a feller doesn't like to miss out on it."

She smiled. "I wish you well, Private Whittacker, and I will be sure to write to your commanding officer, informing him of your kindness and gallantry tonight."

He blushed. "There's no need to do that, miss."

"There's every need." She took out some coins and pressed them into his hand. "Please accept this."

"Oh, no, miss! I wouldn't dream of it."

She smiled again. "Won't you drink the king's health, sir?"

He hesitated and then grinned. "I'm the king's man, miss, and I'm always willing to drink his health. Thank you."

"Thank *you*. Good night."

"Good night, miss."

He assisted her inside and closed the door. The sound of the fair was suddenly and blessedly muffled. A moment later, Jupiter was turning the coach around and trotting slowly back up the lane toward the busy thoroughfares of the city.

30

Guy returned to his house at midnight after dining with Harry Fitzjohn. He handed his hat and gloves to his butler, and then paused for a while to look at Imogen's portrait above the fireplace. Tonight Harry had praised her as the loveliest woman in England, and perhaps he was right, for there was something ethereal about the sweet face gazing down from Lawrence's canvas. The artist had captured her perfectly, and yet was she really as flawless as the portrait suggested?

The butler cleared his throat. "Sir Guy?"

"Yes?"

"A message was delivered earlier." The man held out a silver plate on which lay a folded, sealed piece of paper.

Guy broke the wax and read: "If you go to the seminary immediately, you will find that your niece has flown the nest and that Miss Conyngham is away in the arms of her lover." He looked sharply at the butler. "When did this arrive?"

"Some time ago, sir. I trust it isn't of great importance, for you did say you weren't to be disturbed at Sir Henry's—"

"I know, I know. Who brought the note?"

"A boy, sir, a ruffian who ran off when I tried to question him."

"Have Archer bring my carriage around immediately. With luck it will still be harnessed."

"Yes, sir." The butler almost ran to carry out the order.

Guy slowly crumpled the piece of paper, his dark eyes angry.

*   *   *

The hackney conveying Leonie and Stella halted at last on the corner of Park Lane and Curzon Street. Leonie looked quickly toward the seminary. It was in darkness; there was no sign of any alarm having been raised. They had a chance! She got out and helped Stella down before paying the hackneyman handsomely for his trouble. As she parted with the last of her coins, she sighed inwardly, for now she had nothing left.

The hackney drove slowly away, on its way home at last, and Leonie turned Stella to face her. "It looks as if we'll be able to get away with it, provided we can get inside without disturbing anyone. I know that Joseph often sits up very late in the kitchens, practicing his reading and writing, and I have my fingers crossed that he'll be there now. We'll go in the back way, from South Audley Street."

Stella nodded, and they hurried down Curzon Street toward the corner. South Audley Street was silent and their footsteps echoed a little as they ran to the tiny alley leading to the seminary garden. At last they could see the kitchens, and to their immense relief, a light was glowing there. They crept through the snow, glancing up at the main building all the time, afraid that someone would look out and see them, but then at last they'd reached the kitchens. Peering inside through a crack in the curtains, they saw Joseph, his wig discarded on the table before him, his curly head bent over a book. Leonie tapped on the window and he gave a start, his eyes wide as he stared toward the sound. He couldn't see them, and so she tapped again. Slowly he rose to his feet, picking up a large poker from the hearth before coming warily toward the window. He drew the curtains sharply back and the flood of light illuminated their faces. His mouth dropped with surprise and he hastily discarded the poker and came to unbolt the door. A moment later they were safely inside in the warmth.

"Miz Leonie? Miz de Lacey? Why on earth—?"

"It's a very long and complicated story, Joseph," said Leonie, holding out her hands to the fire. She smiled at him. "Will you promise not to tell anyone we were out tonight?"

"Of course, Miz Leonie."

"And will you do something for me?"

"I owe you many favors, Miz Leonie," he replied, gesturing toward the book. "What do you want me to do?"

"Just go up through the house and see if anyone is up and about. We want to get back to our room without anyone knowing we've been away."

"I'll do that right now," he said, snatching up his wing and putting it carefully on his wiry curls. He hurried out, and it seemed that he'd been gone for ages, but at last they heard his steps at the kitchen door again. "It's all right, Miz Leonie, they're all asleep, there's not a sound from anyone."

"Thank you." She smiled gratefully at him and then ushered Stella out into the passage. They tiptoed through the silent building, pausing only once, their hearts suddenly thundering as something brushed past them, but it was only Mrs. Durham's cat.

They at last reached the sanctuary of their room, closing the door thankfully behind them. They were safe, they'd got back, and no one was any the wiser! But even as the relief coursed through them, they heard a carriage driving swiftly up Park Lane. It came to a halt outside the seminary, and a moment later someone was hammering urgently on the front door.

Miss Hart awoke with a start, getting quickly out of her bed and pulling on her wrap. What on earth was all the noise about? Her curl papers bobbing and her night bonnet slightly askew, she hurried down to the vestibule, where a startled Joseph had just admitted Guy.

"Sir Guy?" she cried in astonishment. "Whatever is the matter?"

"I wish to see my niece."

She stared at him. Was he in drink? "At this hour? But she will be asleep!"

"Then wake her. I wish to see that she's all right."

"Sir Guy, it's past midnight."

"Madam, I am fully aware of the time. I still wish to see my niece. *Immediately*."

She stiffened, her curl papers quivering. "Very well, sir, if you insist."

"I do insist. I also insist upon seeing Miss Conyngham. She *is* in, I take it?"

"In? Of course she is, sir. Joseph, go directly and inform Miss Conyngham and Miss de Lacey that they must come down to the visitors' room." She glanced coldly up the stairs, where a sea of curious faces was peering down. The whole school, it seemed, had been aroused by the commotion. "Go to your rooms," she commanded icily. The sea of faces vanished immediately.

In the visitors' room, Guy took up his position with his back to the fire. His hands were clasped behind him and he looked very severe. Miss Hart felt both bewildered and uncomfortable, and she was aware that she looked a little ridiculous in her voluminous nightgown, the curl papers jutting all around her face.

At last they heard steps. The door opened and Stella came hesitantly in in her nightgown, her bare feet pattering on the polished floor. She was followed by Leonie, who was still tying on her wrap. Their hair was tousled beneath their night bonnets and they looked as if they had just awoken.

Stella's eyes were huge. "Uncle Guy?"

His eyes had lightened the moment he saw her, and now he smiled, holding out his hand. She ran to him then and he lifted her up in his arms for a moment before setting her down once more and looking seriously at her. "Are you all right, sweetheart?"

She couldn't help glancing at Leonie for a moment before nodding. "Yes, Uncle Guy. Why do you ask?"

He took a deep breath. "Because I rather think I've been the victim of a tasteless practical joke. I'm sorry I've woken you, sweetheart. Run along back to your bed now." He kissed her on the forehead.

Tears filled her eyes and she looked guilty for a moment, before gathering her skirts and hurrying out again.

Leonie turned to leave as well, but he called her back. "Miss Conyngham, with your permission I would like a word with you. In private," he added, looking pointedly at Miss Hart.

The headmistress bridled. "Sir Guy, it would hardly be proper."

"I was alone with you a moment since, madam, and I was not aware of your mentioning any impropriety then."

She said nothing more. Dull color tinged her cheeks and she swept out, her nightgown billowing and her curl papers trembling with indignation.

"Please sit down, Miss Conyngham," he said, indicating a chair.

She obeyed.

"I'm sorry to have disturbed you, but believe me, I had good reason."

"I'm sure that you did, sir." She was shaking inside and couldn't meet his gaze. She felt as guilty as if she'd deliberately taken Stella to the fair with intent to deceive him.

"I was given to understand that my niece had run away again," he said.

Her heart almost stopped, and she stared at him. "As . . . as you can see, she is safe enough," she said at last. It was the truth, she wasn't lying . . .

"Yes, and that makes me feel a little foolish for having stormed in here as I did. However, it has at least given me an early opportunity to tell you about my dinner with Harry Fitzjohn. It might interest you to know that he agrees with you about your father, and he tells me that there are others at India House who also feel that way. He is hoping to probe further into the matter, and if anything should come to light, he will see that I am informed immediately."

A glad smile touched her lips then. "Thank you, Sir Guy, I'm very grateful to you for putting yourself out in this way on my account."

He gazed at her for a long moment, and it seemed to her that a veil descended over his eyes. He looked away, turning to gaze into the dying embers of the fire. "I was brought here tonight by an anonymous note which informed me that my niece had run away and that you, Miss Conyngham, had gone to meet your lover." He looked at her then. "Had you such an assignation earlier tonight?" he asked softly.

The room was suddenly very quiet. She was so startled and dismayed by what he had asked that she could only stare at him.

"Well? Haven't you anything to say?"

At last she found her tongue, and it was an angry tongue. "I have indeed, sir, and it is that I don't think it's any of your business what I do in my private life."

He rounded on her then, his eyes flashing. "Not any of my business? Madam, you astound me!"

"And you, sir, astound me!" she cried, caught on the raw

and leaping to her feet. "You aren't my husband. By what right do you presume to question me in this disgraceful way?"

"I may not have the misfortune to be your husband, madam, but I do have the right to question you, since you are in charge of my niece. If you have a lover and are neglecting your duties, then I believe it is very much my business."

"I'm not the one neglecting duty, sir," she replied icily.

"Meaning that I am, I suppose."

"If the cap fits, sirrah, pray wear it."

"Have a care, Miss Conyngham, don't press me too far."

"Why? What will you do? Will you strike me?" She knew she was almost taunting him, but she was so angry and beset with a strange sense of guilt that all caution had been thrown to the winds. "Strike me if you wish," she challenged recklessly, "but it won't make one iota of difference to the facts. You *have* been neglecting your duties, you've placed the spiteful, vindictive caprices of a cold and selfish woman above the needs of a lonely child who has no one else in the world but you, and who loves you with all her poor little heart!" Her voice broke a little and tears suddenly filled her eyes, making her turn away to blink them furiously back.

"Damn you for saying that," he whispered, his eyes very bright.

"And damn you for accusing me of having a lover," she replied, her voice trembling with the closeness of the tears.

He bowed his head for a moment then, and when he raised it again to look at her, his anger seemed to have evaporated. "Forgive me," he said softly, reaching out hesitantly to take her hand and turn her slowly toward him. He saw the tears then, and his fingers tightened over hers as he drew her almost sharply into his arms. "Don't cry," he whispered, "don't cry, for I can't bear to think I've been such a monster that I've reduced you to tears." He stroked her hair, and for a moment he seemed to press her even closer, but then it was as if he realized what he was doing, and slowly he released her. "Forgive me," he said a little awkwardly, "I did not mean . . ." He left the rest unsaid.

She felt weak, as if the few seconds in his arms had drained her of all her strength. Her cheeks were warm and her eyes dark, and the ache of loving him was almost too much to endure.

"Forgive me too for making unwarranted and insulting accusations. What makes it worse is that I knew in my heart that you were innocent, but still I felt compelled to ask you. I don't know why . . ." He paused. "No, that's not strictly true, I know damned well why I asked you, and you were correct to tell me to mind my own business, for what you do in your private life has nothing whatsoever to do with me. I have no rights over you and should not conduct myself like a jealous husband. I trust that you can find it in your heart to forgive me, for I would be grateful if we could both put my disagreeable conduct tonight from our minds."

She managed to smile, and she even managed to make her voice sound light. "Of course it is forgotten, Sir Guy. No doubt we are both tired and that is why we both said things we would prefer not to have said."

When he had gone she lowered her eyes again, the tears welling from them. How could she forget that tonight he had taken her in his arms? That his heart had beaten for a moment close to hers? She could never forget. The anger and recrimination would not endure, but that tender moment would live on forever.

31

Stella had fallen into an exhausted sleep when Leonie returned to the bedroom, but on waking the next morning she at last revealed what Imogen had said that had so devastated her. Evidently wanting to provoke an act of defiance which would alienate Guy for a long time, she had told Stella that he had decided she must remain at the seminary until she was at least eighteen, after which, provided the war in Europe permitted, she would be sent to a finishing school in Geneva. Leonie listened sadly, appalled that even Imogen could be so heartless, for she must have known how much misery would be inflicted by such news. It seemed that there were no depths to which that lady would not sink in order to have her own way, and it was small wonder that poor Stella, frightened and alone, had become so hysterical.

Leaving the matter of Imogen's visit, Leonie pressed Stella to tell her who had put her up to going to the fair, although even before the girl admitted that it had been Nadia, Leonie had suspected that this would prove to be the case. Stella was still reluctant to break her word to Nadia, and only did so in the end because she felt she had been tricked and that Nadia had never had any intention of accompanying her. The fact that Leonie herself had been deliberately drawn into it, they put down to Nadia's jealousy and Imogen's dislike, and they thought that Edward had been involved because he wished to assist his sister. They also guessed that Edward had been the author of the anonymous note which had brought Guy so swiftly to the seminary in the middle of the night, for Stella remembered looking out of the window and seeing him give a piece of paper to a small boy, who had run away in the direction of Curzon Street; Lansdowne Passage lay that way. . . . Leonie knew that only the fact that Guy had been dining out with Sir Henry Fitzjohn had prevented him from receiving the note at the correct time, for if he had been at home when it had been delivered, he would have come to the seminary and found both his niece and her teacher absent, and the note's lies apparently only too true! The plan, elaborate as it had been, had so very nearly worked.

Before going down to breakfast, Stella reiterated her promise of the night before. Leonie smiled at her. "Are you still as sure this morning?"

"Yes."

"It won't be easy for you with Imogen there all the time, for we both know only too well how hard and unfeeling she is capable of being."

Stella nodded. "I know, but I still promise. I just want to go home again, Leonie."

Leonie hugged her. "I'll go and see Sir Guy today. I don't know exactly when, but I'll go."

Edward strolled elegantly along frozen Curzon Street and into Park Lane, his cane swinging idly in his hand. He paused outside the seminary, glancing up at Leonie's balcony. Last night had been a miserable failure because somehow she'd recognized him and realized it was a trick of some sort. As a consequence, his chances of winning the wager were now nonexistent; she would be too much on her guard where he was concerned, but Rupert was still very much in the running, and that wouldn't do at all. It was time to spike friend Thornbury's guns. Smiling a little, Edward stepped up to the door and rapped smartly on it with his cane.

Leonie came very reluctantly to the visitors' room when told that he wished to see her, and at her request Joseph waited in the passage outside. She left the door open and advanced only a little way into the room. "You wished to see me, sir?" she inquired coldly.

"That is correct." He glanced at Joseph and gave a short laugh. "I assure you that you need no protection, Miss Conyngham. Not now."

"Say what you have to say, sir."

He allowed his glance to move slowly and appreciatively over her. "You are indeed a very desirable woman, and in my opinion worth every penny of ten thousand guineas."

"Ten thousand guineas? What do you mean?"

"The Duke of Thornbury and I have that handsome sum resting upon the surrender of your virtue."

She stared disbelievingly at him, hot, humiliated color flooding into her cheeks. "How dare you," she whispered.

"How? Oh, with the greatest of ease, I assure you. I'm only telling you because I would no longer appear to stand a chance of succeeding with you. Placing you in full possession of the sordid facts would seem to me the best way of ensuring that he is at an equal disadvantage."

"Get out of here," she breathed, her eyes filled with utter loathing.

"Certainly." Still smiling, he made an elegant bow and then strolled out past her, pausing in the doorway to look back. "By the way, should you choose not to believe me, I suggest you ask someone to look in White's betting book; it's all written down there, in Thornbury's own fair hand." Touching his hat to her, he strolled on out. She heard the front door close behind him.

Later that morning, before she had had time to go to see Guy, she and Katy were ordered yet again to take some of the pupils for an airing in the park. As they emerged from the seminary, they came face to face with Rupert, who was on the point of calling upon Leonie once more.

He smiled. "Good morning, I—"

"Don't waste your breath, sir!" she interrupted coldly. "I now know exactly what you are about."

The smile faded from his lips. "About? I don't quite follow you."

"Your associate has failed abysmally, and now has protected his interest by informing me all about the wager. My instincts concerning you have always been correct, and I wish to have nothing more to do with you. Please leave me alone from now on, sir."

He quickly caught her arm. "It's not true, I swear it. Edward Longhurst is lying."

"Is he? I mentioned no name, and yet you know perfectly well to whom I am referring." She shook her arm free. "I find you totally despicable, my lord duke."

"Leonie—" he began, seizing her arm again.

It was the last straw. Furiously she dealt him a stinging blow across the cheek, much to the incredulity of the watching pupils and several passersby, who halted to watch the scene on the seminary steps.

Anger leapt into his eyes, and in that brief moment his desire for her died. He loathed her now for publicly humiliating him. A nerve flickered at his temple, and he took a step toward her, but he knew that too much attention had already been drawn. Without another word, he turned on his heel and strode away.

Edward looked up from the billards table at White's as Rupert came into the room, his face still dark with anger. The man with whom Edward had been playing immediately detected the strained atmosphere, and discreetly he withdrew, leaving them alone.

Leaning on his cue, Edward smiled a little. "What's this? A tête-à-tête?"

"No, Longhurst, it's the formal ending of our friendship."

"Is it indeed? I'd put you down as many things, Thornbury, but never a poor loser."

Rupert kept his fury in check, but only just. "I don't mind losing fairly, but I will not be cheated."

Edward's smile faded. "Don't go too far," he said warningly.

"You were the one who went too far, Longhurst, and since you've now laid down new rules, let me warn you that I've learned them very thoroughly indeed."

"And what is that supposed to mean?"

"Simply that I fully intend to have my revenge for your cheating. The heavy betting on my marriage plans is about to prove your undoing. You'd have been wiser keeping your mouth shut instead of whispering that you believed I would marry Nadia Benckendorff in September."

Edward felt a cold finger deep inside, but he gave a light, incredulous laugh. "I was joking, and they knew it, for they know as well as I that no man in his right senses would take a woman like Nadia as his wife!''

''It seems they took you seriously, dear boy, as I pointed out to you some time ago.'' Rupert gave a cool smile. ''They aren't going to be very pleased when I announce at Poyntons that I am married, are they? Especially when it is first rumored, and then proved, that you have secretly laid a small fortune on precisely that.''

Edward stared at him. ''I haven't laid anything on your damned wedding plans,'' he said shortly.

''Oh, I know that, and you do—but they don't, and I've employed the services of a very discreet but very reliable undisclosed agent. Word will gradually get about concerning your duplicity, dear fellow, and it won't be long before you're *persona non grata.*''

Edward flung down his cue, his face pale now. ''You've taken leave of your senses! Your anger I can understand, but not that you'd actually encumber yourself with Nadia Benckendorff simply to be avenged.''

Rupert smiled. ''Enjoy the coming days, Longhurst, for by midnight on the ninth of February your name will be spoken of as contemptuously as Richard Conyngham's, and it seems to me that there is some poetic justice in that. Oh, maybe your crime will not be on exactly the same level, but if there's one thing society doesn't take to it's a lying cheat, and you will be seen as just that.'' Inclining his head, he left.

Edward remained by the table, his blue eyes both angry and uneasy, for he could remember some of the names he'd seen in the betting book. It wouldn't do to be ostracized by such men as those; too many doors would be closed. But then gradually the alarm and unease began to fade away, to be replaced by his usual clever confidence. A great deal could happen before the ninth of February was out, and Thornbury's ring was far from being on Nadia Benckendorff's finger yet. . . . He picked up the cue again and eyed the ivory balls on the green baize table, but as he bent to make a stroke, the door opened once more and his partner returned. Edward glanced up at him and saw a rather hostile look on his face. ''What is it, James? You look as if you've lost a sovereign and found a farthing.''

''The analogy may not be far out.''

Edward straightened. "Meaning?"

"Meaning that there are whispers about your financial dabblings, Longhurst."

"Dabblings?" Edward laughed. "I don't dabble, dear boy."

"No, you connive."

Edward's smile began to fade. "I take it you're referring to this business of Thornbury's marriage?"

"I am."

"Well, let me assure you that whatever you've been told is untrue. I haven't placed any secret bets, nor do I know who or when the fellow intends to get spliced. I do know one thing, though, and that's that no one will be expecting the actual announcement made at Poyntons on the ninth of February."

"What do you mean?"

"Patience, dear boy. Oh, and do have more faith in me, it's very tiresome having you scowling at me like that." Edward smiled and gestured toward the table. "Your shot, I believe."

He watched as the other hesitated for a moment and then went to take up his position by the table. As the ivory balls struck one another and then rolled silently over the baize, Edward's unease returned a little. Thornbury had thought carefully about gaining his revenge, and the only way of defeating him was to see that at midnight on the ninth Nadia Benckendorff remained a free woman.

As Edward planned his next careful move, Nadia was standing on the pavement outside the embassy in Harley Street, watching as her sleigh was unloaded from the flat-topped wagon on which it had been conveyed from the ship. She huddled shivering in her fur-lined cloak, thinking that there was something decidedly incongruous about *carrying* a sleigh across ice-covered streets which were ideal for driving it along. It was, she decided, typical of the eccentric and incomprehensible English.

She watched the unloading with little pleasure. She had been looking forward to the sleigh's arrival, but the complete failure of the plan the night before had left her in a very sour mood. She couldn't believe that after everything, Leonie and Stella had somehow succeeded in eluding the trap, or that they had actually managed to convince Guy de Lacey that they'd never been out. It was so galling to have to remain silent, for to say anything would mean risking awkward questions, which might lead to embarrassing facts coming out into the open. So Leonie Conyngham remained where she was, and as far as Nadia was concerned, that meant that she was still available to Rupert.

A carriage drove carefully over the hard-packed snow and ice toward the embassy, and Nadia's face cleared as she recognized it. Dorothea! At *last*! Now something could finally be done about Leonie.

The travel-stained carriage halted and Dorothea alighted, followed by a maid carrying Baryshna, the pug dog, in her arms. Dorothea shook out her skirts and then thrust her hands deep into the warmth of her fur muff. She wore crimson, and looked radiant and content. Lord Palmerston was evidently good for her temper. She offered her cheek for Nadia to kiss, and then she smiled. "Nadia, *chérie*, how good it is to see you again. I've so much to tell you. Ah, I see that your troika has arrived at last. What a dash you'll cut now, to be sure."

"Dorothea, I must speak urgently with you."

"Urgently? Nadia, I've only just arrived back after a very tiring and cold journey."

"It's very important."

Dorothea sighed. "By which you mean it concerns the Duke of Thornbury."

"I want Leonie Conyngham removed from the seminary, and only you can see that she is."

"My, my, how your tune has changed," murmured Dorothea. "When I left, you were delighted to keep her there. I presume that all this is because your wretched duke is still pursuing her. Well, I did warn you."

"I don't want a lecture, I simply want her dismissed."

"There's no need."

"No need? What do you mean?"

"Let him bed her, it's of no consequence, since he doesn't intend to marry her. He's going to marry you."

Nadia's breath caught. "You've heard something?"

"Yes, I've heard that he intends to marry on the ninth of February, and the bride is a lady who hasn't long been in the country."

Dismay lanced through Nadia. "Marguerite St. Julienne! It's *her*, not me!"

"No, my dear, I'm assured that it is you."

"Assured? By whom?"

"Lord Palmerston."

Nadia gave a disbelieving laugh. "And what does *he* know about it?"

Dorothea was at her haughtiest. "He knows a great deal. On our return to town, we came here by way of White's, where Lord Palmerston had some private business to attend to. The place is seething with rumor because a certain anonymous bet has come to light in the book. It's for a vast sum of money and wagers that the duke will marry on the ninth. It is firmly believed that the bet was laid by Lord Edward Longhurst, although he strenuously denies it. When the duke himself was challenged to say if there was any truth in the matter, he did not deny it; he said that he was indeed intending to marry a lady new to England. Like you, many believed he was referring to Miss St. Julienne, but he merely laughed and said that he liked his women pretty. So there you have it, Nadia: everyone at White's is convinced that you will be the new Duchess of Thornbury on the ninth of February. I'm further convinced that it is true because Lord Edward is very ill-thought-of at the moment, since he is believed to have deliberately misled a number of gentlemen simply in order to make a financial coup himself."

Nadia wasn't interested in Edward Longhurst. "Lord Palmerston is certain Rupert did not deny planning to marry me in a week's time?"

"Quite certain. There can be little doubt, my dear Nadia, that you are soon to be the next Duchess of Thornbury."

Nadia's eyes shone. She hardly dared believe it. From the depths of despair she was suddenly raised to the heights of joy. Nadia, Duchess of Thornbury. . . .

"By the way." Dorothea glanced a little coldly at her. "What's all this I hear about you and my rubies?"

Nadia's smile faded. "Oh. Dorothea, I can explain—"

"I trust you can," replied Dorothea, sweeping past her and into the embassy.

32

Early that afternoon, Leonie was at last able to set off to walk to Berkeley Street to see Guy, but at that moment he wasn't at home; he had gone to a repository of fine art in Bond Street with Imogen, who was undecided about which of two landscapes to purchase.

Imogen was struggling to appear all amiability and sweetness, but inside she was seething with anger because of the way things had gone wrong the night before. She was also uneasy, because Guy had once again believed what Leonie Conyngham had told him. Like Nadia, Imogen was frustrated at not daring to tell the truth, for fear of inviting unwanted questions about her own complicity. She knew even more than Nadia now, since Edward had confided in her the previous night about the wager, and the last thing she wished was for Guy to realize how much she was remaining silent about. It was all a great strain, but she was endeavoring to go on as if there was nothing wrong. She only pretended to study the landscapes, for neither of them was to her liking. "I don't know," she murmured thoughtfully. "Perhaps they're both too dark. What do you think?"

"Mm?"

She laughed lightly. "Guy de Lacey, I do believe you haven't heard a single word I've said to you this afternoon."

He smiled a little ruefully, quickly raising her hands to his lips. "Forgive me, my mind is still on that wretched business of last night."

"Oh."

He didn't notice her reaction. "I can't help wondering who thought it amusing to send me on such a wild-goose chase."

Suddenly she couldn't bear it anymore. "Are you so sure that it was a wild-goose chase?"

"What else could it be? Neither my niece nor Miss Conyngham had even been out."

"They had. Edward saw them both." She'd said it almost before she knew the words were on her lips. A hot color flushed swiftly to her cheeks, but she knew she had to go on now that she'd started. "They've made a fool of you, your beloved niece and your precious Leonie Conyngham!"

He was very still and unsmiling. "If they have, they do not appear to be the only ones to do it to me, do they? Well, since you've embarked upon this confession, I trust you intend to finish."

She looked quickly, wishing that she hadn't let her jealousy and frustration get the better of her, but it was too late now. "I . . . I didn't want to say anything, I wanted you and Stella to come together again, and so I thought it best not to say anything."

"Did you?"

"Yes! I did!" She felt trapped, both by her own foolishness and by the chill in his eyes.

"What, exactly, did your brother tell you he saw?"

"He was alighting from his carriage outside the house. He saw Stella drive past in a carriage with two strangers, and then he saw Leonie Conyngham in a hackney—she was obviously going to meet her lover."

"Obviously? How can it have been obvious?"

"Because she does have a lover. Oh, if you must know, Edward and Rupert have a wager of ten thousand guineas on which of them can seduce her first, and naturally they made it their business to find out all they could about her. That's how they discovered that she has a lover, although they don't know who he is. She's been meeting him for some time, leaving the seminary after Stella has fallen asleep and then returning before she awakens, which is why Stella knows nothing about what's going on." She met his gaze without wavering as she told him such a monstrous lie.

For a long moment he didn't reply. His eyes remained cold

and his lips a thin line. "You knew all this and yet said nothing to me?" he asked softly at last.

She couldn't meet his eyes then, looking quickly away, the color heightening on her cheeks.

He gave her a glance which verged on the contemptuous. "I thought not. You cannot even begin to justify your silence!"

"You're being unfair and unreasonable!" she cried.

"*Unreasonable!*" He raised his voice incredulously, ignoring the astonished glances of several people nearby. "My niece, a child of only twelve, was out last night with complete strangers, while the woman who has charge of her apparently kept an assignation with a lover. You knew all this but chose to keep silent, and now *you* accuse *me* of being unfair and unreasonable!"

"How dare you speak to me like that! I *will* not be treated in such a way!"

He suddenly snatched up his hat and gloves. "I think I'd better go before either of us says something we might later regret."

She stared after him. "Guy!"

He didn't reply or look back. The doorbell tinkled loudly in the silence long after he'd vanished among the crowds of Bond Street.

He returned to Berkeley Street. He'd considered going straight to the seminary to face both Stella and Leonie, but he knew he was too angry. It was better to wait awhile, until his temper cooled. But as he entered the vestibule of his house, he was informed that Leonie was waiting in the drawing room upstairs. His face darkened and he glanced toward the staircase.

The butler looked uncertainly at him. "She said she had something of importance to tell you concerning Miss Stella, Sir Guy, and so I took the liberty of bidding her wait until your return. Did I do wrong?"

"Wrong?" Guy glanced at him, shaking his head. "No, it's all perfectly in order. I'll go to speak with her now."

He went up the stairs without once having glanced at Imogen's portrait.

The drawing room was furnished in the Grecian style, with wallpaper striped in shades of pale blue and all the woodwork painted white. There were golden velvet curtains with blue cords and tassels, and Grecian chairs and sofas with golden upholstery. It was a light, elegant room, very large and spacious, and Leonie looked very small seated on a chair close to the white marble fireplace.

She rose quickly to her feet as he entered, and the smile of greeting died on her lips as she saw the dark anger burning in his eyes. "Sir Guy? Is something wrong?"

"Yes, madam, I rather think it is. What have you come to tell me? That you've just remembered that you did slip out last night after all? Oh, and maybe my niece did as well? Perhaps it all escaped your memory last night when I spoke to you."

She stared at him, the color draining from her face. "How did you find out?" she asked, her voice barely above a whisper. "Was it Lord Edward Longhurst?"

"It doesn't matter *how* I know, madam, it matters only that I do. Where are the tears today, Miss Conyngham? Surely you can squeeze a few for my benefit!"

She stiffened then. "I see no point in replying, sir, since I'm obviously accused, tried, and condemned already."

"Might I remind you that I asked you for the truth last night, and you chose to lie to me. I don't like being made a fool of, Miss Conyngham."

"I didn't make a fool of you, nor did I lie, I simply omitted to tell the whole truth."

"How gracious of you," he replied sarcastically, "but I'm afraid that in my book you lied, and I find that quite unforgivable." He paused, his dark eyes sweeping scornfully over her. "Well, aren't you going to eloquently protest your innocence once more?"

"Sarcasm is the lowest form of wit, sir."

"Oh, forgive me," he said acidly, bowing a little, "but I'm afraid that my fury is rather getting the better of my politeness."

She raised her chin defiantly. "Do you want to know exactly what happened last night? Or do you merely wish to condemn me unheard?"

He met her eyes for a moment and then nodded. "Very well, tell me."

She told him everything, except the truth about Imogen's visit. She left nothing else out, not even the humiliating wager which had been made on her virtue, and when she had finished she looked challengingly at him. "That is what happened last night, Sir Guy, and the only reason I did not admit it then was that I knew that Stella had at last accepted what she must do. She learned a dreadful lesson at the fair and realized that no matter what, she wanted to go home to you. I protected her in order to avoid exactly what has happened now. Answer me one thing, sir: had you not learned the truth, what would your feelings be now on being told that Stella had at last given the promise you've sought?"

He didn't reply.

"Have you nothing to say, sir? Maybe you don't really want her to come home after all, no matter how nobly you've protested in the past!"

"Damn you!" he cried then. "You *know* I want her home!"

"Do I? Why am *I* expected to take your word for granted, while *you* choose to believe what you will as the mood takes you? I omitted to tell you the truth last night because I hold you in very high regard and because I love your niece. I wanted to assist in bringing you both together again, and I honestly believed that that was the best way of achieving that end. All would have been well, had someone not chosen to whisper in your ear. I think it best if I leave now." She began to walk past him, but he suddenly caught her arm.

"Please, don't go."

"I will not stay to be further accused of lies and deceit, sir."

"There will not be any, for I know the truth when I hear it. If you'd told me last night, I'd have known it then. How can I be expected to believe you when you don't trust me? Look at me, Leonie."

Slowly she turned to face him. The fact that his eyes had softened and he used her first name did not release her from the pain he had yet again inflicted. She was cool, concealing the hurt she felt inside. "You know the truth now, sir, and you know that Stella has at last given the solemn promise you so desperately sought. What happens next is entirely up to you, isn't it?"

He looked deep into her eyes and slowly his hand fell away from her.

She swallowed, close to tears suddenly and determined that

he should not realize the fact. "What do you wish me to tell Stella?" she asked.

He turned away. "I wish to be reconciled with her before I leave for Poyntons, and so I will come for her in the morning."

"Very well. Good afternoon, sir."

"Good afternoon."

He watched from the window as she hurried away from the house, her head bowed. He waited until she was out of sight and then turned to ring for the butler.

The man came running. "Sir Guy?"

"I'm going out. If anyone calls, tell them I do not know when I will be back."

"Yes, Sir Guy."

Edward was alone in his box at the crowded theater. The box was in shadow, and in the whole auditorium only those close to the brightly lit stage could be seen clearly. He lounged back in his chair, gazing at the players without really seeing them. He was thinking of what had happened at White's, where the atmosphere was already extremely unsociable. He trusted that he could play his cards cleverly enough to eliminate the hostility and turn it instead toward Thornbury, but it would require extremely delicate handling, that was for sure.

He didn't hear someone enter the box behind him; he knew nothing at all until someone suddenly wrenched him out of his chair and flung him roughly against the beautiful gilded plasterwork of the wall at the back of the box, where the shadows were darkest. Almost choking from the tight grip upon the knot of his cravat, Edward found himself staring in amazement into Guy's cold, angry eyes. "De Lacey!" he squeaked. "Good God above, have you taken leave of your senses? Unhand me!"

"When I'm ready, my fine lordling," breathed Guy. "I haven't taken leave of my senses, but I promise you this, if you make one more move toward Leonie Conyngham, or say one more word against her, then I will believe you to have taken leave of yours."

Edward's eyes were like saucers. "I don't know what you mean," he said quickly.

Guy's fist tightened on the cravat, almost stopping the

other's breath. "Don't you? Then let me refresh your memory. I'm referring to your wager with Thornbury concerning the lady's virtue, and I'm here to warn you both to stay away from her or you will regret it."

Edward struggled to wrench himself free. "Dammit, de Lacey, it's my sister you're marrying, not the schoolteacher, and—" He got no further because Guy almost lifted him from his feet by the knot.

"I tolerate you, Longhurst, no more and no less, and if you're foolish enough or vain enough to disregard this warning, then so help me I'll nail your foul hide so close to the damned wall that they'll never prize you free again. Do I make myself quite clear?"

Edward's eyes goggled and he nodded. "Yes! Yes! For God's sake, de Lacey, let me go!"

Guy flung him disdainfully aside. "Don't forget it," he said softly, gazing down with utter contempt as the other lay winded where he'd fallen.

Edward rubbed his bruised throat, closing his eyes with relief as Guy left the box. At that very moment the play ended, and rapturous applause broke out.

After being so summarily left by Guy, Imogen had returned to Longhurst House, where she waited, confident that soon Guy would call upon her to make amends. But time went by, darkness fell, and still there was no sign of him.

At ten o'clock she heard someone at the front door. Quickly she rubbed her eyes to redden them, and then she lay gracefully back on the chaise longue, her pale pink skirts carefully arranged to spill beautifully to the floor. A lace handkerchief was held delicately in one slender hand, and she presented a picture of gently reproachful melancholy. But the careful preparation was in vain, for it wasn't Guy who was announced, it was Miss Hart.

Irritation flickered over Imogen's face and she sat up again. What on earth was that wretched woman calling at this time of night for?

Miss Hart bustled agitatedly in, the hem of her taffeta skirt damp from the snow. "Oh, Lady Imogen, I'm so relieved to find you at home."

"Whatever is it, Miss Hart?"

"It's Miss de Lacey."

The blue eyes narrowed. "What about her?"

"She's leaving the seminary first thing tomorrow morning to return to Sir Guy. She's packing at this very moment. Oh, Lady Imogen, I did my very best to see that she remained at the seminary, I sent no favorable or even vaguely encouraging reports, but Sir Guy has been taking Miss Conyngham's advice. *She* convinced him this afternoon that Miss de Lacey was now ready to go home."

Imogen was staring in shocked incredulity. "This afternoon? Are you sure?" she demanded.

Miss Hart was taken aback at the sharpness in the other's voice. "Why, yes, quite sure. I overheard her telling Miss de Lacey on her return."

"Return? From where?"

The headmistress lowered her glance a little uneasily. "From Sir Guy's house. She went to see him about Miss de Lacey."

Imogen rose furiously to her feet. "You permitted that . . . that *creature* to call upon Sir Guy?"

"But what could I do?" protested Miss Hart. "Sir Guy had personally placed her in charge of his niece, and he wished to be informed of her progress."

Imogen turned restlessly away. "Thank you for coming to see me, Miss Hart. I will not keep you."

The headmistress was offended at being so abruptly and ungratefully dismissed. Gathering her damp skirts, she walked stiffly out.

As the door closed, Imogen commenced to pace agitatedly up and down, her silk skirts hissing over the floor. Things weren't going at all as she wished, and if she wasn't careful she'd find herself losing Guy to Leonie Conyngham! She halted suddenly, a gleam entering her blue eyes. Leonie didn't yet have the upper hand, and she wasn't going to be permitted to gain it. Guy couldn't possibly be aware yet that news of his niece's homecoming had reached Longhurst House, so there was time yet to mend the rift. He was about to receive a call from his penitent, transformed future bride, who was going to express her shame and remorse and beg him to send immediately for Stella. Yes, that was what must be done; she must appear to have suffered a change of heart *before* discovering that the girl was going home anyway.

She reached for the bell. Guy de Lacey was hers, *hers*, and she wasn't going to surrender him.

Guy was in his library when Imogen was announced. She hesitated in the doorway, as if pathetically unsure of what her reception would be. She looked fragile and vulnerable, twisting her lace handkerchief anxiously in her hands. There were imploring tears in her magnificent eyes and her lips moved tremulously. "Guy?" she whispered. "Oh, Guy, I'm so very sorry, I didn't mean to . . . to . . ." She allowed her voice to trail away.

He went quickly to her, sweeping her into his arms and kissing her on the lips.

She clung to him. "I've been so miserable because I know I've been wrong, but I thought I was doing it for the best, Guy, truly I did. I know now that Stella must come home, she should be back with you and not in the seminary, where I know she's dreadfully unhappy. I feel so ashamed to think that I was responsible for her being sent there, but I *did* believe it was right at the time. You do know that, don't you?"

"Of course I do."

"I'll be a good wife to you," she whispered, twining her slender arms around his neck. "I'll be all you could ever wish." She reached up to kiss him.

He drew her closer, but as her lips yielded beneath his, her rich auburn hair became the palest of silver-fair, and her blue eyes darkened to the deepest of browns. He hesitated.

She felt the hesitation, and knew that all was still not well. She had regained her ground, but she wasn't safe yet. . . .

Nadia walked with Rupert in the conservatory at the embassy. They paused by the macaw in its elegant golden cage. She had seldom felt more happy, for she was convinced that what Dorothea had told her was the truth. Rupert had not said anything in so many words, but he had hinted a great deal about a surprise he had in store for her on her first day at Poyntons. If he wished it to be a surprise, then she would not spoil it for him, especially as he had seldom been more loving and masterful than he had been tonight.

She watched as he fed the macaw. "What time will you

come here tomorrow night?'' she asked, linking her arm through his and resting her golden head on his shoulder.

''Tomorrow? Ah, that is a little difficult. You see, I have to leave town tomorrow. I'm going to visit a friend in Sussex.''

She looked at him in surprise. ''But why did you not mention this before?''

''I only made the arrangements today.''

A sixth sense began to stir warningly within her, although she could not have said exactly why. ''Do you have to go?''

''I've given him my word, and a fellow's word is his bond.''

''How long will you be away?''

''Several days—I'm not exactly certain.''

''But we were to travel to Poyntons together.''

He smiled quickly. ''It only matters that we are there on that day; it doesn't matter if we don't arrive together, does it?''

She stared at him. ''No, I suppose not.''

''Perhaps it would be better if you arranged to travel with Dorothea. I'll see you there.'' He drew her suddenly cold hand to his lips.

''You . . . you *will* be there, won't you?'' she asked.

''Oh, yes, you may count upon it, for I have something very special planned.''

''Concerning our future?'' It was as far as she dared hint.

''Yes,'' he said softly, kissing her on the lips, ''most definitely concerning our future.''

Stella had at last succumbed to sleep, after lying awake in a frenzy of excited anticipation about going back to Guy in the morning. Outside, the moon was high in the starry sky, and Hyde Park shimmered with ice-blue shadows.

For Leonie, sleep was as far away as ever. She stared up at the bed hangings. Tomorrow Guy would take his niece away, and he'd never again give a thought to Leonie Conyngham.

33

Leonie stood alone at the bedroom window. Stella had left and the room felt very empty. She wondered how long it would be before she was banished to the upper floor once more.

It was another crisp, clear day, and the crowds had once again been drawn to the Serpentine. They all seemed so happy and carefree, but here, in the quiet bedroom, she was sad. She had avoided meeting Guy's glance when he came, and he had made no effort to speak to her, beyond a very formal, distant expression of thanks for all that she had done for Stella. With those few words she knew that she had become part of the past. It had been a hollow moment, devoid of any show of emotion, and only Stella's bubbling enthusiasm masked it. The girl had been torn between joy and tears, for if she was at last going home, she was also leaving Leonie behind.

Leonie stared out over the park, in her mind's eye watching Guy's carriage driving away from the door, but then she became aware of a stir of interest among the people close to the park gates. They seemed to be looking toward Tyburn. Curious, she opened the window and stepped out into the crisp, flawless snow on the balcony. The ice-cold air seemed to snatch at her after the warmth of the bedroom, and she shivered as she looked up the busy street to see what was attracting all the attention. It was a sleigh, a troika drawn by three cream-white horses harnessed abreast. Bells jingling, it glided smoothly toward her, and she immediately recognized its two occupants, Nadia Benckendorff, displaying a surprising skill with the ribbons, and beside her, lounging among the warm furs, Edward Longhurst. His lips were, as always, curved in that perpetual half-smile which Leonie loathed so very much, and today there was an extra dimension to that smile, for he seemed slyly pleased with himself, as if something was going exactly as he wished.

Afraid that they might glance up and see her, Leonie stepped back into the bedroom, looking out again to see the troika turn in through the park gates, the small group of onlookers parting to allow it through. Nadia maneuvered it expertly, swiftly bringing the team up to a brisk pace. The sleigh slid away over the snow, drawing admiring glances from all who saw it. Even the skaters on the Serpentine paused to stare as it swept magnificently by, the team kicking up the snow like glittering sugar. Leonie watched it for a while longer, and then left the room to go about her duties.

Edward held on to his top hat as the sleigh flew across the park, the runners whining and the bells jingling to the swift rhythm of the horses. The speed was almost alarming, and he glanced at Nadia's unsmiling face. She wasn't gleaning the satisfaction she should from the troika's first triumphant appearance in London; she should have been basking in all the envious admiration, but instead she hardly seemed to notice it. Her mood was almost brooding, and her mind was most definitely on something else—on Thornbury, if Edward was any judge. He smiled to himself, for he knew that he was responsible for her lack of spirit, having very carefully over the past day or so hinted at Thornbury's untrustworthiness. Perhaps she was now ripe for the plucking. He smiled at her. "I'm honored today, am I not? Shouldn't it be Rupert beside you in your hour of glory?"

"He's out of town," she replied abruptly.

"Ah, yes. He's returned to his family seat with his mother and Miss St. Julienne, hasn't he?"

"No, he's visiting a friend in Sussex or some such place."

"I think you are mistaken, for I saw them departing from Grosvenor Square and they most definitely took the Oxford road."

"Perhaps Sussex is that way too."

"No, Sussex is to the south, across the river. Oxford is to

the west. I don't know who told you about Sussex, but it was untrue, I promise you."

She reined the team in and then turned to him. "Rupert told me himself."

Edward shrugged. "Well, I have the evidence of my own eyes. There's no mistake, I assure you. I don't know why he told you something else . . ." He allowed his voice to trail provocatively away.

"Why are you doing this to me? Why do you continually try to make me unsure of him?" she demanded, her tone angry because of the uncertainties milling around inside her.

"Perhaps because I don't wish to see you hurt."

"Hurt?" She stared at him. "Why should I trust you, milord? In the past you haven't been a friend to me, no matter how much you've denied it since. Why should I believe you now instead of him?"

He held her gaze for a moment, managing to make his blue eyes very reproachful. "Oh, Nadia, that was unworthy, but I will not take offense, for I know you are upset. Very well, you doubt my veracity, and so it seems to me that the only course open to you is to go to Grosvenor Square and inquire."

Without another word, she whipped the team into action again, turning the sleigh around and driving back across the park the way they had come. Edward settled back, his clever eyes shining, for he knew what she would be told; he'd made certain of his facts before embarking upon anything.

Grosvenor Square was quiet, the neat paths of the railed formal garden in the center covered with unblemished snow from which rose a gilded statue of the first George. The sleigh bells tinkled prettily as Nadia drove the troika toward Thornbury House, which occupied a prime corner site. It was a handsome red-brick building, with tall, symmetrically arranged windows and a pedimented door which was approached up a shallow flight of steps.

Edward remained in the sleigh as Nadia went to the door. He saw the footman shaking his head and then the door was closed once more. She walked slowly back toward the sleigh, dismay written clearly on her lovely face. He hid a smile. It was all so easy, especially when Thornbury was so overconfident that he didn't take the elementary precaution of priming his servants to lie on his behalf. He'd gone on the Oxford road with his mother and the Jamaican Gorgon, that much was true, but if Edward's information was correct, he'd subsequently gone to spend a day or so in the arms of a certain lady of dubious character, whose residence was in Amersham. A friend in Sussex, be damned! Well, friend Thornbury's unfaithfulness was going to prove his undoing, and he was a fool ever to think he could so easily triumph over Edward Longhurst! And Nadia was also a fool, urged on by ambition, but without the wit to see the traps placed so skillfully before her.

He gallantly alighted to assist her back into the sleigh. She said nothing for a moment, but then she looked at him. "You were right, he hasn't gone to Sussex, and neither the duchess nor Miss St. Julienne is at home. Why did he lie to me?"

He held her gaze, trusting that he looked sincere. "He lied because he's gone away to marry Marguerite St. Julienne."

Her face, already pale, lost still more color. "No. No, I will not believe you. Everyone knows he's going to marry me," she whispered.

"Has he said so?"

She hesitated. "Not in so many words, but—"

"Has he actually said he is going to marry you?" he repeated.

"No, but he gave me to understand . . ." Her voice trailed away.

"Yes?"

She took a deep breath. "That there would be a surprise concerning our future awaiting me at Poyntons."

"An ambiguous statement if ever I heard one," he said softly. "Oh, my dear, can't you see? The surprise he has in store for you is his marriage to someone else. Think of him: has he ever been completely open and honest with you? Well, has he?" He leaned across suddenly, taking one of her hands. "Forget him, Nadia, for there is someone who loves you more than he ever did."

She stared at him. "Milord?"

He drew her hand to his lips, turning it palm uppermost. "Forget Thornbury," he murmured, his eyes warm and dark, "for I'm here now."

*   *   *

For the next two days he laid siege to her, although he was always careful to keep the fact a secret from the rest of society, since he had no wish as yet to disprove Thornbury's clever tale. The denouement, as originally planned, would take place at Poyntons on the ninth, but it would not be the one friend Thornbury fondly imagined it would be!

Nadia was more cautious than he had expected, and showed a desire to be as secretive about things as he was himself, thus conveying to him that she was not yet ready to finally cast Thornbury off, but he knew her confidence was very badly shaken and he offered her the salvation of her search for a wealthy, titled husband. Maybe being the future Countess of Wadford was not quite as grand a prospect as being the Duchess of Thornbury, but it would do.

Imogen watched the proceedings with growing disquiet, not having been taken into her brother's confidence and therefore believing him to be in earnest where Nadia was concerned. Imogen was forced to examine very closely her own feelings toward her friend, feelings which had changed considerably of late, for it was one thing to encourage Nadia in her pursuit of Rupert, it was quite another to contemplate her as a sister-in-law. For Imogen, this latest development would have been bad enough, but there was also the irritating and galling presence of Stella de Lacey in Guy's house. The child constantly eulogized Leonie Conyngham, and Imogen thought she detected a lingering interest in the schoolteacher on Guy's part. The situation was intolerable, and by the evening of the third day Imogen had reached the end of her tether. She could do nothing about Edward and Nadia, she didn't dare move yet against Stella, but something could most certainly be done about Leonie Conyngham! In a cold fury, Imogen set off in her carriage for Harley Street, to call not upon Nadia, but upon Dorothea.

Dorothea was in her boudoir, preparing to go out to meet Lord Palmerston. She was holding up her rubies to see if they went well with the dainty neckline of her revealing white silk gown. She put them down in surprise as Imogen was announced. "Ah, Lady Imogen, what a pleasant surprise." Her smile faded as she saw the expression on the other's face. "It would seem that this is not merely a social call."

"Forgive me, I did not mean to offend you."

"I am not yet offended, since I do not know what is in your mind."

Imogen took a deep, quivering breath. "I want you to see that Leonie Conyngham is immediately removed from the seminary."

"I see. May I ask why?"

"If you had endured nearly three days of Stella de Lacey prattling on and on about her, deliberately turning the conversation toward her, and all the while bringing Guy into it, then you would feel as I do now. I know what that brat is up to: she wants that Conyngham creature to take my place. Well, I don't intend to let it continue. That is why I want you to see Miss Hart—she'll do as you ask."

Dorothea nodded. "Very well, if that is what you really wish."

"It is, and I want it done as quickly as possible. Like you, I leave for Poyntons the day after tomorrow, and I want that woman gone from the seminary before I set off. I wish to be able to go to Poyntons safe in the knowledge that I am free of her."

Dorothea studied her. "Your uncertainty where he is concerned surprises me."

Imogen stiffened a little. "I'm not uncertain, I merely wish to rid myself of a tiresome creature who believes she has a chance of luring him if she flutters her eyelashes often enough. I'll rid myself of her now, and the child later. He's mine and I mean to keep him, and I do not intend to share him with anyone."

Dorothea smiled then. "My dear, how very Russian of you. I vow St. Petersburg would adore you. I admire such determination and unswerving resolve, and so I will do all I can to assist you. I will call at the seminary this very evening on my way to Lord Palmerston."

Imogen smiled too. "Thank you. I will be forever grateful."

Withdrawing from the boudoir, Imogen encountered Nadia at the top of the stairs. There was a very slight air of coolness in their greeting, for Imogen's manner over the past few days had not gone unnoticed.

A carriage was arriving outside, and Imogen knew that it was Edward. She looked quickly at Nadia. "You shouldn't trust him, you know—he isn't capable of an honest act."

"You don't think I'm good enough for him, do you?" replied Nadia icily.

"I merely wish to protect you. I know my brother only too well.".

"No, my lady, that isn't it at all."

"Believe what you wish," said Imogen, beginning to descend the stairs.

"I believe that you've been masquerading as my friend," called Nadia after her. "It amused you to think of me with Rupert, but it displeases you greatly when I am with your brother."

Imogen paused, turning briefly back. "You are an adventuress, Miss Benckendorff, and not in any way fit to aspire to my brother. I consider our friendship to be at an end. Good night." With that she went on down, passing Edward in the doorway and not saying a word to him.

34

Leonie saw Dorothea arrive and go with Miss Hart to the visitors' room, but although she wondered what the visit was about, she didn't give it a great deal of thought. The matter of writing the promised letter to Private Whittacker's commanding officer had to be attended to, and so she took a candle and some writing implements into one of the deserted classrooms, where the fire still warmed the air. Setting the candle on the teacher's desk, she settled down to write, but she had hardly commenced when Joseph came to her.

"Miz Leonie? Miz Hart wants to speak to you straightaway."

"But she's with the countess, isn't she?"

"Yes."

A sense of foreboding seized her then, and as she went toward the visitors' room, she couldn't help remembering the last time she had faced both the headmistress and Dorothea Lieven. Her hand trembled as she opened the door, and the sense of foreboding increased as the murmur of voices inside ceased abruptly.

Dorothea, glittering with rubies, was seated in the same place she had been on that other occasion, and as Leonie entered, she deliberately looked away, making no sign of acknowledgment or even recognition.

Miss Hart rose from her chair, her hands clasped before her as she faced Leonie. "I will not waste any time, Miss Conyngham. There have been serious complaints about the standard of your teaching, which is evidently far from satisfactory. In view of this, and after due consultation with the countess, I have no option but to request you to leave the premises immediately.''

Leonie stared at her, a horrid coldness seeping slowly and inexorably through her. Leave immediately? But where could she go? What would happen to her? Incongruously she thought of the outstanding fees. "But I haven't paid all that is owing."

"Your debt is to be waived."

"Waived? But it was once considered of sufficient importance to make me sign an agreement!" She paused, her eyes flying from one face to the other. "If I'm to be dismissed, I wish that contract to be returned to me."

The headmistress glanced at Dorothea, who gave a barely perceptible nod. Miss Hart then went to the drawer, unlocked it, and drew out the document. She gave it back to Leonie. "That will be all, Miss Conyngham," she said coldly.

Leonie met her gaze. "My teaching hasn't been unsatisfactory at all, and you know it. This is merely a ploy to get rid of me, isn't it?"

"I said that will be all, Miss Conyngham."

Leonie knew there was no point in protesting anymore. "Do . . . do you wish me to leave tonight?"

Miss Hart hesitated. Such haste would, if anything untoward befell Leonie, reflect poorly upon the seminary, which might be judged overharsh and unchristian. "No, that will not be necessary," she said. "You may leave first thing in the morning."

Without another word, Leonie left the room. She felt numb and very, very cold as she went slowly back to the empty classroom, where the glow of the solitary candle on her desk threw only a feeble light. She moved automatically, almost as if in a dream. Sitting at the desk, she continued writing, and she had finished the letter and sealed it before she could no longer ignore the awfulness of her desperate situation. Tears pricked her eyes and suddenly she hid her face in her hands, her shoulders trembling as she wept.

The candleflame swayed suddenly as the door opened and Joseph came in once more. "Miz Leonie? You have some visitors." He smiled, not seeing her tears in the half-light.

Hastily she dabbed her handkerchief to her eyes, rising to her feet just as a small figure almost hurtled into the room and into her arms. It was Stella.

"Leonie!" she cried joyfully. "Oh, Leonie, I've missed you so, and I've been simply *longing* to see you again!"

In spite of her tears, Leonie smiled, holding the girl close for a moment, but then something made her look toward the door, and her heart seemed to stand still, for Guy was there. Their eyes met and she felt a wild emotion tumbling through her. For a fleeting moment nothing else mattered but that he was there, and just to be able to look at him again brought her an immeasurable joy. Oh, how she loved this man. How she loved him. . . .

Slowly she released Stella. "Good evening, Sir Guy." Her voice sounded calm, but she was anything but calm.

His dark eyes rested shrewdly on her tearstained face. "Good evening, Miss Conyngham."

Stella caught her hand excitedly. "I've so much to tell you, I just don't know where to begin!"

Leonie smiled. "You've been gone for three days, not three years."

"Sometimes it feels like years," replied the girl, glancing deliberately at Guy.

He raised an eyebrow. "Thank you for the compliment."

"I wasn't meaning you."

He took a deep breath. "Stella—"

"It's all right, I'm not going to start anything," she said quickly. "Besides, there's something much more exciting and interesting to talk about."

Leonie inwardly sighed with relief, for it had seemed for a moment that Stella's rattling tongue and impetuous personality were once again going to lead her to speak disparagingly of Imogen, who was evidently the real subject of the brief exchange.

Stella looked up at her again. "Leonie, we've come to ask you to stay with us at Poyntons during the celebration. You must say yes, you really must!"

Leonie stared at her, completely taken aback. "Stay with you?"

"Yes. You'll be a guest, and you'll go to the ball and enjoy all the other diversions. I want you to come, and I simply won't let you refuse!"

"Stella," reproved Guy a little sternly, "you are supposed to be inviting Miss Conyngham, not ordering her."

Stella lowered her eyes, biting her lip a little. "I know, but I couldn't bear it if she refused. You won't, will you, Leonie? You must be there, you simply must."

Leonie looked slowly toward Guy. "It . . . it's very kind of you, sir, but I couldn't possibly intrude—"

"It wouldn't be an intrusion," he replied.

Stella was aghast that the invitation was not going to be accepted. "Leonie! You can't refuse! You mustn't!"

Leonie shook her head. "No, Stella, I don't think it would be right."

"Why not?"

Leonie couldn't reply, for how could she say that apart from the fact that Imogen would hardly be pleased if she was present, there was also the matter of being in love with Guy?

Guy studied her. "Miss Conyngham, believe me, I would like you to join us. I know that maybe we last parted on a bad note, but I have no wish to remember that."

"It . . . it isn't that, Sir Guy."

"Then what? Do you think Miss Hart will refuse permission? I will speak to her."

"It isn't Miss Hart."

He smiled then. "If it isn't either of those things, I do not believe there can be any reason of sufficient importance to make you refuse. Please come, Miss Conyngham, if not for my sake, then certainly for Stella's."

Stella's hand tightened around Leonie's. "Please," she begged. "I do so want you to be there, and I shan't enjoy it at all if you aren't."

Leonie turned to Guy. "If . . . if you're sure you wish me to come . . . ?"

"I'm quite sure."

"Then I accept. Thank you."

Stella was ecstatic, dancing around the room like a wild thing and setting the candleflame gyrating.

Guy went a little closer to Leonie. "You've been crying," he said softly. "Will you tell me why?"

"I haven't been crying," she said quickly.

"You're an appalling liar, Leonie Conyngham. Tell me what's wrong."

"There's nothing wrong." To tell him the truth would look as if she was throwing herself on his charity.

He searched her face for a moment. "I won't press the matter, but remember that you once promised to come to me if anything was wrong."

"I haven't forgotten."

"Maybe not, but will you act upon it, I wonder. Still, no matter, for the moment there are other things to discuss—the arrangements for tomorrow, for instance. I'm leaving a day earlier than expected because my agent has requested me to. It seems he's concerned about the effect of the long hard winter on a bridge adjacent to my estate." He smiled a little. "It's my misfortune to be responsible for said bridge, which carries the highway and is therefore much in use. Since I will therefore be closeted with my agent, and since the other guests will not arrive until the day after, you might find it rather dull at Poyntons at first. We will be the only three there."

"Oh. Sir Guy . . ."

"Yes?"

"What of Lady Imogen?"

"She will be coming on the ninth, as originally planned."

Leonie was a little surprised, for it wasn't like Imogen to allow something like this to slip by.

"We will be leaving directly after breakfast, Miss Conyngham. I trust that that will be too inconvenient."

"Not at all."

"And if you are in any doubt at all about Miss Hart—"

"She will not prevent me from coming with you."

"You seem very certain."

"I am."

He nodded. "Very well. Until tomorrow morning, then. Good night, Miss Conyngham."

"Good night, Sir Guy."

His attention was suddenly drawn to the letter she'd written. "You're a woman of your word, aren't you?" he murmured.

"I like to think that I am."

"Lieutenant Colonel Mainwaring will also be receiving a letter from me, for I too have cause to be grateful to Private Whittacker. Had it not been for him, I might have lost not one, but two people who mean a great deal to me." He took her hand suddenly, drawing it swiftly to his lips.

She stared at him, but almost immediately he had released her hand and was walking to the door, addressing Stella as he did so. "Come on, young lady, it's time to get you home to your bed. We'll be rising early in the morning."

Stella flung herself into Leonie's arms once more, stretching up conspiratorially to her ear. "It's going to be all right, Leonie, I have it all planned," she whispered.

"Stella . . ." began Leonie uneasily, but the girl had gone, running out in Guy's wake.

The outer door of the seminary closed behind them and silence returned to the classroom. Leonie gazed at the slowly moving candleflame, a million emotions tumbling through her. She could still feel the touch of his lips on her hand, and still hear his voice. *Had it not been for him, I might have lost not one, but two people who mean a great deal to me.*

35

Leonie said nothing to Miss Hart about being invited to Poyntons; indeed she did not speak to the headmistress again before leaving the following morning. Her sudden departure caused a great stir throughout the seminary, some of her young pupils bursting into tears on being told. In the kitchens, where she spent the remainder of her last evening, everyone was very sad, especially Katy and Joseph.

Guy's carriage arrived very early, and there was still a thin mist clinging between the trees in the park. It was strange to walk out of the front door for the last time, and she couldn't help remembering how in the past she'd often dreamed of this moment. If fate hadn't intervened, she would be stepping down to her father's carriage now, a bouquet of flowers and two inscribed prayerbooks in her arms, Miss Hart's farewell words of praise ringing in her ears, and the whole school gathered to wave her off. Instead she was leaving like this, with only Katy and Joseph to say good-bye to her.

It was bitterly cold outside, but there was the promise of another fine day in the glowing sky to the east. Guy's coachman was well wrapped against the cold, and the team of bays stamped and snorted impatiently, their breath standing out in clouds. She paused on the pavement, watching as Joseph loaded her two valises in the trunk. Two half-empty valises, that was all she had to show for all her years at the seminary. . . . She glanced back at the building again, in particular at her balcony and the tree growing up toward it, then she turned away forever.

Guy held his hand out to her, assisting her into the carriage, where an excited Stella sat, warmly tucked out with traveling rugs. The carriage pulled slowly away, Leonie waved to Katy and Joseph until they were out of sight, and then the carriage was turning a corner, and part of her life was over. She did not know what lay ahead; she only knew that while she was at Poyntons she would live each day as it came.

Miss Hart arose just in time to see the carriage draw away. Astonished, she stared at it, and then she rang quickly on the bell. Joseph came hurrying in. "Yes, Miz Hart?"

"Where has Miss Conyngham gone?"

"With Sir Guy and Miz de Lacey, ma'am. She's to be a guest at his country house."

The headmistress stared at him and then waved him away once more. She took a deep breath, wondering if she should inform anyone of this unexpected development, but then she decided not to. She had done her duty by dismissing Leonie at Dorothea's command; the matter was now out of her hands. Besides, the only one who might expect to be informed was Imogen, and after that lady's rudeness the other night, the headmistress no longer felt disposed to assist her in any way whatsoever.

They were nearly at Poyntons now, for the stark silhouette of Windsor Castle could be seen in the distance. The sun was high above the snow-covered countryside, where wisps of smoke rose straight from cottage chimneys and herds of cattle stood huddled together in the fields. It was bitterly cold, the trees hanging frozen over the wide road, where the passage of countless vehicles and horses had packed the snow to a smooth, glassy, dangerous surface. The carriage moved slowly, the horses picking their way carefully as they turned in between massive wrought-iron gates by a lodge. The lodge-keeper removed his hat and bowed as it passed.

They drove on between an avenue of oaks. Leonie saw deer moving near a wood, and then, at last, she saw Poyntons itself. It was a beautiful, classical mansion, with an immense portico and symmetrical wings ending in pavilions, and it stood on rising ground beyond a lake. The lake was frozen, smooth and white, and from its center rose an island on which had been built a temple of Apollo. All around, the park stretched away in serene winter beauty, and Leonie could only stare at it all in admiration, for Poyntons was surely one of the loveliest estates in the whole realm.

The carriage halted before the house, and a butler and two footmen came hurrying out to it. Guy alighted and handed Stella and then Leonie down. He held Leonie's hand for a moment. "Welcome to Poyntons, Miss Conyngham."

All the servants were gathered in the vast entrance hall to welcome them, and after the small staff at the seminary, Leonie felt as if she was facing an entire army. The entrance hall was quite magnificent, with pale green walls decorated with gilded plasterwork and niches with statues. A wide, sweeping double staircase rose up between great Ionic columns to a half-landing, where she could see a number of gilt-framed portraits gazing down at her. There were more statues on the landing, and guarding the foot of both staircases, and there was a roaring log fire in an immense pink marble fireplace. Before the fire lay three large hounds, and they rose to their feet immediately they saw Guy, their great paws pattering on the black-and-white-tiled floor as they too came to greet him.

The butler assisted Guy with his coat, hat, and gloves. "Welcome home, Sir Guy."

"Thank you, Belvoir," Guy replied, fondling the long ears of one of the hounds. "I trust all is in hand?"

"It is indeed, sir. Everything is in readiness for the arrival of the guests, and all arrangements have been made for the ball tomorrow night."

Leonie was a little startled. The ball was tomorrow night? Somehow she'd thought of it as being some days away yet.

"Did you receive my instructions about arranging a shoot?" went on Guy. "I understand a party of gentlemen guests will be arriving fairly early tomorrow, and there must be some diversion for them."

"The keepers have been alerted, sir, and word has been sent out all over the neighborhood. A considerable number of gentlemen have indicated their intention to attend, and so it should be an excellent day's sport."

"Good. Now, will you please have someone attend to my niece and Miss Conyngham? I trust you have set aside the adjoining apartments at the front of the house?"

"I have indeed, sir, just as you instructed." The butler bowed and then beckoned forward two maids, who immediately bobbed curtsies and turned to lead Stella and Leonie toward the nearest branch of the staircase.

Stella followed them quickly as far as the half-landing, but there she stopped, thus ensuring that Leonie and the maids halted as well. The girl grinned impishly at Guy for a moment and then very deliberately began to study one of the portraits Leonie had noticed earlier, that of a very handsome young man in the full wig and lace collar of the Stuart period. "That is my ancestor, Sir Edwin de Lacey," she said, raising her voice so that Guy was bound to hear from the hall below. "I really must ask Uncle Guy to tell you all about him, Leonie."

"Really? Why?"

"Well—"

"Stella!" Guy's voice echoed sternly up to them. "Not one more word, is that quite clear?"

"Oh, but—"

"That's enough."

"Yes, Uncle Guy," she said meekly, but Leonie knew full well that she would return to the evidently contentious subject of the handsome Sir Edwin.

Leonie glanced curiously at the portrait again, and then followed Stella and the maids.

The adjoining apartments Guy had spoken of occupied prime positions at the front of the house, overlooking the lake. The rooms were furnished luxuriously and were very warm from the glowing fires which had been lit in every hearth. The walls were hung with silver-gray brocade, and the ceilings were richly coffered and painted. There were chandeliers, elegant chairs and sofas, some exquisitely inlaid, and the carpets had been woven especially for each individual room, the designs softly echoing the colors of their surroundings. The bedrooms were next to each other and were connected by a folding door. Stella's bed, an immense four-poster in which she looked totally lost, was draped with crimson velvet, while Leonie's was of golden brocade. Both sets of rooms were indeed very grand and could have been a little intimidating, but someone had thoughtfully placed bowls of flowers in each room, and somehow this seemed to make everything more personal and friendly.

Stella lay delightedly on her bed, gazing up at the intricate draperies. "I'm here again at *last*! What do you think of Poyntons, Leonie?"

"It's very beautiful indeed," replied Leonie, gazing out of the window at the island in the center of the lake.

"I knew you'd like it," said Stella softly, an anticipatory gleam in her eyes.

Guy's business with his agent did not take as long as expected, for the bridge was no longer causing alarm, and that afternoon, when the winter sun was just beginning to sink toward the western horizon, he took Stella and Leonie for a drive in the park.

The tracks had all been cleared in readiness for the house party, and so the light phaeton moved easily, drawn by four high-stepping chestnut horses which Guy drove with consummate ease past the frozen lake. The trees were hung with icicles which glittered like crystal in the dying sunlight as the phaeton crossed over a small Chinese bridge where a small stream flowed into the lake beneath a lacework of ice. There were rhododendrons and azaleas on either side of the track now, and great evergreen trees which soared majestically into the lilac sky, and then suddenly Leonie saw ahead, set in an Oriental garden, a beautiful pagoda, its roofs painted gold, crimson, and sapphire, its dragon carvings gazing so fiercely down that they seemed almost alive.

Stella sat forward excitedly. "Oh, please stop, Uncle Guy, I'd like to climb up and ring the chimes."

He reined in. "All right, but don't take a long time, it will soon be dark." He helped her down and she ran away through the snow, disappearing into the pagoda. He turned to Leonie then. "Are you ready yet to tell me what's wrong?"

The question caught her unawares. "There isn't anything," she said quickly and very unconvincingly.

"You don't fool me, Leonie Conyngham, I can see in your eyes that you're unhappy about something, it's there in your expression when you think no one's looking." His shrewd glance seemed to peel back all the veils she'd placed so determinedly between them.

"I'd really rather not talk about it, Sir Guy."

"Am I going to have to shake it out of you?"

She lowered her eyes. "I . . ."

"Yes?"

She took a deep breath. "I've been dismissed from the seminary. When I left there this morning, I left for the last time."

"Where will you go?"

She didn't reply.

"You haven't anywhere, have you?"

"No."

"You have now. You can stay here, as Stella's governess."

She stared at him, and then quickly shook her head. "Lady Imogen—"

"Cannot possibly find anything to object to in such a sensible arrangement. It's quite obvious to me that my niece's education is far from complete. She's had governesses in the past and I was about to engage another one when Stella's misconduct brought about thoughts of sending her to the seminary. You're good for my niece, and you are in need of a roof over your head; the solution seems to me to be quite obvious. Will you think about it?"

At that moment Stella appeared at the top of the pagoda, reaching out to ring the chimes which hung from the eaves. The melodious sound rippled out over the snow-covered park.

In London, well after sunset, Edward was in the drawing room at Longhurst House, pouring himself another glass of cognac. He glanced at the clock on the mantelpiece and then took out his fob watch. It was six, and still Imogen hadn't returned home. He wondered if she'd already found out about Leonie Conyngham being invited to Poyntons, but then he heard her carriage entering the porch outside.

A minute or so later she came a little angrily into the room, still wearing her fur-lined cloak. "Edward, what's the meaning of your order that my carriage is to prepare to leave immediately for Poyntons?"

"I take it that you haven't heard, then."

"Heard?"

He swirled the cognac. "Leonie Conyngham is there, with Guy and the brat."

She stared at him. "If this is your idea of a jest—"

"No jest. Fact." He leaned one pale hand against the mantelpiece, an elegant foot resting on the gleaming fender, studying her for a moment. "You may take my word for it."

"How do you know?"

"I have my methods, in this instance a cooperative kitchen boy who has proved useful in the past. Arrangements for the visit were made last night, and Guy called for her this morning. She has, therefore, had him all to herself today."

Imogen threw her reticule furiously onto a table. "I can't believe it!" she breathed. "After all my efforts, the creature has actually got herself ensconced at Poyntons! Damn her! And damn Guy too!"

"Perhaps now you understand why I left orders concerning the carriage, for I imagine you'll wish to set off immediately." He paused. "Or maybe you feel safe leaving the two of them alone all night as well."

"I would as soon trust you not to cheat at cards."

He bowed. "Thank you for those few kind words." He drained the glass of cognac then. "But I forgive you—you are under something of a strain, are you not? Shall we go, then?"

"We?" She looked sharply at him.

"My dear Imogen, I wouldn't miss this for the world."

"I thought you were *persona non grata* with Guy at the moment—at least that is what I presume from the coolness between you."

"He is being a little disagreeable, but it will take more than that to deter me."

"I trust you don't expect Miss Benckendorff to join us."

"Miss Benckendorff? My, my, it was 'dear Nadia' not so long ago."

"That was before you became so smitten with her."

He smiled. "You don't really believe I am, do you?"

"What else am I to think? She's been practically your only companion for a number of days now."

"She's unwittingly serving a purpose, that's all."

She relaxed a little. "A purpose? Is it something to do with your quarrel with Rupert and this wretched business at White's?"

"Yes. Need I say more?"

She smiled then. "No, I understand perfectly. But do you really think she will settle for a future earl rather than a present duke?"

He spread his hands innocently. "She will if she believes he's about to marry someone else. Marguerite St. Julienne, for instance."

Imogen gave a short laugh. "Even Rupert wouldn't go that far—the wretched creature should not go out without something over her head to stop her from frightening the horses. Besides, everyone knows that he intends marrying Nadia; he more or less admitted it at White's."

"I know that and you know that, but dear Nadia has become woefully uncertain. You see, he told her he was off to Sussex for a few days, but he actually toddled off to a new *inamorata* and at the same time Mama and the warthog toddled off as well. It played sweetly into my hands, especially as he's so damned cocksure of himself that he doesn't even suspect I might think of wooing Nadia away from him. His attempt to compromise me and have me ostracized in society can only succeed if he and Nadia actually do marry on the day he's claimed I've set a fortune upon. If the lady don't do it, he ain't won." He raised his empty glass, turning it expressively upside down. "Is all quite clear to you now, sis?"

"Perfectly."

"Good, for I was beginning to fear for your intelligence. Now then, let's be off to see what they're up to at Poyntons, hm?" He offered her his arm and they went down to the waiting carriage.

36

At Poyntons, Leonie was ready to go down to dinner. She wore her white silk gown, and the maid had dressed her hair up into a beautiful knot from which tumbled several long curls.

She turned as Stella tapped at the adjoining door. "Can we come in, Leonie?"

"Yes, of course."

The door was folded back and Stella came in with Guy. He wore a black velvet evening coat and there was a diamond pin glittering among the folds of his neckcloth. Stella had on a pretty blue velvet dress with a white sash, and she twirled for Leonie to admire the huge bow at the back. "Do you like it?" she asked.

"It's lovely, Stella. You look very pretty and very grown-up."

Stella flushed with pleasure. "You look beautiful too, Leonie. You don't seem to need lots of jewels."

"You're being very kind, but thank you."

Guy shook his head. "She isn't being kind, Miss Conyngham, she's merely telling the truth." His dark eyes moved slowly over her.

She felt her pulse quicken and her cheeks felt suddenly warm. "Thank you, Sir Guy."

Stella turned to him. "Can we look at the ballroom before we go down?"

"If you wish, but it isn't ready for tomorrow yet."

"I know, I just want to look at it, and when we arrived the doors were closed."

The ballroom stood at the head of the double staircase. Leonie hadn't known it was there because, as Stella had said, when they had passed it earlier the great white-and-gold doors had been closed. But they were open now, giving onto a wide flight of marble steps above the immense polished floor. It was a lofty, elegant chamber, its lower walls paneled, while above they were painted with magnificent murals of gods and goddesses. To one side there were many crimson velvet sofas and chairs waiting to be placed evenly all around the floor, while from the gilded ceiling far above were suspended six glittering chandeliers. The chandeliers had been lowered to the floor on their heavy chains, ready to be cleaned in the morning.

Stella's eyes shone as she gazed over the ballroom. "It will be my very first ball," she breathed, "and I can hardly wait. Oh, I wish I could stay up until the very end."

"You'll be allowed up until midnight," replied Guy firmly.

"Oh, but—"

"Midnight, and not a minute later."

"It's not fair."

"It's very fair, Miss Grizzle."

Stella glanced slyly at him then. "Let's go on down, I'm starving," she said, catching Leonie's hand and drawing her away toward the staircase. On the half-landing, by the portraits, she stopped again, glancing mischievously at Guy and then at the painting of Sir Edwin. "Leonie, don't you think he's very like Uncle Guy?" she asked with seeming innocence.

Leonie was uncertain how to respond, for she knew that Guy had forbidden his niece to mention the portrait. "Well, I . . . Yes, I suppose he is."

Guy came down to the landing, toying with the spill of lace at his cuff and giving his niece a dark, warning look. "Stella, I thought I made it plain—"

"Oh, please, Uncle Guy!" she begged. "I just want her to know the story—it's such a strange coincidence that her name and a previous Lady de Lacey's are the same."

Guy glanced at Leonie and then nodded resignedly. "Very well. But, Stella, if you embarrass Miss Conyngham even remotely, I shall extract a very humble apology from you."

"Of course, but she won't be embarrassed, I promise you." Stella was filled with impish delight, clearing her throat and then striking a very melodramatic pose, one arm extended toward the portrait. "Behold, Sir Edwin, so dashing and handsome, and so unhappily married to the Lady Maria." She turned in an aside to Leonie. "A dragon, and, as it so happens, an ancestor of Imogen's." She cleared her throat once more and moved on to the next portrait, that of a grim-faced woman with a thin mouth and a bony figure, who rather reminded Leonie of Dorothea Lieven. "Behold the Lady Maria," went on Stella. "Dragon, tyrant, and all-round miseryguts."

"Stella!" reproved Guy.

"Well, it's true, she was awful."

Leonie felt the urge to laugh, but she struggled to hide it, gazing steadfastly at the portrait and thinking that Lady Maria did indeed look a miseryguts. Looking away from the painting, she happened to catch Guy's glance, and she saw a flash of devilment in his eyes. He wasn't as angry as he was pretending to be.

Stella gave Lady Maria's portrait an arch look and then moved on to its neighbor, this time a likeness of another woman, a shy-faced creature with rather wistful eyes and lips which seemed as if they would often tremble. Stella struck her dramatic pose again. "Behold, the Lady Penelope, Sir Edwin's mistress and then his second wife." She turned to Leonie. "And this is the coincidence: Lady Penelope's name, before she married him, was Cunningham." She surveyed the portraits again, stepping back thoughtfully, but then pulling a dreadful face at Lady Maria. "Oh, isn't she just too much? She'd make a splendid gargoyle, wouldn't she?"

Guy looked in all seriousness at her. "Actually, there's a miniature somewhere of her when she was your age. She looked exactly like you—it could be a portrait of you, in fact."

Stella's eyes widened with horror and she looked quickly at Maria's picture again. "You don't really mean that, do you?" she whispered.

It was too much for Leonie, who suddenly burst into a fit of the giggles. Stella stared at her, much offended, but then she saw how Guy was concealing a smile as well. "You beast!" she cried. "You've been teasing me!"

"You deserved it," he replied, laughing. "You get far too big for your boots at times, young lady. Perhaps that will teach you not to force your wishes upon others."

"I didn't force them, I knew Leonie would like the story You did, didn't you, Leonie?"

Leonie had to nod, still laughing. "Yes, Stella, I did. It was very funny."

Stella was at her most wicked then. "There you are," she said to Guy, "Leonie thinks your ancestors are hilarious."

"I didn't say that!" protested Leonie.

He turned to her at that, putting his hand to her chin and making her look at him. "I trust, madam," he said sternly, "that you do not find my family history a matter for mirth?"

"Oh, no," she said quickly, "I wouldn't do such a thing." But there were still tears of laughter in her eyes.

He smiled, bending down quickly to kiss her on the cheek. "Then you are forgiven," he said softly.

At that moment the main door of the house was slammed and with a start they all three turned to look down into the entrance hall. Imogen and Edward stood there, and by the flash of cold fury in Imogen's eyes, she had witnessed everything.

Dinner was a very strained affair, after being delayed for some time while Guy and Imogen were closeted alone together in the drawing room. No one knew exactly what was said, but Imogen's raised voice could be heard from time to time and it was evident that she was requiring a great deal of placating. Leonie and Stella waited uneasily in the entrance hall with Edward, who seemed to find the whole business secretly amusing. He didn't address a single word to either of them, and for that at least Leonie was grateful.

At the table, when Guy and Imogen at last emerged from their discussion, it soon became evident that Imogen had decided upon a plan of campaign. There was no sign of her anger, but Leonie knew her well enough to know that that was only because she'd chosen to mask it for the time being. Imogen had seldom been more witty and amusing than she was that night; she positively sparkled with brilliance, her tinkling laughter ringing out time and time again, but through the dazzling display, the real Imogen shone out, and always to devastating effect upon Leonie and Stella. Stella tried to avoid catching her attention, but to no avail, for Imogen was intent upon provoking her if possible, and she did it simply by correcting the girl, finding mild fault, and then smiling almost apologetically at Guy.

Leonie was subjected to different treatment. Imogen made a point of frequently mentioning people from society whom she knew perfectly well Leonie had never met; then she asked Leonie's opinion about them. Leonie could only admit having no knowledge of them, at which Imogen raised a surprised eyebrow and then moved on. After a while it began to seem that Leonie Conyngham knew nothing at all and was a very dull creature.

Guy was strangely reticent throughout. Only once did he react sharply to anything, and that was when Edward very unwisely made a cutting remark at Leonie's expense. Guy turned quickly on him. "Have you been to the theater recently, Longhurst? I understand there are some very amusing spectacles to be seen."

Edward stared at him, color rushing into his pale cheeks; then he quickly applied himself to his meal and didn't say another word.

By the end of the meal, Imogen was alone in still managing to recount witty anecdotes and generally appear unconcerned by the atmosphere that had descended over everyone else. Stella was looking rebellious and resentful again, Leonie wished she was anywhere but at that table, and Edward seemed to find the structure of the epergne of immense interest. Guy was hard to read. Leonie had watched him from time to time, but only when he had rounded on Edward had he shown his feelings; beyond that, he was a mask.

The meal over, both Leonie and Stella seized the opportunity to excuse themselves, pleading tiredness after a long day. They escaped, going hand in hand up the staircase and not even glancing at the portraits; it was as if all the shared laughter of earlier had taken place in another lifetime. Stella was struggling not to cry, her lower lip quivering, and she looked a different child from the bubbling, carefree girl of a few hours before.

Leonie helped Stella undress, and when the girl was sitting in the capacious bed, sat beside her for a moment, hugging her tightly. "Don't give in, sweetheart," she whispered. "Don't let her win so easily."

"I hate her," cried Stella, her voice muffled as she hid her face in Leonie's shoulder. "We were so happy before she arrived. We *were* happy, weren't we?"

"Yes, we were."

"You won't go away and leave me, will you?"

"I'll only be in the next room."

"I don't mean that, I mean leave Poyntons."

Leonie gently cupped the girl's face in her hands, kissing her on the forehead. "I don't think it would be right for me to stay, Stella."

"Why not?"

"It isn't easy to explain."

"Tell me. Please. I want to understand."

"Stella, I mustn't stay here because I love your uncle."

Stella stared at her. Slowly Leonie got up from the bed and went back into her own room, leaving the folding door slightly ajar so that she would hear if Stella called her again, but there was only silence.

Leonie didn't undress straightaway; she sat by the fire, Lord Byron's *The Bride of Abydos* unopened in her lap. It would be so easy to accept the post of Stella's governess, for it would make Stella happy, it would mean being close to Guy, and it would mean security. But it would also mean seeing Guy with Imogen, and it would mean Imogen's constant spite and jealousy, jealousy which, as far as Leonie herself was concerned, was only too well-founded.

The door from the passage opened suddenly and Imogen walked in unannounced, her jewels glittering in the candlelight.

Leonie rose slowly to her feet, glancing briefly toward Stella's room.

Imogen was icily contemptuous. "I want you out of this house, madam, as quickly as possible. Oh, I suppose you think you've been very clever, not only persuading him to invite you here but also somehow managing to receive the offer of the post of governess. Well, I don't intend to let you continue, do you understand?" She came a little closer. "I've never liked you, Leonie Conyngham, and the last thing I intend to put up with is your presence in my house. I know your Achilles' heel: you'll do as I wish if you think it will benefit Stella. Stay and I'll make her life a misery. Go, and I'll soften my attitude quite considerably. Guy de Lacey is mine, and I don't intend to surrender him to anyone, least of all a nonentity like you. Be warned, Leonie, and if you have any thought in your head at all for Stella, you'll leave this house tomorrow.'' Her skirts rustled as she turned and went out once more.

A small sound from Stella's room made Leonie turn sharply. Had the girl been listening? She hurried to the door and peeped inside. The room was very quiet, but she saw the crimson bed curtains moving just a little, as if someone had at that moment slipped between them. Stella *had* been listening.

Leonie hesitated for a moment, wondering if she should go to the girl, but the continued silence from the bed made her feel that for the moment, at least, Stella did not wish to talk about what she had heard. Turning from the door, Leonie went slowly to the window of her own bedroom, looking out at the park, which was bathed in moonlight, the shadows deep blue on the snow. On impulse she opened the window, shivering a little as the icy air swept over her. At first she heard no sound in the iron stillness, except for the distant wavering call of an owl, but then she heard the soft drip-drip of melting snow. She took a deep breath. There was a difference in the air, a dampness which hadn't been there before. A thaw had set in.

She remained by the window for a while longer, thinking of what Imogen had said. Could her word be trusted? Would she indeed be more kind toward Stella if Leonie herself was not there? She lowered her eyes, loath to believe that Imogen would abide by her word. She didn't know what she should do; but she knew that in her heart she wanted to stay at Poyntons. She wanted to look after Stella and be near Guy . . . just be near him. . . .

37

After a restless night, Leonie woke early the next morning. Outside there was every sign that the thaw was going on apace, but as she looked out she heard Stella calling her from the other room. She hurried through to find the girl looking very pale and wan. "What is it, Stella? Aren't you well?"

"I have a headache."

"Is there anything I can bring to you?"

"No. I'll just stay in bed today. I want to feel well again in time for the ball."

Leonie looked at her in concern. "Stella, is this because of what you overheard last night?"

The girl looked away. "It's because of all last night, *her* especially!"

"Stella—"

"I'll be all right, truly I will." The girl struggled to appear brighter then. "Are you going to go down to breakfast now?"

"Isn't it a little early?"

"Breakfast's always very early at Poyntons, very early indeed."

Leonie looked at her in surprise. "Is it?"

"Oh, yes," replied Stella earnestly, "Uncle Guy makes a point of it."

"Well, I suppose I'd better go down, then." Leonie hesitated in the door. "Do you want any breakast sent up?"

Stella thought for a moment and then nodded, a shade of her old self suddenly shining in her eyes, as if she'd suddenly

259

thought of something. "Yes," she said, "I'd like lashings of scrambled egg and bacon."

Leonie stared at her. "I thought you were wilting with a headache."

"I am," replied the girl quickly, "but my nurse always told me that food was good for such things."

"Did she indeed. All right, lashings of scrambled egg and bacon it is." Leonie looked curiously at her for a moment more and then left.

The servants were all busy preparing for the arrival of the guests, and the ballroom was a hive of activity in readiness for the ball that night. The sofas and chairs had already been put in place, and the chandeliers were receiving a very thorough polishing.

She found a footman and inquired where breakfast was served. He looked at her in some surprise and then directed her to a room on the ground floor, facing the east and therefore catching the full force of the early-morning sun. It was a handsome room, with blue-and-white Chinese silk on the walls and a huge log fire burning in the immense hearth. The hounds she had seen on arriving were stretched lazily before the flames, and they looked up with quick interest as she entered. The butler, who had been standing by the sideboard with its array of silver-domed dishes, stepped forward to greet her.

"Good morning, Miss Conyngham."

"Good morning. Oh, Miss de Lacey has a headache and will not be coming down to breakfast, but she would like some to be taken up to her. Some scrambled egg and bacon."

He smiled and nodded. "Lashings of both, madam?"

She smiled too. "Most definitely."

"I will attend to it immediately. If you will excuse me . . . ?"

"Oh, yes, of course. I can serve myself."

"Thank you, madam." He bowed and withdrew.

She glanced around the room, but no one else appeared to be there, and so she went to the sideboard and lifted the first silver cover.

Guy's voice spoke from the deep armchair by the fire. "Good morning, Miss Conyngham, what an early riser you are."

She gave a gasp and dropped the cover with a clatter, whirling about. "Sir Guy! I didn't know you were there!"

"So it seems. I thought for a moment you would jump out of your skin," he said, folding his newspaper and rising from the chair. The sunlight had been streaming from behind him and that was why she hadn't seen him. He came toward her, taking her hand and raising it to his lips. "Shall we begin again? Good morning, Miss Conyngham."

"Good morning, Sir Guy." She smiled. "From what Stella said, I was expecting to be practically the last one to arrive, but it seems that I am the first."

"From what Stella said? What, exactly, did she say?"

"That breakfast was always served early at Poyntons."

He raised an eyebrow. "Did she indeed? Well, let me assure you that it isn't served any earlier here than anywhere else, especially not when there are so few guests, and those there are, yourself excluded of course, are prone to lie in bed until all hours. Personally I cannot abide lolling about in the mornings, and that is why I always come down at this hour, but everyone else will come as and when they please."

She felt a little embarrassed. "If . . . if I'm intruding—"

"Intruding? Far from it. I'm delighted to have your company. I usually have to sit in solitary splendor." He smiled.

It was one of those smiles which made her heart seem almost to turn over, and she had to look quickly away, pretending to examine the contents of the domed dishes. She stepped back a little as she lifted one and the strong smell of smoked fish rose up over her.

Guy laughed a little. "I take it that kedgeree does not appeal to you this morning."

"Nor any morning."

"Ditto, but I fear that Lord Edward Longhurst finds it very much to his taste and so it is always served when he is here. I think I will settle for bacon and egg, what do you say?"

"Yes, I think so too."

"But not lashings of it, as my disgusting niece would say."

"Oh, I don't know," replied Leonie, eyeing the deliciously crisp bacon.

"Miss Conyngham, I'm surprised at you," he murmured, forking large quantities onto her plate.

"Oh, that's more than enough!" she gasped.

"Are you sure? I realize that the country air has a diabolical effect upon town appetites."

"Not *that* diabolical," she replied, replacing some of it.

"Do you still like taking walks, Miss Conyngham?" he asked, drawing out a chair for her at the long polished table.

"Yes."

"Then will you walk with me afterward?"

She looked quickly at him. "But what of your guests? And then there is the shoot."

"Are you placing obstacles in my path, by any chance?"

"No. No, it's just that I thought you would have much to do."

"Guests are capable of arriving without me to guide them, and shoots invariably take place without my presence. I would much prefer a quiet walk with you, while there is still a little solitude here. By this afternoon it will be like Bedlam itself, I promise you." He poured her some coffee from an elegant silver pot. "So, it is agreed that we walk together?"

She smiled. "Yes, I'd like that."

"So would I."

Their eyes met for a moment, and again she had to look away.

"Miss Conyngham . . . Leonie . . . Have you thought any more about my offer yesterday?"

"Yes."

"And?"

"I don't know." She looked at him then. "I don't think I should, Sir Guy."

"Just 'Guy' will do. Why don't you think you should?"

She took a deep breath. "Because I think I stand in the way where Lady Imogen and Stella are concerned."

He studied her for a moment. "Is that your real reason?"

"Yes."

"I don't think it is, but for the moment I will accept it." His eyes moved slowly over her pale face. "But only for the moment."

"Please . . ."

"I'm embarrassing you?"

"Yes."

"Then let's talk of something else. Do you mind attending the ball tonight without any jewelry?"

She was taken aback. "I beg your pardon?"

"It seemed to me last night that you wished you had a necklace, or a jeweled comb, something like that. Mind you, it also seemed to me that you had no need of such things, you are very beautiful without them, but I know that such things do matter. I was wondering therefore if you would like to choose something from among my mother's jewelry."

"I thank you most deeply, sir, but I couldn't possibly accept." She felt a warmth creeping over her cheeks.

"Why not? I promise you that my mother, if she were still alive, would be very cross indeed with me if I did not attend to the matter."

"I was thinking more of Lady Imogen," she said quietly. "She might—"

"Misinterpret?"

She colored a little more. "Something of the sort."

"But there is nothing to misinterpret. Is there?"

"No."

"Well, then, I don't think there is anything more to be said, do you? The moment we've finished breakfast, I will take you to inspect the jewelry, you may choose what you wish to wear, and then we will go for a walk." He smiled then. "My, how masterful I am this morning—the country air must have gone to *my* head as well. Eat up, if we dally much more we might run the risk of Edward Longhurst and his wretched kedgeree, and that I simply could not stomach. He is odious in the extreme, without any good quality to commend him at the best of times, but when set beside a mound of kedgeree, he's quite beyond belief."

She laughed. "I can quite imagine that he is."

"So we'll make ourselves very scarce indeed, comforting ourselves with the hope that maybe he'll be abominably sick afterward, or maybe that he'll take himself off on the shoot where some shortsighted fellow will mistake his elegant posterior for a pheasant and pepper him accordingly."

"I'll drink to that, sir," she replied, still laughing, and raising her coffee cup in salute.

Shortly after that they left the breakfast room and Guy conducted her to the library, where his mother's jewelry was kept in a secret place. The library was a long, narrow room lined with shelf after shelf of books and sporting a very handsome wooden gallery reached by a wrought-iron spiral staircase. The secret place was a cupboard hidden among the shelves and disguised by having false spines, purporting to be a set of rather obscure Italian poems, fixed cleverly over the door. Guy carried the key in his pocket at all times, and he took it out now to unlock the little door. Inside there was a chased-silver casket, which he took down and opened on a nearby table. It contained a magnificent collection of jewelry, some in velvet-lined boxes from exclusive London jewelers, some just loose.

Leonie's breath caught at the beauty of some of the pieces, for they were quite exquisite, and the settings the most intricate and dainty she had ever seen, but there was one diamond necklace in particular which immediately caught her eye. She lifted it carefully out and held it up so that it caught the light from the window, flashing with all the colors of the rainbow.

"There are matching earrings," he said, searching through the casket and taking them out.

"No, I think it is perfect on its own."

"Try it on. Here, I'll help you." He took the necklace, standing before her to slip it gently around her neck and fasten it. His fingers were very warm against her skin, and she was very conscious of him. She felt the spell coiling softly around her again. She felt breathless. After a moment he paused, his hands resting where they were. He hesitated, but then slowly bent his head to kiss her on the lips. He lingered over the kiss, his lips moving very softly, arousing every sense within her. She felt almost weightless, swept along by the heady desire which coursed through her veins. She no longer cared if he knew the truth about her love for him, and she put her arms around him, returning the kiss. He drew her closer then, his lips more urgent and demanding, and her body yielded against his.

A madness seemed to seize her for a while then; she wanted him so much that all thought of resistance was gone, and there was only a need to surrender to him, but then a cold, sober sanity settled abruptly over her and she broke away. "No!" she cried.

"Leonie—"

"No. It's wrong. You're going to marry Imogen and tonight there's to be a ball to celebrate your betrothal. Soon all the guests will be here and society will be toasting your future with her. You belong to *her*, not to me." She was trembling with emotion, still almost intoxicated with the sweetness of his kiss, but also so very sober because her conscience reproached her. "I must leave here. I . . . I will stay until tomorrow," she said, struggling to sound more calm. "I would go today, but I know that that would disappoint Stella—she wants me to be there at her first ball. But I *will* leave here in the morning. Please, don't say anything, for I think I've said all that should have been said." Tears shone in her eyes, and gathering her skirts, she hurried out.

She didn't see Edward Longhurst's stealthy figure slip quickly out of sight behind a velvet curtain in the passage outside. He watched her hurry away toward the entrance hall, and he heard the smothered sound of her sobs, but then she had passed from his sight. He glanced back toward the library. She had left the door ajar and he could see Guy quite clearly, standing motionless, his face very pale as he closed his eyes for a moment. Then he picked up the casket and slowly replaced it in the secret cupboard.

Edward heard someone at the main door of the house, and then there were voices in the entrance hall. Footsteps approached swiftly, the heavy sound of a man's boots, and Edward shrank back once more as Guy's agent hurried toward the library, the damp hem of his cloak dragging on the black-and-white-tiled floor. The agent paused nervously in the doorway, as if uncertain of his reception, then took off his hat, turning it anxiously in his hands. "Sir Guy? May I have a word with you? It's important."

Guy turned sharply, having been so deep in thought that he'd been unaware of the man's arrival. "Ellis? What in God's name brings you here at this hour?"

The agent took a deep breath. "The Hartwell road bridge, sir."

"Dammit, man, that bridge brought me down here a day early, and then you informed me that it was a false alarm and there was no need for concern after all! Am I now to take it that there *is* some trouble with it after all?"

"There may be, sir, but I cannot be certain, and I would

feel much more at ease about it if you would examine it yourself."

"What's happened since yesterday, then?"

"A thaw. The ice has moved on the river and now there's new pressure on the center piers of the bridge. I believe there's a crack, and if there is, then the middle of the bridge might sink or even collapse completely. I'm no engineer, Sir Guy, and I might be quite wrong, and that's why I'd be grateful if you could come and take a look."

Guy turned exasperatedly away. The bridge was on the very far perimeter of his land and was his responsibility, and if there was any danger, then the road would have to be closed. He knew he had to go, but it was the last thing he wished to do when he had so much else on his mind, for it would take him away from the house for practically the whole day. He glanced back at the agent, nodding. "Very well, I'll come immediately."

"Thank you, Sir Guy."

Edward watched as they hurried away. He heard Guy calling to the butler to have his horse brought around as quickly as possible, and then after a moment all was quiet again. He slipped from his hiding place and into the library, smiling a little as he picked up the key which he had seen Guy leave forgetfully on the table. He opened the secret cupboard and took out the casket, searching through it until he found what he was looking for, the earrings that matched the necklace Leonie had chosen. He put them quickly in his pocket, replaced the casket, and locked the cupboard once more. He left the key where he had found it on the table, then slipped out of the library as silently as he had entered it.

Leonie was in her room when she heard the sound of horses outside. She looked out in time to see Guy hurry out and mount; then he rode away across the park accompanied by his agent, whom she had seen the previous day.

Stella came quietly to stand beside her, slipping a little hand into hers. "You're going to leave, aren't you?"

"I have to, Stella," whispered Leonie, watching him still. "I love him too much, and now . . . Now it is no longer a secret from him."

"I thought this morning, when first you awoke and then

went down to breakfast, that you wouldn't do as Imogen ordered.''

"It isn't because of that, it's because I know I must go."

Stella stared up at her. "I won't let you leave," she said. "I'll make you stay here somehow!" She ran back into her own room then and closed the folding door firmly behind her.

The carriage conveying Nadia and Dorothea to Poyntons was almost at the lodge now, having left London before dawn due to Nadia's impatience to be with Edward again. A note from him had been delivered at the embassy the night before, having been written before he and Imogen left for Poyntons, and it left Nadia in no doubt that he intended to propose to her at the ball that night.

Dorothea was not amused by such a very early journey, for she liked to rise late and do things as and when *she* pleased, not at the whim of others. She sat huddled among furs, feeling cold and sour-tempered. She wore a very dark blue pelisse with a high military collar, and her hat was also in the military style, with tassels and braid. It was a very stylish outfit, but somehow it emphasized her long neck and beaky nose; many women it would have flattered, Dorothea Lieven it did not.

Nadia wore white, and as always she looked very beautiful. Her hat was of white fur, and her pelisse had the same fur on its collar, cuffs, and hem. Her hands were plunged deep into a white fur muff, and the only relief from this dazzling whiteness came from the amethyst-studded gold brooch pinned to her breast.

Dorothea gave an irritated sigh as Nadia leaned forward yet again to see if they were almost there. "Do you *really* believe Edward Longhurst is about to make an honest woman of you?"

"The note he sent last night—"

"Said absolutely nothing. It was a lot of words which conveyed no real information at all. He missed his vocation; he should have gone into politics."

Nadia flushed a little. "You are just furious that Lord Palmerston was seen out last night with Lady Cowper again."

"I'm nothing of the sort. I was tired of him anyway."

"Really?"

"I hardly think you are in a position to throw stones, my dear, for Edward Longhurst is no safe anchoring ground, of that you may be sure."

"I'm satisfied that before today is out I will be his wife."

"Then you are very easily satisfied," replied Dorothea acidly. "May I remind you that you were once equally as satisfied that the Duke of Thornbury would come up trumps?"

"I've heard nothing from him since he lied to me just before leaving town. Lies and silence are not the actions of an ardent lover. I've already forgotten him. My future now lies with Edward."

"For your sake I trust you are right, but let me warn you of one thing. I will brook no trouble from you, I want no requests for my intervention, no embarrassing scenes, and no covert attempts to do anything to Leonie Conyngham, for in my experience covert too easily becomes overt, and I've risked too much already where you are concerned. I have my own reputation to consider, and it may be irreparably damaged if I pay heed to you anymore. Do anything, anything at all, Nadia, and I will cut you, do you hear me?"

Nadia was seething with anger. "Oh yes, Dorothea," she said icily, "I hear you. Well, you've served your purpose as far as I'm concerned, and now you can go to the devil."

Dorothea quivered with fury, but she bit back any further retort and looked away. Not another word passed between the cousins as the carriage drove along the avenue of oaks toward the house. The horses kicked up slush now, and from time to time the wheels splashed through puddles. As the carriage passed the lake, there was an occasional flash of sunlight upon water, as the ice began to melt.

The noise and bustle at the front of the house drew Edward to look out. There were carriages arriving all the time now, and he saw Nadia and Dorothea alight from theirs. Close by, the shoot was gathering, a large number of men and gun dogs, and Guy's keepers explaining the lie of the land and the sport they could all expect. But none of this activity in the foreground really caught Edward's interest, for he quickly noticed a solitary figure in the distance, walking along the far shore of the lake. It was Leonie. He recognized her because she had flung back the hood of her cloak and the sun was shining on her silvery hair. So, he pondered, for the moment at least nothing more could happen, for she was out on her own and Guy was away somewhere inspecting bridges. Imogen had yet to be informed of the interesting events in the library, but she would be told the moment she deigned to wake up. There were times, he thought, toying with the stolen earrings in his pocket, when his sister almost deserved to lose de Lacey to the schoolteacher.

He heard the door open and close softly behind him, and he turned to see Nadia standing there, her magnificent figure outlined by the clinging folds of her white muslin gown. He smiled and held out his hand to her. She came quickly into his arms, her lips full and warm as she kissed him. Her perfume enveloped him as he drew her close. Today was the day Rupert had set for his revenge, but Rupert wasn't even here yet. Was he still so cocksure that he thought he could turn up when he chose and produce his special license? Did he intend to make a dramatic appearance at five minutes to midnight, with a clergyman in tow, and then make sure of his revenge with barely seconds to spare? Yes, that was probably how he meant to do it, but he had reckoned without the craft of his opponent. Midnight would come and go, and Nadia Benckendorff would still not be Duchess of Thornbury, but then, nor would she be the future Countess of Wadford either. . . . Until the witching hour, though, she was still of interest, and in the meantime he had every intention of enjoying the charms she used so calculatingly to further her ambitions.

38

Imogen was at last awake, and she was sitting up in bed when her maid showed Edward in. "Edward? To what do I owe the pleasure of such an early visit?"

"Early? Dear girl, it's gone midday."

"Since I intend to dance until dawn tonight, I think I deserve to be lazy."

"That isn't all you might deserve. I must speak with you in private."

She waved the maid away and then looked curiously at him. "What's wrong? Don't tell me Rupert Allingham has married Nadia Benckendorff after all."

"No, but unless you take a few precautions, dear creature, you'll forfeit de Lacey to Leonie Conyngham after all."

Her blue eyes sharpened. "Why do you say that?"

"Oh, perhaps because I witnessed a very tender and passionate scene in the library early this morning."

She stared at him. "I cannot believe that they did anything while you were present."

"They didn't know I was there, they left the door ajar. You have much to fear, Imogen, for although she is intending to do the right thing, as they say, and has told him she's leaving first thing in the morning, I wouldn't bank on it if I were you. *She* may intend going, but I'm not so sure he intends letting her."

Imogen had gone very pale now. "Are you quite sure of what you saw?"

He gave a brief laugh. "Quite sure. It was no mere peck

on the cheek, it was a full-blooded kiss. To be sure, it made me feel quite hot.''

Her eyes flashed. "This is no time for your notion of clever humor!''

"It wasn't humor, it was wistfulness,'' he replied smoothly, "for I'd have paid handsomely to have been in his place.''

Furiously she flung back the bedclothes and got out of the bed. "Yes, you'd have paid ten thousand guineas!''

"Correction, I'd have *won* ten thousand guineas.''

"Damn you, Edward, can't you be serious for once? I've just woken up on the day I'm to be betrothed, and you tell me Guy has been making love to Leonie Conyngham! The very least you can do is be helpful, instead of just cynical.''

"My dear, I'm about to be very helpful indeed, far more helpful than your present mood deserves.''

"What do you mean?'' She looked quickly at him.

He took the earrings from his pocket and held them aloft so that they glittered. "The schoolteacher is wearing the matching necklace tonight.''

"Oh no,'' breathed Imogen, "for she will be out of this house before then!''

"How do you intend to achieve that? Will you bundle her out in person, with all the guests looking on in astonishment? No, I think not, especially when there is another way. Guy opened the secret cupboard in front of her—''

"What secret cupboard?''

He raised an eyebrow. "Don't you know? Well, Leonie Conyngham now does, that's for sure. It's in the library—he keeps his mother's jewels there. Leonie chose a necklace to wear tonight, and then they were . . . er, sidetracked . . .''

"Oh, do get on with it!'' she snapped.

"Well, she left him, and then almost immediately his agent arrived, twittering about a collapsing bridge somewhere, and he and Guy left to examine it. Guy left the key of the cupboard on the table.''

"And so you took the earrings.''

"Correct. It would seem to me a simple matter to hide them somewhere in her room and then choose an opportune moment on Guy's return to accuse her of theft. She will be sweetly compromised, and I don't think her protestations of innocence will win him over on this occasion.''

At that moment Imogen thought she heard a sound from the next room. "Someone's there!" she whispered urgently, going to the door. But the room was empty. Slowly she turned back to him. "I could have sworn I heard a noise. If someone should have heard—"

"Well, they didn't, did they? Now then, I'm anxious to get rid of these earrings as quickly as possible, and since Leonie is at this moment still out walking—she has a great deal on her mind, you understand—I think it an ideal moment for us to secrete these somewhere in her rooms."

"Us? I see no reason for me to—"

"The brat is in the next apartment. I'll need you to keep watch."

Imogen took a deep breath and then reluctantly nodded. "Very well. But it must be done quickly. I don't want to risk being seen."

Shortly afterward, they slipped along the passage to Leonie's door. The house was full of noise and bustle now, but it was quiet where they stood. After glancing quickly all around, they slipped into the empty apartment. Imogen hurried quickly to the folding door into Stella's rooms. It was tightly closed, and there was no sound from beyond it. Edward looked quickly around for a suitable place to conceal the earrings, then smiled as his glance fell on a many-branched candelabrum standing on a table. He removed two of the candles, dropping an earring into each holder and then replacing the candles. Imogen's eyes gleamed and she smiled; then they both slipped out again.

It was almost dark now, and there was a torrent of water roaring beneath the arches of Hartwell Bridge. Torches flickered on the bridge and along the riverbanks as the men watched the engineer, who had at last arrived from London, being slowly lowered on a makeshift cradle to examine the center piers. Guy leaned wearily back against the trunk of a tree, his top hat pulled forward and his heavy cloak drawn tightly about him. The ground was soft and wet now, and there was a dampness in the air which seemed to seep right through him. The roar of the water was deafening, and the dancing torches looked demonic in the encroaching darkness. He watched as the engineer gave the stonework a minute examination, his lantern held close, his cloak billowing in the bitter draft of icy air sweeping up from the foaming, thundering torrent sweeping by barely inches beneath the cradle. At last he had finished and signaled to be raised once more. Guy straightened, leaving his place by the tree to go and hear what the man had to say.

"Well? Is it safe?" The noise of the river almost drowned his voice.

"I think so, Sir Guy."

"You only *think* so? Can't you be more specific? Is the damned thing going to collapse or isn't it?"

"I'm not sure."

Guy turned exasperatedly to the agent. "Close the road."

"But, Sir Guy—"

"I said close the road. If there's any doubt whatsoever, I will not take any chances."

The engineer looked embarrassed. "Sir Guy, I'm sure it's in order to leave things as they are—"

"And have someone killed? I don't know what standards you are used to working to, sir, but they do not come up to mine. I bid you good night."

The engineer stared at him, his mouth opening and closing, and then he turned on his heel, splashing away through the slush and puddles to where his chaise waited.

Guy's riding crop tapped angrily against his mud-stained boot. He watched as some men hurried away to place barriers across the road by the nearby fork. The closure of the bridge meant a long detour for anyone unfortunate enough to be traveling this way, but a long detour was better than the risk of death.

He went to stand on the riverbank again for a moment, watching the swollen waters rush by and disappear beneath the bridge. Water under the bridge. Time slipping inexorably away, like sand through his fingers. Could he let Leonie slip through his fingers and vanish from his life forever, like the water vanishing beneath the bridge? Tomorrow she'd be gone. He closed his eyes for a moment, and it was as if she was in his arms again, her lips on his, her body close to his. . . . He whispered her name, but the roar of the river drowned his voice.

*　　*　　*

As darkness fell at Poyntons, the house was ablaze with lights. The guests had nearly all arrived, and everyone was preparing for the ball. Among the guests who hadn't yet arrived was Rupert, Duke of Thornbury, a fact which Edward, glancing shrewdly at the time, was careful to note. There were others who noted it too, and there was much talk about the bets at White's.

The hour of the ball arrived at last, but there was still no sign of Rupert or of Guy. Imogen, wearing a gown of sheer silver-blue gauze sprinkled with tiny satin spots, took up her place at the foot of the ballroom steps, greeting each guest who entered. She murmured excuses for Guy, mentioning his anxiety about a dangerous bridge, and she was, to all intents and purposes, the mistress of the house. She looked magnificent, her red hair dressed up exquisitely beneath a turban around which was twisted a long string of pearls, and there was something about her tonight which struck everyone who saw her, an air of almost exultant anticipation which shone most noticeably in her blue eyes. Everyone put it down to the imminence of her betrothal to Guy, but Edward, dancing with Nadia, knew that it was the prospect of at last striking out Leonie Conyngham.

Nadia danced on air, and she had never looked more beautiful than she did tonight, the hundreds of sequins on her white gown flashing in the light from the chandeliers. Her golden hair was adorned with a jeweled comb, and there were opals at her throat and in her ears. She moved gracefully to the music, constantly seeking Edward's eyes and smiling yearningly at him. Tonight he would be hers, he had whispered so, he had left no doubt at all. . . .

Leonie and Stella appeared at last in the entrance of the ballroom, looking over the crowded floor, where jewels flashed against pale throats and tall plumes swayed, and where the dark velvet evening dress of the gentlemen formed the perfect foil for the delicate pastel shades worn by the ladies. The strains of the orchestra rose sweetly above the babble of conversation, and it seemed that even without Guy's presence the ball was a resounding success.

Stella's hand crept nervously into Leonie's, and Leonie smiled down at her, thinking that she looked particularly pretty in her best blue velvet dress, a golden locket given to her by Guy around her throat.

Leonie wore her white silk gown again, but this time it was enhanced by the beautiful diamond necklace, which looked quite perfect, as she had instinctively known it would. Her hair was dressed up into a knot, and once again there were several long curls tumbling down from it, just as she always liked. She took a deep breath and then squeezed Stella's hand before nodding at the waiting master of ceremonies. His staff rapped upon the marble floor and he announced their names. There was a brief stir of interest and many faces turned quickly toward the steps, but then the moment was over and they were forgotten again.

At the foot of the steps, Imogen turned slowly to look up at them both. There was no smile on her lips and her eyes were like ice. She watched as they slowly descended, and at the last moment she turned away. They walked past without being formally greeted, and they were the only two in the whole room to have been dealt such a snub.

The snub had not passed unnoticed, for a number of people had witnessed it, including Edward, who thought his sister's action very foolish, for it drew attention to the fact that there was some acrimony between herself and Leonie. People were not dull-witted; they would put two and two together and arrive at the correct answer. Soon it would be being whispered that Imogen Longhurst was jealous of the schoolteacher, and Imogen would have only herself to blame on this occasion. He glanced again toward the steps, where Imogen was now all smiles to greet the next guests. She'd never hold a man like Guy de Lacey, she wasn't clever enough, she couldn't see beyond the immediate. But Leonie Conyngham was clever without even knowing it, so Imogen was at the crossroads now: one false step and Guy would turn to Leonie forever.

Leonie and Stella made their way around the edge of the ballroom until they found a vacant sofa. For Stella's sake, Leonie tried hard to be lighthearted, but it was quite difficult when she felt the very opposite, and she knew that the girl wasn't deceived by the pretense. "I'm sorry, Stella, I'm spoiling your first ball for you."

"No, you're not," replied the girl quickly. "You're not spoiling anything. It will be all right, honestly it will."

"You said that before."

"But this time it's true," was the mysterious reply.

Leonie looked quickly at her, but at that moment the master of ceremonies' staff rapped importantly and he made an announcement which brought the ball to a standstill.

"The Duke and Duchess of Thornbury, and the dowager Duchess of Thornbury."

There was a buzz of astonishment as all eyes went to the three people at the top of the marble steps. Rupert wore a blue coat with flat brass buttons, and white breeches with silver buckles, the accepted clothes of a bridegroom. Beside him, looking very happy indeed, stood his diminutive mother, resplendent in primrose brocade. On his other side, her hand placed a little possessively through his arm, was Marguerite St. Julienne, looking as dreadful as ever in mauve satin. It was toward her left hand that all eyes were drawn, for there, displayed for all to see, was a wedding ring.

A babble of conversation broke out as they descended the steps to be greeted and congratulated by Imogen. On the floor, Edward and Nadia had immediately stopped dancing. Nadia glanced briefly at the new arrivals, a cold anger passing fleetingly through her as she remembered Rupert's deceit and the way he had made love to her on the last occasion they were together, but then she turned with a smile toward Edward, who was all that mattered now. Her smile faded at the pale fury she saw written on his face.

"Edward? Whatever is it?"

"He's tricked me," he breathed, his gaze not moving from Rupert's smiling face.

"Tricked you? I don't understand. You told me he was going to marry her, and now he has, so why do you—?"

His cold eyes swung to her puzzled face then. "You fool, you still don't realize, do you? You thought you were using him and then me, but we were using you."

She flinched a little, her fan snapping open then and wafting swiftly to and fro before her hot face. Alarm was spreading through her, but she still didn't understand. "How has he tricked you?" she demanded, her green eyes meeting his.

"Because I thought he intended marrying you. I thought I was lying when I told you he was marrying the Jamaican."

She stared at him. "You thought . . ." Her voice died away. "You aren't going to marry me, are you?"

He gave a mirthless laugh. "I'm amazed that you ever believed I would. Women like you are two a penny, my dear, and I don't want soiled goods when I marry."

Hot color sprang to her cheeks then and she dealt him a furious blow to the face, leaving a stinging mark on his pale skin. He put his hand slowly to touch the place where she had struck him, but then he merely bowed to her and turned to walk away, pushing his way through the guests who had all turned with interest from the group by the steps to watch this other disturbance instead.

Nadia stood where she was, waves of dismay and humiliation sweeping over her. She turned desperately, seeking Dorothea's eyes, but Dorothea turned deliberately away. With a cry, Nadia gathered her skirts and fled, and the crowd parted before her, watching as she hurried up the steps and out of the ballroom.

Edward made his way toward the steps as well, but Rupert saw him and moved into his path. "I trust you aren't leaving without congratulating me."

"Go to hell."

Rupert grinned. "Come now, I do hate a poor loser. You've always thought me the fool, Longhurst, but this time the dunce's cap is yours. I didn't say I was going to marry Nadia, *you* presumed that I was referring to her. You thought it definite when I didn't deny it on being questioned, but if you think very carefully, you'll remember that I didn't admit it either, I was at my ambiguous best. You thought that by stealing Nadia you'd defeat me, but you were wrong, for I never had any intention of marrying her, and if you'd checked very carefully among the bets that were being made, you'd have known it. I told you that I'd had a large wager made secretly on your behalf, and so I have, but it is that I would marry Marguerite today, not Nadia. That very secret wager is already becoming painfully public, I've seen to that. Society doesn't like a sharp, Longhurst, and you're going to appear a prime one indeed, double dealing to the disadvantage of your friends to fill your already bulging pockets. There's no excuse for that. They'll think you've deliberately misled them twice, and that's not playing the game. All's fair in love and war, but the same doesn't go for cheating on one's friends. Every door of consequence is going to be closed to you." He smiled and stepped out of Edward's path. "I bid you good night. I do trust you will enjoy the remainder of the ball as it will be the last social occasion of any importance you'll be attending for some time."

Edward's eyes were like flint. "Be on your guard from this moment on, Thornbury. I'll make you pay, of that you may be sure."

For a moment Rupert's smile faltered, for there was something in the other's gaze which instilled a deep cold in him. He turned quickly away, returning to his new bride and his mother.

Edward went slowly on up the steps, pausing at the top to look back at the ball; then he went on out, beckoning to a footman who stood near the staircase. "Have my carriage made ready, I shall be leaving soon."

"Very well, my lord."

At that moment the main door of the house closed, and looking down into the entrance hall, Edward saw that Guy had at last returned.

39

Guy came slowly up the staircase, pausing as he saw Edward. "I can think of other faces I'd rather see than yours, Longhurst."

"To be sure, I feel more or less the same myself, de Lacey, but on this occasion I rather think it is as well that you've seen me first, and not, shall we say, a certain pretty schoolteacher?"

Guy's eyes darkened. "And what do you mean by that?"

"Mean? My dear fellow, I don't know what you think I'm insinuating, but the truth is that I've discovered the lady to be a thief, and I rather think you will have to agree, when you see the proof."

Guy looked at him for a long moment. "I warn you, Longhurst," he said softly, "I'm in no mood for—"

"She's a thief, de Lacey, and Imogen and I can prove it."

"Imogen?"

"She has seen the proof."

Guy took a deep breath. "I don't believe Leonie Conyngham is a thief, Longhurst, and I don't really care if you and Imogen have proof ten times over."

"You're touchingly trusting, dear fellow, but if you will leave keys lying around after you've shown penniless schoolteachers where you keep your mother's jewels, I rather think you're asking for trouble."

Guy's eyes narrowed then. "And what would you know of it?"

"I saw her go into the library, pick up the key from the

table, and open the cupboard. She took out the earrings which match the necklace she's wearing tonight, and she hid them in the candelabrum in her bedroom. If you don't believe me, I suggest you go and look for yourself.''

"Where's Imogen now?"

"Receiving your guests for you."

"No, I'm not," came Imogen's voice from the entrance of the ballroom. The satin spots of her gown shimmering, she hurried toward Guy, linking her slender arms around his neck and stretching up to kiss him.

He drew back slowly but firmly. "I wish to speak with you in private," he said.

Edward stepped quickly forward. "De Lacey, I suggest that this other business is too important to delay. You have many guests here tonight, the house is filled with valuable jewelry and so on, and I hardly think it wise to ignore the fact that there is a thief among us."

Imogen took the cue. "He's right, Guy, she has to be removed, and as quickly as possible."

"I would prefer to speak to you first."

"No!" she replied angrily. "I insist that you throw Leonie Conyngham out of this house!"

Guy looked at her for a long moment and then at Edward. "*If* she is a thief, I will deal with the matter in my own way."

"I demand—" began Imogen furiously.

"You aren't in any position to demand yet, madam!" he snapped.

She recoiled as if he'd struck her, and she looked with alarm at Edward, who gave her a barely perceptible shrug.

Guy turned wearily to the nearest footman. "Have Miss Conyngham come to see me immediately."

"Yes, Sir Guy."

"Imogen, I suggest you and your brother wait elsewhere."

Edward inclined his head coolly. "We'll wait outside her apartment, for that is where you will find the proof, de Lacey." Taking Imogen's cold hand, he drew it through his arm and they moved away.

Guy leaned his hands on a console table, his head bowed. A nerve flickered at his temple, but beyond that he didn't move. It seemed an age before at last he heard the rustle of

Leonie's skirts. He turned quickly then, to see that Stella had come out with her.

"Stella, I would prefer you to go back to the ball," he said.

"No, Uncle Guy, because I know what they've told you. I've been waiting for you to come home so I could tell you what they've been doing. I didn't tell Leonie because I knew how upset she'd be."

Leonie stared at her. "What are you talking about, Stella?"

Guy nodded as well. "Yes, young lady, I think you should explain."

Stella took a deep breath. "I heard Edward and Imogen plotting this morning. I was listening in the next room and they almost caught me. Edward saw you and Leonie in the library, Uncle Guy, and he saw that you'd left the key on the table. He took some earrings and then he and Imogen hid them in a candelabrum in Leonie's bedroom while she was out walking. I saw them through a crack in the door, and when they'd gone I took the earrings out again. Here they are." She went to him and pressed them into his hand. The diamonds flashed and winked in the soft light.

Stella looked anxiously at him. "You do believe me, don't you? Leonie isn't a thief, Edward and Imogen did it all. I'm not fibbing because I don't like Imogen, truly I'm not."

Guy smiled, ruffling her hair. "I believe you."

She turned gladly to Leonie. "There, I told you it would be all right, didn't I? Now will you believe me?"

"Stella," said Guy, "you've helped a great deal, but now I want you to go back to the ball."

"Oh, Uncle Guy!"

"Please, for I would rather you were out of the way for the time being."

"I want to see what happens."

"I'm sure you do, but you're not going to. Now, then, will you go back, please?"

She sighed. "I suppose so, but it isn't fair."

They watched her walk slowly back into the ballroom, and then Guy turned to Leonie. "I've been thinking a great deal today, Leonie."

"Guy—"

"No more talk of wrong, Leonie, for I'm about to do

what's right. There is something I have to do now, but afterward I must speak with you. Will you wait in the library?'' He put his hand gently to her cheek. ''Please do as I ask.''

She nodded. ''I will wait there for you.'' His fingers seemed to burn against her skin.

It was very quiet in the library, which was one of the few rooms in the house not bright with lights. Only firelight flickered over the shelves of books, the gallery, and the spiral staircase.

How long she had been waiting, she didn't know, but it seemed a very long time. She could hear the sound of the ball echoing through the house, but then, quite suddenly, everything was silent. Several more minutes passed, and then she heard cheers, after which the ball proceeded as before.

A carriage was brought to the front of the house and she looked out to see Edward Longhurst hurriedly entering it. It drove away at speed, and as she watched, she saw another carriage coming toward the house. It too was being driven swiftly, its panels travel-stained and its horses tired. It came to a standstill before the house, but she heard the library door opening behind her and she turned away before she saw who alighted.

Guy had come to her at last. He wore his evening attire now, almost as if he'd been at the ball throughout the evening. He took her hand, drawing it palm uppermost to his lips, and then he pulled her into his arms, kissing her on the lips.

She drew breathlessly back, staring up at him. It couldn't be happening, it couldn't. . . .

He smiled at her. ''It's no longer wrong, Leonie,'' he said softly, ''for I am no longer going to marry Imogen. All thought of the match has been dropped. No, don't say anything, for I have so much to explain to you. I've ended the match with Imogen not only because of what she tried to do tonight but also because I no longer love her. Neither she nor her brother denied what they had done with the earrings, and I ordered Edward to leave Poyntons immediately. I could not deal so harshly with Imogen, for although she is guilty of a great deal, I cannot with all honesty say that my own conscience is clear.''

"Your conscience? But surely—"

"Oh, I haven't schemed and plotted, at least not in the same way. I have done things I shouldn't, though, and if I wasn't unfaithful to her in fact, I was a thousand times over in my thoughts after meeting you. That was why I spared her tonight, and why everyone at the ball was told only that she and I had come to a mutual agreement not to proceed with the betrothal. If you noticed a silence a little earlier, it was when she and I were making our announcement. It was greeted with a little initial astonishment, but they were all more than glad to toast our good sense with my best champagne, I assure you."

"Where is Imogen now?"

"At the ball."

"She loves you, Guy."

"I don't think so. I don't think she is capable of real love, not the sort of love which will make sacrifices." He cupped her face in his hands. "You would have left here in the morning, wouldn't you?"

"Yes."

"I could not have borne it without you. I've been selfish, I've wanted to be with you, I've been jealous, I've been all manner of things, but I haven't been honest. I've known for some time that I was falling in love with you. I tried to fight it, but I couldn't. This morning I at last gave in to temptation, a temptation which has been there since the first moment I saw you. If I hadn't known before that you loved me, I certainly knew then. If only you'd looked into my eyes, you'd have seen how I felt about you."

She still hardly dared believe that it was happening. Her fingers crept slowly up to rest over his. "I thought you loved Imogen, that I was merely—"

He stopped her words, his lips as warm and filled with desire as they had been earlier. "I love you, Leonie," he whispered, "and if I haven't been honest with you before, I'm being honest now. I want you to be my wife, the mistress of my house, and the mistress of my heart. Will you have me?"

In answer she raised her lips to his again, clinging to him as if she feared even now that she would suddenly awaken and find it all a dream.

There was a sound at the door and they drew quickly apart when they saw Stella peeping in, a smile of delight on her face at having caught them together in a passionate embrace. She came farther in. "Sir Henry Fitzjohn has called, Uncle Guy, he says it's very important."

Leonie held her breath. Sir Henry Fitzjohn? Did he have word about her father?

Stella stepped aside and Harry Fitzjohn came in, grinning a little sheepishly at Guy. "I trust I haven't called at an inconvenient time, Guy."

"Is it about Richard Conyngham?"

"It is indeed."

"Then this is the lady you should talk to. Leonie, this is Harry Fitzjohn, of whom I've spoken. Harry, this is Miss Conyngham."

Harry's quick glance noticed how Leonie moved closer to Guy, her hand slipping into his. "Miss Conyngham, it's a privilege to meet you, although I vow you're much more beautiful than even Guy admitted to me."

"You have news for me, sir?"

"Yes, and I'm glad now that I came rushing out here into the sticks at this time of night, for it's very good news. Your father's name is cleared, for his partner has confessed to being the guilty party. Your fortune is fully restored to you and you are once again a very wealthy young lady. That is it, in the proverbial nutshell. Congratulations."

Tears of joy leapt into her eyes and she flung her arms around Guy, who held her tightly to him.

Harry grinned again as he watched them. "Evidently congratulations of another sort are in order as well," he said, turning to wink at Stella.

About the Author

Sandra Heath was born in 1944. As the daughter of an officer in the Royal Air Force, most of her life was spent traveling around to various European posts. She has lived and worked in both Holland and Germany.

The author now resides in Gloucester, England, together with her husband and young daughter, where all her spare time is spent writing. She is especially fond of exotic felines, and at one time or another, has owned each breed of cat.

More Delightful Regency Romances from SIGNET

*Prices slightly higher in Canada

**Buy them at your local
bookstore or use coupon
on last page for ordering.**

Delightful Regency Romances from SIGNET

SIGNET Regency Romances You'll Enjoy